RIVER RISING

BOOK THREE: THE LOSS OF CERTAINTY SERIES

~

RIVER RISING

~

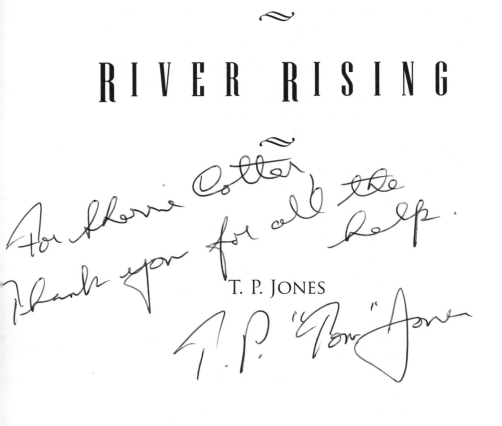

T. P. JONES

Synergy Books

River Rising
Book Three: The Loss of Certainty Series
Published by Synergy Books
P.O. Box 30071
Austin, Texas 78755

For more information about our books, please write us, e-mail us at info@
synergybooks.net, or visit our web site at www.synergybooks.net.

Publisher's Cataloging-in-Publication
(Provided by Quality Books, Inc.)

Jones, T. P., 1941-
    River rising / T.P. Jones.
    p. cm. -- (The loss of certainty series ; bk. 3)
    LCCN 2010921706
    ISBN-13: 978-0-9842358-8-9
    ISBN-10: 0-9842358-8-4

    1. Floods--Iowa--Fiction. 2. City and town life--
Iowa--Fiction. 3. Local government--Iowa--Fiction.
4. Iowa--Fiction.   I. Title. II. Series: Jones, T. P.,
1941- Loss of certainty series ; bk. 3.

    PS3610.O6298R58 2010   813'.6
                        QBI10-600034

This is a work of fiction. Many of the scenes in this as well as the earlier volumes
are written from the points of view of people who are technically trained. The
author has attempted to be as accurate as possible in his portrayal of these pro-
fessions, but if any errors have managed to slip through, they are the author's
responsibility entirely. Furthermore, the characters themselves are fictitious. Any
resemblance to actual people is purely coincidental.

10 9 8 7 6 5 4 3 2 1

For the citizens of Dubuque, Iowa. Thank you.

PART I

CHAPTER 1

$\backsim$

In the lee of the warm front and the first rains, temperatures climbed into the low fifties, fog boiling off the snowpack. Behind this would come a second front, cold, bringing more rain and the first thunderstorms of the spring, perhaps wet snow, temperatures falling back into the mid thirties.

Walter Plowman drove through the fog with the window down and his elbow stuck out. Clumps of ice frozen to the undercarriages of cars had dropped off and lay in the street like the erratics of a retreating glacier. He drove south out of town, up the long grade past the airport, and onto the Iowa prairie, the view normally of a rolling empty vista punctuated with farm compounds but now shuttered by the mist.

He crept through it, counting the mailboxes. At the third, he turned right and parked beside a small, neat cottage.

Mary Herrig came to the back door, adjusting the pins in her white hair. She always looked relieved when Walter stopped by. Someone else to deal with Fred for a bit.

"Out to check on my instruments," he said.

"Come in, come in." Her gnarly old fingers worked impatiently at the bun.

Walter scraped his feet on the entrance mat and pulled off his woolen touring cap. "How you?"

"Oh, fair to partly cloudy. Yourself?"

The speaker wasn't Mary but Fred, creeping across the kitchen, looking anything but fair to partly cloudy. He fumbled with the mugs next to the coffeemaker. "Here, pour yourself a cup," he said.

Mary, her chore with her hair completed to her satisfaction, patted Walter's arm. "I'll do it," she whispered. "You go sit down."

Fred lowered himself into his chair, which occupied the middle of the floor, in uncertain relationship with the other objects in the room, the room itself cramped but tidy.

"We saw El on the TV there," he said, "wasn't but an hour ago." The set was on, an ancient black-and-white job. It sat on the counter, canted toward the center of the room.

"She got up at five and drove down to the Quad Cities, closest NBC affiliate," Walter told him. *The Today Show* had wanted to interview her about David Duke's visit to the city and everything else that had happened.

"How's that work?"

"How did she get on the show? Got a call from New York. They arranged things."

"That right? Bryant what's-his-name's idea, was it?"

"Gumbel," Mary said. She had been looking disapprovingly at the cup she was about to pour Walter's coffee into and set about washing it.

"Probably his idea, Gumbel there, him being a Negro and all," Fred opined.

"To have El on?" Walter asked.

"Yup."

"Maybe, Fred. Dunno." Nothing happened but what Fred had a theory about it. "She's off to go on the Donahue show this afternoon."

"The hell you say. Phil Donahue?"

"She and a bunch of the others from the city."

Fred just continued to shake his head at the wonder of it.

"We'll be sure to watch," Mary said.

"Expect he was damn disappointed," Fred commented.

"Who?"

"Bryant Gumbel."

"Why's that, Fred?"

"You know them reporters, always trying to get you to say stuff. And El there pretending like she's the mayor of Disneyland or something. Here we got this Duke fellow comes to town, all hell breaks loose, reporters all over the place calling Jackson practically the racist capital of America. And there's El saying everything's just hunky-dory, givin' them politician's non-answer answers, and…"—he made a ricocheting sound and caromed the palm of one hand off the other—"… that's it!"

"Nonsense. She did a good job," Mary said as she brought Walter his coffee.

Fred harrumphed.

"The hell she did. No offense there, Walter, but everything ain't exactly hunky-dory. I mean, El acts like she thinks she can keep the snow from falling, or something, know what I mean?"

Walter laughed. Fred and Mary were Walter's first Weather Family, way back when they still had the farm, and Fred, like all farmers, had a meteorological turn of mind, although in Fred's case it was, if anything, even more so. He made Walter look positively indifferent where the weather was concerned.

"Yup," Walter agreed and left it at that.

"Well, I think she did a fine job," Mary repeated, plunking down the cream and sugar harder than necessary.

"Got to be careful, Walt, what you say around a woman's libber like Mary."

Now it was Mary's turn to harrumph. "I'll tell you one thing. If people listened to El, we wouldn't have the likes of David Duke coming around and appealing to what's worst in folks."

"But they don't listen," Fred said, "that's the whole point there. It's what I call the eternal verities." Fred set great store by the eternal verities. "Might as well go outside there and talk to the wind, ain't that right, Walt?"

"Guess I better be careful what I agree to here, Mary being such a rabid feminist and all," Walter said, although, despite Fred's warning about his wife's imagined radical nature, Fred himself liked to needle her a good deal. "A man's got to have a little trouble in his life," he'd once explained to Walter.

"Say, Fred, you gonna join me in a cup or what?" Fred sat with his hands on his knees, elbows sticking out, as if he was thinking of getting up.

"Can't. The wife cut me off."

"Two cups is plenty," Mary said from the sink, back to washing dishes although hardly any were dirty. "Freddie talks too much as it is."

"That's because I got somethin' to say."

"You talk to the TV, plenty, Freddie, but I don't see you on *Today* there. El's trying at least. Good for her, I say." Mary looked meaningfully back over her shoulder at her husband. "And, yes, she is a woman, and we women think a little bit different from you men. About time you start paying some attention, you ask me."

Fred winked at Walter. "See, a woman's libber. I married me one of them bra burners."

Mary didn't react to this. Over her print housedress, she wore an old cardigan, brown and furrowed and sagging, like the loping Iowa farmlands she'd lived on for nearly eighty years. Fred could talk about the eternal verities all he wanted…

As Walter was leaving, Fred warned him, "Watch yourself driving back. Them truckers don't slow down for nothing."

"Obliged," Walter said and touched the bill of his touring cap, two fingers, the Boy Scout's salute.

Before he got back on the road, however, he needed to check his instrument platform, the reason for his visit. He'd already forgotten Fred's warning as he crumped through the old snow with the Herrigs' shovel slung over his shoulder.

His ankles crackled, like ice breaking. He felt the warm air prickling against his skin and envisioned the great mass of it sweeping eastward, advecting over the cold snow cover between two vast fronts, the warm front past, the cold coming.

It had been a couple of storms since he'd been out there. He began to reopen the path to the platform, the shovel biting into the sodden snow with a gravelly sound, each shovelful heavy, lifted only with effort as if against a vacuum. Soon he was winded.

At one point, as he rested, he cut into the side of the trench, peeling away the slumped snow, and crouched down to count the strata marking the sequence of winter storms, separated by gray ice lenses and layers of soot. He knew how many, of course, could date them with a precision a geologist would envy. The pattern pleased him, and he ran his gloved fingers down it, feeling the texture through the leather. A good deal of water stored in the pack, he nodded to himself. More up north.

He thought about all of Ellie's problems. Poor girl, charging all over the countryside trying to settle things down. Well, David Duke had come and gone, stirred up the hive, but he wouldn't be back. The journalists might poke the nest as much as they wanted, to see what else would fly out, but not much, Walter guessed, not this go-round. As Fred Herrig might say, where storm systems were concerned, Mr. Duke wasn't much more than a squall. Yup. But the storms that had laid down *this snowpack*, well, they were an entirely different situation. Synoptic.

Walter stood up and stretched, arching his back to ease the ache, then setting to shoveling once more. Poor Ellie would lose the election just as things were quieting down again.

The sun, a perfect disk, bored through the mist, casting toward him over the snow a white-hot column of light. Fog drifted across his path. The temperature had topped out and begun its backward slide.

Finally the instrument shed materialized at the crest of a low ridge, the fenced enclosure a snippet cut from the cornfield, which once had been farmed by Fred, now by his son. The shed cast a smudgy shadow in the eerie sunlight.

Walter paused again and admired the scene. Out of the shed, the tubes of his snow and rain gauges rose barely above the deep snowpack. He'd installed them only the previous fall. Walter always used up-to-date instruments—paid for out of his own pocket.

Atop the shed the cups of the anemometer turned slowly, barely overcoming the subtle friction of the spindle on which they were mounted. Beneath, the direction arrow pointed a few degrees west of south. Walter imagined he could see the cups beginning to accelerate, the vane veer around with the approaching storm. Of course, it wasn't true, his eyesight wasn't that good. But still—and this, after all, was the point—sometimes, just sometimes, the future could be foretold.

He took the shovel off his shoulder again and went back to work.

Chapter 2

~

Deuce Goetzinger's mother brought him the beer. He was playing poker in the dining room of the farm with a bunch of guys he knew from somewhere. He had to take a wicked leak. His mother gave him the beer and said that Aggie would call back later. At that moment, the phone began to ring. He got up and started to look for it. He crawled under the table. He had to answer before his father did.

The phone brayed again, so loud it might have been inside his head. Deuce struggled to wake up, still held in the web of his dream.

Eyes closed, he fumbled on the bedside table for the receiver and mumbled into it.

"Found your water," the voice on the other end of the line said.

The words didn't register. They could have been part of his dream.

"It's me," the voice said. J.J. Dusterhoft.

"What?" Deuce yawned.

"Your water, remember? That you lost. From the plant."

Deuce dragged himself up onto his elbow. "What time is it?" he yawned again.

"Ten thirty."

"Morning or night?"

J.J. laughed. "Middle of the morning, my friend, time to rise and shine." His voice, distant, faded in and out of street noises. "Figured you might be interested."

"Yeah." *Shit*, he thought, *so soon*. It'd been barely a week since he'd been snooping around in the old lead mines with Seth Brunel, the city engineer, looking for the water that had gone missing from the city's intermediate system. "Where?"

"Murphy's Way."

The cold floor stung the soles of Deuce's feet as he sat up. He needed to take a leak. His alarm clock read 10:35. He couldn't have been asleep more than an hour. That was the problem with working rotating shifts. Nobody ever knew whether you were asleep or awake. "Murphy's Way? Where the hell's that?" Deuce thought he knew every street in the city.

"Back alley, up near the old cable car tracks at Tenth. It collapsed. Car went into it. The driver's messed up pretty bad. They just hauled him off to the hospital."

"That what it's called—Murphy's Way? Never knew it had a name."

Deuce yawned again and rubbed his face, remembering the dream, remembering that his mother was dead.

"You interested in the water or what?"

He'd given up any idea of finding the leak in the system. A fantasy, he'd decided. He'd wanted to stick it to that horse's ass, Frank Lacy, he'd decided. That was all. Nothing to it.

"Yeah. Where you at?"

"The scene."

"Who else?"

"The commissioner. We're waiting on Chuck Fellows."

"Okay."

Deuce hung up.

But for a time, exhausted, he didn't move. He went back to thinking about his mother. Except during snowstorms, when he imagined her still wandering through the woods and felt the pity of her fate, his grief had deserted him. Only a blank remained, and a pain in the pit of his stomach, a dull twitchy thing, most likely the beginnings of an ulcer. His mother had died and he had an ulcer.

"Shit." He forced himself to stand up, yawned again, stretching, pushing aside the powerful desire to lie back down, and started to dress.

~

"The locals use it as a shortcut."

Deuce and J.J. were standing near the foot of Murphy's Way, a steep, makeshift affair, more alley than street, descending from modest, respectable houses at its brow to ratty, wooden tenements where it emptied into a second alley leading downtown. Street department barricades had been set up at either end. More barricades, as well as yellow police tape, surrounded the hole.

Herbie, the police photographer, had been there earlier and taken his pictures and left. Hank Kraft, head of the street department, had left when Fellows didn't show. The rubberneckers had gotten bored and gone away, too. The damaged car had been towed. J.J. and Deuce were alone.

"City street?" Deuce asked.

"Yup."

Deuce could spot no hydrants that he might have tested. Anyway, he and Seth Brunel hadn't been there. He seemed to remember looking down here from up above. Why they hadn't checked it out he had no idea.

He couldn't see any water running in the hole. Helluva big hole.

"I take it Frank Lacy's been here."

"Like a flash, you know Frank. He valved off a bunch of streets up above, until he found the right one."

"We all know Frank." When any honchos were around, the foreman of the water distribution crew hopped to it, the consummate professional.

Several of the old street's cobbles had been scraped loose and teetered on the upper lip of the hole. No guarantee, of course, that Deuce's missing water was the culprit. Depended. They'd have to see what happened to pumpage at the plant, whether it came back down to what the operators thought it should be. Probably would.

"The guy in the car? Hurt bad, you say?"

J.J. nodded. "Screwed up his back, looked like. They had him immobilized—head on a board, one of them straps around his forehead. Scared shitless, the poor bugger."

They contemplated the scene.

Deuce imagined what it would be like to break his back, to suddenly find himself in a different life. "You think of that happening and it makes your own problems look pretty goddamn insignificant."

"Well," J.J. said consolingly, "you work with what you got."

A couple of old beaters had been abandoned to the snow. Deuce stared at the turn-of-the-century tenement across the way, wooden stairs zigzagging up its back, disappearing into the fog.

J.J. had followed his gaze, for he said, "It's interesting how we notice a place like this. The ass end of people's lives."

Deuce could imagine the run-down apartments inside, filled with the disgruntled, the lame, the incompetent—his father's natural constituency, when the old man had been mayor. "Places like this just irritate the hell out of me."

He said this because it was the sort of thing he'd always said, but at the moment he wasn't feeling irritation or anything else.

J.J., looking downhill, posed a question. "Well, well, what have we here?"

Two men had parked a city vehicle at the foot of the street, behind the barricade, and were making their way up toward the site. Paul Cutler and Chuck Fellows.

Ignoring Deuce and J.J., they halted on the far side of the collapse. Fellows, the head of public works, squatted down on his haunches and peered intently into it, while the city manager merely shook his head. He wore a neatly-cut camel's-hair coat. *Nice coat*, Deuce thought. A bit odd on the manager, though, who was generally a lousy dresser.

"Let's go on over." He wasn't going to waste an opportunity like this. The manager would never stoop to negotiating with the union himself, leaving the dirty work to Aggie Klauer, but every once in a while...

J.J. hesitated, then tagged along. "I suppose you're gonna make a scene."

"You're the one suddenly all hot on the subject of employee participation, remember?" Deuce said quietly over his shoulder.

"An idea with some merit," J.J. conceded, "but requiring a certain subtlety for implementation. Trying to chat up the manager? I don't know."

"Screw subtle," Deuce said.

Behind him, J.J. sighed. The union's most recent ploy—thanks to J.J.—had been to prepare a counter-budget to Cutler's pillage-and-burn version. Even the guys at the shit plant had offered their suggestions of ways to trim wastewater without layoffs, although Bob One and friends hadn't gone so far as to actually rejoin the union yet. All in all, a nice little publicity gimmick. Of course, it made no discernible impression on the city manager.

Chuck Fellows, the public works guy, moved along the edge of the collapse, looking at it from different angles. Cutler stayed put. Clearly, holes in the ground were not his thing.

By the time Deuce and J.J. reached the manager, Fellows had completed his inspection.

"Not much to see, no sign of services," he said. He was looking back and forth along the bluff-line now. The street descended sharply, then almost leveled out at the point of the collapse before angling down again but more gently. "Maybe used to be a bench along the river," he mused. "Wonder why the guy didn't see the hole. Unless the street collapsed under him."

Cutler glanced at Deuce, his look freezing for a moment—the shock of recognition—before moving on to J.J. "What do you know?"

J.J. explained the situation. Cutler pursed his lips and nodded, torquing his body slightly as if to symbolically exclude Deuce from the conversation.

Deuce had no intention of being excluded. "Too bad Lacy didn't look for the leak earlier."

Cutler cocked his head toward Deuce, just enough to squint suspiciously at him. "What's that supposed to mean?"

"The operators at the water plant have been telling him for months there's a leak somewhere in the intermediate system. Told Wayne, too."

"How much water?" Fellows wanted to know.

"Thirty thousand, maybe thirty-five. Guess you didn't get the word." Deuce turned his attention back to Cutler. "You see, Paul, that's what happens. Somebody fucks up, and Chuck here doesn't find out. You got your hierarchy. You got no backup." The rock-bottom argument in support of participatory democracy, of Cutler giving up just a little bit of his precious power.

"Need anything else here?" Cutler asked Fellows, who shook his head. Cutler turned to Deuce. "I'll see you in my office. This afternoon. One o'clock."

To his retreating back, Deuce continued, "That's why you oughta give rank-and-file guys more of a say-so, you ask me. Give us a real stake, then maybe this sort of thing won't happen. Talk to us, Paul." The manager moved steadily away, as if he had not heard.

"Well, that's interesting," J.J. mused when the other two were out of earshot. "It never would've occurred to me that we might want to make matters worse."

Deuce looked back at him and smiled. "You work with what you got."

CHAPTER 3

~

Walter Plowman was just settling down to work in his tiny room at the TV station when Chuck Fellows stormed in.

"In the building," he said in the abrupt way he had, "decided to drop in for a sitrep. Don't have much time." He stopped dead in his tracks and peered intently at Walter. Fellows had who-knows-how-many irons in the fire. His manner contained equal parts aggression and expectation and irony.

Walter knew, of course, the genesis of this stew of humors. He leaped up and set to work ripping the most recent National Weather Service products off the NAFAX machine and spritzing them with his water bottle so he could smooth and pin the broad curling sheets to the corkboard. As he went about it, he said, "The ice is out of the river below Bellevue." Twenty-five miles south of Jackson.

"When?"

"This morning. Early."

The maps in place, Walter explained the current situation, pointing out the highs and lows across the western states, showing the shifts in the two jet streams, and talking about the oscillation—unseen off the left-hand edges of the maps—of the massive permanent high in the Pacific Ocean. The winter weather pattern was quickly breaking down.

"What about the temperature?" Chuck asked. "Gonna hold?"

"There's a system moving in. Big but not particularly cold. Moist air flowing up from the Gulf."

"Stay above freezing?"

"Stay above freezing."

"And afterward?"

"A warming trend." They were now looking at each other, not the maps.

"So all that's left is the rain," Chuck said.

Walter remembered the previous November, the first time Chuck had appeared, out of the blue, come to ask how long he had before freeze-up on the river, and they'd ended up discussing spring floods, or more precisely what the preconditions were for a massive spring rise on the Mississippi—autumn rains, hard freeze, winter storms with their ice lens, sealing the snowpack and tamping it down, forming the geological-like strata that Walter had observed out at the Herrigs' that morning.

And now came the warm weather, which, if it held, if temps stayed continuously above freezing, would send the rotted snow slewing off the land in a single pulse, one continuous melt. Which would leave…

"That's right," Walter said, "just the rain."

Chuck had already taken a step toward the door.

"Still might not happen?"

"Still might not happen." Walter reached back and tapped the map in the desert southwest. "Watch the Four Corners. Watch for storms coming off the Pacific and reorganizing there."

"Okay. One more question. The Corps of Engineers is saying a twenty-five-foot crest, just about a flood of record..."

"Couple feet below."

"Close enough. A shitload of water, at any rate."

"But still five feet below what the system is designed to handle," Walter pointed out.

"Yeah, the city would be okay. But we'll have plenty to do out at the dog track. Anyway, what I want to know, Walt, is what do you think?"

"About the Corps's prediction?"

"Yeah."

Walter had been mighty reluctant to make any sort of prognostication when he'd first encountered Chuck, not knowing the man. Now he knew him. Liked him, too. And trusted him, at least as much as he trusted any man, which wasn't 100 percent.

"Corps's got the best equipment available. If anybody should know…"

Chuck ducked his chin down and looked up at Walter from beneath his eyebrows, not buying.

"Off the record?" Walter asked.

"Yeah."

"Gut level?"

"Yeah."

As one precondition after another had been met, Walter knew he'd started to anticipate, just as patterns in the random tossing of a coin can trick the mind into certain expectations. That was one thing. But Walter liked making forecasts other professionals shied away from. He'd been collecting data for more than a quarter century, adding to the baseline. All well and good, except what use was data without a theory? Floods follow droughts—that was his theory, or hypothesis, or conjecture at least. Might be right, might be wrong. Walter knew what he thought.

But a flood of record? No one could predict outliers like that. The unique event. The singularity. Pure experience. As individual as a human life. Had nothing to do with theories or conjectures or anything else in the scientist's toolkit. Sometimes, however, they weren't necessary. Sometimes a man, if he had spent his entire life attuning himself to the nuances of his experiences, the subtle fields of energy flowing through him…sometimes he knew more than he knew. Walter could, of course, keep it to himself. But knowledge not shared was hardly knowledge at all.

"I think," he told Chuck, although not without a twinge of uneasiness, "that the Corps of Engineers has got it wrong. I think what we're likely to have here is the worst flood in the history of the white man on the Upper Mississippi."

As Chuck headed out the door, Walter remembered himself and called after his friend, "Off the record. That's off the record."

But Chuck was already gone.

CHAPTER 4

~

As they took their seats in the city manager's office, Deuce checked out the others—Paul Cutler, Chuck Fellows, the city attorney Harvey Butts, the managers of water and streets, Frank Lacy, and finally Deuce himself. Six cowboys and one Indian.

Lacy had shown up in his work togs, looking particularly filthy. A hard worker, that Lacy. Deuce wasn't worried. He had the SOB dead to rights.

"Okay," Cutler said finally, "let's get this over with."

Hank Kraft began with an account of the accident.

"Do we know anything more about the condition of the driver?" Cutler asked no one in particular. Nobody knew.

Next Lacy told the tale of his heroic search for the main break and the patching of the system. The break, he claimed, could have just occurred. In the spring, when the frost came out of the ground, his crew was out straight dealing with ruptured pipes all over the place, this year already the worst he could remember.

"What evidence," the manager asked Deuce's boss Wayne Gourley, "do you have that this isn't what happened?"

"None," Wayne said at once, a little too eagerly to suit Deuce, although what could you expect? Wayne always tried to smooth things over, as if cause and effect didn't exist.

"We'll need a few days," Deuce interrupted, "to see if the pumpage stabilizes at the lower level. Probably it will."

"But even then," Cutler questioned.

"There's no way of knowing for sure," Wayne told him.

Chuck Fellows helped Deuce out a bit. "It didn't just happen. It's not simply the frost coming out of the ground. Hole's too big."

Frank Lacy challenged him. "You'd be surprised how fast erosion can occur. There could've been a mine shaft. Or a seam in the limestone."

"No sign of either," Fellows countered.

"Suppose you're right," Cutler told him. "Could it have happened gradually then, over a very, very long period, say from groundwater?"

"Of course," Fellows agreed brusquely. Cutler was just trying to make a record. He knew the answer to the question.

"So it still might not be this so-called lost water."

Deuce began to feel a little less easy in his mind and said, "It's not *so-called*. We've been missing water out of the intermediate system for months."

Cutler ignored him and turned to Harvey Butts, the city attorney. "What's our exposure here, Harv?"

"Depends." Deuce shifted his attention. From time to time, when he'd gone up to the mansions on the bluffs to play poker with the mucky-mucks, Harvey would sit in. Didn't play a bad hand, either, although not as good as he imagined. But good enough so that Deuce enjoyed beating him. Didn't mean squat at the moment, however. Butts had ambled into the city manager's office, the last to arrive, without so much as a nod in his direction. In situations like this, Butts didn't condescend to know Deuce.

"Basically," the lawyer said to Cutler, "for the city to be liable you have to have been notified of the problem...or for sufficient time to have elapsed during which you could reasonably have been expected to discover it for yourself." Deuce noted the formal, well-organized statement, more like written than spoken language. Butts used the second person plural, delicately distancing himself from the whole matter, the first faint rumbling of what was sure to be a storm of ass-covering.

Cutler turned to the street department chief. "Did we know, Hank?"

Kraft shook his head.

"Do we have any idea when the collapse occurred?" Cutler asked.

Again Kraft shook his head.

Cutler turned back to the lawyer. "This was a city street, Harv, but it was an alleyway, and for all we know, the collapse occurred as the car drove over it."

The lawyer nodded, as if agreeing. "Need to find out."

"What about the seat belt?" Fellows suddenly piped up.

"Wasn't wearing one?" Butts asked the manager.

"So I understand."

"I suppose it doesn't make any difference," Fellows said.

Butts smiled pleasantly at him. "Not at all. The folks down in Des Moines agree with you. A man ought to be responsible for his acts, you betcha."

Fellows looked skeptical.

"If it's true and he wasn't wearing one," Cutler asked, "what are the chances that we could get out from under?"

"Well," Butts said, lifting his chin and stroking his neck, "I'd have to check, but if memory serves, a certain percentage of the fault can be attributed to the driver. We'd have to prove his failure contributed to the injury. That might be admitted to mitigate damages." Like a witness coached to answer no more than asked, Butts stopped. That was the way he played poker, too. Maybe if he'd been a courtroom lawyer, he would've had a little more flair, but he was one of those back-room guys.

"And?" Cutler prodded again.

"Assuming we could do all this, well, then, damages might be reduced as much as…oh, 5 percent."

The others groaned, except Fellows, who laughed.

"So," Cutler pressed on, "it comes down to whether we knew about the problem."

"Or should have known," Butts amended.

"Not possible," Frank Lacy interrupted. "Situations like this just happen. No warning, then boom, you've got a huge friggin' hole to deal with. As soon as we find out, me and my boys are on it, middle of the night, weekends, makes no difference."

"And the missing water," Fellows said, turning to Deuce, "you didn't find any trace of it yourself, when you looked?"

"The fuck…," Lacy said.

"What?" Cutler snapped.

Oh, shit, Deuce thought, *here we go*. "No," he said to Fellows, "I didn't find it."

"What were you doing looking for the water?" Cutler demanded.

"It was thirty, thirty-five thousand gallons a day we were treating, Paul, and then sending who the hell knows where. Money flushed down the toilet. I thought somebody oughta go look for it. Lacy was sitting on his ass."

Now Wayne Gourley rushed in. "Frank called me to complain that Deuce had been harassing him. I talked to Deuce and told him to lay off. I told him explicitly not to have anything to do with Frank and his operation."

"And you went and looked for the water anyway?" Cutler said to Deuce.

Cutler was royally ticked off, but Deuce at the moment was feeling none too accommodating himself.

"Yeah, I did."

"What does this do to our situation?" Cutler asked Harvey Butts.

"Oh, I suppose it doesn't help. All this information will come out in the depositions, of course, if we get that far. As for the rest…juries tend to take a dim view of this kind of infighting."

Cutler turned back to Deuce. "And you thought you were trying to do what, make Frank here look bad, was that it?"

"I was trying to save the city a few bucks," Deuce countered, although he certainly wouldn't mind sticking it to Lacy.

Cutler continued. "You disobeyed a direct order." He glowered at Deuce, an I'd-love-to-fire-your-ass-on-the-spot glower. "You don't know how much potential damage you've done."

At the thought of millions of dollars in jury awards, Deuce's stomach got queasy, but he wasn't about to back down.

"The water *was* missing. The operators at the plant knew it. We'd been saying it for months. And we were right."

"What I'm interested in," Fellows interrupted, "is why I didn't know about this. Why did I have to find out from Goetzinger here and Seth Brunel?" He directed this inquiry at Wayne, and then explained to Cutler that Seth had gone around with Deuce looking for the water.

"I didn't think it was a big deal, Chuck," Wayne told him. "Frank couldn't find it."

"It is a big deal. It's become a big deal. And whatever you and Frank think, the operators obviously think different."

Deuce, suddenly finding himself with an ally, took heart. He barely knew Fellows, but the man had a rep for bluntness, just the sort of person who could disturb the repose of Wayne's last few months before retirement.

"The only reason the operators noticed anything," Wayne now claimed, "was because it was in the intermediate system. In either of the others, a discrepancy that small would've been swamped by the normal variation in the pumpage."

"I don't care about the details," Fellows countered, "I care about the disagreement. If you've got a disagreement in your operation, I want to know about it."

Gourley's cheeks twitched and eyes blinked. "I didn't think it was significant."

At this point, Paul Cutler put an end to Deuce's boomlet of hope.

"I expect my people to exercise judgment," Cutler said. "Whether Chuck should have known is immaterial. Wayne made a determination. It was up to him"—pointing at Deuce—"to follow orders, not to go off half-cocked looking for the water on his own."

"And you didn't find it, did you, Goetzinger?" Lacy pointed out with a big grin.

When Deuce tried to continue, Cutler cut him off. "I've heard more than enough from you."

Lacy was enjoying himself. From his crotch, in which one of his hands was dangling, hidden from Cutler's view, he gave Deuce the finger.

CHAPTER 5

~

At the end of the meeting, Chuck Fellows walked out with Goetzinger and told him that whatever else had happened, he appreciated his initiative in the matter. Goetzinger studied him, as if making a judgment, then merely insisted again that the water was missing.

"Well, we're gonna find out," Chuck told him.

Wayne Gourley would try to sweep anything smaller than a blue whale under the rug, Gourley nothing but timeserver.

Back at his desk, Chuck tried to concentrate on the routine stuff that had continued to pile up during his many absences, but the scene with Goetzinger and the others bothered him. Shit flows downhill. Goetzinger got reamed out because he disobeyed an order and yet, of the lot of them, he was the only innocent party. How damn ironic was that? Well, fuck, Chuck couldn't just leave it at that.

When he got back to Cutler's office, the door was open, so he walked in. Only Harvey Butts remained. The manager stopped talking to him in midsentence and impatiently turned his attention to the intruder.

"Yes?"

"Deuce Goetzinger isn't the problem here."

"Oh?" The manager's evident hostility might have had some other cause, but no doubt he'd made a note of Chuck walking out with Goetzinger earlier.

"It's well known," Chuck told him, "that Frank Lacy runs his operation as he damn well pleases. And as for Wayne Gourley, he's as good as retired."

"Goetzinger disobeyed a direct order."

"Maybe the water's missing, Paul, and maybe it isn't, but Gourley and Lacy just blew the operators off."

"If Goetzinger was unhappy, he should have come to you."

Cutler set considerable store in doing things by the numbers, so this suggestion reeked of hypocrisy.

Chuck told him, "If you need whistle-blowers, then they're not the issue, it's the organization that's fucked up."

"Anything else?"

"Nope."

"Then you'll excuse us."

Harvey Butts, displaying his usual psychiatrist's demeanor, had witnessed this exchange without offering comment. No doubt that would wait until he and the manager were alone again. As for Cutler, well, he obviously wanted to bury Goetzinger in an anthill up to his eyeballs and didn't give a shit about anything else.

Chuck executed an about-face and left.

~

At the end of the afternoon, he stopped down at the city garage, where he found Hank Kraft, head of the street department, comfortably settled in at the end of his workday. Having been at the roasting of Goetzinger and that dustup obviously still on his mind, he was ready for a little pleasant consideration of the troubles of others. Chuck had no time or patience. He had things to do.

He told Kraft that he needed somebody who could operate a dozer. The job would last about a month. Seven days a week. Six p.m. to three in the morning. Starting the next day. When Kraft tried to return to the Goetzinger business, Chuck ended the conversation.

From the garage, he drove out to the dredge, which continued to vacuum sand off the bottom of the Mississippi River for the dog track's parking lots and access road. The discharge line had been shortened so that they could pump more sand, stockpiling the stuff near the southeastern corner of the construction site. They'd use a scraper to haul and place it.

Chuck stopped first at the harbor tug, idle and anchored at the far side of the open water. Soon its job would be done, no more ice to keep away from the dredge, and it could go on home. He found Orv Massey napping below decks, the tight quarters not quite as shipshape as usual and smelling of old man. Asleep, Orv resembled a corpse and reminded Chuck of his earlier fear that one day he'd arrive down at the site and find the ninety-two-year-old tug skipper dead and frozen on his boat. But Orv had survived, had even managed another birthday and become ninety-three, each year like another virtue. A commendable old man. Everything that Wayne Gourley was not.

Orv slowly roused himself, coming up from his sleep as from a great depth and gazing at Chuck without recognition, his memory only gradually catching up with his consciousness.

"The ice is out of the river south of Bellevue," Chuck told him.

Stiffly, Massey sat up on the edge of the narrow bunk. His waking did, indeed, resemble a man coming back from the dead. He tried out his voice.

"Yup. Heard."

"We're gonna have ice moving on the river up here before long."

"Hand me those, will ya?" Orv motioned toward the package of tiny cigars on the galley table. Chuck fetched them, and lit one with a wooden stove match, Massey's hands being too unsteady to accomplish the task at the moment. Orv tilted his head back and, eyes closed, blew out a stream of smoke. The drag revived him. The aroma of the smoke mingled with the other odors.

"Way ahead of you, Chucky lad."

"Good. All we need is for a floe to take out one of the swing wires. Or worse."

Orville reached out one of his ancient hands, the finger bones veering this way and that, and tapped the cloth on Chuck's trousers. "We got you this far, my friend," he said.

Chuck paused for a moment to admire the old man, so straightforward in his vices and virtues, a man who would be alive until the day he died.

Massey's great-grandson Billy ferried Chuck out to the dredge.

The temperature had been dropping, the fog thinning, white streamers drifting and hesitating above the water, making the breezes visible. A light rain had begun to fall.

Chuck and Billy flipped the fenders over the side of the workboat and climbed aboard the dredge, where the great humps of accumulated ice had begun to waste away, gleaming with meltwater. In the machine shed, Billy went back to his OJT with Sid Furlong, and Chuck climbed up into the lever room where Bud Pregler continued to perform his endlessly repeating ritual as he swept back and forth across the cut.

As soon as he spotted Chuck, he slid off his tall stool at once, relinquishing the controls. "All yours."

Chuck started to protest, but realized at once that this was just Pregler's little joke, a test of Chuck's presence of mind. If he was really serious about operating the dredge himself at night, let's see how quick he could pick up the rhythm of the setting and releasing of brakes and winches.

Chuck scrambled up onto the stool. The dredge was rotating to port, at the very end of its swing, no time to assess the situation. In a reflex, he reached to disengage the port winch, which pulled the cutterhead to the left. His hand closed around the ball atop the lever, his muscles already tensed to throw it into neutral. Parts of his mind worked at different speeds, like gear wheels, the small accelerating gear, his desire to act, countered by the flywheel of caution. The cutterhead continued to move to port, bearing down on the anchor it pulled against, nearly underneath the anchor boom. Chuck closed his eyes. He had no time, but he took time anyway, the few moments required. The starboard brake! Set that first!

He opened his eyes and removed his hand from the lever of the port winch long enough to cinch up the starboard brake. Then, the brake set, no danger that the winch, which had been running free, would spool and snarl its wire, he went back and disengaged it. The dredge paused at the very outside of the cut.

Chuck exhaled, a small puff of wind at the close call, and smiled back at Pregler, just to show that he wasn't put off by the stunt Pregler had pulled. Pregler nodded slightly.

Before he began to pull across the cut in the opposite direction, Chuck asked, "Do I need to lower the head?"

"It's fine for the moment."

Chuck performed the necessary steps and the dredge began its slow, steady sweep back to the right. He watched his gauges and didn't speak again until he'd lowered the right spud and raised the left at the center of the cut.

"I'm getting somebody from the city garage to handle the dozer," he told Pregler. That would complete Chuck's crew for the night work, himself as leverman, young Massey in the engine room, and the dozer operator.

"You sure you wanna do this, boss?" Pregler asked, for about the tenth time since Chuck had announced his intention. "I'm not gonna be here to hold your hand."

Pregler was an agitator. He liked to needle people.

At the right-hand edge of the cut, Chuck went through the reverse series of procedures, and the swing began back to port. His attitude was, what happened happened. Situations would come up. So what? The worst he could do was sink the damn dredge. He liked the idea of working twenty hours a day. It appealed to him. The object of the work was never as important as the work itself.

He asked Pregler about the production he'd been getting now that they'd shortened the line. They talked about that.

CHAPTER 6

~

After the debacle in Cutler's office, Deuce had stopped by the Riverview, one of his haunts, and nursed a cup of coffee and his grievances. Finally, sensing the passage of time, he looked at his watch. After two. The graveyard shift last night, the swing shift today. He needed to think about going back to his apartment and getting ready.

But at the moment movement was out of the question. He slouched in the booth and stared at the empty cup. Scraps of ideas drifted through his mind. How easy it would've been to blow the job off. He could. But then what?

Time ticked away. Up at the front, someone entered, and he glanced idly toward the soft concussion the door made as it swung shut. A woman, her head momentarily bowed as she dusted rain from her hair. Below the bright patchwork parka, her dress fell in sober gray folds. Nice calves. She stamped her feet and sparks flew off, water droplets catching the light. Then she looked up, and he started. Aggie Klauer.

She seated herself at the counter and plunked her shoulder bag down on the empty seat next to her. Deuce slid farther back in the booth, where he could observe unobserved.

Darlene took her order. The two women exchanged comments, and Dar walked away laughing. He wondered if maybe they knew each other.

Aggie seemed to remember something and scrounged around in her bag until she found it, a campaign button, which she pinned to her coat, tucking her chin into her collar so she could see what she was doing.

She relaxed, shucking the coat off and draping it casually over the back of the stool. Two o'clock on a Wednesday afternoon, a strange time, he thought, for her to be stopping at a place like the Riverview.

Not conscious of being watched, she went about making herself comfortable, like a woman at the end of her workday. She undid the button at her throat, giving her collar several little tugs to free and puff out the silky material of her blouse. She tentatively patted her short, strawberry blond hair, then gave it a quick, irritated raking over. Finally she sighed and let her body sag back in the chair, smiling wanly as Darlene served the coffee.

These simple acts fascinated Deuce, so used to her public, formal, scripted persona. She seemed to be unveiling the real Aggie—taking off her attitude and setting it aside—and he imagined that if he could have spoken to her just at that moment...

At once, he realized this was not a fantasy with a happy ending. Who the hell in his right mind wanted to catch a woman unawares and find out what she was really thinking? Not him, no way.

Aggie, her toilet complete, her coffee sugared and creamed to her satisfaction, had begun to look curiously around the room. Here was, he understood, another chance to strike a blow for the union cause—to fire some more blanks, at least—but at the moment he just wasn't up to it. He slid deeper into the booth.

He toyed with his coffee cup and tried to imagine a conversation with Aggie that didn't have anything to do with the union.

Then he contemplated the union's situation again and thought, what the hell, he might as well drag himself back to the firing line. One last time. He motioned for Darlene to come over.

"Has the woman at the counter paid yet?"

Darlene arched her eyebrows. "Well, well, well."

"Tell her the gentleman's picking up her tab."

"Gentleman?"

"Don't give me a hard time, Dar. Just tell her, okay?"

A half minute later, Aggie was standing next to his table, cup in hand. Wordlessly, he gestured toward the other seat, and she slid in across from him.

"So," she said as she settled herself.

"So."

They inspected each other. Aggie's face was still slightly flushed from the outdoors, her hair damp, as if it had been moussed, her expression full of curiosity. The aura of a woman relaxing had disappeared. She was back on duty.

"So...," she repeated, "tell me, where are you in your day?"

"Off at seven. Back on at three. What about you?"

"Going home to watch *Donahue*." She glanced at her watch and shook her head sympathetically. "I don't envy you, having to take different shifts all the time."

"Harder on the married men."

She nodded. "I expect. And anyway, you're a tough guy, right?"

"Regular John Wayne."

They stopped speaking. Where this conversation might go was anybody's guess. But Deuce didn't mind the silence. Their relationship hadn't exactly been a crashing success, but at least they'd never rushed into the gaps with mindless chatter. Beneath the freed collar of her blouse, the end of her collarbone was visible, winter pale. Her oval face, small and also pale, its features comfortably spaced but another man's idea of pretty, was rescued by her array of expressions—amusement, wonder, incredulity, irony, boredom, amusement again. Before he had begun to deal with her across the negotiating table, she'd seemed waif-like, insubstantial, not the sort of person to let her own ideas stand in the way of anybody else's, the city manager's, for instance. Those preconceptions seemed less important now.

"You talked to Cutler recently?" he asked.

"Not since yesterday. I took a personal day. Why?"

"Not important." Her expression remained alive as she waited for him to elaborate. She studied his face. With Aggie, Deuce always felt seen. When he offered no explanation, she changed the subject.

"Took my mother to Mass. First Wednesday."

"Exciting."

"You'd be surprised."

"Which parish?"

"Nativity. Your family belongs to St. Columbkille's, I believe."

"That's where my mother went."

She registered the significance of this, then asked, "How is your father, by the way? How's he doing? We don't hear much about him down at the Hall."

Deuce gave her his best how-the-hell-should-I-know shrug.

"I see," she said. "I understand you two don't get along."

"We've had our moments." He didn't like talking about the old man. When people asked him about his relationship with his father, it was always his father they were interested in.

"Nevertheless," Aggie persisted, "I'd think you'd want to check up on him from time to time, just to make sure."

"Just to make sure what?"

The sharpness of this reply stopped her. She shook her head and looked down, seeming to discover her coffee cup. She took a sip.

He considered launching an attack on his father, but discarded the idea.

"The old man and I have a perfect relationship," he said instead, "until one of us opens his mouth."

Her smile had just a trace of mocking in it. "Just like you and me, then."

This seemed to be a cue, so they lapsed into silence once more.

Dressed for Mass, all her negotiating outfits with their whiffs of military readiness home in the closet, Aggie radiated a surprising gentleness of manner. Even her vigilance, given present company, did not completely hide this, and if he had found her increasingly attractive before, as they went mano a mano over articles in the union contract—there was, indeed, something satisfyingly erotic about negotiating with a woman—now he found her even more so, more feminine, certainly, which was okay, but more complex, too, which was even better.

"So then," she asked, "when I see Paul, what's he going to tell me?"

Deuce didn't want to talk about Cutler and the business of the missing water. How much more enticing a round or two of sparring on a more intimate level.

"Don't tell me you've been trying to negotiate with him again," she said.

He might not want to talk about the water, but only a moron, Deuce realized, would give Cutler the first crack at defining reality here. So he briefed her, told the tale without embellishments, forgoing the urge to justify himself. He didn't even bother to criticize Frank Lacy and Wayne. Aggie knew what these people were like; she didn't need Deuce telling her. If he had, it would've just sounded like poor-little-me. She asked some questions. He answered them.

"I suppose," he said finally, "this won't help with the union proposal."

"The committee? Not to worry," Aggie reassured him, "this will have no effect upon your prospects for getting that approved."

"Well, that's good news then."

"Watch him," Darlene warned as she came over with refills, "he's a regular Casanova."

Deuce laughed. "Yeah, and I got a new line, Dar. You'd love it."

Aggie laughed, too. She looked at Dar, curious, and Deuce could see what she was wondering. Which was okay.

Alone again, they quietly regarded each other.

Finally, she said, "A pretty woman."

"Darlene?"

"Yes."

Never what you'd call svelte, Dar had put on more pounds since she got married and started popping out kids. Still, she was handsome in her way. The two women made quite a contrast.

"I understand you're very successful," Aggie said all at once.

The boldness startled Deuce. "Very successful at what?"

She laughed lightly and rescued herself. "Well, at your job..."

"Other things, too."

"No doubt... Of course, you're not such a great negotiator."

"I'm not, huh?"

"You're a very good poker player, I'm told."

He couldn't quite pick up her intonation and responded with the barest of gestures, meant to be interpreted any way she chose. She leaned back and crossed her arms and looked at him seriously.

"Tell me," she said, "what's the attraction?"

"Cards?"

She nodded.

"You don't approve?"

It was her turn to make a gesture of uncertain intent.

"You don't have to talk when you play," he said.

She nodded at this answer, which was in character if nothing else. "I've often wondered," she said, "why you took over the negotiations. A man with your particular interests."

The question unexpected, Deuce hesitated. His impulse was to tell her the truth, but you started telling the truth and pretty soon things got out of hand. They were looking at each other quietly again. Although the irony remained, everything they said laced with it, a level of understanding seemed to have come into their exchange, too, some recognition of the interior spaces from which they observed each other.

"It's curious," she continued. "You're pulling all these stunts, kamikaze-style, as futile as they are amusing. The casual observer might think you were actually serious. But I don't think so. I don't think you believe in any of it, not even the committee with no instructions."

"Really? And do you have to believe in something to do it?" he asked. "I don't believe in poker. I just play it."

"If you don't believe in something, what value does it have?"

"Judging by all the demented beliefs people act on, I'd say the whole idea of believing has been pretty much discredited."

"And what do you put in its place?"

"Nothing. As far as the committee's concerned, an argument can be made for it, it's worth trying. Why do you need more than that? If it doesn't work out, so be it. Just as well you never believed in it."

She had leaned forward, and he could see the words of protest rising up in her, but all at once she stopped and leaned back and smiled a little shit-eating smile. "What a crock."

"Makes sense to me," he said, delighted.

"Of course it makes sense. Still, it's a crock. Did you ever really think you might win?"

"Get the committee?" Here truthfulness was easier. "First I didn't know, then I figured probably not. Haven't given up. Never give up." And he hadn't, although as she said, his chances of success were approximately zilch.

She pushed her cup forward so she could lean toward him again, both elbows on the table. Her eyes were serious, asking him for something besides his usual line of bullshit. "If not out of conviction, if not because you think you can win, then why?" This was, in another form, the same question she had asked at first—why was he involved in the negotiations at all?

He stared over her shoulder and considered the matter. There was his mother, of course, but even there... He let his gaze rest on her once more. He liked the intelligence in her face. He thought of all the time people wasted doing things that weren't worthy of them.

"I don't know," he said.

She tipped her head to one side and looked at him more intently, but she didn't say any of the obvious things she might have, consolidating her small victory. She didn't say anything at all for a time and then merely, "Of course, you don't have to know."

And it was true. At the deepest level, he had no idea why he'd taken over the negotiations. Or continued to fight for the committee with no instructions. His root system didn't extend down that far.

For the rest of their brief time together, they said little, doing mostly what they did best together.

The parting was awkward. All their previous separations had been in their official capacities, terminating sessions abruptly, leaving in a huff, and so forth. Now Aggie put her coat with its campaign button back on, her small breasts straining for a moment against the silkiness of her blouse. They exchanged incomplete sentences and she began to leave. "But," Deuce said, as much to get her to turn around so he could see her face one more time as to score a last point, "it was a good idea. You know it was a good idea."

She did turn, and their eyes linked and held. Hers were gray, flecked with gold, like an unmined vein of ore. She wore almost no makeup, and her light eyebrows were barely visible, her skin almost too pale.

"Yes," she said, "it was a very good idea."

CHAPTER 7

∼

When Chuck got home just after seven, expecting his last home-cooked meal for a while, he discovered Diane in the living room watching the *Donahue* show (which she had obviously taped earlier) and no sign of culinary endeavors, unless popcorn counted. Gracey sat on the couch next to her mother, with the popcorn bowl on her lap. She giggled when she saw her father, and put her hand over her mouth.

Diane was much engrossed in the show. She glanced at Chuck, as she might toward a strange noise and, having satisfied herself that it was nothing, went back to *Donahue*. Despite her obsessive home-maker streak, she was capable of saying to hell with it every once in a while and ordering out.

She was also capable of taking a remarkably blasé attitude toward what another person might consider a fairly unusual circumstance, certainly one requiring some explanation. For she and Gracey were not alone on the couch. Next to them sat a young black woman that Chuck had never seen before. "This is Francine," Diane informed him. End of story.

"Hello," Francine said, looking very uncomfortable.

"How you?" Chuck motioned for her to stay put and reached down for a perfunctory handshake. Francine, unsure whether she should be looking at him or the TV screen, shifted her gaze back and forth several times and finally settled on the TV. Chuck asked no questions, determined to be unsurprised.

"Hi, Li'l Bit," he said to Gracey, wedged between the two women, and she lifted the bowl toward him, cradling it unsteadily her little hands. He reached over for a handful of popcorn and began to toss the kernels into his mouth one after the other.

Maybe, he thought, *Diane had encountered the woman at the clinic and brought her home with the idea of exposing the kids to another black.*

31

From where he stood, looking almost directly down, Francine's features were foreshortened and very little visible. Stray hairs curled up from her short Afro. The toes of her woolen socks poked out, her shoes nowhere to be seen. She sat with her back straight, leaning slightly forward, and something in the fixity with which she watched the TV suggested sadness.

Diane told Chuck, "You can rewind it later and watch the whole thing, if you want."

"Pass," he said and would have left at once except for his curiosity about the young black woman.

On the tube, Donahue's guests sat in a semicircle, each chair with a small space around it, a sort of waterless moat symbolizing the basically adversarial nature of the proceedings, the chairs occupied by their assortment of Jacksonians.

"Where's Todd?" Chuck asked.

"Upstairs. He was expecting a man."

Chuck would have followed up on this curious statement, too, except for the fact that the camera had lit for an instant on one of the guests.

"Sam Turner? He's out of the hospital?" When Chuck had visited him, Turner had looked like hell. He still looked awful. A pair of crutches lay on the floor behind him, which Chuck just glimpsed, the camera shifting away almost at once. And landing on somebody else he knew.

"Oh, sh—how did they find him?"

"I've been explaining to Francine," Diane said, "who the Vasconcelloses are." Lonny was the one on the TV screen, seated next to the mayoral candidate Roger Filer, Filer looking like his dog had just died. Phil Donahue asked a question of one of the other guests and the camera shifted again, to Reiny Kopp this time.

The popcorn was making Chuck thirsty, so he went into the kitchen for a beer and took the last cold one out of the fridge. He pried the cap off, but, before he put the bottle to his lips, stared at it and decided, what the hell, if he was going to be working twenty-hour days, he might as well give up booze for the duration. This idea pleased him. He took a slug, the beer tasting particularly good, and went back to the living room in a better frame of mind. He pulled a footstool out and sat on it and watched the show.

"Who's winning?"

"The women," Diane said. "Wouldn't you say the women, Francine?"

"Definitely the women," Francine agreed. She sat with her hands pressed between her thighs, the coke on the coffee table in front of her barely touched.

The women Diane and Francine thought were winning turned out to be El Plowman and Johnny Pond's wife, Chloe.

Two of the cross burners were on the show, too, the older ones, not Lonny's brother. Out on bail, they were not allowed to travel, but a camera had been set up in one of the conference rooms at the Way-farer Inn out on the highway so that they could appear via remote. One was large and quiet, the other small and loud and called Dwight.

"A white speaks out, why that's racist. We can't say a thing," Dwight was ranting. "It's the NAACP that's the real racists, you ask me, wanting everything for the blacks."

Johnny Pond's wife listened, sitting perfectly still and composed, and then responded, "The NAACP seeks equal treatment for African-Americans in this society, nothing more."

"What about whites," Dwight blurted out, "what about equal treatment for us?"

And so it went. Chuck observed the way the camera grouped people, the two cross burners together in their motel room, of course, but more interesting, Lonny bracketed with Filer and El Plowman with Kopp, while the blacks were mostly shown in isolated shots, a student from the U. and Sam Turner and the thin, handsome Chloe Pond. These shots set the general tone, but there were telling variations. As Chloe Pond tried to speak about the NAACP, Dwight interrupted her repeatedly, and the two of them were shown in split screen. And a short time later, as Lonny was mouthing off about cross burning as a form of free speech, the camera panned back to include the battered Sam Turner.

Phil Donahue, the white-haired host with his pleasant let's-you-and-him-fight expression, hardly opened his mouth, this not being a group that required a kick in the ass before they'd do their performing bears routine for the edification and amusement of his audience.

Whether El Plowman and Chloe Pond were winning or not, clearly Dwight and Lonny were the stars of the show, just the sort of loudmouth dipshits that drove up the ratings. Lonny had established himself as the theoretician of the pair, trying to build a case for cross burning as nothing but free speech, like pornography and flag burning.

El Plowman laughed and asked him if he approved of flag burnings, and without waiting for a response suggested that free speech didn't include the right to make threats and cross burnings were certainly threats. To which Lonny retorted that he felt threatened when somebody burned a flag.

All this was too abstract for Dwight. "You wanna know what threats are? Drive-by shootings. Them's threats. You can't go out at night, you're afraid of getting slaughtered in your bed. You want that?"

At this point, Roger Filer decided to provide some perspective. "There's a real concern here," he began and then launched into a story about a fellow he'd met at a supermarket who'd told him that he didn't mind responsible blacks moving to Jackson. It was their ragtag relatives sure to follow that gave him the willies. "That's not the way I would have put it, but it *is* the perception…"

Gracey had the right idea. She was ignoring it all and picking through the popcorn, making a collection of old maids.

"Their ragtag relatives?" Plowman asked, clearly incredulous. "I didn't know we had a policy about relatives. What a wonderful idea. I'm sure we've all got some relatives we'd just as soon keep out of Jackson."

"I'm just saying—," Filer began, but he didn't get a chance to finish before Dwight had leaped to the attack again.

"People wanna live with their own kind."

"Is that so?" El Plowman retorted. "Perhaps you'd like to keep all blacks out of Jackson, then."

"We got our place, they got theirs. We don't wanna go where they live, why do they wanna come here?" As Dwight spoke, the camera returned to Filer, shaking his head.

El said, "This young man doesn't represent the people of Jackson."

"The hell I don't," Dwight yelled. "We're gonna have an election. We're gonna find out who represents the people. It ain't you."

Filer rushed back in, hoping no doubt to salvage something from this disaster. "If African-Americans want to come to Jackson, that's fine. But there's an element of fairness here, too. Lots of young people have had to leave the city to find jobs somewhere else, not to mention all the people out of work. Tax dollars shouldn't be used to attract blacks. It's not fair. If anything, the money should be used to create jobs so that our young people could come back." This was, of course, code for exactly what the loudmouth had just said, but it created the pleasing illusion of being calmly reasonable. As he spoke, Dwight was shown on split screen nodding in agreement.

Chuck said, "When Filer watches the rerun of this, he's not going to like it."

"It's his own fault," Diane countered. "He should have known enough not to appear with the cross burners. He was even worse at the beginning. He kept on trying to tell his stories and getting cut off."

Chuck snickered. "No doubt he prefers the city council, where he can yap all he wants."

"I like your mayor," Francine said, the first words she'd spoken since Chuck had sat down. "If I lived here, I'd vote for her."

Diane agreed. Chuck voiced no opinion, but he supposed that he'd end up voting for Plowman, too, like it or not. In state and national elections, he usually went for the Libertarian or Green or somebody else who refused to sacrifice principle to political expediency, but local elections, being nonpartisan, didn't provide such satisfying handles to grab hold of. And the other candidates for mayor were an even sorrier lot than Filer.

As Chuck considered this, his attention had lingered on Francine and the mystery of just who she might be. Her face was very broad, almost dished, as if it she had been punched while the flesh remained malleable, her nose flattened and the tip of it turned down. Her cheeks flared outward. Her eyes squinting at the TV and her body canting forward gave the impression of someone advancing into a stiff headwind. She wore strictly utilitarian clothes, jeans and a loose red pullover with a pouch on the front into which she could have tucked her hands for warmth.

Chuck recalled Diane's odd comment from earlier, explaining why Todd had gone upstairs—he'd expected a man.

Ahhh, he thought, *of course*. Obvious. He should have guessed it right off the bat.

"You work for Dexter Walcott. You're one of his carpenters."

"I told you," Diane said to Francine, "that he'd get it if we gave him enough time."

"Daddy's smart," said Gracey, who had been in on the joke.

Francine herself turned toward Chuck. "I'm not a carpenter, Mr. Fellows, just an apprentice. I haven't been with Mr. Walcott but a few months now."

Diane used the remote to switch off the TV. "We've put her stuff up in the spare room. She's going to share the bathroom with the kids. Isn't that right, Gracey?"

"Yeah," said Gracey, grinning and twisting around in her shy delight, the old maids disappearing from her lap down between the seat cushions.

"I'll be out of the bathroom early," Francine assured Chuck. "I won't get in their way."

"Don't worry," he told her. "We're glad to have you."

And he was, although, like Todd, a little disappointed that Walcott hadn't seen fit to send along one of his men. No doubt he had his reasons.

"So," he said, "tell me, Dex's got most of his crew on the job site now, does he?"

"A few of us. He's building it up a little bit at a time."

Chuck nodded. Made sense. "And you know who Lonny Vasconcellos is? Diane told you?"

"Yes, sir."

"Don't call me sir. I'm not your superior officer."

"Yes, sir."

Now that she was talking, Francine's nervousness became even more apparent. But they continued chatting, and after a time the pizzas which Diane had ordered came, Todd storming downstairs to greet the delivery boy.

Later, in the messiness of eating, all of them together, Francine asked, "Could you pass me another piece, please?" Carving out a slice, Chuck caught Diane's eye and smiled.

Chapter 8

~

The three of them bounced down a rutted dead-end street. "Not too cherry, is it?" Bob Two observed. Bob One parked at the end, next to The Jackson Country Club. Deuce, with more determination than enthusiasm, had been talking up his democracy scheme as they drove around. The guys from the shit plant—it didn't make any difference how damn difficult they happened to be—remained too valuable a resource to be ignored, the mother lode of malcontents.

They all got out and waded through the sodden snow alongside one of the fairways to a lift station set between the golf course and a cluster of small frame houses. Big, lazy snowflakes fluttered through the gloom.

"Go shut her down," Bob One told his partner. The wellhead was outside, and Bob One peered down and swore.

"Cutler loathes the idea of the committee, Bob," Deuce said, continuing the exchange begun in the truck. "That should tell you something."

"Yup, sure does, Houdini. Grant you that much… Look at that." Bob One gestured with disgust down at the dull coat of scum floating on top of the sewage. "Goddamn country club." He obviously had some vision of what proper sewage should look like.

Two electrical lines hung down, one disappearing into the goop, the other limp, its end floating. Bob One dipped the second up and down until it broke through the surface and a pool of bright brown light appeared in the middle of the dullness. "Electrodes," he said, and began to haul the line in, on the end of which was suspended an object the size of a shotgun shell. "All the grease and shit they put into the system plugs 'em up."

"Okay," Bob Two said, returning.

Bob One took out a penknife and scraped the electrode and dug out the end containing the sensor, used to cycle the pumps on and off. He worked barehanded, his fingernails ruined, shiny black oil on his palms.

"I'll say one thing for ya, Goetzinger," he conceded, "none of us would've thought up such a cockamamie scheme, not in a million years."

"Maybe it ain't cockamamie."

Bob One grunted. Deuce recalled his encounter with Aggie the day before, admitting to her that he didn't really know why he was doing the thing, why he kept on pushing it, cockamamie or not. He'd been considering the matter, mulling it over in the hours since, but all this cogitation had totaled up to precisely zip. Nothing remained but to play out the cards he'd dealt himself.

But...on the other hand, if he could con the shit plant guys into rejoining the union and they came armed with the typical nutso enthusiasm of new converts, who knew what might happen... Something interesting, maybe. Deuce had no plan, of course. He'd never had one, or much of one. He did something, waited to see what happened, then did something else. Spontaneity was the pleasing name he had for his ignorance, the feather he stuck in his cap.

When Bob One was satisfied, he dropped the electrode back into the well and pulled up the second line, longer than the first, and repeated the process. "Sometimes, on wash days," Bob Two said, "you can smell detergent." At the moment, the odor was of rancid grease. Sewage never smelled exactly like you expected it to smell.

When both lines were back in the well, Bob Two went to restore the power while Bob One wiped his hands off with snow. They waited until the pump cycled on, pumped the well down to the lower electrode, and cycled off.

In the truck again, Bob One turned around, and they headed back on out.

"Okay, Houdini, I'll tell ya, this is the deal," he said after they were well under way. "We just don't see what it gets us. Slimy bastards like Cutler will figure some way to weasel out of anything this committee of yours dreams up. What guarantee you got it won't be...well, fuck, just a committee, just like every other goddamn, do-nothin' committee we ever heard of?"

"You want guarantees?" Deuce asked, incredulous. "Shit, did you just get off the boat? I'm Houdini, not God."

Bob One laughed.

"All I'm saying," Deuce told him, "is this—we get the committee, we can shoot back. Who the hell knows if we'll hit anything?"

"You can bet that's for sure."

"Mostly we probably hit nothing, you're right. But not always. It's like damn voting. Most of the time nobody goes to the polls. Too much trouble. Who gives a fuck? But every once in a while something big comes along, some big fucking deal, like *this* goddamn election, for instance, and suddenly everybody's up in arms, and people start thinking about voting the bastards out. That's the same thing here. When a real shitstorm hits, we got a weapon. If it wasn't true, Cutler wouldn't be so damn set against the thing."

"We'll never be able to vote Cutler out of office," Bob One said, determined to be contrary. He stopped the truck. They were on Grandview Avenue, not near any of Bob One's outlying stations.

"Fuck, not again," Deuce said. He remembered only too well having to hump all the way back from the shit plant the first time he'd tried to recruit them. "I gotta be someplace."

"You shoulda thought about that before ya agreed to take a ride with people like us. Anyway, you ain't got so far to walk this time, Houdini. That means you got our attention. But you ain't our friend yet."

"The game's almost over, Bob."

"Not my problem."

Bob Two knew when it was his turn to speak. "Have a nice day," he told Deuce, the words trailing off down the road, for Bob One had already put the truck in gear and was barreling away.

CHAPTER 9

~

El's attention was split, half on the hurried sounds of Walter overhead, half on Aggie's tale of her chance encounter the previous day with Deuce Goetzinger. When Walter rushed, something uneven and galumphing in the rushing, El always felt a touch of anxiety, such as an older woman might have for an elderly husband. His footsteps came stuttering down the back stairs. El waited for him to successfully arrive at the bottom, but managed a smile at Aggie, who was obviously enjoying her telling so much.

Aggie was rushing, too, but verbally. "That's all he said—'I don't know.' But...it was like all his masks had, you know, like, fallen away or something. The way he has of always watching for you to put down the wrong card, the devious little poker player—gone. It was like, I don't know, like we were together for the first time. God, did I say that?"

"Well!" El said. Here was something new.

Her friend's wide-eyed quality wasn't at all like credulity, just a capacity for wonder. And humor, too, for the next thing she said was "Fortunately, the restaurant didn't provide beds or I'd have been in the sack with him in a flash." She was obviously ecstatic to be able to confess this. Here *was* something new.

Walter, in transit through the room, had paused to listen. "I say 'I don't know' all the time. Haven't noticed the ladies lining up to get in bed with me."

He disappeared into the mud room. "It doesn't count if you do it all the time," El called after him.

Walter grumbled at this injustice but didn't tarry long enough to comment further. He was running late and human foibles were no match for the siren song of bad weather. The storm door had already slammed shut before El realized she had something else to say to him. She hurried to the door and thrust it open.

"Remember you said that, dear, when people start asking you how high the water's going! 'I don't know.' Remember!"

She couldn't tell if he heard, not that it made any difference. Walter was too single-minded to be prudent.

"And get something to eat!" she yelled, just before the car door slammed. Outside, the fog remained, but the rain of yesterday had turned to snow, flakes as large as half dollars.

She returned to the kitchen, shaking her head. "Good grief." She plopped herself back down in front of her tea. "He won't keep his mouth shut. He never listens. He won't eat. He never remembers his raincoat. He's a weatherman, for God's sake, you'd think he'd remember his raincoat."

El leaned back, her wrists crossed limply in her lap, a gesture of resignation.

"I suppose I should be happy for him. He's been scouring through all his precious data and talking to his buddies up and down the river and doing who knows what all. It's like he died and went to heaven…

"But," she decided, having second thoughts, "he'd *better* watch his mouth. I won't have him getting all caught up in the middle of things."

They paused to absorb this possibility, Walter getting all caught up in the middle of things, and then Aggie asked, a hint of genuine concern in her voice, "Does he really think water might go over the wall? I mean, really go over the wall?"

"Pfff, who knows? If he does, he hasn't told me. What he's saying to others I have no idea. Speaking of which, you'll never guess who called him up the other day."

Aggie shook her head.

"Fritz."

"Is that right? Wow. I asked Deuce about his father yesterday, but didn't get anywhere. He could've been dead for all the son knew."

"Well, turns out Fritz is very much alive…although, based on past experience, I'd have to say that's a decidedly mixed blessing." El immediately disavowed the sentiment with a wave of her hand.

"What did he want?"

El shook her head again. "Walter's so damn vague, who knows. The long-range weather pattern, for one thing…although Fritz has asked about that in the past. Something to do with when he plants his corn. He also asked about the river. Of course, under the circumstances…" El had cautioned herself not to read too much into the fact.

"Fritz Goetzinger," Aggie said with wonder, "the unsinkable Fritz."

Having brought Fritz up, El now discovered the ex-mayor wasn't a subject she cared to pursue. Unwillingly, she recalled her last, thoroughly unpleasant exchange with the man, when he'd shot the pig.

"Let's talk about somebody else, please."

They resettled themselves. The old steam radiator hissed softly. The humidity in the room was 100 percent, and El's walking outfit smelled pleasantly of damp wool.

"So what about the son?" El asked. "Is he throwing in the towel then?"

Aggie nodded. "I suppose. I've got a mediation scheduled with Fire tomorrow. We're pretty close. There's the staffing issue. And the EMT guys are pretty pissed because they'll have to go back on the trucks. The Association's been stonewalling, but it's mostly for show, I think."

Once one of the unions settled, the others could be counted on to come around. Police and Fire would get a little and no layoffs, everybody else nothing and some layoffs. Morale would sink even lower.

"It's over, then," El said. "Except maybe there'll be a thing between you and Mr. Deuce Goetzinger."

"Swell. After everything, what happens? I end up with a boyfriend. How pathetic is that?"

"It's about time you had yourself another beau."

"What a quaint word. Anyway, boyfriend, beau, who's got the time? I have a campaign to run."

"Hmm."

"I think you're going to win. You just don't realize how great you were yesterday." They'd already done the Phil Donahue debriefing during their walk, but however wonderful Aggie imagined El's performance, El was sure it would change nothing, except maybe improve Roger Filer's numbers, poor Roger now the victim of the liberal media establishment.

"All I care about," she told Aggie, "is putting the whole business behind me. I'm almost glad I'm going to lose. Let somebody else have the grief." That night the council would pass the miserable budget that they'd managed to cobble together. A victory for Paul. And there was the very real possibility of a flood, which would at the least

threaten the dog track project. And there was Ultima Thule, the cata-
log retailer, even less likely to come to Jackson after everything that
had happened. El should try to talk to Deke McKeown, the Ultima
CEO, again, while she was still mayor.

Anyway, losing the election made no difference. Being mayor
had turned out to be less than met the eye. And El had all her other
organizational ties in the city. She'd still have them. As mayor, she'd
attempted to operate without a consensus. Silly. A feverish dream.
Fortunately, fevers pass.

She told Aggie, "Getting a boyfriend might not seem like such
a great thing at the moment, but I think it would be wonderful if it
worked out. A genuine gift. I'd rejoice with you." It would perhaps
mean children, another generation.

Aggie remained unconvinced. "I'm not Deuce's type. He likes the
chesty kind, if the waitress at the Riverview is any indication."

"You have many other virtues, my dear. If your friend can't see
them, he doesn't deserve you."

El tried to imagine Aggie and Deuce together, but she didn't know
the younger Goetzinger very well and the image of Fritz kept intruding.

Aggie had, in the meantime, turned perfectly serious. "We could
have tried it, El. Deuce's idea. Maybe it wouldn't have worked. But we
could have tried it."

"Sorry I wasn't more help."

El remembered the scene with Paul, when she mentioned the
union's proposal and he hinted that he might quit if the committee
was forced on him. Probably he'd been bluffing. Anyway, she hadn't
pushed it. She'd been more interested in avoiding layoffs. She didn't
just want to bring more blacks to the city. She'd wanted to do things
for the people already there, too. Help everyone.

And what had happened? What had resulted from this laudable
sentiment? They were going to cut the bus service. There would be
layoffs. They'd do pretty much what any other city would do in similar
circumstances.

"I didn't mean to depress you," Aggie said, reading her expression.

"It's not you, dear. And I'm not depressed, not clinically, at least.
Probably I should be." She laughed. "My real depressions never have
anything to do with what's actually going on in the world. A year from
now, all this will have passed, everything will be hunky-dory, and I'll be
in the dumps. Go figure." El stared at her friend, who looked so festive
dressed in her bright walking outfit. "But this scheme of Deuce's, I

wonder... There's no reason it has to be in the union contract, is there? The city could simply do it."

"That's right. Of course, Paul…"

"To hell with Paul. We could just go ahead and do it."

"But…," Aggie said thoughtfully, "after all the trouble Deuce has gone to… I mean, shouldn't he get the credit?"

"Yeah, yeah, spoken like the girlfriend you claim not to be. But if it's a good idea, what difference does it make who does it? The council could just go ahead and authorize the committee, if we wanted."

"You could."

Or El could simply keep her mouth shut and bow out gracefully. Did she want to do that, bow out gracefully? Without her pushing, nothing would happen, that's for sure, and she could simply stop pushing, simply go through the motions. Then again, though a mayor might not succeed, though success was never guaranteed, there was nothing to keep her from continuing to try...

"And perhaps, my dear, we will."

CHAPTER 10

～

J.J. Dusterhoft was taking his ease down at the city garage when Deuce Goetzinger showed up. The snow continued to fall, but melted at once on the roadways. A number of Hank Kraft's people had stood down and were lounging in his office, J.J. among them. The golfing paraphernalia, stored for the winter, gave the place the aura of a pro shop, and most of the guys present were Kraft's golfing buddies, derisively known as the Street Elite by the guys who played euchre in the back room. J.J. didn't golf. He didn't play euchre, either. He kibitzed.

They had arrived at the matter of Reiny Kopp, Brian the mechanic introducing into consideration the rumor going around town that Kopp had orchestrated the pirate radio station business and most of the other stuff that had come down. David Duke got wind of the possibility somehow and was claiming he'd been hosed and demanding an investigation by the feds.

J.J. sat back and let the conversation ricochet around him and considered the logic of the situation. Kopp had pulled all sorts of stunts back in the sixties. There must be some unreconstructed sixties types still running around, and no doubt, the FBI had a file on Kopp, which might be resurrected should anybody care enough.

"David Duke's problem," he opined for the benefit of the others, "is that he's got no friends in D.C. The Dems hate him, that goes without saying. But the Republicans, too, worse if anything. After all, Duke's trying to make himself into one of 'em. How would you feel if he suddenly decided to become your friend? So you ask me, he can scream all he wants, nothing's gonna happen. And anyway, the interesting question isn't Reiny Kopp and David Duke, it's Kopp and El Plowman."

In this way, J.J. tossed out a matter he'd given some thought to, the speculation that Kopp and Plowman had cooked up this whole scheme just to discredit Roger Filer.

"You've gotta be kidding, Dusterhoft," Brian the mechanic said. "Plowman's a Girl Scout. She's even been sending back the out-of-town campaign money she's been getting."

J.J. hefted one of the woods from a set of golf clubs as if he was considering taking up the game. "Well, I'll grant you, she certainly gives the impression of over-the-top rectitude. On the other hand, maybe she's just very, very sly. Think about it—if Filer becomes mayor now, Jackson's rep as the heart of white-bread America will be set in concrete."

"We don't give a shit what anybody else thinks."

J.J. selected another club, a short iron, for an approach shot.

"At least you don't *think* you do."

In the midst of this, Deuce had stuck his head in the door.

"Speak of the devil," J.J. remarked upon spotting him, "we were just talking about you." Actually Deuce had been considerably earlier on the conversational agenda, but no matter. "We're told you've been harassing poor Bob Mikulec again."

"Is that what you're told?" Deuce had a wonderful capacity for remaining unmoved in the face of what must have been startling information, the rapid dissemination of his discussion that morning with the shit plant guys, another of his attempts to lure them back into the union.

Deuce surveyed the room, Kraft and the Street Elite, as he might look around a poker table to judge what cards the players held, then turned back to J.J. "Got a minute?"

"Say, Deuce," Brian the mechanic put in as J.J. was rising and he and Deuce on their way out, "word is that the city has offered police and fire 2 percent. If that's true, we better damn well get it, too."

Deuce paused long enough to glance at Hank Kraft and then gave Brian a look. "Is that what you hear?"

"That's the word."

"I see."

As they stepped out into the equipment storage barn for their private word, Deuce asked, "Tell me, J.J., do you people make a habit of talking about union matters in front of Kraft? He's management, for Christ's sake."

"Well, yes, you got me there. I don't myself, but it's true, the Street Elite and Kraft are awfully tight, talk about pretty near everything."

"Do me a favor. Tell Brian to keep his trap shut."

J.J. preferred to avoid unpleasant situations, but he supposed, under the circumstances...

"Since when," J.J. wondered out loud, "were you such a stickler for union etiquette?"

"Since always. You're gonna do something, do it right."

Deuce had lowered his voice. In the barn, words echoed around, like radio waves bouncing off the ionosphere. They shielded themselves behind the trash trucks, lined up nose-to-nose, their routes finished for the day.

"I was gonna tell you about my meeting with Mikulec," Deuce said. "I took a ride with the two Bobs this morning. Mikulec's acting like some damn Valley girl playing hard to get. But obviously you already know. I could've saved myself the trip."

"Bad news travels fast."

"I guess the hell it does. I suppose you know about the meeting in Cutler's office yesterday, too."

"'Fraid so. Hank can't keep his mouth shut any more than Brian can. Of course, we all love a good story."

"Cutler would fire my ass if he could."

"Never happen."

"Maybe. But he would if he could."

J.J. considered the implications of such a consequence. "Then you'd become a saint. A martyr to the sacred union cause."

Deuce snorted. "Sainthood. Now there's an idea."

"And here we were, thinking we'd run out of options. Let's see... what about a hunger strike? Like they do in Northern Ireland? All the locals of Irish persuasion could certainly appreciate that."

"Starve myself for the likes of Brian back there?"

"Well, yes, Brian doesn't inspire, I'll grant you. But let's face it, American unionists have never been really serious about their causes, not like the Irish. You could change all that. Think of all the marvelous publicity. And imagine the good things people will say about you after you're gone."

"Right."

"And it's said that saints give off a sweet scent after they die."

Deuce just laughed, and they stood in the gloom, J.J. musing on the delights of martyrdom, and Deuce musing on whatever he was musing on.

Finally, obliquely, Deuce returned to the matter of Bob Mikulec and the failure to get the shit plant guys to re-up.

"Hardly anyone gives a rat's ass about the committee. Two percent, that's what they want. Two percent! How friggin' boring is that?"

"Our fellow unionists are, to be sure, somewhat deficient in the imagination department. On the other hand, and I hope you'll take this in the spirit in which it's offered, perhaps you're not the best of salesmen."

"I'm a shitty salesman. I'm still trying to sell myself." Deuce grinned and shook his head and suddenly, out of nowhere, he seemed in a good mood. "Screw this, we're up shit creek, J.J. You know it and I know it and what the hell, let's go get a beer."

"Work. Still got a long day ahead of me. Hank has given me a new assignment."

"Yeah?"

"Down at the river. Actually I volunteered. Something a little different. I'm gonna drive a dozer for Chuck Fellows." He described the situation. At 6:00 p.m. he was meeting up with Fellows at the dredge.

Deuce listened and then said, "Did Kraft tell you that Fellows came up to me after the meeting yesterday?"

"No."

"He was standing practically right there. Had to hear. Fellows told me I'd done the right thing, looking for the water. Here Cutler had just finished reaming me out, and along comes the public works director and starts telling me I did the right thing. Man, how weird is that?"

"Sounds like typical Chuck Fellows to me."

"Yeah? Well, the man's an idiot. Must have a death wish."

"Yet he said something nice to you."

"I suppose. He's still an idiot. The words change nothing."

"I'll pass it along."

"No... Shit, no. Thank him for me, will ya? He didn't need to say what he did."

This decided, Deuce returned to the matter of the beer. "It isn't even three yet, Dusterhoft. You're not going to drive the dozer into the river if you have a couple. I'll tell you about my little scheme."

"Your little scheme?"

"The last arrow in my quiver."

"Not martyrdom?"

"Hell no. And a miserable crooked little arrow, it is. But what the fuck, I'll shoot the damn thing anyway."

"What is it?"

"It'll cost you a beer."

J.J. pushed back the sleeve of his coat so he could read his watch. "Well," he said, curious, for he had, indeed, thought they were out of arrows, miserable little ones or sleek high-caliber jobs, "okay, maybe just one."

As they went off together, Deuce added, "Here's something else I bet you haven't heard about. I ran into Aggie Klauer yesterday. We had an interesting chat. Aggie's okay, Dusterhoft. Unlike a lot of the women I've known, she improves with familiarity."

J.J.'s heart sank a little at these words. "Now," he said, "if only you did."

Deuce laughed and agreed at once, almost eagerly. Just like a man, J.J. decided, who was beginning to fall in love.

Chapter 11

≈

Harry Steadman, of Steadman and Associates, manager of the dog track project, was busy assuring the city council that the track was perfectly safe. The construction site had been raised to the height of the floodwall and was being armored with rock. It would be as secure as the city itself. They were elevating the access road, too. Whatever the river did, work would continue.

Paul Cutler felt pretty good. The river was a concern, protecting the track a concern, but Paul felt pretty good, considering. Tonight—finally!—the council would pass his budget, the climax of any city manager's year. After all the alarums and excursions, he was going to get what he wanted. The required cuts had been made, and he'd contrived to save some money for Ice Harbor Place. The city was still in the business of economic development. He'd been hired by the council as an economic development guy, and if most of his other initiatives had withered, the festival mall survived. He hadn't been reduced to just another city manager quite yet.

As for the flood... Well, he had no direct experience of major natural disasters, so they remained somewhat abstract. But not without their virtues. As with wars, they provided the mediocre an opportunity to rise above their mediocrity, the situation suddenly clarified, the covert, divergent human trajectories of everyday life replaced for a moment by a shared and relatively uncomplicated purpose.

And floods were, he imagined, in their own way, a time of healing. After the budget fight, after everything else that had happened recently, healing was required.

At the council table, El Plowman was talking about Chuck Fellows.

"He isn't here tonight, and I understand that relates to the attempt to keep the dog track site open," the mayor noted, which was Paul's clue and so he roused himself from his reverie.

"He's down on the dredge." Paul described Chuck's moonlighting as dredge skipper in an attempt to place more sand for the access road before water could cut the site off. There wasn't time to train someone else. Seth Brunel, the assistant city engineer, had come to the meeting in his stead and could answer any of the council's questions.

The exchange—El's comment and Paul's elaboration—had been contrived before the meeting as a way of letting the general public know the city was proactive here. Although whether it made sense—this pumping of sand rather than trucking in clay or gravel—was anybody's guess. Paul didn't have much faith in Fellows at the moment. But he wasn't in the business of second-guessing decisions he paid others to make, even loose cannons like Fellows.

Paul reminded himself to ask Aggie how many responses she'd had from the ads that had been placed in technical journals seeking applications for the permanent position of public works director.

Finally they got back to the business of passing the budget, and Paul could return for the moment to his private pleasure.

~

Near the end of the meeting, the city council went into closed session to discuss a matter related to the union negotiations. El had requested this. It disturbed Paul. There was no reason for a closed session. Negotiations had been difficult, but they were back on track, except with the big union. Mediations were scheduled with police and fire. Once somebody settled, transit would come around. And with the budget now safely passed, the amounts for the departments locked in, they could tell the unions, "No more money, folks. That's all there is. Take it or leave it." The big union would have no option but to settle. There was no earthly reason for the council to worry about this anymore.

But there they were, in closed session, and, as it turned out, El back on her high horse and young Goetzinger's damn proposal for a committee with no instructions dragged out for further airing.

El turned to Harvey Butts, the city attorney. "We could form this committee the union has proposed, we could give it free rein, isn't that right?"

"So long as you don't abandon your statutory responsibilities," the attorney agreed, giving no hint of what he might think of the proposal.

Paul said, "The unions are on the point of settling. There's no need to offer them anything more."

"I'm not talking about tit for tat, I'm talking about the idea on its own merits," El replied, speaking to the council members. "Paul expects to be inundated with the equivalent of frivolous suits from the city employees. I say, nobody has time to waste. This could be a clearinghouse for ideas on how to improve city services."

"We don't need a clearinghouse."

El leaned toward him, her eyes blazing. He liked her better when she was depressed. "I say we do. I say there's too much distrust. We all know there is. How do we deal with it? Maybe this way. Anyway, it's worth a try." Halfway through this brief speech, her attention had returned to her fellow council members.

Paul sat steaming. Maybe he should let them go ahead. What the hell. What difference did it make? He was sick to death of the whole business. Let them do whatever they wanted. How many times, during the interminable debates over this scheme, had he considered simply stepping aside? There was more than one way to deal with such a half-assed proposal.

"Of course," he told them, "you could set the committee up, and then I could ignore it. That would be one way to proceed."

"Are you saying you *would* ignore it?" El challenged.

Paul sighed. He had gone too far. He was just so pissed. This was not necessary, this was absolutely unnecessary. "No, of course not. I manage at your pleasure. I'll attempt to do anything you instruct me to do. But look, this scheme is nothing but a duplication of efforts. First, we've already got the Spirit program. Second, it was never anything more than a negotiating tactic on the union's part. If we'd accepted, and demanded givebacks as a quid pro quo, you'd have seen Goetzinger and his friends backpedaling fast enough... And last, but hardly least, it's a distraction. It's going to use up my time, my staff's time. We've got an economy to rebuild here. The last thing we need is a bunch of chronic complainers—and, believe me, these are the ones you're going to get—second-guessing every move we make."

"Paul, of course, is painting a worst-case scenario," El countered. "I'm concerned about a lot of things, but hardly the possibility that people might actually end up talking to each other more. I'm concerned about the deterioration of city services as we lay people off. The problem is distrust. We as a council need to take some ownership in that. We hired Paul for his expertise in economic development, fair enough. But I keep on hearing complaints that nobody ever sees him outside city hall—"

"That's not true."

El simply ignored this. On and on she went, and then around and around Paul and the others went until he tried to end matters with, "All I'm saying is that democracy might be the best system we've come up with, but that's no reason to stuff it into every nook and cranny. If you're going to insist on doing this thing, why not make families and churches democracies, too? It makes about as much sense. Or science, what about that? Let's vote on what's true and false. Why not?"

"I don't accept the analogies," El said. "*Democracy* is just a swear word as far as you're concerned."

Paul, transfixed by this outrageous accusation, failed to react at once. El elbowed ahead. "Let's forget about democracy, forget about loaded words like that. The proposed committee is given no instructions. We might end up with something like an ombudsman. Who knows? We just don't know. And that's the point. This isn't a top-down thing, it's bottom-up. That's the key idea. And that's what sticks in Paul's craw."

"You don't know what sticks in my craw," Paul told her, but El just ignored him.

"This is what I suggest," she said to the others. "You don't want to put this in the contract with the union. Fine, to heck with the union. I don't think that's such a good idea myself. But why do we have to? We can do the thing ourselves. Make it a council initiative."

"Wonderful," Paul said.

El looked at him. "I wasn't talking to you."

"Okay." Paul sat back, hands in the air, surrendering. One of the pleasures of closed sessions, of course, was the opportunity for frankness. Paul preferred frankness that didn't involve him.

For a brief spell, none of the other council members rose to the occasion.

Then Sister Jean said, "I think it's an intriguing idea. I mean, who knows what we might come up with? How refreshing to do something so open-ended." The nun could be counted on the side with El. The two women seldom disagreed.

Next, apparently feeling that his status as mayor-in-waiting required some sort of response, Roger Filer said, "I don't know. Maybe it's a good idea. Could be, I suppose."

Paul started to suggest that maybe Filer should try it out at his Chevy dealership first. He caught himself just in time.

"But this is the first time I've heard about it," Filer stumbled on, "I mean, setting up the committee ourselves. I'd like to think about it before I start making any commitments."

"Perhaps we need a committee," Sister Jean suggested. Sister had a sense of humor, sly and even wicked on occasion, but here only slightly satiric. Committees on committees on committees, like Russian dolls.

"Perhaps," Paul said, seeing the joke although hardly appreciating it, "but if you people *are* serious about doing this yourselves, it's a matter to be discussed in open session, not here. Right, Harvey?"

The city attorney concurred, after his usual delay for dramatic effect. "If it's no longer a matter of the negotiating strategy, it's hard to see how you could justify a discussion in camera."

"Fine," El said, "I agree. Let's do it in public. I want this on the next agenda, Paul."

Paul understood at once that El had foreseen this denouement, what had just occurred merely a tactic in the larger strategy which she had devised, having decided to support Goetzinger's scheme full bore.

She stared at him. "Tell me you're going to put this on the next agenda."

"Of course."

As he said this, Paul allowed himself a mental reservation. The election was in less than two weeks, before the next council meeting. El would be gone, what she did or did not want no longer pertinent.

This was a matter he'd have to think about. Perhaps he could bury it among the consent items next time, with a recommendation to refer to staff. And once he had the idea back in his custody, he could, like the English kings of yore, imprison it in the tower and strangle it at his leisure.

The council went back into public session to take any comments from the handful of hardy citizens that remained despite the late hour. El questioned them closely, dragging the meeting out even longer, her last chance to hold the gavel and determined not to go gracefully. For a moment, inserted among his less kindly thoughts, Paul remembered how it had once been. El had done some good work. They had done some good work together. A shame it had to end so badly.

Chapter 12

~

They began hopefully enough. Chuck had a plan. "I'll swing her across the cut slowly at first and pump just water," he told J.J., "then speed up and add sand to the mix a little at a time. As we go along, you'll get a feel for the percentage in the slurry." J.J. would drive the dozer, Chuck be the leverman, and young Billy Massey patrol the engine house. The dredge would sweep back and forth across the cut, sucking sand off the bottom and pumping it through the discharge pipe to J.J., his job simply to push the stuff off to the side, berm it up, and keep the makeshift spillway that the day crew had built clear so that only water passed over the flashboards and back into the river. That was the theory, simple enough.

At six fifteen, only a remnant of early spring daylight remained, darkened by the continuing storm. J.J. watched Chuck and Billy motor out to the dredge in the workboat. Then he turned on the generator, which powered the light plant used to illuminate the work site, and climbed up onto his machine to familiarize himself with it, a D7 with a side boom as well as a blade.

The light plant flooded the scene with a white glow, carving a space as vivid as a movie set out of the dim early evening. Through this brightness the snow fell, thicker than during the day but still wet and melting, the temp stubbornly holding in the thirties. J.J., in his sou'wester gear, felt quite comfy and waited pleasantly, enjoying the romantic aura cast by the lights over that mundane scene. Thinking of movie sets and romance, he was reminded of Aggie Klauer and his hopeless fantasies where she was concerned, and this put him into a rather more melancholy frame of mind.

It took quite a while, but eventually, over the noise of the generator and light plant, J.J. heard the dredge engines being engaged, and the air around him seemed to take on a certain subtle vibratory quality. Hesitantly, at the far horizon cast by his work lights, the elaborate, awkward-looking craft began to pivot back and forth around the brace of tall poles at its stern, one pole rising as the other fell, like someone marching very, very slowly in place.

After a few minutes, water appeared at the end of the discharge pipe, first a trickle, then semen-like spurts, and finally a steady arc. The water splashed down into the sand and flowed in an oxbow around and down into the drop structure, where it rose by degrees up the flashboards. J.J. still hadn't bothered to fire up the dozer. When the water changed color, becoming a slurry mixed with sand, would be soon enough.

It never happened. The moment he thought the color had begun to darken, the flow suddenly slowed and then ceased altogether.

He got on the radio. Chuck's irritated voice explained the situation tersely. "Backpressure went way the hell up. Slugged the line."

"What now?"

"I'm shutting her down. If we get lucky, the backflow will clear it out."

J.J. waited for Chuck to get lucky, but it didn't happen. In a few minutes, he and Billy came motoring back to shore to pick J.J. up, and the three of them drifted along the floating discharge pipe—which Chuck called the limber line—banging on the pipe, waiting for the echoey reverberations to become dull thuds, which ought to be diagnostic of the blockage. After disconnecting and reconnecting three sections, the first two false alarms, they finally managed to find and clear the sand plug. It took nearly an hour.

Having managed to get back to the status quo ante, Chuck and Billy returned to the dredge and J.J. to his dozer, where he once again waited for the clear water to begin to discharge and then the telltale signs of sand in it. And once again, the water did begin to flow and did change color only to abruptly slow and then stop altogether, and in a few minutes Chuck and Billy came motoring ashore to pick up J.J. once more, and they went back to gunkholing along the pipe, looking for the new blockage. The first pipe they disconnected wasn't it. They tried again.

The pipes were locked in place by chains hooked around metal ears, and as Chuck, showing signs of irritation, yanked at the chain of the next section they had decided to disassemble, he dragged his thumb across the ragged edge of the metal.

"Aaah, shit!" He shook his hand in the air and then looked at his thumb, a gash from the tip diagonally to the joint, the blood already coming fast. He clamped his other hand over it.

Chuck cursed his own stupidity.

J.J. pulled off his glove and reached into his back pocket for the tissues he carried. "Here."

The wound wrapped temporarily, they returned to the dredge and used the first aid kit there.

"This isn't gonna be enough," J.J. said.

"I know. Stitches."

And so J.J. took him up to the emergency room at St. Luke's. Chuck said, as they drove, "Off to a good start." After that, they chatted about other matters.

"You had a tetanus shot recently?" the ER doc asked as soon as he saw the first aid job they'd done. When he was sewing Fellows back up and discovered just who he was and what he was trying to do, he suggested that maybe Chuck should leave the dredging to the people who actually knew what they were doing. Much of the doc's clientele, no doubt, consisted of folks who had recently taken leave of their senses.

J.J. picked up on this theme when they were ready to leave and suggested that it might be a good idea to call it a night. Chuck was, after all, down to one opposable thumb, and given the success they'd had so far...

Chuck wouldn't hear of it. Back down to the dredge they must go.

And once more to work, although the rest of the evening could hardly be called an improvement on the start—more water pumped, more slugging of the line, although it was true they were becoming better at pinpointing the blockages. Toward the end, J.J. seemed to perceive more sand in the water reaching the end of the pipe, although it could have been his imagination.

He started the D7 and drove it around a bit, just to get the feel.

At three a.m., quitting time, the three of them stood on the shore looking out toward the shadowy pipeline and dredge. "Could have been worse," J.J. supposed. "We only went to the hospital once." Chuck laughed, a single bark. J.J. killed the lights and they stood silently for a few moments in the pitch darkness.

"Tomorrow," Chuck said.

PART II

CHAPTER 13

~

In the cold rain, Walter Plowman and Vern Gunderson, the lock-master, stood on top of the sidewall, exactly where they'd been on a sub-zero night in December, three and a half months earlier. Their view was the same, too—the towboat, Dixie Darlin', trapped in the ice as Corps of Engineers personnel worked with pikes and chain saws above the upper lock gates trying to free her.

A skeleton crew had remained on board the tow all winter, and diesel fuel had been hauled out over the ice so her engines could be kept idling. Now, with the river open below the lock and dam, the corpsmen were back at work.

The ice remaining above the upper gate had been partially cut away. Foot-thick slabs, with hearts of light blue, like quartz crystals from some outsized world, lay scattered across the ice sheet.

"If it was just the tow, Wally, I'd leave her sitting there until the damn ice melted." Vern was no happier having to set his people to the task of freeing the tow on a spring day, only rain to worry about, than he'd been at midnight in the frostbite cold of early December. Barge companies that played Russian roulette with the river deserved what they got. But Vern had his orders.

"Another storm reorganizing over the Four Corners," Walter told him, while all around them, rain from the present one dropped straight out of the sky.

Vern shook his head. Helluva year.

The temperature, for the past week above freezing around the clock, stood just a skosh over forty, although the rain made it feel colder. Winter had broken across the entire upper basin. Snow had begun to melt everywhere.

Below them, the men in their orange life vests moved gingerly, prodding the water-slick ice like mountain climbers searching for crevasses.

The lockmaster retreated to his tiny control shelter, even smaller than Walter's office at the TV station, and once again began the tedious process of cracking the gates open and shut as the lockmen maneuvered small floes through with their long pikes. The towboat hadn't moved yet, its tow, nine barges of grain, angled into the guide wall.

Ice bobbed under the blows of the pikes and slipped between the open jaws of the gates and inside the lock drifted forlornly, barely moving.

Above the lock and dam, the snowfield covered the river yet, but beneath it, the current would be working steadily. At places the snow had been sandpapered away by the wind, exposing the frozen surface. A ragged fault line extended far out into the pool, disappearing into the misty rain, resembling a geological seam ripped across the earth.

But despite these traces of movement and stress, the snowfield lay perfectly silent. Walter would have liked to linger until the scene fractured and flotillas of ice began to move over the dam's spillways. But ice-out might take days. It didn't happen, didn't happen, didn't happen, and then the ice was gone.

Whenever he left, now or later, it made no difference, it would be with the same regret. He could never turn his back on the river without that subtle sense of loss. And so he stood there for a little while longer.

~

At the dog track construction site, Mitch Mitchell, the grading contractor, said, "Track sand you're looking for—there's a farmer I know up on the Balltown Ridge thinks he's got some stuff worth looking at." He switched his wad of tobacco from one cheek to the other and spat.

The rain had nearly stopped for the moment, and through the tangle of trees and undergrowth, Jack Kelley, the construction manager, watched the towboat approaching, moving steadily southward.

"Barge company got its tow back," he remarked offhand. He felt…he wasn't sure what he felt…a desire to be on board and heading south himself maybe. To put all the complexities of his life behind him. To find other problems to deal with. Other problems always seemed simpler than his own.

"Damn expensive load of grain." Mitchell switched the chaw back to the first cheek and spat again.

Chuck Fellows, the public works director, said nothing. Jack was conscious of Fellows saying nothing.

The three of them had walked out to the northern tip of the job site from which they could inspect the low, swampy upstream end of the island and watch Mitchell's crew excavating from the borrow site, scooping black earth for the track infield, rushing because they had to finish armoring the slope with riprap.

"The Balltown Ridge?" Jack asked. Once upon a time, his mind would jog effortlessly among the swarming details of a project. Now nothing happened without some overcoming of resistance. Sand? Oh, yes, that—the special material the racing secretary was making such a stink about, so the dogs wouldn't hurt their feet.

Mitchell said, "Yeah. Guy I've known forever. Dairy farmer."

"No shells in it."

"So he says. I haven't seen it. He claims it's a kind of loess maybe."

Fellows spoke. "Loess is full of silt."

Jack said, "If it's like that, then we've got a problem. According to the spec it's supposed to be 3 percent silt, maybe 4, something like that." He couldn't quite remember. That was another problem—his skepticism about the value of a racing facility. He worked at the project from the time he got up until the time he went to bed, but some part of his mind remained indifferent, discarding information with barely a glance.

Mitchell said, "Mostly you find loess out in the western part of the state. I don't know what this stuff is."

"Worth a look," Jack agreed. He didn't want to truck in material from way the hell and gone if he could help it.

Below them, the backhoe dug into the soil of the burrow site in the snow-encrusted wetland, the subject of long mitigation talks. Frost had melted from the top layers but remained frozen below, and prying the soil free with the teeth of the machine's bucket struck sparks from the earth.

～

They walked along the rim of the job site. Through the trees, Jack scanned the broad reach of the river to the north, now empty, the tow gone. During the winter, the ice capped the river, seeming to hold it in place and reduce it. But with the ice gone, the river had swollen, filling its banks. During the flood, it would rise higher in midstream than at the shores, like a massive water beast beginning to breach. Jack knew that much about floods.

Farther upstream, the lock and dam, a long, low dentition of gates, reached from shore to shore, insignificant in the distance, useless for flood control, never meant for flood control, only to maintain the nine-foot navigation channel so commercial outfits could move product. The scant barrier and the tremendous sweep of open water, placid and waiting, random flecks of light the only evidence of its impatient flow and latent power, filled his field of vision, and Jack whispered to himself, "Jesus, Mary, and Joseph."

At the northeast corner of the plateau, beyond the kennels, he and the others stood for a brief time and sighted along the eastern slope and watched a truck dumping its riprap, the rock beginning to creep out of the box only to finish its descent in a rush, with a concussion, kicking up a plume of dirt.

∼

In the construction trailer, Jack called Nick Boxleiter, the racing secretary, the man responsible for the welfare of the dogs, and told him they had maybe found the sand he was looking for. Boxleiter, very excited, wanted to know where, what it looked like, when he could see it. Right now? Later in the day? Jack told him he'd try to arrange something.

After he hung up, Jack sat musing, ignoring the contractors assembling for the usual Friday meeting, ignoring Sean, his gofer, who was saying something to him. Boxleiter's excited voice echoed inside his skull. Jack had no idea why he had lost the gift for such enthusiasm, never so unalloyed as Boxleiter's, perhaps, never so completely absorbed in his vocation, but a hell of an improvement over his current state of mind. Then again, maybe this loss of desire was nothing special, nothing to get upset about, just the relentless whittling down of life over the decades. Maybe his grinding dissatisfactions were to be expected, and his failure to accept them gracefully just the typical naïveté of people growing older, only the mirror images of the delusions of immortality in the young. And whatever he'd lost, he still had his faith…a little threadbare, to be sure, but no less real for that… One mustn't ask for too much. Perhaps that was it.

His young helper spoke again, and Jack turned toward him. "Yes, Sean? What did you say?"

~

All the contractors except the kennel guy were behind schedule now.

Jack asked if anybody subscribed to a long-range weather forecasting service.

"Precip above normal," according to Jim Bergman, the foreman for the steel contractor. He was enclosing the grandstand, weeks behind. Once that was done, they could go like hell, but until then, they were stymied, reduced to nibbling around the edges.

"Okay, but how much?" Jack asked him.

"The National Weather Service doesn't like to put numbers on their long-range predictions."

"What does the Corps say? They must be factoring some sort of rainfall figures into their forecasts for the river."

Fellows spoke up. "Thirty percent above normal." Fellows didn't look so swell. He'd been operating the dredge at night, and the second job didn't seem to be agreeing with him. "But I've been talking to Walt Plowman. He thinks we're in for a rough ride."

"Plowman?" Jack said. What did Plowman know? "He's just a local TV guy." Although it was true, Jacksonians set great store by the weatherman's forecasts. For them he was—Jack didn't know—a shaman or something. Jack wasn't impressed. The locals liked antiestablishment types, the little guy who got it right while all the big guys were screwing up. They cut people like Plowman too much slack, remembering the forecasts he nailed and forgetting all the ones he blew.

Fellows said, "We've been talking about the possibility of a big spring flood since last fall. Tracking the preconditions. They're all there. It's weird, as a matter of fact, absolutely uncanny."

"How bad?" Bergman asked.

"Flood of record. Water near the top of the floodwall maybe. Maybe higher. It's not unthinkable. The wall and levees were only built for a two-hundred-year event."

Jack didn't want to hear this. He said, "Walter Plowman might be the darling of the locals, but he's a bit of a flake, you ask me. He thinks it's possible to tell how high the river's gonna go by where the mud daubers build their nests." Jack looked at Fellows as he spoke. Fellows was an engineer; what in God's name was he doing giving credence to the likes of Walter Plowman? "And anyway, he hasn't got the Corps's resources."

Fellows had crossed his arms. "Walt might be wrong," he agreed. "But he might be right, too. The Corps's got no patent on the truth."

"In that case, we can just pack up and go home," Jack said. "There's always a worst-case scenario. There's always an excuse to give up."

"Who's saying anything about giving up?"

"You are." Jack had imagined that his relationship with Fellows had improved some. Apparently not.

~

When they got around to matters requiring coordination among the contractors, Mitch Mitchell said, "We've finished our underground work at the track. We're placing loam on the infield now and expect to bring in the specialty sand for the track surface as soon as we can get our hands on it."

These words were clearly meant for Tony Vasconcellos, the electrical contractor, who had his own underground to put in—for power out to the tote board, the light standards, the starting boxes, the track railing. Tony had a load of conduit to install beneath Mitch's finish work.

He rose to the bait. "You wanna be outta here before the water comes up, is that it, Mitch?"

"I might not have a choice," Mitchell told him. "Lots of people along the river got no protection. I'm already getting calls wanting to know about the availability of equipment."

Jack didn't like hearing this any more than Walter Plowman's end-of-the-world-as-we-know-it scenario. The last thing he needed was contractors starting to pull out on him. But he understood the priorities. And it wasn't just them. Construction workers who had family or friends near the river might abandon the project at some point. He might be left with a handful of guys trying to fend off the water with nothing but shovels and sandbags.

"We don't know what's gonna happen," he told them. "I can live with that, I can live with the uncertainty. We don't know what the river's gonna do. Okay. What I can't live with is people turning their backs just because they've got an excuse. Flood or no flood, this project's important to the city. And believe me, if anybody simply bails on me, I'm gonna remember."

To this, Tony Vasconcellos said, "People got their responsibilities, Jack. And nobody likes to get threatened." He didn't raise his voice, speaking in a manner which Jack could only describe as sincere.

Jack stared at him. "No, that's right, Tony, nobody likes to get threatened."

~

Dexter Walcott, the black contractor from Waterloo putting in the interior systems, told them that most of the studding had been accomplished in the paddock building, ready for plumbing and electrical rough-ins.

The conversation continued and Jack listened, disturbed by it, although he only half knew why. It was like a thousand other meetings he'd been in. And these men weren't so bad. He'd worked with worse. Even Tony Vasconcellos, since the arrest of his young son for the cross burning, had been giving a decent imitation of zeal. His eldest son, too, even Lonny, who Jack understood was potentially more dangerous than his father, seemed to have gotten with the program. Tony might do nothing, but Lonny had the capacity to make matters worse. And his appearance on the *Donahue Show* had given him a certain stature among the troublemakers. But he had been watching his mouth of late, around Jack at least. Not that Jack actually expected to get much more work out of the Vasconcelloses. Oh, no, that would be asking too much.

He listened to the others and reminded himself again that these were not bad guys and that jobs like this required the kind of coordination which human beings didn't necessarily find congenial and that you could only ask so much.

In this way, Jack rationalized, trying to accommodate himself to the views of the others. For it was true, they were not bad men.

~

At the end of the meeting, when he asked—as he did every week—if they had any other comments relative to the project, no one spoke up, although the silence seemed a little more charged than usual. So, he thought, that was it, another meeting gotten through. He looked around, deciding who he needed to have a private word with.

And suddenly he knew what had been bothering him all along. It had been, quite simply, the very ordinariness of everything. These men were thorough-going professionals and realists. They had their handbooks of procedures. They had payrolls to meet. They had families to think about. They had every reason to do a professional job here, and no reason to do anything more. Yes...right...

"Then I've got something to say," he told them.

But he didn't continue at once. He felt the burden of himself, of his own uncertainties, and so he paused and wondered if it wasn't best simply to let matters take their course. It was just a dog track, after all, whatever its economic importance. Why not let it slide? The world wouldn't come to an end. Why this drive to keep going?

He didn't know. He only knew what he felt.

"The position I'm taking," he told them, "is that we forget about the flood. The flood isn't our problem. We deal with the problems we know we've got. Number one—buttoning up the grandstand. We don't get that enclosed, doesn't make a damn bit of difference what else we do."

He looked around. Nobody was saying anything. The rain, having started up again, pounded on the roof of the trailer. The gray pall of cigarette smoke hung motionless in the trailer.

At last, Jim Bergman, the steel guy, said, "If I could get two full weeks, I could finish the roof. I got a problem with the rain. I got a worse problem with the wind. If it gets up to 10 or 15 miles per hour, my men can't work with the sheets. You bend one, you might as well take it over and throw it in the dumpster." Bergman was a good man, and two weeks didn't seem like such a big deal. But construction site time was like psychological time—you could forget about measuring it with a clock.

"What if we rig up some sort of canopy?" Jack asked.

"To work under? You'd have to fly it with the cranes."

"Why not?"

"That might take care of the rain, but what about the wind?"

They talked about that briefly, coming to no conclusion. Jack threw out a couple of other ideas, also greeted with a good deal of skepticism. But skepticism was an improvement over resignation.

"Enclose the building, gentlemen," Jack repeated at the very end. "Forget about Walter Plowman and his doomsaying. Forget about everything else. Enclose the damn building. The rest is easy."

～

Later, when Jack was alone, and the jolt of energy he'd felt had vaporized, and he was imagining how pleasant it would be to lay his head on the desk and have a little snooze, a woman entered the trailer, holding the door open behind her for a man with a camera.

"Excuse me," she said, "I called earlier. I'm looking for Dexter Walcott."

Oh, shit, Jack thought. He'd forgotten.

For a moment they regarded each other without speaking. Jack had read enough of Rachel Brandeis's stories in the *Trib* over the last six months, but he'd met her face-to-face only once and briefly. He remembered that encounter; no doubt she did, too, and this pause before speaking seemed to be filled with a mutual calculation of whether it served any purpose to acknowledge that earlier contact. Jack would have let the matter slide, but the reporter came to a different conclusion.

"When I was here before," she said, "you were just beginning construction. You were with Mark O'Banion."

"That's right." She'd just arrived in town, come from the East Coast somewhere, and was being shown around by Len Sawyer, the *Trib* publisher. "Mark and I, as a matter of fact, thought it rather strange, old Len not in the habit of taking such an interest in his new hires."

"Is that right?"

"Yes, although, of course, we found out the reason later." Forewarned of her intention to talk to Dexter, Jack had given the matter some thought before other issues had intervened and he'd forgotten she was coming. This was a public project and he couldn't keep her off the job site, but he didn't have to be happy about it.

"You mean," she said, "to do the stories on the attempt to save the Pack."

"That's one way to look at it." There were people in town that laid part of the responsibility for the failure of the packing company at her doorstep. She was a reporter, of course. Reporters seldom improved the situation. Anyway, she immediately registered the hostility underlying Jack's comment, and paused again, only briefly, only long enough to decide apparently that bringing up the past had been a mistake. She went back to the reason for her visit.

"Is Dexter Walcott around? I'd like to talk to him. How's he doing, by the way?"

"Fine," Jack told her. "He's doing just fine."

She looked at him with her reporter's sharpness, then asked a couple of innocuous questions, a kind of tactical retreat, before returning to the more inflammatory stuff.

"I understand there have been several incidents already, tension between the white and black construction workers."

Jack had been expecting Brandeis to show up for some time, now that the Pack had closed and she seemed to be taking up race relations as her special interest. Too much to hope she'd leave him alone.

"We've had no trouble," he told her. "I don't know where you're getting your information."

"None at all?"

"Not a speck."

"That's not what I've been told."

"Somebody's been feeding you a line, then."

She looked at him, her gaze unbelieving, and then probed in a different direction. "When Walcott won the contract, there was a concern he might not have the necessary experience to handle a job this big. How's his performance been?"

"Fine. And you're wrong about a concern. We were never worried. He wouldn't have gotten the contract if we didn't think he could handle the work."

She gave Jack another calculated look. "I see. Can you tell me where I can find him, then?"

"I'm not sure," he told her.

"Where *might* I find him, then?"

The photographer stood waiting in the open door. Brandeis had come a half step farther into the trailer. She had a dark complexion and strong, full features. Some of the reporters on the *Trib* were harmless enough, Jack supposed, young people of modest ambition. Brandeis obviously wasn't one of those.

He looked at his feet, then back up. It wouldn't do any good, but he had to try.

"What I'm gonna say now is off the record. We haven't had any trouble, Miss Brandeis, but that doesn't mean we won't. You've written all these stories, and you know the situation in the city. I can't imagine what you think one more's gonna accomplish. And, to be honest, Dexter Walcott's position on the job site is...not that easy. You can only make matters worse."

She nodded and had a ready answer. "I don't want to make matters worse, Mr. Kelley. I just want to do my job."

Like contractors, reporters obviously had their overweening personal agendas, particularly the tough, ambitious ones like Brandeis.

"You just want to do your job, do you?" he said. "Just like with the Pack?"

She didn't react to this. Nothing more Jack could do, except hope that Dexter would know how to deal with her. "You'll need hard hats," he told her and the photographer, "if you're going to walk around the site."

When she was gone, he decided that the problem didn't signify. The racial stuff was minor now, too. Everything minor. Only enclosing the grandstand mattered.

∾

Later, wondering what had happened, he went over to the paddock building where Walcott's people had started to put up sheetrock. The vivid white glow from the temporary lights, nodding at the top of tall stands, pushed the gloom back into the corners. Work proceeded quickly, the rooms taking shape, but Jack took no pleasure in it. They should all be working on the grandstand.

Walcott wasn't there. Probably over on the deck, one of his people told Jack, and so Jack went back through the rain and made his way up onto the grandstand deck and gingerly along what would eventually be the concourse between administrative offices and concession stands, but now lying open to the skies, slick with water and crowded with gang boxes and stored construction material and the stays used to stabilize the steel.

He found Dexter at the far west end—where the roof was on and some stud work therefore possible—framing in the public johns. With him were his foreman, the grim-faced fellow with the Muslim name, and a couple of laborers Jack hadn't seen before, one a woman. Each day, it seemed, a few more blacks were on hand. If they managed to get the building buttoned up, there'd be blacks all over the place, young black males, which, if Jack hadn't decided not to worry about such things anymore, would have made him nervous as hell. He looked at Walcott's people, the expressions on their faces, and understood that Dexter had the same problems all contractors had.

On a rolling scaffold, the male laborer riveted struts used to brace the tops of the studwalls to the joists overhead. Below, the woman checked the alignment and moved the scaffolding.

"Reporter find you?" he asked Walcott.

"Expect so."

"She give you a hard time?"

Walcott paused. He always paused, his responses considered, reminding Jack of the old carpenter's adage: measure twice, cut once. "Nobody gives ol' Dex a hard time… They can try."

"Good," Jack said. "She talk to anybody else?"

"The whites? Yup, she walked around a bit. Don't know if she got any good quotes, though."

"Wonderful… Well, okay," Jack decided, "we're not gonna worry about it. We're gonna worry about getting the roof on. You just keep on the studs. Do as much as you can."

"Intend to. Gonna run outta work before long."

"When we're buttoned up, there'll be plenty. You'll be able to go like hell. It's twelve weeks to substantial completion, which I'm still calling June 15."

Jack read doubt in Dexter's lack of response.

"We might have industrial caterers lined up outside selling beer and brats, Dex. We might have to use shuttle buses to get people onto the site. Hell, maybe water taxis. I don't care. The doggies are gonna be up and running." Walcott nodded slowly, without conviction. He didn't believe it. Nobody did.

But Walcott was okay. He and Jack had come to a private understanding, just between the two of them. Dexter ran his jobs through Jack. Dexter was Jack's foreman, for all intents and purposes. He had a problem, he came to Jack. He didn't have a problem, he still came to Jack.

As Jack walked across the deck, from the protected area back into the rain, he thought about the woman laborer he'd seen. Black construction workers, he imagined, were even more chauvinistic than whites. Then again, women were beginning to turn up all over the place; no reason to think black men could hold back the tide any more than white men could. And a woman on Walcott's crew might be a plus, men more apt to watch their behavior around her.

He reminded himself again that it didn't make any difference; he wasn't going to worry about garbage like this. Just the building. Enclose the building. Let the rest take care of itself.

A black man was coming diagonally from one direction, a white construction worker from the other, the two bearing down on each other. For an instant, they seemed to merge. Then they had separated, the gap between them quickly widening. Neither had slackened his pace. Neither had acknowledged the other's existence. Jack exhaled.

The black passed by him without so much as a nod.

⌘

Next Jack went over to the steel contractor's trailer to have a word with Jim Bergman. Bergman was the point man here. If Jack couldn't get him to buy into a hopped-up effort to complete the grandstand shell, putting pressure on the others to perform—the steel stud contractor, the glazier—would accomplish nothing. The building would never be enclosed in time, and June 15 would, indeed, become a meaningless date.

Bergman's trailer was rather fancier than Jack's, gussied up with curtains and imitation wood paneling, although if he had designs on appearing in *House Beautiful* he'd have to get Janelle in there. At the moment, the man himself stood frowning by the drawing board. He wasn't alone. Ironworkers milled around who had come down off the steel because of the slippery conditions.

Bergman had taken a sheaf of drawings from the plan rack and opened them.

"Lookee here," he said, pointing at a section of the roof. A blunt man, he never greeted Jack, merely picked up one of their previous conversations where it had been left off.

"What?" Jack moved up beside him and stared down at the plan but didn't see anything amiss. "We've been looking at this for two months."

"That's just it. I still haven't got what I need."

Ah, Jack thought, *that again*. His eye moved to an area devoid of detailing. The concessionaire still hadn't indicated where he would need penetrations for his equipment.

"We're gonna finish and go away, Jack," Bergman said, immediately and genuinely angry, "and somebody else'll come along and screw up our roof."

Jack's boss, Harry Steadman, was supposed to be coordinating with the concessionaire, but Harry, as usual, had been avoiding unpleasantness. "I'll see what I can do," Jack assured Bergman. "Of course, if we don't get the roof on, all this is academic."

"As for that, your idea about using a canopy…we've been talking about it."

"Yeah?"

"Doesn't work, no friggin' way," one of the ironworkers piped up behind Jack. Jack turned around.

"Why not?"

"The wind would get it as easy as the roof panels," the man said. Jack only knew his first name: Mattie. Around ironworkers, physically fit men, men who walked beams hundreds of feet in the air, Jack always felt a certain reduction of matters to their essences.

"Might be we could secure it in some way," he suggested.

"If you can do that, why can't you secure the panels and forget about the canopy?" another asked.

"Okay," Jack conceded. "If not the canopy, then what?"

Nobody responded. Jack still thought the idea had some merit, but he'd have to think about it later. Anyway, only a fool would try to ram it down the throats of men like these. On top of which, they weren't locals but over from Rockford, headquarters of the steel erector. This was just another paycheck for them. Jackson could wash down the river for all they cared.

"No thoughts on the matter?" Jack spoke into the silence. "I see. Well, what can I say? You're right, it's something of a poser. Gonna be tough coming up with a solution… Real tough… Maybe can't be done."

"Maybe," Jim Bergman said testily. "Let me tell you something, Jack, just so you'll know." Bergman was obviously PO'd at Jack's implication, the challenge he was flinging at the feet of this proud lot. "The weather gets bad like this, I don't decide who goes up. The men do. I'm not about telling a man to take his life in his hands just because somebody like you is all hot to set product and doesn't give a shit what the conditions are like."

Jack was stung. "Is that what you think, Jim—all I care about is setting product?"

"As a matter of fact. Finishing the project—that's what you're all about, tell me you're not. Everything else can take a flying fuck as far as you're concerned." This, particularly the tone with which it was uttered, could have come straight out of the mouth of Chuck Fellows.

Jack tried to think. What was the right answer here? He couldn't back down in front of this crowd. He couldn't talk them into the effort, either. They'd have to talk themselves into it.

So he said, "You're right, Jim, I wanna finish the project. I'm pretty damn obsessive about it, too, come right down to it. What's wrong with that? And it's true, every man's got to decide for himself. That's the deal. This doesn't get done unless people commit to it. I'm committed. What about you? Or is it just another fucking job? You tell me. Is this thing doable? I think it is. I think you've got a problem. There's always some sort of fix—you're determined to find it. So you tell me. If the canopy idea doesn't work, what does? You decide. It's your call."

There was always a technical solution of some sort, if people were clever enough and determined and willing to spend the money. And it wasn't just Bergman's call, not a chance. Jack was damn well going to think about it himself, to put a solution out there. Give them something doable to reject.

But as he left, satisfied with his performance, and walked back toward the construction trailer, he asked himself how he'd feel if some ironworker, goaded by him, went aloft in a storm and fell to his death.

⁓

Three hours later, and fifteen miles to the north, the rain had quickened once more as Jack and the others picked their way down a slope in single file, keeping between the muddy heart of the path on one side and an old, pockmarked, abrading snowbank on the other. Behind them rose the top of the Balltown Ridge. In front, farther down, lay a curtain of trees, beyond which the complex eastern Iowa landscape of low hills and valleys loped westward, lost in the storm.

Mitch Mitchell led the way, with his friend, a farmer named Verlyn, and the track secretary Nick Boxleiter close behind. Jack lagged farther back. They could have waited for better weather, but who knows when that would arrive. Anyway, Jack didn't want to waste decent conditions on some wild goose chase.

Verlyn carried a shovel and Nick Boxleiter an umbrella, which he shifted back and forth over his head like a tightrope walker as he descended. Jack sidestepped down the fringe of muddy field grass. Meltwater purled along the edge of the snowpack.

"Anywheres around here," Verlyn said, but he kept on going. He was an old man and badly overweight and walked with effort, rocking from side to side. "We was having trouble with our fencing. The animals kept getting out. So we dug down a bit, but all we found was this stuff. Finally decided there was nothing for it but to move the fence."

Near the bottom, close to the trees, they circled a low hummock, which had been partially excavated on its downslope side. Verlyn stopped.

"I had my boys clear away the snow." The signs of recent disturbance were all about. Peering into the scalloped-out excavation, Jack immediately noted the lack of shells in the exposed soil.

He looked around to orient himself. Behind, a creek, in full flow, added its continuous but ragged sound to the steady drum roll of the storm. The ashy bark of the nearby trees, full of narrow, irregular ridges and valleys, resembled a mountain system seen from a great height. Jack had no idea what kind they were. He could identify many types of lumber by the grain, but only the most obvious trees in the wild, and virtually nothing without its summer leafage. In the breathless air, the rain plunged straight into the ground. It had soaked through his raincoat.

But at the moment he wasn't thinking of his discomfort. Or even the scene around him. He was watching the rain fall straight as a plumb line and thinking that if only the wind stayed away, they would certainly find a way to put the roof on the grandstand.

Shielded by Nick Boxleiter's umbrella, Verlyn was spading the soil away from the back of the shallow cavity, prying it loose more than digging, revealing the dry, light-colored material where the rain hadn't penetrated. There was little frost in the ground here, for the soil gave way easily beneath the probes of the blade. Boxleiter leaped in as soon as there was enough room and, down on both knees, plunged his hands into the material, forking it up and letting it sift through his fingers.

"Where did this stuff come from?" he wanted to know. Jack listened to the enthusiasm in his voice.

"Got me," Verlyn told him. "From somewheres else, I expect, like most of the soil around these parts. Got a lot of what they call glacial till." Verlyn had an adenoidal wheeze from the effort of digging.

"How much is there?" Boxleiter asked, his excitement increasing.

"Don't know that, either. But it goes down to that pond there, maybe farther." The farm pond lay at the foot of the shallow valley drained by the stream behind them.

"Look at this!" Boxleiter fingered the soil, showing Jack and the others how easily it crumbled, holding it up for Jack and Mitch to feel. Jack rolled the material, silky and grainy at once, across his fingers, the rain staining it a deep brown, and then watched as Boxleiter balled up a fistful and balanced it on the open palm of his hand.

"See," he said. He gripped the ball and attempted to throw it, but like a snowball made of too-dry snow, it flew apart as it left his hands. "Perfect," he announced. He looked up from the hole. "This stuff's *great*!" He balled up and threw another handful, which disintegrated immediately, knocked down by the rain. "Fantastic! Absolutely fantastic!"

Jack felt only relief at the thought of another problem solved, one less thing to worry about.

Boxleiter was still down on both knees, digging deeper into the back of the tiny excavation, pulling out scoop after scoop of the sandy material and peering intimately at it. Finally he looked around at the others, grinning, his face slightly canine, a pug or boxer, not a greyhound. The raindrops slid off his cheeks. They could have been tears of joy.

As Jack returned with the others, he carried this ecstatic image of Boxleiter and, as he had earlier in the day, set it against his own dulled life. Boxleiter's joy might have been profane, but it seemed to Jack pure and complete in its own way. Even if the man was a son of a bitch the rest of the time, he was St. Francis where his dogs were concerned.

∾

After five, Jack stopped by Steadman and Associates, hoping to catch Harry before he left for the weekend. No dice, his boss gone, not so much as a word left behind for Jack's benefit. About the concessionaire or anything else.

Jack sorted through memos and mail and faxes, wrote some memos of his own, and brooded over the absence of Harry, who was running several jobs and had been gradually distancing himself from the track project, as one might from someone with a communicable disease. He'd even begun talking in-house about when they ought to shut down and wait for the flood to go by. Harry was another of those guys who parceled out his life between the professional and private, with a little spillover of mutual back-scratching for the benefit of his special pals.

Jack felt an unpleasant feeling in his throat, the onset of a cold or the flu, and thought, shit, on top of everything else, just what he needed. He rummaged around in his desk for some cold tablets. Finding none, he went out to Marge the secretary's desk, but it was locked. He considered going down to the nearby convenience store. He could sometimes dodge an illness by taking pills at the first telltale sign. But if he left, he'd never be able to drag himself back. And he had project manager work to do, his day up to that point filled with field manager stuff.

He went back to his desk.

∾

By the time he got home, the intimation of an illness had swollen into a full-fledged sore throat. His own fault, he decided. He should have gone down for the pills. Or better, he should have gotten his damn raincoat waterproofed. He'd been walking around in the rain all week. Now he'd suffer the consequences, his only hope that he could get some more work done before the worst set in.

When he went into the kitchen, however, intent upon getting a quick bite—he hadn't lost his appetite yet—and then back to work, he found Father Mike Daugherty in possession, sitting with Janelle.

Mike was the last person Jack wanted to see at that moment. He'd been avoiding the priest. He'd gone so far as to stay away from Mass the previous Sunday, which he never did. And now here was Mike, looking like his own pleasant self, as if nothing had happened between them.

Janelle had supplied him with a cup of coffee. The two of them seemed to have been having a chat; Jack couldn't imagine about what. Janelle was looking particularly ironic. Why became immediately clear, as Mike, spotting Jack, brightened up and said, "I've been trying to get Janelle to drag you to one of our couple's weekends."

Jack couldn't think of a thing to say confronted by such an absurd undertaking. He forgot about food and instead contemplated an escape. "I'll leave you two to your negotiations, then."

"No, no, no," Mike countered at once, grinning, "I came to see you both, to pass along a bit of good news."

"Good news?" Jack noted that Mike had on his collar. What, he wondered, could the priest conceivably say that might be construed as good news?

Mike, however, put off the moment. Instead he looked intently at Jack, as if noticing something for the first time.

"How you doing, Jack?"

"Coming down with something."

"Ahh, sorry. Miserable time for a cold. Must be the weather… You know, my friend, I've been thinking about you—down there on the island, the rain, flood on the way… A flood of all things." He shook his head sympathetically.

Jack swallowed. His throat hurt and he was breathing through his mouth. The cold bearing down on him seemed to have gotten suddenly worse.

"What's your news, Mike?"

"Yes. Well…it's young Leo Vasconcellos—looks like we're gonna be able to keep him out of juvenile detention."

"This is good?"

"Yes, most definitely, most definitely good. They were talking about one of the halfway houses, but frankly, between the three of us, those places are breeding grounds for even worse behavior. Fortunately, we've avoided that. It's taken a lot of talking."

Jack didn't give a fig about the fate of Leo Vasconcellos. It wasn't very Christian of him, maybe, but there you were. At another time he would have made a stab at pretending. Not now. He decided he was really pissed that Daugherty had shown up. They were on the outs. Mike should respect that.

"And just why is this good news, Mike?"

Janelle explained. "Father imagines the son will have a good effect on the rest of the family."

"Is that right?"

"That's right," Mike agreed, choosing to ignore Jack's tone. "We've had a lot of people talking to young Leo, Jack. We've piled on, so to speak, and, believe me, he understands now why what he did was so bad, he really does."

"Umm."

"And that's not all. You change one member of a family, you change the rest. A child shall lead them, Jack… I wouldn't even be surprised if you've already started to see some positive things out on the job site."

"From Tony and Lonny?"

"Have you? Maybe?"

Jack closed his eyes and breathed through his mouth and swallowed painfully. "Well," he said, "it's true, they've changed their tune some."

"See, there you are."

"Words, Mike, nothing but words."

The priest was not deterred. "Perhaps it'll take some time. But things are changing in the Vasconcellos household, Jack, rest assured."

"I'll tell you what's happened, Mike. Tony's found it expedient to fall back on the typical contractor's ploy—say anything, agree to anything, promise the world. Doesn't mean a thing."

"Well," the priest said, "let's just wait and see."

He stayed a few more minutes, bringing them up-to-date about other initiatives in the parish. Mike always had a lot of irons in the fire. The exchange had the feeling of a public encounter. Mike continued to wear his mask of pleasantness, playing his elevated priestly role. But he wasn't what he seemed to be, Jack had decided. No, indeed. He was exactly like Jack and Janelle, just another fallible human being, driven by his demons, trying to arrange the world to suit his own needs. If Jack hadn't been such a dyed-in-the-wool, old-style Catholic, he would have seen the truth long ago.

~

When Mike went away, Janelle said in her take-it-or-leave-it voice, "I made a casserole."

"Maybe a little soup. I'm not feeling so great."

Jack went to get pills and came back to the kitchen and took them with water from the tap. The time lapse seemed to make talking about what had just happened more feasible, so he said, "I've turned my back on Tony Vasconcellos and his brood. I leave them to Mike."

"Father's a social worker, not a priest," Janelle responded.

She made the soup, and she made her case. She had many reasons for the accusation. Janelle was always full of reasons. Sometimes Jack made the effort to challenge her, but not tonight.

Later, upstairs, he got out a pad and sat at his drawing board and sketched some preliminary ideas for a protective canopy for the iron-workers at the track.

He felt steadily worse. He couldn't concentrate. Even his eyesight seemed to be closing down, forcing him to focus piecewise on his drawings, like trying to read words one letter at a time. Finally, he gave up and went to bed, shivering under the bedcovers, sleepless, and taking what comfort he could from the dream that life had, despite all appearances to the contrary, gotten simpler.

Enclose the grandstand. The rest would take care of itself.

Chapter 14

~

Harvey Butts hadn't seen much of Goetzinger *fils* in these poker games recently, and he figured there could be only one reason for his sudden reappearance tonight. The kid had come to pitch the union's side in the tussle with the city, an end run around Cutler and the council, although, so far, he hadn't tried to slip it into the proceedings. He hadn't had much of anything to say.

The razzing he'd taken at the beginning of the game hadn't set him off, not so much as an offhanded, snide comment. The fellows sitting around that table, none of them being friends of organized labor, lamented the fall of a perfectly decent poker player into the degraded pursuit of trade unionism. Deuce took his buffeting in silence, a man who knew how to conserve his nut and wait for the main chance.

The button had come around to Harvey, and since he'd won a couple of decent-sized pots and was feeling expansive, he decided to loosen things up a bit and said, "Lowball, gentlemen," as he shuffled and began to deal.

Goetzinger smiled at this, Harvey had no idea why. Didn't make any difference. Neither one of them won the hand.

Later, during a piss break, Harvey wandered over for a chat with Goetzinger, to see what he'd have to say for himself in private, expecting at the least some remark vis-à-vis their encounter in Paul Cutler's office, when the manager had reamed Goetzinger out over the so-called lost water. Harvey waited. Goetzinger seemed to be waiting, too. About the set-to in Paul's office, about the union business, he said nothing. The game resumed.

And Harvey resumed winning. Goetzinger, contrariwise, couldn't buy a card, dumping his hands with hardly a look. Yet bad hand after bad hand, he remained quite at ease, in no rush to win, in no rush to do anything, and as the chimes of the antique clocks in the surrounding rooms tolled the passing hours, Harvey finally began to think that just maybe the kid had no ulterior motive after all. Maybe he'd heard that El Plowman had taken up his cause with the council. Of course, that meant nothing. Plowman would soon be gone. But maybe Goetzinger had heard; maybe he was just there to play cards.

This possibility, for some reason, didn't particularly please, although Harvey had little interest in listening to the union's sad, sad story. He was more interested in Paul Cutler's adamantine opposition to the union's proposal for a committee, the proposal a minor matter as far as Harvey was concerned, nothing to get your gonads in an uproar over.

Almost relieved when dealt an absolutely worthless hand, he folded and turned sideways in his chair, draping one arm over the back and letting his mind roam.

A faint sound, someone moving, filtered from a far precinct of the house. The mysterious Alice. Her husband Bill, the host for these Friday night games, was a man, on the other hand, rather not mysterious enough. At the moment, he held a good hand, this fact betrayed by his casualness. Harvey had known him forever, by birth a grandee in Jackson, but always something of a disappointment. Bill and the mysterious Alice lived well within their means, proving that that was not always a virtue. The furniture in the lived-in part of the large room was mass-produced stuff—off-blue, stained, skewed. Family heirlooms occupied the margins, waiting stolidly for the next inheritor.

Harvey's attention drifted back to Goetzinger, who had tossed in his hand, too, and sat waiting, ever-patient, for the next. What, Harvey wondered, would happen if the right opportunity to plead the union cause never surfaced? What would Goetzinger do then? An interesting question. Probably nothing. Probably he'd just keep his yap shut. You didn't start betting wildly because the cards weren't falling your way. Goetzinger would go away and that would be that. Despite himself, Harvey felt a certain respect for the man. What a shame, he thought, that the little twerp wasn't one of the good people.

"Read 'em and weep, gentlemen," Bill said as he triumphantly laid down his full house and raked in a pot smaller than it should have been.

The game continued. When Harv won the next hand, he looked across at Goetzinger and said, "Looks like it's not your night, my friend."

"Looks like." Goetzinger picked up a poker chip and rubbed it and then idly tumbled it back and forth across the knuckles of one hand.

After midnight, Goetzinger began to catch some cards and Harvey cooled off a bit. But he still felt strong. He played smart, didn't try to climb uphill like some players when a streak turned sour. He waited, as earlier Goetzinger had waited.

And sure enough, after a time, things swung back in his direction once more. He congratulated himself on his patience. He began to feel expansive again.

And so, between deals, the union matter popping once more into his mind, he said to the silent figure across the table, "You know, my friend, you'd do yourself a favor if you got off your high horse and just negotiated the damn contract."

They were playing Texas Hold 'Em, the big money game popular in Vegas. Deuce lifted the corners to inspect his two hole cards. "That right, Harv?"

"You better believe it."

The flop was dealt, three community cards faceup—two, four, seven, all puppy feet. One of Harvey's hole cards was also a club, the king.

"Possible flush, gentlemen," Bill, who had dealt the hand, said. They bet, everybody but one staying.

Bill dealt the turn card, faceup. Another club, the jack this time. *Lookee here*, Harvey thought. He had his flush, the second nut. Only the ace could beat him.

On the betting round, Harvey limped, but the others started to drop out anyway. Except Goetzinger.

"Heads up," he smiled. With only two of them left in the hand, the limit on the number of raises was gone.

Harvey tossed two ten-dollar chips into the pot, and waited for Deuce to raise. On a raise, he would have dropped, certain that Deuce held the missing ace and was looking down his throat. Goetzinger, however, merely called.

"Possible flush," Bill needlessly repeated as he dealt the last card, the river card, faceup. An irrelevant diamond.

Deuce's bet. He tapped the back of his hole cards and studied Harvey speculatively.

"So the union ought to fold, is that what you think, Harv? Give up our wonderful idea to improve city services?"

Harvey sniffed. "You're kicking against the pricks, my friends."

Deuce regarded him with a little grin, a hint of derision.

"So bet already," one of the other players complained—the CPA Luther Muller.

"Tell you what, then," Goetzinger suggested. "Why don't we make this interesting?"

"Interesting?"

"Yeah. What say we bet on it?"

Harvey laughed silently, but he didn't quite understand what Deuce was proposing.

"Anybody can bet money," Goetzinger went on. "Money doesn't mean anything. Let's bet something that's important."

"Oh?"

"I'll drop my demand, go back to the table, and negotiate the contract…if I lose this hand."

Harvey crossed his arms over his chest. This was an idea he already didn't care for. "And me?"

"If you lose, you come over to our side."

"You're kidding."

Goetzinger shook his head. "Dead serious, Harv. C'mon, let's bet something got a little juice to it. Why not?"

"You seem to forget that I'm the city attorney. I represent the city."

Goetzinger shrugged. "I'm not talking about going public, Harv. Talking about the council, talking about Cutler. Talking about what you do best, the back-channel stuff, greasing the skids."

"Shit, this is stupid," Luther Muller said. Luther sat to Harvey's right. He had always been a man for the proprieties. The others at the table seemed nothing but interested in this little pissing contest between Harvey and Goetzinger.

Harvey, for his part, wasn't thinking about Deuce's ploy, stupid or not. He was thinking, *The son of a bitch's got the damn ace.*

"But I don't agree with the union position, Deuce," Harvey told him, summoning up as much casual pleasantness as he could under the circumstances. "Now tell me, what could possibly have led you to imagine I might switch sides, under any circumstances?"

"Since when do lawyers have to believe their clients are innocent?" Goetzinger asked.

Harvey smiled at this jibe, but he was thinking, Shit, if he refused the bet, that just proved he lacked cojones. But if he took it, he lost. Either way, he was fucked.

"It's stupid, Harvey, don't do it," Luther said, the voice of conscience at Harvey's elbow. The prissiness in the tone annoyed Harvey. Needlessly, he looked at his hole cards again, then at Goetzinger. They held each other's gaze, Harvey with his arms crossed, feinting sleepy indifference, the kid with forefinger tapping his hole cards, betraying no expression whatsoever. Sincerity perhaps.

Goetzinger surely was an inscrutable bastard. It occurred to Harvey that maybe he'd been folding his hands all along, good and bad alike, just waiting.

"There's another problem," Harvey said.

"And what's that?"

"You've got the ace."

"Maybe, maybe not. Why don't we bet? Then you'll find out."

In spite of everything, Harvey was tempted. What a nice story it made. Harvey wins, beats union head at own game, union settles.

Harvey took a deep breath and exhaled slowly. Then he shook his head.

"So you're folding, then?"

Harvey shook his head again. "Bet."

Deuce's expression changed, from mocking to a kind of dismissal and finally resignation. He reached for his chips and bumped the pot five bucks, a lousy nickel. Another surprise.

Harvey called. "What you got?"

Goetzinger flipped his hole cards over: six of spades and a club, the ten, not the ace. His smile returned. "You see, Harv, you could have won."

Harvey showed his king and raked in the pot. "I believe I did win."

Deuce just continued to smile.

~

Goetzinger's gaze—amused, speculative, interested, coolly indifferent, unreadable—returned to Harvey from time to time as the game wore on. Harvey was ticked off. The little shit could have forced him to fold but didn't. He ran that goddamn bluff just to make him look bad.

Goetzinger picked up his few surviving chips and let them cascade back onto the felt. Harvey told himself to forget it. Let him have his little victory. Didn't mean a damn thing. Luther was right—don't mix business with pleasure.

But it stuck in Harvey's craw; he couldn't leave it alone. He brooded, a good deal of the joy gone out of the evening for him, the small cityscape his own chips made beside the point. He supposed that in some twisted way, Goetzinger was trying to take revenge after getting fucked over by Paul Cutler. He had a damn strange way of doing it. It just irritated the hell out of Harvey. *Okay*, he thought finally, *two can play at this game.*

Support for the union versus an end to this crap about workplace democracy, that was the proposition. Suppose he'd surprised the kid and taken him up on it? Suppose, even, that the little cocksucker had had the ace? Harvey tried to imagine himself championing the union cause. A stretch. Still, it occurred to him, he might get something done to move the process along. Support for the union? Well, maybe, but whatever he did, it would be on his own terms, not according to the dictates of the likes of Deuce Goetzinger. He felt a familiar surge, uncertainty thrust aside.

He weighed the risks. Nothing without some risk. Did he have the cojones? The cards had been falling his way. And, whatever happened, he couldn't really lose.

As the game was breaking up, and Bill moved to put the cards away, Harvey reached out and placed his hand over the deck, looking at Goetzinger.

"Okay, we'll cut for it. I win, you settle. You win, I'll talk to Cutler."

Goetzinger, surprised, mused over this turn of events, then asked, "Talk to Cutler, that's all?"

"Take it or leave it." Hobson's choice, but that was the whole point.

Goetzinger's smile this time was inward, the smile of recognition. "Sure," he said, "why not."

"What happens stays here in this room." Harvey lifted his hand from the deck. "High card, aces high."

Most of the others had already gotten up from the table. Movement and chatter died away.

"Luther," Goetzinger asked, "how about you shuffle for us?"

"Not me," Muller said, "I don't want any part of this."

"I'll do it," Bill volunteered.

Harvey watched Bill split the deck, tap the halves on the felt and riffle them together. Once, twice. Then he laid them dead center on the table.

Goetzinger cut first, as casually as he seemed to do everything. He turned his card over at once—the jack of diamonds. *Damn*, Harvey thought, and quickly, just to get it over with, he reached out and cut himself. He had to grip the cards twice to get a firm hold. He looked without showing the others, then, disgusted, tossed away the cards he'd picked up. Another diamond, a deuce.

"Great," Luther said, "just great."

"If you want some arguments to use on Cutler," Goetzinger offered, "I've got plenty."

"You can keep 'em. They're no use to me," Harvey told him.

~

Harvey felt like shit. He told himself again that this was a no-lose proposition, remember? But that made no difference, not at the moment. Despite all his fine rationalizations, Harvey felt lousy—mad at Goetzinger, mad at himself, mad at the whole sorry business.

As they were leaving, Luther pulled him aside. "Should I be worried, Harv?" the accountant asked.

"About what?"

Muller nodded back in the direction of the departing Goetzinger. His tone irritated Harvey. Luther worshipped at the shrine of his own maturity. Since he'd gotten his instrument rating, he'd become even more of a pill, always flying at night and calling up everyone he knew while he was in the air. He was as tiresome and self-righteous as the city manager.

"I'll honor the bet," Harvey told him, "but that doesn't mean Goetzinger will much care for the result."

Luther considered this elliptical assurance. "Why don't you give me a call?" he suggested.

But this was not a matter Harvey had any intention of strategizing over with the likes of Luther Muller.

"I'll take care of it, Luther. It's none of your business."

Luther paused and read the expression on Harvey's face. He let the matter drop.

CHAPTER 15

~

Two men and a boy worked their way slowly along the outside of the city's floodwall, the men avoiding where they could the billows of rotting snow, while the boy, wearing snowshoes, sought them out, the time left for winter fantasies quickly slipping away. The river reflected the intense blue of the sky, the storm of the previous days having finally moved east and leaving a brilliant, if brief, interregnum. For the harbingers of the next onset of heavy weather were already visible on the western horizon. Since ice-out, the Mississippi had risen several feet, excavating along the edge of the snowpack, marking out a sharp seam between blue-reflecting water and white land. The temperature stood in the low forties.

Walter Plowman could hear the meltwater running beneath the snowpack. Tonight, again, the temperature wouldn't fall back to freezing, the patch of clear weather too brief to bring radiational cooling. The water would continue to run.

"There are people around here who question your credentials as Jeremiah," Chuck Fellows said.

"My what?"

They had stopped while Chuck inspected the massive rusty hinges on one of the concrete gates that would have to be shut to seal the wall should the water begin to threaten the city.

"Your prediction. A flood of record."

"You've been talking? That was supposed to be private, between the two of us," Walter said.

Chuck looked around and called his son Todd over and explained how they'd go about closing the gate when the time came. Walter, his thoughts disturbed by the idea that Chuck had been nosing about what he'd been told in confidence, let his eye move from the shore up the riprap and then to the top of the wall. He envisioned water beginning to move in the tribs and main stem to the north. You couldn't nick the body without drawing blood and now you couldn't nick the countryside without cutting across one of the countless veins of snow-melt and rainfall, sending a vast flux of water pell-mell toward this narrow throat.

After they were again under way, Chuck said, "Sorry. I mentioned it at the dog track. They're outside the wall. If you're right, they've got all kinds of problems."

Good reason or not, Walter still didn't like it. "But they didn't believe you?"

"The construction manager, Jack Kelley, he didn't. Don't know about the others."

Certain people in the city had never taken Walter seriously. For the most part, he knew who they were—big men with small beliefs—and didn't waste his time on them.

"So how's it look now?" Chuck asked. They hadn't spoken about the situation in several days. "Anything changed?"

Walter decided he wasn't quite ready to say, his ardor for talking to this man cooled for the moment. Nobody, he reminded himself, could be trusted 100 percent. Anyway, he was willing to tell Chuck what he'd been doing. "I keep on checking conditions and asking around. According to my friend at the ag extension, you dig down a foot or so, you still got frost most everywhere. Widespread. No place for water to go but into the rivers. Been talking to the snow survey people up in Minne-apolis, too. They've never seen this much water in the snowpack, about twice as much as normal. It looks bad. But you already know that… Everybody knows, it's no secret… So what's gonna happen? Maybe nothing. Maybe the fellow out at the track is right."

The water-saturated snow had clogged the webbing of Todd's snowshoes and he stumbled along, quickly losing interest in his game of frontier trapper and Indian fighter.

When he complained, Chuck merely said, "I told you not to bring them. Take them off and carry them if you want. They're your responsibility."

They started up again, and Chuck turned his attention back to Walter. "But nothing's so unlikely that it might not happen."

They turned a corner. The floodwall unfolded before them, upright concrete panels in straight runs and abrupt veers where it jogged, fol-lowing the winding shoreline.

Walter said, "If your wall here doesn't fail, we should be okay. I don't know about the dog track."

Chuck stared at the floodwall, as if perhaps to locate the point where a twenty-five-foot stage would reach, the Corps's current prediction.

For the past couple of weeks, Walter had been up until two or three almost every morning, running regression analyses on data he downloaded from the mainframe at the U., comparing his current data with his master file, then going through the historical material year by year, looking for the closest match he could find, the key that would unlock the pattern.

Todd had taken the snowshoes off and was dragging them along, their tails tracing a pair of raggedy lines behind him.

Chuck waded around the next corner, kicking his way through a ridge of wind-gathered drift and sighting down a reach of the wall. "Okay, then tell me this, Walt. What's a two-hundred-year event?"

Walter knew the genesis of this inquiry. Chuck had changed his tactics. The wall was designed to protect the city from the worst flood expected on average every two hundred years. Five-hundred-year events, millennial events, well, they were a future you didn't bother to prepare for. Not cost effective.

But Chuck obviously understood this. During his engineering training, he would have taken a hydrology course somewhere along the line. No, his question had nothing to do with the definition of a two-hundred-year event. It went to the heart of the climatologist's trade. And it was aggressive, too, filled with the rough, good-humored challenge Walter had come to understand marked Fellows's character.

"You're right," he conceded. "We don't know what a two-hundred-year event is. We've got maybe a hundred years of decent data. And the whole twentieth century—not just this year—has been an outlier, warmer than any time over the past several hundred years." Walter had thought about this stuff for decades, and he knew the situation might be stranger still. "Could be even worse. Suppose, just suppose, there ain't no such thing as a climate. Ever considered that?"

Chuck had stopped and was staring back at his son. Todd had been walking aimlessly behind them. The snowshoes had disappeared.

"Where are they?" Chuck demanded.

"Aw," Todd complained.

"Go get them." For a few moments, the kid looked like he might try to give his father a hard time, but he thought better of it and went back to fetch the abandoned footgear. When he returned, he tried to hand the snowshoes to his father, but Chuck just shook his head. Walter thought the kid was awfully young to be held to such strict account. If it had been his son, he surely would have taken pity on him.

At the entrance to the Ice Harbor, they went up a ladder onto the concrete gate-wall, atop which stood the machine shelter for the pump and gate motors. Chuck climbed with his bandaged thumb stuck out. Walter looked at the thick swathing and imagined the gash underneath and felt a tingling sensation around his testicles.

The harbor gates were open, folded back against the wall and frozen in during the winter. Now the heat of the sun had warmed the concrete and melted the ice and snow around them. In the harbor, the ice had been lifted from its footings and floated like an area rug, gray and sodden.

"You close the gate at seventeen feet, isn't that right?" Walter asked. He had read the city's flood drill, but it had been years ago.

"At sixteen when the stage is going to seventeen." Chuck contemplated the harbor entrance. "Got to clear off the sills first. Thinking of getting out my scuba gear."

In the shed, Chuck showed his son the engine with its elaborate gearing for sealing the harbor, talking about the gear ratio—two thousand to one—which allowed the tiny three-horse motor to close the massive gates. Then he explained how the pump would force the storm water, which drained from the city into the harbor, over the wall.

As they climbed down and continued on their way, Walter asked, "You ever dive in the Mississippi?"

"Nope."

"Not exactly the Caribbean."

Todd dawdled behind, experimenting with different ways of carrying the snowshoes and finally throwing them down in disgust. Seeing that his father had noticed, he sullenly picked them up again.

"It's tough on a kid," Walter ventured gingerly, "having to lug them all this way."

"He's got to learn," Chuck responded, his tone brooking no contradiction. *A hard man*, Walter thought, liking Chuck less now than before. He should take it easier on his kid. And he shouldn't have talked to the construction workers.

People all had their loyalties, Walter reminded himself, and you couldn't really know how much to trust a man until you understood where you fit.

They detoured by the old river terminal building, inside the flood-wall. Metal placards affixed to the brickwork, one above the other like the various heights of a child growing up marked on a kitchen door-post, memorialized the highest stages of notable floods in the city's history, before the Corps built the wall.

Mostly for Todd's benefit, Walter told them a couple of the famous stories about these disasters—the 1951 flood in which scour in the Mines of Spain south of the city uncovered an ancient Mesqua-tie Indian village, and in 1965, the flood of record, when firefighters actually had to dive beneath the floodwater to attach a hose to a fire hydrant in order to fight a fire in a building surrounded by water. Walter pointed out the building, nearby and still standing.

After he finished, Chuck added, "When I was hired and Mark O'Banion was showing me around town, he brought me down here."

"That's right, he would. Mark was an old-timer. He had respect. He knew what the Mississippi could do. Hardly anybody remembers anymore. Not like before they built the wall. Back then, come spring, everybody kept his eye on the river."

Outside the wall again, they passed under the approach to the Mesquatie Bridge. Above them the tires of traffic crossing the river whirred over the metal roadway grid. Walter pointed out where one year he'd found a mud dauber's nest in the fall and what the folk-lore said about the height of the wasp nest above the river. "Last year found one up on Apple Island. According to the wasps, we're gonna have a twenty-seven-foot crest."

"You believe that?" Chuck asked.

"That wasps can predict flood crests? No, of course not," Walter assured him.

South of the bridge, Chuck inspected the joint where the Corps, having more land to work with, had built a levee, tying it into the wall. There were a number of holes nearby in the outside slope of the earth-work, which would have to be plugged before the water started to rise.

"Probably groundhogs," Walter said. "I know a woman who traps them. Uses apples. Releases the critters where they won't do any damage."

"Oh, yeah?" Chuck obviously wasn't sure what he thought about that, but he said, "Give me her name. She'll have to hustle."

Finally, they climbed to the crest of the levee and followed it southward.

Todd had fallen way behind, but still he carried the snowshoes. At the moment, he was trying to balance them on top of his coonskin cap. Chuck kept an eye on him but made no attempt to get him to go faster.

Finally, at the southern limit of the levee, they waited for him to catch up. Here the bluffs pinched down to the river, leaving a bench just wide enough for the Illinois Central tracks, which pierced the protection works. If the water rose far enough, they'd have to stop running trains and sandbag the gap.

"Okay," Chuck said as Todd straggled up to them, "I'll take those. You did good. I'm proud of you." He reached down and lifted the snowshoes off his son's shoulders. Walter felt as if the burden had been lifted from his own.

Todd's spirits rose at once—he'd endured his penance—and father and son walked along side by side, Chuck's hand resting lightly around the boy's shoulder. Todd was the image of his father, his chest puffed out, walking jauntily beside his dad.

The three of them were retracing their steps now. Walter could just make out the point where the levee met the floodwall, and beyond, the stem of the first gate valve. And beyond that, the sweep of the city, from the bluffs in the west to the bluffs in the east, on the Illinois side of the river. The sun had been reduced to a pale disk behind the scrim of approaching clouds.

"So, tell me, Walt—you *do* think we're in for one hell of an event, right?" Chuck said after a time. "You told me. You're not backing down, are you?"

Walter hesitated and then said, "No, I'm not."

"But you haven't told me your rationale. What do you know that nobody else does?"

The camaraderie between father and son had restored some of Walter's esteem for the father, but there was still the matter of Chuck having betrayed the earlier confidence. Probably Walter should have kept his mouth shut. Too late now. And if his predictions were to become public, probably his reasons should, too.

"Let me tell you about what happened a few years ago, down south," he began.

The three of them continued slowly along the levee. The child after a time broke free from his father's embrace and skipped backward ahead of the two men, whose pace slackened even further, until they had stopped altogether and turned toward each other to continue their conversation. The boy, caught in some boy's fantasy, danced far ahead of them.

Chapter 16

~

Aggie and El abbreviated their morning walk, hardly a walk at all, just a lick and a promise, before the two of them hightailed it back toward the Plowmans' old Vic. Cold rain whipped into their faces, the sidewalks were mined with slushy puddles, and overhead clouds scudded, grim and determined.

In the mudroom, Aggie shivered as she shucked off her parka and jogged in tiny steps into the kitchen, flapping her arms to warm up.

Walter looked up mildly from his breakfast.

"A little chilly out there, girls?"

The shades were drawn.

"Coffee," Walter gestured with his fork. He had a tie on. He and El were going to the earlier service at the Presbyterian Church to give El a little more time to ring doorbells, the election only two days off now.

Aggie fixed herself a cup and sat down. She had badgered Lucille, her mother, into going to the Saturday night Mass at Nativity and so had the whole day free. She was meeting with the volunteers at ten thirty. The big last-minute push. They were blowing their tiny media budget on radio spots over the next two days. She had plenty for the volunteers to do. Besides the lit drops, rides had to be arranged to the polls for voters who needed them and crews assigned to collect lawn signs and take down posters on Wednesday.

Outside, the wind rose and fell, making a sound like the air being sucked out of a container, rattling the storm doors in their frames. She shuddered sympathetically.

"All this weird weather," she said.

El shook the teakettle to see if there was enough water in it, then deposited it on a burner. Walter got up and took his dishes over to the sink, and Aggie watched the two of them, husband and wife, moving around the kitchen, filling the vacancies each other left. Despite the stuff still left to do, Aggie already had a kind of postpartum feeling about the election.

El went back to the stove and shook the kettle again, impatiently. "If it was only the weather."

To this, Walter sniffed but said nothing. He'd sat down again, staring at his coffee cup with a distracted air. His presence always seemed provisional.

El said, "I'll tell you what annoys me, Aggie. This election really *has* turned into a vote about whether or not to keep Jackson closed."

"Roger Filer can't do that. People will come. To the U., for instance. And if Ultima Thule moves here, they've got black employees."

"If," El immediately countered. She sighed and looked off into space. "Deke McKeown hasn't returned my calls." She turned back toward Aggie, and Aggie felt the considerable power of her attention. "The damage has been done. Now everybody thinks we're the bigot capital of America."

"Nonsense. This isn't Idaho or something. We haven't got survivalists running all over the place."

"I've got an aunt in Virginia," Walter chimed in, "who thinks Jackson is in Idaho."

"You're no help," Aggie told him.

El snorted. "But Walter's right, Aggie. Iowa, Idaho, Ohio—people out East can't tell the difference."

Aggie switched tactics. "All that means is, okay, so we've got a problem. But we're hardly alone. There are lots and lots of other places in the same fix."

"We are alone," El insisted. "People don't know about all these other places, they know about us. Thanks to all this publicity. The *Donahue Show* was going to be a disaster no matter what happened. And it was. Just an out-and-out disaster. What black in his right mind would want to move here now?"

"Perhaps ones who want to do something about the problem," Aggie said, trying to muster a little defiance in the face of El's certainty.

"You think there are any of them left? Aside from Jesse Jackson and a few like him."

"Well, Jesse Jackson *is* coming here," Aggie pointed out. Jackson was, indeed, coming, and some other black activists, and even a contingent of Guardian Angels, a counterdemonstration to protest the David Duke visit and the beating of Sam Turner and all the other racial stuff of the past few months.

"You think that helps?" El said. "All it does is make matters worse."

Walter pushed himself away from the table with much scraping of chair legs and propped his hands on his knees. "Doesn't make any difference. A month from now everybody will have something else to talk about."

El turned around and gave at her husband a sharp look. "Oh?"

"After I walked the floodwall with Chuck Fellows yesterday, I called up Mick Kilmer."

"Who?" Aggie asked.

"One of Walter's buddies in the Corps of Engineers," El informed her with a disdainful little jut of the chin.

Walter expanded on the topic. "Mick's down at Rock Island. He runs the Corps's data collection operation. A neat guy."

"Data," El said archly. El was bipolar, but in her own way. When she wasn't depressed, she was super-focused and of most definite opinions.

Walter decided to talk to Aggie rather than his wife. "According to Mick, if we get just average precip from now on, the river will top out at twenty-five feet."

"That's what they've been saying all along, isn't it?" Aggie asked. She wasn't into floods. Lucille lived down in Little Wales, practically the lowest point in the city, and Aggie dreaded having to get her mother to evacuate if the time came. Lucille had always hated the flood protection system, but now, no doubt, she'd say, "Well, they were determined to put the thing up. Let's see it do its job."

"Twenty-five," El said. "The floodwall's ten feet higher than that." She was leaning with her back against the sink and staring at her husband. Nearby, the kettle made a rustling sound, a grumble of discontent.

Walter fixed his gaze on a point somewhere between El and Aggie. "Eight feet," he said, "and the last three are freeboard."

"Whatever."

"Anyway, that's not the point. Mick's beginning to come around to my way of thinking."

"Is he, now? And what's that, pray tell?"

"Things could get a lot worse. Expect you're going to see the Corps's prediction go up in the next few days. We both think so. We were trying to put a number on it last night, but it's tricky under conditions this extreme."

"What's this 'we' business, Walter?" El demanded. "How did you suddenly become part of the equation?"

Ignoring this question, Walter said, "Way above average, that's what the precip looks like over the next few weeks. Might be looking at a crest at least twenty-seven feet. That'd be two-tenths above '65."

Aggie did the arithmetic in her head. "But still three feet below trouble."

He nodded. "But a minute ago Eleanor here was trying to say we had ten feet to spare. Didn't take long to get that down to three, did it?"

"This is none of your business, Walter," El told him. "You stay out of it."

Walter continued to ignore El. To Aggie, he said, "Jet streams seem to be stuck. If they stay that way, we could have a series of storms. Could just keep coming." His words were determined. The tension in the room felt not like something beginning from scratch, but rather taken up where it had been left off earlier. El's look had intensified, but Walter didn't see it. On the stove, the kettle began a few experimental attempts at whistling, a kind of uh-oh noise.

El bore down on her husband. "But you can't tell, isn't that right? After four or five days, forecasts are pretty much worthless. Isn't that right, dear?"

Instead of conceding this point, Walter parried. "The long-range is a different breed of cat." His annoyance mounted.

El paid no attention to it. "But you can't tell. You're always saying that. You just can't know for sure what's going to happen."

"*Can't ever* tell for sure what's gonna happen." Aggie had the impression this remark was meant to be pointed, but El didn't react to it. She said what she was determined to say.

"You're just going to get in trouble, Walter, if you start making predictions for the river."

"'Course," Walter said, his voice suddenly rising, "*you'd* predict there *won't* be a flood."

El gave Walter one of her characteristic what-planet-are-you-from looks. "I'm just saying, Walter, stay out of it. I'm telling you, you'll get in serious trouble. Leave it to the National Weather Service, leave it to the Corps, to your friend Mick there. Leave it to the people who get paid for this sort of thing."

"I'm not gonna predict nothin'," Walter told her, calming down a little, but still more angry than Aggie ever remembered.

"You know what I mean. You'll say something you'll regret. Stay out of it." Aggie imagined El was right. As a weather forecaster, Walter was a local legend. People believed him. He could rile them up and maybe get into a lot of trouble.

But Walter at the moment was conceding nothing.

"I'll do what I damn well please," he snapped. "I know what I know."

"No, you don't. When it comes to people, Walter, you're too trusting. You're naive."

"I'm naive? Like hell. If anybody's naive around here, it's you, Eleanor. We could be in for the biggest damn flood this city has ever seen and you want to bury your head in the damn sand."

El looked briefly away, the gesture of someone taking a moment to gather her forces. Walter didn't wait.

"Okay," he said, "okay, I've had enough. You wanna know? This is the deal. I bust my hump. Every day, I'm studying the charts, looking at old data, new data, every goddamned piece of data I can lay my hands on! I got data up the ying-yang! Where's your data?!" Aggie winced at the intensity of Walter's attack. She'd never seen him like this.

"Good grief," El said and looked at Aggie and shook her head. *Do you believe this?* the look said.

"I'll tell you! You got no data!" Walter yelled at her.

"Apples and oranges," El responded, unperturbed.

"Like hell!" He dragged his chair around in a quarter circle, an act of separation, then twisted his body back toward El to fire off a broadside. "Take this election of yours. You keep on saying you're gonna lose. You don't know. You got no polling data. Even if you did, people lie all the time. You got nothing."

"Data is just the plural of anecdote," El sniffed.

Walter stampeded on. "Yeah, right. You're so damn sure of yourself. To hell with data, who needs data! But me, I got all this stuff, been collecting it for years, hell, been collecting it for decades, and all I'm trying to do is predict the damn weather! Not trying to change anything! Just say, like, tomorrow we got a 10 percent chance of frogs or whatever the hell!" El's derisive laugh slowed Walter not one jot. "But you, you got nothing, not a damn thing! Working with human beings to boot! Who the hell can predict what human beings'll do?"

"That's right," El said, still pretty calm, but Aggie could tell that Walter was beginning to get to her. "And that's exactly my point, Walter. That's why you'll get in trouble. You can't tell how people will react."

"Like hell!" Walter brushed this statement aside. The teakettle was whistling like crazy now, steam shooting out of it. Aggie crept over and moved it off the burner. "It's arrogance," Walter practically yelled, "that's what I call it, arrogance! You're an arrogant woman, Eleanor Plowman! You got not a shred of data and here you are spouting off like you know it all! Bullshit, that's what I say, bullshit!"

El abandoned the effort to reason with him. She drew herself to her full height, smoothed out her rumpled clothing, and said, "Fuck your data."

"Fuck your non-data," Walter retorted.

"What a stupid thing to say."

"Okay, then, fuck you. How's that? Fuck you."

"Fuck you, too, then."

"Fuck you."

"Fuck you."

All these "fuck yous" were delivered not at a feverish pitch, but with a certain dignity, each one slightly less intense than the last. The two of them glared at each other, then sniffed with mutual disdain and turned away.

And that was it. The fight had ended.

El went over and made a great show of fixing her tea. Walter got up and stomped out into the hallway.

Very soon El had abandoned the attempt to make the tea and turned toward Aggie and smiled, her smile not on quite straight. "Expect this is a little more than you bargained for this morning."

Walter had returned and plopped back down in his chair, still scowling, all hunched up.

During the exchange, Aggie had been staring from one to the other, completely lost to herself. "I'm just thinking, 'Wow!' I thought you guys never had fights."

"Used to not. Walter's a great avoider, isn't that right, dear? But I've been working on him." Walter was admitting nothing at the moment. El came around behind him and leaned down to give him a bear hug and nuzzle. "Making some progress, too, by the look of it, ain't I, dearest?"

Walter just grumbled, all this sudden sweet talk no good for his newfound image as a brawler.

Aggie shook her head, thinking of the substance of the brief battle. "Pretty serious stuff."

"Bah," El said, standing up and setting partially to rights the mess she'd made of Walter's hair. "We've been having this fight for years. Haven't we, sweetie? Walter's just getting a little more demonstrative is all."

Walter, the tough guy, seeing his chance, said, "Eleanor's been wrong for years."

El cuffed him playfully, with the flat of her hand, mussing his hair once more. "But Jackson's not a weather system, dear." Now she placed one hand on top of his head, the second on the first, and rested her chin on both. Walter squirmed, but El applied enough pressure to hold him in place.

Aggie wondered how many people had witnessed a scene like that between them. "I'm honored," she said.

"As well you should be," El agreed. Walter was still trying to act the tough guy, but a satisfied little grin had begun to peek through, a tic enlivening his resolutely-plain, going-about-its-own-business face.

El stood up, releasing him, giving him another love pat. "But what I said goes, dear. Stay out of the flood forecasting business."

"I'll do what I damn well please," Walter said, beaming.

Self-conscious now, Aggie looked wistfully at the two of them. Who could she have such a satisfying fight with? Her mother? Paul Cutler? Not a chance. A fight had to be fair to be any fun.

What about Deuce? This idea popped, unbidden, into her head. The sum total of their relationship so far had been a handful of negotiations. Fights of a sort, she supposed, but hardly like the set-to between El and Walter. She remembered the accidental meeting in the cafe. She had been remembering it, adding to and subtracting from its meaning in the days since.

And then there was the fact, she reminded herself over and over, that Deuce was a specialist in brief dalliances. And on top of everything else, look who his father was. Who in her right mind would want Fritz Goetzinger as a father-in-law? And what was she doing thinking about fathers-in-law anyway?

And on and on her thoughts careened in typical Aggie fashion, until with a little mental stamp of the foot, she told herself to shut up.

El was humming as she finally completed making her tea. Walter had raised the window shades to inspect the storm. They were both radiant. Aggie got herself some more coffee, a half cup. She had a few minutes before she had to go back to her condo and get ready to meet the volunteers.

CHAPTER 17

~

In the eighteenth century, the building had been a mill on the Merrimack River outside Lowell, Massachusetts. When the farmers moved west and the milling business collapsed, it had become an inn. Finally, at the turn of the century, it changed hands once more, purchased by one G.N. Phelps, a wealthy wagon maker in Jackson, Iowa. The old mill had been taken apart and, like the farmers before it, moved west, where it was faithfully reassembled, numbered board by numbered board, to become the clubhouse of The Jackson Country Club.

Paul Cutler looked with disapproval at the old machinery—the millstones and troughs and gearing—reduced to ornamentations in the country club bar. He and Harvey Butts skirted around them. Nothing in the building was quite in plumb—the skewed post-and-lintel doorways; the low-ceilinged rooms; the broad, knotty floorboards, which made Paul conscious of his manner of walking.

The two of them were following the host of the club's restaurant, Harvey joking about putting up the spring pictures to encourage good weather. At the moment, the walls were covered with Currier and Ives winter scenes. The prints were changed to match the seasons. Such coinages irritated Paul. Practically everything his eyes fell on irritated him, including Harvey.

This little luncheon audience with him was strictly a home game for Butts, who served on the club's board and was reputed to be a hell of a golfer. As he ambled along, large and stoop-shouldered, he resembled nothing so much as a man addressing a golf ball.

In the dining room, the spindly tables and Hitchcock chairs were set generously apart, ensuring a measure of privacy for club members and their guests. The host, after a quiet word from Butts, led them to a dining alcove well off to the side. Paul had no idea what Harvey had in mind, which was typical.

The server was at the table immediately, a man of about Paul's age. Harvey ordered only coffee. Paul could have used a good stiff drink, certainly not coffee. He settled for a glass of white wine. The server wore a starched white jacket, which gave him a faintly medical look. Harvey chatted him up, as he had the host.

"Well, Harv," Paul said as soon as the drinks had arrived and they'd ordered their meals, "what's up?"

With a shake of his head and the toss of his hand, Harvey fended him off. He would not be rushed. Instead, he settled back and gave Paul the once-over. "You're looking a little dog-eared, my friend."

"It's been a lousy winter. It's still a lousy winter."

Harvey smiled. "Got to get those damn pictures changed."

Paul thought about the potential for a big spring flood and said, "Why don't you go straight to summer."

Paul left his glass untouched for a time, a small act of abstinence. They talked about calamities.

Finally, the waiter rematerialized and laid the food before them with surgical exactness. Paul noticed the closed expression on his face, suggesting not so much a mask as self-absorption, as if his whole being centered on those simple, menial acts. Something about the performance depressed Paul, although he could not have said exactly what, and something about it made him envious, as well.

Harvey asked if the scrod was satisfactory—fresh? cooked okay?—and then commenced a brief narrative about the problems they'd been having finding a new executive chef for the club. Paul let him go on. This was Harvey's show. Paul had been in a rush at first, but now he found his mood had changed. If Harvey never got around to what was really on his mind, that was soon enough.

But finally the attorney stopped eating for a minute and went through a series of minute adjustments that suggested the time had arrived. Paul waited.

"I've been thinking…," Harvey started and then hesitated, returning to his New England boiled dinner. "Now I don't want to meddle here," he said between bites.

Hearing this disclaimer of meddlers everywhere, Paul laid down his fork.

Harvey sliced off a morsel of corned beef and inspected it critically before popping it into his mouth. "I've been giving the business with the unions some thought."

Paul said nothing. The unions? What did Harvey care about the unions?

"A shame," he said, "all this divisiveness...at a time, you know..."

Paul listened to these sentence fragments and wondered where in God's name this could be going. "I'm not the one you should be talking to."

"I know. Unions. Worst thing that ever happened to this town." Even as he made this ritual denunciation, Butts's mind was obviously elsewhere. "So tell me, Paul, what's the current status?"

"In the negotiations?"

"Yup. Up to the minute."

"Well," Paul hesitated, reluctant to say anything he didn't have to before he knew just what was afoot. "Police and fire have put on their usual Alphonse-and-Gaston act. But we're close. By the end of the week."

Harvey took a bite of salad, then vegetables, organizing his food as he went and paying equal attention to each item. "And transit, what about them?"

"Transit? Yes, well, they're waiting for somebody else to do something. But as soon as they do..."

"Good. And the big union?" With this question, Butts glanced up at Paul, for an instant.

"When young Goetzinger wants to get serious, we'll get serious. Aggie tells me he's clueless."

"I see."

Harvey stopped eating abruptly. He patted his lips with his napkin—a fastidious gesture—and eyed Paul. "And what about this business that keeps on coming up, this, what do they call it, workplace democracy?"

Harvey knew perfectly well what they called it. "What about it? You were at the meeting last week. You heard El Plowman. It'll be on the next council agenda."

Paul couldn't believe that Harvey Butts would have the time of day for such a cockamamie proposal, but apparently he was wrong, because the lawyer next said, "El Plowman's tenure as mayor is coming to an end. Her initiatives no longer pertain. So, I was just wondering...what if? Suppose we just gave Goetzinger his committee?"

Paul picked up his fork again and ate a bite of scrod. He allowed himself a sip of wine, savoring it on his tongue until the sharpness began to fade.

"You're kidding."

Harvey smiled slowly. "Not at all. Of course, it's a small matter. And it's your show. But why not?"

What on earth, Paul wondered, was going on here? In moments such as this, a chasm opened before him—interests, accommodations, all the back channels in a place like Jackson. But each time this matter had come up, each time he'd been blindsided like this, Paul's resolve stiffened.

"You heard what I said to the council. Do I really need to repeat myself?"

"No, I suppose not."

"You know what's ironic about this whole thing? The only one who ever really liked the idea was Aggie Klauer. I blame her. She's been way over the line. It was Aggie, if you want to know, who put the bee in Plowman's bonnet. But I don't get it, Harv, you're no friend of the unions. What's this all about?"

Butts popped another square of corned beef into his mouth and chewed thoughtfully before he said, "Think of it this way. It's what we lawyers like to call a declaration against interest. As you say, I'm no friend of the unions."

"I still don't get it." Paul was too annoyed at the moment to have any time for Harvey's witty formulations.

Butts's expression changed, becoming slightly cooler. He said, quite serious now, "Have you considered the possibility that the committee might provide you with an independent source of information? Hierarchies, after all, are not without their bottlenecks. Something to be said for that."

"Perhaps," Paul allowed. "But I don't think it'd be worth the grief."

"I see… Well, of course, it's a small matter."

Efficiency wasn't sexy, so people generally discounted it, even people who should have known better. "If we talk everything to death, Harv, not a damn thing will get done."

"I suppose… Okay, so you don't like the pluses of the thing. Then what about this?" Butts smiled. "You're a man who can appreciate the value of a failed experiment. Did you ever think of that?"

This argument, the obverse of the first, pleased Paul even less. He shook his head. "Please, spare me." Again, he wondered what was going on. Who the hell had Butts been talking to? "After the union's settled, okay, maybe we can do something. Not before. And not the committee, no way." The very idea of the thing, pushed in his face like this, over and over, just pissed Paul off no end. And coming from Harvey of all people. Paul said bitterly, "I didn't become a city manager to do this sort of thing, Harv. It's not part of my program."

Butts, who had attended to this retort carefully, at its end merely frowned briefly and went back to his meal. "It's a small matter," he said. "Just thought I'd bring it up. Whatever you want."

The server had returned, bringing a postprandial cup of coffee for Paul and a refill for Harvey. After he had performed his practiced routine and left, the two of them went on to other matters.

～

As Harvey dialed the number, he mused over what Paul Cutler had said. *It's not part of my program.* A damn curious turn of phrase. It occurred to him that for some time now Paul and the city had been falling out of love.

Not that it would do Deuce Goetzinger any good.

"Yeah?" the voice on the other end of the line said.

"Butts here. I talked to him. No go. You want my advice, you'll settle."

Goetzinger said nothing.

"You held the marker. I honored it. We're even."

"Yeah, sure, Harv."

"Now do everybody a favor, go back to the table and settle."

Again, Goetzinger said nothing.

"The ship's about to sail, my friend. You damn well better be on it."

Harvey hung up. Let him chew on that for a while. Harvey thought about this and nodded, satisfied. Then he went back to the matter of Paul Cutler.

It's not part of my program, the man had said. Yup, no doubt about it, a mighty curious turn of phrase.

CHAPTER 18

~

The odor of lime seemed to clot in Ned Pickett's nostrils. The floor of the room in the water plant was stained, a ragged skirt of white around the bottom of the slaker. Heat swelled from the machine. The cop kept his distance. He had to go on duty in a few minutes and didn't want to mess up his clean uniform.

No purpose to prolonging things, he thought. *Get this over and get out of here.*

So he said to Deuce Goetzinger, "We're going to settle." The police association had a tentative agreement with the city.

Deuce went over to a small bench made of rough planks. On a pair of upright pipes at the end, plastic gloves had been mounted, like hands raised in surrender. He put these on and carried a tray over to the back of the slaker, where he removed a cover and let lime from the conveyor drop onto a tray as he timed it.

"For what?"

"One percent."

Back at the bench, Deuce weighed the lime on a scale, and nodded, satisfied. He walked from the small room out to one of the clarifiers.

"It's just a token," Ned told his back, "but under the circumstances…"

Deuce stared into the large, circular basin, which filled the room, the water in it a clear pastel green. The soft, moist air cleared the clotted lime odor from Ned's nose. A low murmuring filled the room, the air alive with reflected light.

Deuce wasn't much of a man with the emotions, so far as Ned could see. Scorn sometimes. A guy with a good grip on himself. He would have made an all right cop.

"Anyway," Ned said, "I wanted to tell you. You deserved that much." Among the other cops, Ned had talked up Deuce's idea for a kind of shadow government. He liked it. Of course, power being what it was, no way Cutler wouldn't fight it tooth and nail.

On a small platform at the side of the basin stood a submersible lamp. Deuce lit this and then lowered it into the basin. The cord had markings measured along it, one mark after another descending into the water until, near the bottom of the basin, a cloudy layer became visible, curling and drifting and parting like smoke to swallow the lamp. Deuce took his reading off the cord.

"Bed's down half a foot since the last time I checked it. Haven't decanted. Haven't blown off. Haven't done a damn thing. That's life, Ned, full of all kinds of strange, mysterious shit." And here he looked up. "Unlike the police association. I knew you guys would settle."

Ned made the small mental adjustment necessary not to react with anger to this sneering comment. "Yeah," he agreed. And it was true, the cops supported each other; they didn't have much time for the other city employees.

As Deuce hauled up the lamp, hand over hand, he said, "Bob Mikulec stopped by earlier. You know Bob? Works at the shit plant."

"I know Bob."

"Yeah, well, then you know what a contrary fuck he is. I suggested to him maybe the union could get something done if his people re-upped."

"I heard."

Their footsteps made soft clanging sounds on the grating of the catwalk out to the center of the basin, where Deuce stooped down to feel the housings of a pair of electric motors. He spoke without looking up this time.

"Two months ago I asked him. So tonight, what happens? Just like you, suddenly he shows up, big as life. Except he's not here to bail. He tells me, yeah, sure, what the hell, they'd decided to join the union again. Can you believe that? What the hell you suppose they been doing for two friggin' months, besides playing with their dorks?"

Ned couldn't say he was surprised, union solidarity in the city being what it was. "All those people down at the shit plant are head cases," he said consolingly.

"They sure as hell are something… Well, no matter, I'll tell you what I told Bob, 'In, out, it doesn't make a damn bit of difference. It's over. The fat lady's sung.' Cutler wins, we lose, simple as that."

They stood silently at the center of the basin. The milky slaked lime purled down an open pipe and into the shroud beneath their feet, where it mixed with the water to start the softening process. The two electric motors made quiet, steady sounds, one lower than the other. Treated water slipped over the weirs into the collector channels. Beneath Ned's feet, the platform vibrated, just the slightest wavering motion. Reflections from the water shimmered in the air.

He paused a little longer and composed himself before he spoke.

"I got something else to say."

"Yeah?"

Deuce didn't seem much interested, but Ned hadn't come there merely as a courtesy. That, but something else, too.

"Yeah. It's this: I like your idea. I can see the point, even if most of the other guys didn't. And okay, you're right, it didn't work, not this time."

Goetzinger retreated down the catwalk, leaving Ned again talking to his back.

"Nothing like this takes the first time around, Deuce. You gotta give people time to get used to it. Let them get screwed over a few more times and then they'll start to think, 'Well, shit, maybe Goetzinger's got something there.'"

Over his shoulder, Deuce said, "That's what's going to happen, Ned?"

"Sure, it might. Why not? Take some effort is all. Got to keep people thinking about it."

A rotten egg odor suddenly engulfed them. They were passing by a room containing stacks of trays down which water cascaded. Deuce paused only long enough to close the door. "Damn guy on the other side leaves this open all the time," he said.

They walked into the room where a second clarifier stood, and Deuce began to repeat the same sequence of checks.

"You can still get it done, Deuce, maybe next year, maybe the year after, who knows, sometime," Ned told him. "It's like down in Des Moines there. Bills come up year after year, but eventually they get passed. You see what I'm sayin'? Think about it."

Watching the submersible lamp disappear into the bed at the bottom of the tank, he waited for Deuce to react to this proposal.

CHAPTER 19

~

*O*kay, Aggie Klauer thought early the next afternoon—Tuesday, Election Day, but just another workday for her, or not quite just another workday—*Okay*, she thought, *this is it, this is absolutely, positively the last new outfit I'm going to buy myself.* She stood before the mirror in the ladies room, reviewing her white ruffle-front blouse and skirt with maroon flocking, in a fit of nerves, on the point of marching herself down to the negotiating session with the big union. And Deuce.

She tried to remember what she'd seen in his eyes. Her own heart felt anesthetized, so she had no idea what she was actually feeling at that moment. The new outfit, which had seemed so right when she tried it on in the store, surrounded by other clothes, looked grotesque surrounded by nothing but bathroom fixtures—the earrings entirely too dangly, scarf too neon, belt too...too too. She looked like a Gypsy.

Impatiently she stripped off all these accessories, but the dress, over-fancy before, sagged into something suitable for prison wear. She put the belt back on. Better. She hadn't noticed before how retro the dress looked. Disapprovingly, she inspected the neckline. Too much skin showing, pale, ugly. She tied the scarf around her neck again. That left her ears. Well, ears are not something that bear scrutiny. The earrings returned.

She seized the pouch with her papers in it and fled.

Outside the door to the meeting room, she paused and took a deep breath, filled with the uneasy feeling that she'd forgotten something essential.

Too late, nothing to be done. *Okay, now, be serious, Agnes*, she warned herself, *this isn't a date.*

And into the room she went.

She tried the trick she'd used the first time she'd negotiated with Deuce. She didn't look at him right away. Instead she deliberately placed her papers on the table and then settled herself in her chair, nodding to the finance director on one side and lightly touching the wrist of the secretary who took shorthand on the other. Only then did she let her gaze come up and across the table.

Deuce wasn't there.

In his place sat J.J. Dusterhoft.

Her breath caught. Her confusion made it impossible to speak for a few moments. Then, flailing around for something to say and seizing upon a joke J.J. had made on the day Deuce arrived, she managed, "No relief ace?"

J.J. read her face and smiled sympathetically. "Never let your closer pitch more than two innings."

"Too bad." She struggled to sound breezy and unconcerned.

"We're all sad," J.J. assured her.

Aggie stifled her urge to apologize. Barb Amos was there, as usual. The other original members of the negotiating team had returned. It was like waking from a dream and finding the world as you left it.

"Well," Aggie said, her voice still not as steady as she would have liked, "shall we get down to it, then?"

Chapter 20

~

The rain had eased somewhat, but the solid overcast remained, hardly seeming to move, the gray of unpolished silver.

El sat at Camp 17, the nose of her car pointed at the river. Only on Apple Island, outside the dike system, was it still possible to drive right down to the edge of the Mississippi, to sit just a few yards away and contemplate the great river.

She'd been giving voters a lift to the polls all day and hardly had the time to spare, but was taking it anyway, treating herself to a little silence. She'd decided that she wanted to see the river, Walter's river. She hardly saw it anymore, just glimpses of the levees or floodwall as she drove around town. The predictions of a great spring flood seemed like rumors from a far-off country. Once upon a time, that wasn't so. Once upon a time, the river was a familiar in her life. She needed to see it again, to feel its reality.

She'd followed the road around the rim of the island, past the dredge pumping its sand up under the causeway leading onto the Wisconsin bridge and into a storage area for the dog track. On the other side, she drove along the eastern edge of the track site, where trucks were dumping stone, and finally down the short slope into the deserted park, stopping as close to the water as she dared.

The low embankment, which normally served to divide land from river, had been drowned, the surface of the water now a perfect continuation of the surface of the land, as if the land no longer constrained and channeled the river but rather floated in it.

Yet what stunned her most wasn't this eradication of boundaries but rather the pace of the current, the quick slipping along of the gray reflected light—a sense of urgency, as if the very river itself fled from the massive flood following in its wake, like animals before a fire. She'd forgotten.

The nearshore current moved not so briskly, but was tugged at by the rapid flow in midstream, like a garment about to unravel. The river seemed to exist beyond reason, intent upon its own needs, indifferent to all else.

As she watched, the rising water appeared to creep across the ground toward her and her impulse was to back the car farther away. But it was a trick of the eye, surely, she told herself. Even in the worst of floods, the Mississippi rose barely more than a foot a day. For all the water's power, its oncoming stretched out with insidious slowness. In her suddenly hypersensitive state, she imagined the car becoming lighter, river water moving stealthily through the soil beneath her, the parkland liquefying. She took a deep breath and looked around, seeking the familiar.

She still thought of the place as Camp 17, not Conservation Park as it had been officially dubbed. For her, the river was inexorably linked to the city's past, a historical landmark no less than the old Vic she and Walter owned. So she still remembered the little park by the Depression-era name it had borne when government laborers building the lock and dam system had bivouacked there: Camp 17.

She imagined the old-style flood fights now beginning to take shape upstream and down. And because discord had been so much on her mind of late, she reminded herself that some disasters did, after all, pull people together. Despite the exhaustion, despite the anxiety, they would forget politics for a little while, concentrate on the shared peril, and recognize, since it did no harm, the common humanity in one another.

But then again, perhaps she was just kidding herself. Perhaps it was never that way, not really, but only remembered as such.

She turned back to the river and let her mind become quiet, so that she might see it truly and not obscured by the veil of her worries. Across the complexity of its surface, current and countercurrent clashed, here disturbed by the wind, there by some deep bottom structure reflected to the top, until it was impossible to know what was wind and what part of the internal dynamic of the flow itself.

The rain, sporadic, made exclamation marks on the windshield. The glass had begun to fog up, so she turned on the engine and cracked the side window and started the defroster. Rain spattered against her ear and the side of her face.

She sat there until her mind reached a kind of equilibrium with the panorama before her, a calm held in tension with the water hurtling downstream. Then she put the car in gear and went back to work.

CHAPTER 21

~

At five thirty, the building already emptied out, Paul Cutler walked along the first floor hallway, on his way to vote for Roger Filer before going home. No meeting later, election nights being the preserves of politicians and their supporters. Tomorrow he'd wake up with a new council to deal with, or rather a slightly altered council, containing at least one new face, whoever won El Plowman's old council seat, and—God willing—a new mayor. But even partial and temporary changes like this one came with a certain hope attached, a certain sense of a new beginning.

A light burned in Aggie Klauer's office, and as he passed by, he spotted her, alone, bending over her assistant's desk. Their encounters of late had been mostly in meetings and so at arm's length. Aggie remained unhappy with him. She had become more punctilious in the performance of her duties, a sure sign. When he got to the door at the end of the hallway, his hand on the crossbar that opened it, he hesitated, remembering something he'd been intending to ask her, which, it occurred to him, was a good excuse to go back for a word and perhaps do a little bit of fence-mending.

She had disappeared into her office, where he found her doing nothing, dispirited, slouched in her chair, a very un-Aggie-like posture.

"It can't be that bad," he said.

"I just got through talking to Cliff Wiese."

"Ah." Wiese, one of her drinking problems. "Same ol'?"

She shrugged. "Three times we've set up meetings at Turning Point. He hasn't followed up. He still claims he hasn't got a problem." She shook her head over and over.

"What did you tell him?"

"Either he got treatment or he didn't work."

"And what did he say?"

"Threatened to sue."

"To be expected, I suppose." Police officers were prone to do that when confronted, although no one ever actually followed through on the threat.

Paul said, "Anyway, he knows the consequences. That should do the trick."

"Hope."

Paul asked the question he'd come to ask.

"What's the situation with the public works position, how we coming?"

She roused herself and went over to one of her filing cabinets and pulled out a file, holding it up for him to see the thickness. "These are the apps I've received so far. I've weeded out the duds."

Paul wished now that he'd expedited the process. They could have had a permanent director in place already, and then he wouldn't have had to worry about what Chuck Fellows was going to do next. Too late now.

Aggie held out the folder, offering it to him.

"We're going to wait until we see what the river does," he told her. "After that, I want candidates lined up and ready for interviews. ASAP."

On second thought, he reached out and took the folder, thinking it'd make interesting bedtime reading. He could have a nightcap and dream of a better tomorrow.

Aggie was simply standing still now, waiting for him to leave. The tension between them had gone slack.

"How did the session with the big union go, by the way?" he asked. This was a subject best left out of the conversation, perhaps, but Paul needed closure.

She told him that J.J. Dusterhoft was the negotiator again.

"I hope you're not going to have to start from scratch."

"Oh, no. It won't take long."

"Good."

Good! And finally! The big union had come to its senses. All the contracts would be settled. And Goetzinger sent packing back to the water plant where he belonged. He'd done enough damage.

Aggie, still pensive, was moving stuff around on her desk, going-home gestures. Or going to do whatever she had to do as El Plowman's campaign manager. Another subject best left out of the conversation.

"You're looking very nice today," Paul said, to be agreeable. "A new outfit?"

She nodded and smiled wanly and managed to thank him. He didn't appreciate this hangdog quality. He didn't appreciate a lot about Aggie, of late. But…the contracts would be settled, the election over, and maybe, just maybe, she could get back to doing what she did well—running her workshops and dealing with the Cliff Wieses of this world.

"What about us, Aggie?" he asked. "Can we put all this behind us now?"

"Of course."

"Perhaps something can be done later. Some sort of program to give the employees more of a sense of ownership in what they're doing."

She put on her coat with its "Plowman for Mayor" button. "Sure," she said, "we'll do something later."

Chapter 22

~

Aggie and El were half sozzled in the Wayfarers' lounge. Only a few minutes until last call and still Walter hadn't shown. All the well-wishers had come and gone. All the speculations about the possibility of a recount had been dismissed without prejudice. El's tally—36 percent of the vote; Roger Filer's—36 percent; El's margin of victory—14 votes. The other candidates had divvied up the rest.

Of course, Aggie didn't approve of drinking, any kind of drinking, but martinis were the worst. And it hadn't been but a few hours since she'd told the cop Cliff Wiese that he'd lose his job if he didn't go to Turning Point. And her very own beloved father had died of the drink. And here she was on her second round.

No way they could drive themselves home now, but if Walter showed up like he was supposed to, everything would be hunky-dory. Where was he? He'd finished the weather on TV way over two hours ago. Aggie and the campaign workers had cheered him on as he gave another grim forecast. He'd seemed even more energized than normal, maybe because of the news item that his wife was running neck and neck with Filer. A pretty heavy turnout for a by-election. A *bye-bye, Roger* election.

They'd been hip-hip-hooraying just about anything that moved as the vote came in and *mirabile dictu* it began to look like El might actually win. Win! Who woulda thunk it? Well, Aggie woulda. But not El. She didn't know what to make of it. She'd gotten entirely too used to the idea that she was going to lose. That was when Aggie decided there was nothing for it but to have a drink. A good stiff one. Just this once. Her last official act as campaign manager. And so when everybody else went home from the room they'd rented for the campaign party, Aggie dragged the two of them, still totally sober, down to the lounge. She even bought a pack of cigarettes and began to smoke in public. Just for tonight. Tomorrow it was back into the closet, smoking-wise. If she'd had cigars, she would have passed them out.

She drank her second martini and smoked her ciggies and thought, *To hell with Deuce Goetzinger. Who needs him?* She would've been the cheapest drunk he ever took out. Tough luck for him. Anyway, he was a coward, running out on her like that, afraid to negotiate the contract like a man just because he couldn't have his way. Too bad for him. And anyway, come to think of it, who needed him? Not her. She could go on about her life quite nicely without Mr. Deuce Goetzinger to complicate things, thank you very much.

And while she was at it, to hell with Paul Cutler. To hell with him and the horse he rode in on.

But where was Walter? He was supposed to be there, to share in this shining moment, El's great victory against overwhelming odds.

"You know," El said after a long, thoughtful pause, her words a little bleary, leaning close although they were now quite alone, hidden away in a dim corner of the bar, "you know, I don't mind winning." The booze had made her even more philosophical than normal. Unlike Aggie. All liquor did for Ag was make her drunk. Ran in the family.

"I gotta tell you," she said, hiccupping, "most campaign managers like a little more enthusiasm from their candidates…a little more… razzmatazz." Hic. "That's okay." She patted El's arm. El was a good ol' stick.

"You won," Aggie said, amazed all over again. Every couple of minutes, Aggie was amazed all over again.

～

"So there you are," Walter said when he finally appeared, "I've been looking all over for you two."

"We're celebrating," Aggie explained.

"Looks like." He leaned over and nuzzled his wife and told her, "Atta girl, Ellie." And then, not willing to let well enough alone, he added, "You see, I was right. You didn't think you'd win. That's what happens when you ain't got no data."

"Where you been?" Aggie asked. "You missed the party."

"Running some numbers. On the horn with Mick Kilmer."

"What a surprise," El said. The drinks seemed to be making her morose now, in the determined way she had. Whatever El's mood, her determination never wavered.

Walter told them, "The Corps's putting out a new prediction for the river tomorrow—twenty-seven feet."

Aggie tried to concentrate on the immense significance of this, but decided she was too snockered to summon the proper gravitas. Anyway, that could wait until another day. Today they were celebrating.

"Time to go home, girls," Walter said.

"El won, Walter," Aggie said, amazed once more.

"I know."

"She gave a great victory speech. You shoulda been there."

They were making their way out.

"What I said still goes, Walter," El was warning her husband.

"I'm not predicting anything. This is the Corps."

"Make sure it stays that way."

"Don't you worry about me."

"Short," Aggie said. As they moved toward the exit, she was concentrating on avoiding the furniture. "A real shorty. Just about the shortest victory speech on record. Made the Gettysburg Address look like a positive megillah." She didn't know if that was exactly the right word. Close enough.

They had left their coats in the room where the volunteers watched the election results and so had to go back for them.

"I went down to Camp 17 today, Walter," El said as they walked along an empty corridor. "To look at the river."

"Pretty near bank full."

"Over, where I was. Just barely."

"Now we're gonna start helping other communities," Aggie explained, trailing along behind her friends and feeling a little abandoned.

"That's right," El said to Walter. "That's what I understood when I saw the river again. You forget. You forget its power."

"People do."

"We've got to reach out to others. Communities without protection works. Go and ask how we can help."

"That was her speech, Walter," Aggie explained. "The whole thing. A wonderful speech. You shoulda been there."

They fetched their coats and started back.

Aggie didn't know how many of the volunteers would beat their campaign literature into sandbags, so to speak. Aggie was gonna. She'd go up to Buenie or down to Abbey Station or somewhere like that and fill sandbags or dish out hot meals or whatnot. Ask people what they needed done. El was right, that was the way to do it.

As they trekked back along the empty corridor, Walter leaned close so he could whisper something to El. Aggie couldn't hear what it was. Something endearing, maybe. Aggie hoped so. Boy, was she drunk.

"Look," she said when they got outside, "it's raining."

"You can come back tomorrow and pick up your cars," Walter told them.

The asphalt was slick with the rain, gleaming like ice under the lights of the parking lot. *Wow*, Aggie thought.

Walter's mind was still on the river. He repeated what he'd said earlier, "Twenty-seven feet," and then, as he unlocked the door to his car and they all got in, added, "Exactly what the mud daubers said."

PART III

CHAPTER 23

~

River stage: 12 feet

Chuck Fellows glanced at his watch. Coming up on 3:00 a.m., quitting time. The beam from the spotlight mounted on the roof of the lever room wavered upon the surface of the black water as the dredge swept inchwise across the cut. The ladder, with its cutterhead and suction pipe tilted steeply down, barely reached the bottom now, the river on the rise.

Chuck checked the backpressure and vacuum gauges. They weren't pumping enough material to run a risk of slugging the line. The cutterhead might snag in debris on the bottom; that could happen, but it made little difference, not anymore.

In the distance, the spotlight touched Orville Massey's harbor tug, illuminating parts of the boat with patches of bright, watery light and throwing the rest into deep shadow. The small craft tugged against its anchor line, moving subtly in the nearshore eddies.

Bud Pregler, the day man, claimed to be able to feel the effects of the currents and allow for them by stepping harder in one direction than the other, but Chuck could feel nothing. Pregler might be full of it. Or maybe not. Chuck respected the hypersensitivity possessed by some people. He was too impatient himself. He wouldn't take the time to become really present to the world around him. Except in the woods.

Orv Massey had been using his tug to move the dredge around the permit area as Chuck sought out places where he could still reach the bottom. Pregler, on the other hand, changed positions using only the spuds and anchors and winches of the dredge itself, a point of honor not to let Orv do it. Pretty damn one-way, but Chuck could appreciate that, too, Bud being a man both subtle and in-your-face.

Impatiently, he checked his watch and the gauges again and thought, *Fuck it*, and set the brakes and pulled the cutterhead up out of the water and shut her down.

A few minutes later, he and Billy Massey and J.J. Dusterhoft were standing in the dark next to the river. After the racket of the dredge, the silence felt thick and intense, almost threatening. Each night, they'd taken a few moments at the end of the shift and stood together beside the river and shot the shit, before young Massey climbed back into the workboat to head out to his great-grandfather's tug, and Chuck and J.J. into their vehicles to go home.

The rain began again, making a hollow sound against Chuck's slicker.

"Soup's mighty thin, boss," J.J. ventured.

"Yeah. Another day or two and that'll be that." Chuck had hoped to have a month to pump more sand. He'd managed exactly two weeks. Typical.

"And just when we were getting the hang of it," J.J. said.

Chuck had imagined the worst-case scenario, screwing up so badly that he'd sink the damn dredge, but it turned out that they'd end with a whimper, pumping nothing but water.

The rain fell, heavy and steadily now, invisible in the darkness. He went home to get a few hours' sleep.

∽

In the morning, noises from the spare bedroom woke him. He still wasn't quite used to Francine being there.

As he listened to her moving about, he considered what to do with the dredge. Obvious. Move it down to the Ice Harbor before he closed the gates. Which reminded him he still hadn't cleaned off the sills to make sure the gates would seat properly. Had to get his scuba gear out.

He swung his feet off the bed and sat hunched over, his face in his hands. The gates hadn't been closed in years. Most likely all kinds of crap on the sills. He wondered what the chances were that his wet suit still fit him. Probably he should contract the work out.

When he dragged himself downstairs, Francine was gone.

Diane had the TV on in the kitchen as she prepared the kids' lunches.

"I'm just about done on the dredge," he told her.

"How come?"

"Water's coming up. Can barely reach the bottom. I'll go down tonight, but that'll be it, maybe one more day."

He stopped to watch a news account of the flood fight way to the north, on the Minnesota River. Diane paused, too, and they watched together.

She laid a hand gently on the back of his arm. "How are you?"

"Okay. Tired."

He leaned toward the tiny screen, trying to pick out a detail, but in an instant the picture had changed; a couple of moments later, a third shot appeared, and then a fourth, as if whoever spliced the images together had an attention deficit problem. News stories had a way of irritating the hell out of Chuck.

"All that water," Diane said. "And to think it's coming here. It's eerie, like seeing the future."

"Minnesota's just one trib. There's a shitload of others." The Minnesota emptied into the Mississippi, but so did the St. Croix, the Black, the Chippewa, the Buffalo, the Wisconsin, the Root, the Turkey, and who knows how many more. To the north, the Mississippi drained 85,000 square miles, Jackson the cork in that particular bottle.

As Diane returned to her task, she said, "Four women in a rest home were riding in an elevator, and it failed and kept on going down, into the basement, which was flooded. They all drowned. What a terrible way to die." She spoke sympathetically, but without any trace of a shudder. One of Diane's virtues was the matter-of-factness with which she viewed death, less the result of her job at the medical center, Chuck thought, than the fact that she took her religion seriously. Chuck didn't take her religion seriously, but that was another matter.

"Where?" he asked.

"In a place called Benson."

"Benson? Never heard of it. On the Minnesota?"

"No. I don't remember. I think they said it was the Chippewa."

"In Wisconsin, then."

"No, it was in Minnesota, I'm sure. And I think they did say the Chippewa River. I think so."

"Hmm." Maybe there was a Chippewa in Minnesota, too. All these damn rivers.

Chuck was watching the sandbagging on the television. A dog swimming in the floodwater. Evacuation efforts. A talking head from the Corps. It was, in fact, as Diane had said, a little bit like seeing the future, except, of course, Jackson had its protection system. Jackson wasn't like all these other places with their standard-issue flood fights.

When a story about the previous day's election in Jackson came on, he ceased paying attention.

"So what are you going to do?" Diane asked.

"About the sand? Talk to Mitchell, the grading contractor, tell him to start hauling material for the access road."

"Will he have time?"

Chuck shrugged. "Not important. If the flood gets too bad, we'll shut the project down."

Kelley wanted to keep going. Or did the last time Chuck saw him, nearly a week ago. Since then, conditions had been getting steadily worse.

With a few deft folds, Diane wrapped one of the sandwiches she was making in waxed paper. As if aware of his thoughts, she said, "I'm just afraid Jack Kelley will keep on trying and you'll get roped into it. I know you. As if you don't have enough to do to protect the city."

"Track's a city project."

"I know, but still…"

"Don't worry, forget about it."

Chuck spoke offhandedly, distracted. He was thinking about the old ladies trapped in the elevator. He was visualizing the scene, their helplessness as water forced its way through the seams around the doors and rose inch by inch. How did they behave, he wondered, old ladies without much time left anyway? How would he have behaved, trapped and helpless like that, watching death coming to get him?

It was an interesting question.

CHAPTER 24

~

I'm still here," she said.

"So it would seem."

Paul Cutler beckoned her into his office. He wore a doleful expression, the comic dolefulness of someone making an effort to concede defeat gracefully. Beneath this feigned whimsy, however, real unhappiness could be detected. El understood. Twelve hours ago, Paul had been sure that he was well rid of her, her and her do-gooder streak. Well, he wasn't.

She closed the door, and they settled themselves at the conference table, not speaking, the city manager tilted on an elbow in one of his vocabulary of slouches. They inspected each other, Paul warily, El with chin lifted and eyelids lowered. She was feeling none too chipper after her little celebratory bender with Aggie. Paul had taken off his suit jacket, his shirt still firmly tucked in at this early hour. Later he'd become more disheveled. A man who insisted on the bureaucratic niceties ought to be tall and thin and obsessively neat, not like Paul, shortish and rather overweight. Only his pale eyes betrayed the truer reality.

He began. "I suppose we ought to declare a truce."

After a moment of consideration, she countered, "We ought to sign a peace treaty. I don't know what good a truce would be. It'd just give us something to violate."

He smiled.

"That's okay, Paul," she told him, "let's not worry about it. We'll manage to work together. We'll do it because, basically, we have no choice. But I don't propose to stop annoying you." He lifted a hand and let it drop back into his lap. "For starters, I'm going to remove Deuce Goetzinger's committee idea from the consent agenda where you tried to hide it." The city council met the next night, and El didn't plan to waste any time being nice just to be nice.

Paul made a vague gesture of surrender, but didn't speak, suspecting no doubt that she hadn't come there to listen. She hadn't.

"At the moment," she continued, "there's something else I'm much more concerned about—the flood. We need to be doing something about that."

This perked him up slightly. "What do you mean? We are doing something."

"I'm not talking about us, I'm talking about other people. Other communities. We have our wall, okay, but these small towns up and down the river have no protection. Have you heard the latest prediction?"

"Twenty-five, isn't it?"

"No. The Corps has changed its mind. It's twenty-seven now."

He looked off into the distance and shook his head and exhaled. "Still..."

"A flood of record, even if *still*. It just makes other folks' situations that much more desperate."

"It'll create problems for us, too, probably, out on the island." He meant the dog track.

"Probably... But I'm not worried about that for the moment. I'm worried about people with homes and businesses in the path of this thing. A flood of record, Paul. And I'll tell you what, we're not going to sit on our duffs and watch everyone else struggle. We're going to help."

"I see." Paul nodded, but he was frowning, too. "What do you propose?"

"I'm going to contact people and ask them what they need. We can go from there. It's something we'll want to discuss at the council tomorrow."

"Talk to the county."

"Of course." She planned to talk to the schools, too, and the intergovernmental association and the director of the Red Cross and the captain of the Salvation Army and the local National Guard commander and the archbishop and anybody else she could think of. Get everyone involved. At the moment, however, she wasn't worried about what *she* had to do; she was worried about her anal retentive city manager. "I'm determined that we're going to take the lead here. And if we have to spend money, we spend money. Don't fight me on this one, Paul, you'll lose."

He leaned back, a fist raised in front of his mouth, tapping his lips and silent. It went without saying that he had by now decided she was merely another politician and, of course, politicians just love natural disasters, politically speaking.

She told him, "We might set up a clearinghouse for information and resources. People will want to volunteer. They'll have to be told where they're needed. We could even set up a staging area, maybe at Five Flags. I'll talk to Eddie Trausch."

Paul was massaging his head, mussing his hair, his shirt now partly pulled out on one side. He had begun to assume his daily unkempt look even as El had been sitting there. She could guess what he was thinking. Finally they'd managed to get through the budget fight, the city coffers were all but bare, and here El was, talking about spending money they didn't have to help people they didn't know.

"Of course," he said. "I'll do whatever the council wants me to do."

Chapter 25

～

Jack Kelley still felt rotten. His fever had finally gone down, but a few minutes after he got up, the little store of energy he'd mustered had utterly drained away and he longed to crawl back into bed. He couldn't. It had been five days since he'd done anything about the dog track, the weather continued to be lousy, and he was convinced that in his absence, nothing was happening.

Janelle intercepted him in the hallway, confronting the patient about to check himself out of the hospital. She said, "Have you ever heard of pneumonia?"

"I'm just going down to the office." Best not mention the job site.

"It's raining, you know."

"Only going for a little while. Catch up with some paperwork." This argument didn't sound particularly convincing, so as he fished around in the pocket of the coat for his hat, he added, "I'm feeling a lot better."

Janelle said, "You know, Jack, I was thinking that myself, how much better you looked."

In his car, he turned toward the island and decided that pneumonia or not, he'd work, by God. Anyway, Janelle didn't really think he'd get pneumonia, she was just saying it. They'd always been competitive, although Janelle refused to admit it. He felt a touch of satisfaction when she took a day off, enjoying his work a little more at the thought of her diddling the hours away, and she could pretend all she wanted that women were different, competitive-wise, that they adhered to a higher standard than the lowly male, but Jack knew that secretly she liked the idea of him being sick in bed. It gave her an edge.

He drove through the rain down to the job and parked and shouldered open the car door and sat there, for the moment unable to get out, exhausted. He'd been right. The place looked exactly the same as he'd left it. There were only a scattering of other vehicles, nobody visible up on the deck or in the steel overhead. Raining, of course. But no wind. Not too crummy a day by recent standards.

He exhaled and closed his eyes and felt like he'd been up forever, not just a couple of hours. *Okay,* he told himself, *do the minimum, the absolutely essential. Forget everything else.*

He grabbed the doorframe to pull himself out and walked across the site step by step, hunched over for protection, the rain drumming against his back, and at the construction trailer he grabbed the doorframe there to pull himself up and inside, startling Sean, the young gofer he'd hired out of the engineering school over in Platteville.

Jack's greeting was, "Tell me what's happened since Friday." He'd called down to the trailer the last two days, but remembering the conversations was like trying to remember dreams.

"Shouldn't you be home, Jack?" Sean suggested. "You really look bad."

"Just tell me what's going on."

"Almost nobody here."

"Tell me something I don't know." Jack sat down to listen, since standing up and listening felt like trying to do two things at once.

Sean filled him in, and after a couple minutes, it occurred to Jack how little he cared about these matters which had seemed so critical a few days ago.

"What about Jim Bergman?" he asked finally. The steel contractor Jack still cared about.

Five minutes later, hunched forward, the rain again pounding on his back, he made his way toward Bergman's trailer, where he found the foreman alone.

"I sent my people home," Bergman told him. "You look like hell."

Jack seized a chair and collapsed into it. "I feel like hell." He swallowed and was aware of an irritation in his throat, which probably meant that his fever was returning. Damn it. He said, "Tell me. Our conversation last Friday." Even in his feverish condition the last several days, Jack had considered trying to run Bergman down by phone. He might have. But some matters could not be transacted at a distance. If Bergman intended to blow him off, it was going to be face-to-face.

"Been thinking about it," the foreman said. "Been talking to the guys. Been talking to my boss."

"And?" Jack took out his handkerchief and blew his nose and sat breathing through his mouth.

From the desk where he'd been doing paperwork, Bergman had swung his chair around to face Jack, stretching his legs out and crossing them at the ankles. "Basically, we think it's a stupid idea. Basically, we think you oughta close up shop and wait for the flood to go by and then we can all come back and do whatever needs to be done. That's what any sensible man would do. What's the rush?"

His hands were clasped in his lap, thumbs pointing up, and opening and closing as he made his points.

"Rush is…flood might last weeks, months…could be June before we got back here…could lose the whole racing season."

"Maybe, but you know, an act of God like this, what are you gonna do?" People were always happy to fob calamities off on God.

Jack wasn't in any shape to argue the matter. On the other hand, at just that moment he wasn't in any shape to get up and leave, either. So he let his continuing to sit there be his argument.

Bergman studied him, shaking his head slightly and half smiling. Jack must make a sorry sight. He felt sweaty. His body seemed to be ticking, as if in time with the pulsing of his blood. He could almost feel the blood rushing, like a fire brigade, through his arteries.

Finally, Bergman said, "It's not impossible."

"How?"

"Nothing fancy. Brute force. But if you're bound and determined, my guys are willing to give it a go."

"How?" Jack wished he felt better so he could properly appreciate what Bergman was saying.

"Cranes. We'll have to use them for everything. Hang scaffolding from them for the men, move product, whatever."

"You can get them?"

"Well, we've already got the big machine on site. We were gonna dismantle it, but I suppose we could keep it here for a time. It'd be nice to have another 100 tonner, but under the circumstances we can make do with lighter units. They oughta be available. It's short notice, but it isn't like this is the busy season. Of course, some people might not be crazy about putting their equipment in harm's way. I figure we'll need six—ideally, eight. We'll want to run two crews, working from west to east on both sides of the building."

"A lot of cranes," Jack said fuzzily, but he decided he could lay his hands on some. He knew the locals.

"And that's not all," Bergman said. "It's raining now. The weather forecast looks shitty. Long term looks shitty. That's what they're saying."

"Gotta work when you can."

"Right. Guys on standby, ready to go out whenever. We'll need light plants. We'll need someplace where my people can rack out when they're not overhead. We'll need a weather service to keep us up to the minute. Cost some money, Jack. We won't stiff you, but it'll cost some money."

"Okay," Jack said. He'd have to raid the contingency. There was still some money there, the damn A&E's hadn't managed to use it all up yet. He'd have to talk to Fellows, too. Shit, Fellows.

"So what about it, Jack?" Bergman asked. "You want us to go ahead?"

Jack felt too rotten to have reservations. Probably he should have reservations. "Let's do it," he told Bergman.

Chapter 26

~

Arriving back at city hall after a conversation with Mitch Mitchell, the grading contractor, about hauling material for the track access road, Chuck stopped briefly at the edge of the crowd on the plaza outside and listened to Jesse Jackson, in town for the day. Chuck had no use for Jackson. Off to the side, three Guardian Angels stood at parade rest, wearing berets and looking like they thought they were king shit, and on the platform behind Jackson, El Plowman had joined the president of the local branch of the NAACP and several people Chuck didn't know.

He went inside and climbed the stairs to the drafting room on the third floor, looking for Glenn Owens. He found Sam Turner instead, standing at a window and looking down at the rally on the plaza below.

"Nobody else here?" Chuck asked. He looked at his watch. Lunchtime.

"Who you after?"

"Glenn."

"Up to 16th Street. Got some problem with the pump."

"Okay."

Sam turned back to the window, his thin body pared down by the glare from outside. He was leaning on the cane he'd been using since he had come back to work.

Chuck started to leave, then changed his mind and walked over.

"You're not down there."

"Nope."

"How come?" Chuck found it interesting when people violated his expectations.

Sam considered the question and then merely said, "Thought about going down."

"But didn't."

Sam shook his head.

Chuck remembered their unsatisfactory conversation in the donut shop sometime ago, Sam trying to get time on the CAD machine or, if not that, even go back to hauling trash, and Chuck telling him he had to make a go of the job he already had. Chuck didn't dislike the man. In a way, Sam's isolation reminded Chuck of his own sense of separation, his own dissatisfactions. In other circumstances, who knows, they might have talked frankly about such matters. Become friends. But they didn't have other circumstances, they had these. Chuck certainly wouldn't waste any more words badgering him about upgrading his skills. Sam knew the situation.

And so, that being the case, Chuck walked back across the floor. Now they'd play out the string. No reason for them to have anything more to do with each other than was absolutely necessary.

∼

Sam listened to the retreating footsteps, measuring out the brief time left to speak. He'd always been willing to chat up whites, disarm them with a little of the usual bullshit. But bosses were different. Bosses had a certain slant on situations, and he could never find the right thing to say to them. Nothing seemed interesting enough. Or to the point. Or whatever the fuck.

And a few moments ago he'd been wanting nothing except for Fellows to leave. But now a gesture had been made. Sam felt a need to respond.

"Mr. Fellows."

Sam faced into the room, using his cane for a prop and shifting back and forth teeter-totter fashion as he came around, his leg still bad from the beating he'd taken. Fellows had stopped at the door and turned back.

"Yes?"

Sam tried to think what he wanted to say.

∼

Chuck waited, interested. Sam was looking at the floor, and Chuck imagined him preparing to broach some matter of substance, but when he raised his eyes, all he said was, "Big flood comin', I guess."

Chuck's spate of interest passed away. "Looks like."

"A record, maybe? That's what I heard."

"Maybe."

Again Sam looked at the floor, considering. Without looking up this time, he said, "The other guys are gonna be manning the pumps and stuff?"

"That's right. Not all of them, but some." The draftsmen had various other assignments, depending on the time of year. In the spring, it was pumping runoff over the floodwall and levees when the river rose and the system had to be sealed.

Sam said, "Maybe you got something for me to do?"

"The shape you're in?"

"Might be I could do something."

Chuck looked at him doubtfully. What possible use could he be? Turner cut a sorry figure—average height, thin, the beginnings of a gut, a black stubble growing where he had stopped shaving his head. He leaned against his cane, his shoulders hunched forward, probably to ease the pain from his broken ribs. Ribs healed slowly.

"What's Glenn got you doing now?" Chuck asked across the space separating them.

"Tax maps. The preliminary stuff. Marking out streets. Brad plats out the property lines and uses the planimeter. He'd get mad if Glenn let anybody else do it."

"That's right."

Chuck was a little disappointed that Glenn hadn't been challenging Sam more. Perhaps that would have helped. And there was plenty of work to do without Sam poaching on another man's preserve. On the other hand, they weren't running a drafting school, either, and Sam hadn't shown enough initiative for people to go out of their way to help him.

"There's nothing for you to do," Chuck told him. "What needs to be done is already being done."

At this, Sam looked away.

"Anything else?" Chuck asked.

∿

Sam felt the power of the other man's dismissal. Fellows waited impatiently. Must have a thousand things to do, Sam wasting his time.

Sam thought this and realized the self-pity in it. He looked at Fellows and saw everything he himself failed to be. It was true, he thought. But it was also true that he had no desire to become Fellows. Fellows's life held no interest for him.

Sam didn't know what interested him. A gap existed between himself and the world, and he didn't know how to fill it.

These thoughts passed through his mind in an instant. He repositioned himself, adjusting the cane and shifting his weight until he was slightly more comfortable.

"You gonna lay me off?"

∼

Startled by the bluntness of the question, Chuck started to say something noncommittal, then stopped. How damn easy it was to lie. Like offering a blindfold to a man about to be shot.

"I expect," he told Sam.

The new budget year began in July. There'd be layoffs, Sam among them. Affirmative action wouldn't save his ass this time. Maybe he'd catch on with the private hauler in town. Certainly he'd never get a job as a draftsman anywhere. Might be he'd try to live on his unemployment checks and hope the city would take him back.

At the moment, all he did was nod, as if he had known it all along and only been asking for confirmation.

"Sorry," Chuck told him. And he was sorry. In spite of everything, he sort of liked Turner. Didn't know why.

"Not your fault," Sam told him.

Before he left, Chuck said, "I'll try to find something for you to do." Then he added, to avoid any misinterpretation, "Something might come up if the flood gets bad enough."

∼

But Sam had not misinterpreted. He watched the dying vibrations of the swinging door, and then returned to the window.

In the plaza below, the rally was ending. Sam could see Jesse Jackson shaking hands with others on the platform. At the fringes, people were beginning to drift away, the crowd unraveling, like an old piece of cloth coming apart.

CHAPTER 27

~

The tiny river village of Abbey Station, fifteen miles south of the city, lay at the base of a long defile down through the bluffs. On the upper end of the narrow valley, El Plowman drove past the entrance to the Trappistine abbey, an order of strict observance, which gave the community on the river below its name.

Whenever El and Walter came down to Abbey Station, they would stop to buy the Trappistines' caramels. In a small alcove in the main building of the monastery, they'd put their money in a box like a dumbwaiter and ring the small bell. The door to the box would close and a minute later slide open again, the neatly wrapped candies placed precisely in the center of the container. It had been a long time, but El could still taste the caramels, sweet and chewy and so different from the plain and rigorous lives she imagined the nuns who made them lived.

Through the spitting midafternoon rain, she dropped down the steep, narrow county road. At the foot, her headlights glanced off the abandoned train station. She passed over the humped railroad crossing and along the row of cottages, which formed a dentition at the edge of the slough. When she reached Fisherman's Tap, she parked at the top of the boat ramp.

Inside the door to the bar stood an upright piano, along with several kitchen tables and chairs, a soft drink machine, and a freezer above which had been taped a hand-printed sign with prices for frozen or smoked walleye, catfish, bluegill, crappie. She and Walter used to come down to the feeds that Lester and Margie put on, one of the pleasures foregone in the headlong rush of their public lives.

No one seemed to be around, the place dark except for the gray light coming through the windows. El called out. No answer. She walked through to the back door and opened it and called again. Still no answer. That the cash register had been left unattended didn't signify, the crime rate in Abbey Station being effectively zero, a village lost in time.

Back at the top of the ramp, she looked down to the water and the houses, raised on stilts along the edge of the slough. No signs that a flood fight had begun. The rain nearly stopped for the moment, she took off her hat and stood tapping it against the side of her leg. Probably she should have called ahead, but Les and Margie were always around.

As she lingered, uncertain what to do next, a johnboat swung into view, coming from the north and turning into the ramp, its single occupant a man, who tipped the outboard up as the boat grounded out on the asphalt. He climbed out, tied off, and lifted a bucket out of the boat, which he carried up the ramp, moving slowly, his lips pinched tight, his thin features gathered inward with the effort.

"I was about to leave, Lester. There was nobody around."

"Margie's not inside?"

"Nope."

"Must be off doing something." He set down his burden and flexed his hand, arthritis one of Lester's many ailments. For years he had been in and out of St. Luke's for this, that, and the other. Somehow he survived.

"Fishing? On a day like this?" El asked.

"Lately, it seems every day's a day like this. Once the river rises, you can forget about catching spring walleyes." He hefted the bucket again. "Anymore, we don't see much of you and Wally."

"Busy."

"Gettin' yourself in trouble." He winked using his good eye, the other one, which had many years before got a hook caught in it, a glaucous white.

"C'mon, C'mon," he said. Inside he set about heating up some water for her tea and drawing himself a beer to accompany the cleaning of the fish.

"The mud bars and sand shoals are gone, under water," he told her. "If you had a God's-eye-view, you could watch the islands disappearing from the river, one by one, as she comes up. And once that happens, you can forget about catching anything." He worked quickly, several fish at a time, in conveyor-belt fashion. "Say, Ellie, I'm preparin' to fix one of my chowders. You and Wally oughta come down."

Walter loved Lester's famous fish chowder. As for El, well, she preferred to know exactly what it was that she was eating.

"I'm going around talking to people about the flood, Lester. Finding out what we can do to help."

El sat at the bar watching him clean the fish and telling him who she'd seen so far. Above the liquor bottles, barely legible in the late afternoon dimness, a fading sign announced the annual mountain oyster feed with a date several months old.

"What about East Jackson?" Les asked. "You been over there?"

"Yes. They're building a levee down the center of Main Street. The river side's too low to defend."

"Expect they're none too happy with you."

"Nobody says anything to my face." There had been complaints from certain quarters that floods would be magnified in East Jackson because of the wall and levee system erected on the other side of the river to protect Jackson. "And what about you, Les?" El asked. "What are you going to do down here?"

"Us? Well, I expect what we always do. The river comes up, you best get out of the way."

"Worse than usual this time."

"Yup. Looks to be getting into folks' homes." Lester and Margie and the people of Abbey Station had an accepting nature where the river was concerned.

"What can I do to help?" she asked.

He considered the matter in silence, and El supposed that in the spirit of the independence of river folk everywhere, he might be unwilling to accept any aid. But she was wrong. "Oh," he eventually allowed, in a musing tone, "might be people could use some help transporting and storing stuff, when the time comes. We not all of us as young as we once was."

"Okay, good. I'll organize something." As she'd gone about talking to people, it had become clear that this was the sort of assistance they were most likely to need, trucks to haul furniture and other personal belongings as well as places to store them, and after that places to stay themselves. "There'll be a lot of Jacksonians wanting to lend a hand," she said.

Lester stopped to take a pull on his beer, then set back to work, his words made more emphatic by the swift and certain strokes of the knife. "That's one thing you can always say about a flood. There are lots and lots of folks looking to pitch in. Makes you think there might be hope for us yet."

"Too bad it doesn't spill over into the rest of our lives."

The wet scales of the fish, like mica, glistened in the light.

"You and Wally oughta move down here, El. Then you'd get to see people's better side."

El sat there and sipped her tea and thought about that.

∼

In his weather cubicle at KJTV back in the city, Walter was talking with Mick Kilmer of the Corps of Engineers, Rock Island District. For once, Mick had called him, pleasing Walter. The storm that had been sitting over Topeka, gathering moisture from the Gulf, had finally made up its mind and begun to track northward. A real wet one.

"The jet stream hasn't moved," Walter said. "Looks like the damn thing's nailed in place."

"The congressmen from along the river are trying to pressure the Weather Service into working up a special fifteen-day forecast." Mick was speaking very rapidly. He'd called, but now seemed in a rush to get the conversation over as quickly as he could. "I've been running my model over and over, trying to get a handle on this. We're doing what-if scenarios. All the Corps' advance work's in the crapper. The situation has just gotten too bizarre. It looks now like you might top out at twenty-eight feet in Jackson. That's just between you and me, of course."

Only two feet below the top of the wall, five feet if you added the freeboard. Every time Walter turned around, the prediction had gone up.

"I tell you, Wally," Mick went quickly on, "I got people camping on my doorstep. They're questioning my credibility, my parentage, you name it. We're having conference calls with the Weather Service where all we do is scream at each other. Nobody wants to get in bed with anybody."

Walter believed it. "What I've been thinking, Mick, is it's all so weird. I mean, you and I understand, we understand what can happen. But I never really expected it, not in my lifetime."

"Welcome to the future, my friend. Anyway, this is why I called. Have you got any spare time, any at all?"

"No, not really, but I'll make some. For you. Why?" Walter couldn't imagine what Mick might need done. Made no difference, Walter was up for it. He felt honored.

"I've got a couple of USGS guys from California on their way here to start taking stage-discharge readings off the highway bridge over to East Jackson. Need somebody to provide any support they might require. The Corps and Survey are bringing people from all over of the country, but we're still gonna be mighty thin on the ground."

"They've got equipment?"

"Yeah."

"Can they work over a chain-link fence?"

"A fence? Damn. Since when?"

"They just finished rehabbing it. A federal reg, I think."

"Yeah, yeah, yeah, yeah, shit."

"You wanna take readings off something, it'll have to be the railroad bridge."

"Tougher access."

Mick, thwarted for the moment, fell silent. Walter was thinking, *This is great*, his mind seizing the problem and tearing it at once down to its essentials. "I know a guy works for the Illinois Central. We can talk to him. There aren't many trains going across the bridge. Maybe we could get a handcar to carry the stuff on. Why not? We could store everything in the Ice Harbor. I bet it'd work. Might even be better than using the other bridge, no cars and trucks to worry about."

Mick's silence continued, and Walter prompted him, "Wha'd'ya say?"

After a few more beats, Mick allowed, "Might work," followed by another brief silence before he laughed. "I knew there was a reason I called you, Wally."

"It'll be great, Mick. We can get you your readings, you bet."

Mick waited just long enough for a quick reconsideration, then said, "Let me give you the USGS guys' names and a telephone number."

Walter was jazzed. He'd keep a set of the data for himself, too. The official hydrograph for the biggest damn flood in the city's history. He'd frame it and hang it on his wall.

Very quickly and without ceremony, the matter was settled and the call concluded. Walter sat back in his chair, staring at Hazel, his computer, and grinning. This was going to be absolutely wonderful. He could hardly wait! He took up the slip of paper with the names and contact number on it.

The phone rang.

Probably Mick calling back, Walter thought, *probably he forgot something he wanted to say.*

"Yes?" The person on the other end of the line began to speak. It wasn't Mick. For a moment, not expecting the call, Walter didn't realize who it was.

CHAPTER 28

~

J ack Kelley woke up. He had been dreaming, and when he lifted his head from the table, disoriented, one dreamscape gone, another seemed to spring up in its place, the new one unnaturally vivid—with a strange and hostile everydayness about it—so that he experienced a moment of panic. Then, his glance swinging wildly around, he spotted something he recognized, a photograph on the wall, one of the pavilions up at The Heights, and he realized there was nothing hostile and strange at all; it was just his office at Steadman and he'd fallen asleep.

He looked at his watch—5:50. He'd slept for a couple hours. Or maybe fourteen. Could be either. Somebody was moving around on the floor, and he listened. Didn't sound like janitor noises. Probably somebody working late. Probably it was still Wednesday.

He yawned massively and rubbed his face and tried to remember what he had been doing. He felt like a man with amnesia. Had a tiff with Janelle that morning, he remembered that much. Oh, yeah, then he'd gone down and talked to Jim Bergman about enclosing the grandstand. Decided to backfill around the building, create a highway for the traffic jam of cranes they were gonna bring in.

Slowly the day came back to him. He'd gone looking for Tony Vasconcellos. Couldn't find him, informed one of his people that Tony had forty-eight hours to finish stubbing the conduit out of the grandstand crawlspace for the track and tote board electrical. If he didn't, Jack was gonna bury him. Jack would love nothing better than burying Tony Vasconcellos.

He felt as if all his muscles had been removed. What else had he done? Time was getting away from him. Lunch. He'd stopped to get something on his stomach and fallen asleep in his car. Woke up with a city cop rapping on the windshield and asking if anything was wrong.

He couldn't close his eyes without falling asleep.

How did he get back here? No, Mitch Mitchell first; he'd gone to see him, told him to backfill around the grandstand to create a roadway for the extra cranes, told him about Vasconcellos and the deadline. "Give Tony two days, then bury him." Jack wished he felt better so he could have savored the saying of those words. It had been an all right day so far, but it felt like somebody else's all right day. Jack's meager energy he husbanded to do the bare minimum. Much to be done. Nothing would move unless Jack pushed. Only Bergman and Mitchell on board so far.

And then what had Mitchell said? Oh, yes, his apology because he couldn't provide more trucks. Jack hadn't known what he was talking about.

"The access road," Mitchell told him. "I got a call from Fellows. Water's almost too high to dredge anymore. He was looking for trucks to haul gravel for the road. But no can do. All my equipment's committed to the flood fight over in East Jackson." Across the river, they had no floodwalls or levees. The prediction for the crest had gone up again. They were looking at a flood of record across the river and didn't have a fig leaf's worth of protection. "There isn't a free truck in the tri-state area," Mitchell informed Jack. "Everything's committed to East Jackson."

The access road, Jack thought, *damn*. He was gonna be cut off. He sagged, drained by this recollection. The day hadn't been all that good after all. If he could only concentrate on enclosing the grandstand and forget about everything else. Looked like the flood wasn't going to let him. He'd be cut off if he couldn't figure a way to raise the road higher. Fellows had been diddling around with that miserable little dredge of his. He hadn't pumped anywhere near enough sand. Jack had been a fool to listen to the man.

Jack closed his eyes and immediately his exhaustion flooded back. He was drowning in it. If he could only go to sleep and wake up sometime in July.

He forced his eyes open and sat breathing and staring dully at the wall. He reminded himself that if he didn't feel this crummy, he wouldn't be dreaming about giving up. The situation had changed. So what? The situation always changed. That was the nature of situations.

Okay, then he'd gone to confront Fellows, but Fellows had been off somewhere. Tony Vasconcellos hadn't been around, either. Jack had driven down to Tony's shop, wanting to deliver his message in person. He wrote a note and told the secretary to make sure Tony got it. Then what? He'd come back to Steadman and Associates to start calling around for spare cranes and to tell his boss what was going on. Or rather some of it. He never told Harry everything. All he needed were talking points for his next update to the city council.

"If we can pull this off, Harry…," Jack said and let his boss complete the thought in a way that he would find pleasing.

Then Jack had gone back to his office to start calling crane services. And that was the last he remembered.

～

It was after six when he got down to the dredge, thinking that the dozer operator would be able to communicate with the craft and get Jack a ride out so he could deal with Fellows.

But when he got to the eastern side of Apple Island, the dozer and scraper sat idle, nobody around, and he wondered if Fellows had already abandoned his attempt at dredging. As Jack parked, however, he spotted a woman getting out of a workboat at the shoreline, the new shoreline, for the river was on the rise.

He started down, passing her coming in the other direction—a black woman. She glanced up, giving no sign of recognition, but he remembered her, one of Dexter Walcott's people. *What in God's name…?* he wondered.

Down at the water, he said to the boatman, barely more than a kid, "I'm looking for Chuck Fellows."

"Hop in."

They started out, through the lingering early April light. The little harbor tug that had broken up the ice during the winter was now moored to the dredge, the dredge itself silent and motionless.

Jack thought about the black woman. He'd been surprised when he'd seen her last Friday up on the grandstand deck and now was surprised again to see her down here. The encounters had been brief, but it only took a glance to sense a certain dogged determination in her expression. Of course, if she was going to make it in the trades, she'd damn well better be determined. Not handsome, certainly, not one to be helped along much by her looks. Women who went into construction work, in Jack's view, were often men trapped in women's bodies. Or they were simply looking for a decent paycheck and willing to put up with the abuse. He had a lot of respect for the ones who managed to stick it out.

The kid swung the workboat past the tug and around to the far side of the dredge, where he tied off. On board, he led the way up to the control room.

"Someone here to see you," he said to a person Jack couldn't see as they reached the top of the companionway.

Jack took the last steps into the crowded room and found Fellows with two others, three including the kid.

"Jack," Chuck said.

The space was warm with machine and food smells, the windows fogged. Everyone seemed perfectly chummy, so Jack felt like an intruder. They were eating, each from an identical cardboard box.

Jack said, "I saw the woman coming ashore."

"Francine."

"She's one of Walcott's people."

"Yup." Chuck was fishing around in his dinner box, which he'd jammed between two of the control levers. "Staying with Diane and me."

That was something Jack hadn't heard about.

Fellows told him that Walcott had decided to board some of his people locally, to save the commute from Waterloo.

"She brought the food down to you?"

"Diane's idea."

"Is that right?" Looking around at the others—the kid, along with a very old man, obviously the tugboat skipper, and the third person, equally obviously the city employee assigned to the dozer—Jack couldn't help but feel a little jealous at such a sociable gathering. He wondered if Janelle would do for a crew of his something like Fellows's wife had done for these guys. Maybe. Maybe not. With Janelle, you could never tell.

"So what's up, Jack?" Fellows asked. "You come out to check up on us or what? You look like shit, by the way."

"Flu." Fellows was absolutely at his ease. "I talked to Mitchell earlier."

"Yeah? He's got no more trucks."

"So he says. And you're not gonna pump any more sand?"

"Not much more. Having a helluva time reaching the bottom. River's coming up faster than I thought she would."

"How much longer?"

Fellows consulted his watch. "About eight and a half hours. What you see here is our farewell dinner."

"Great." Fellows, with raised eyebrow and a slight smile, read Jack's expression. "Tell me," Jack asked him, "you haven't, by chance, checked the elevation of the road recently?"

"You're good for a twenty-six-foot crest, give or take."

A foot below the current prediction. "We should've started hauling at once." Jack had known it at the time. But no, not Fellows, he was going to be a hero and run the dredge around the clock. "Mitchell tells me it's too late, no private haulers available. Everybody's over in East Jackson."

"Looks that way. People take precedence over dog tracks."

"What about the city? You've got trucks."

Chuck nodded. "Haven't removed the plows and salt spreaders yet."

"Why not?"

"Last year, we did." This not from Fellows but the one that Jack took to be the equipment operator. "Stripped those babies down on the first of April, all ready for the summer. What happened? Boom, we got nailed with a blizzard. Remember?"

Fellows added offhandedly, "And this year's worse, of course. Who the hell knows what's gonna happen. But I'm way ahead of you, Jack. Already had a little chat with Hank Kraft. We're gonna arrange something."

"Thanks," Jack said. Did he dare hope Chuck might actually be of some use? His general lack of urgency hardly boded well. "We need to talk."

"Shoot."

"What about tomorrow?"

"Do it now if you want."

"Tomorrow." Jack didn't know these guys from Adam. No way he was going to say what he had to say in front of them.

"Don't have my schedule with me," Fellows told him.

"I'll call your office in the morning."

"Whatever." Fellows's tone was enough to drive a man up a wall. Here they were, facing the flood of a lifetime, and the son of a bitch just didn't give a shit.

"I'll call you," Jack said. "Now if I could get a lift back to shore."

It was time to go home.

CHAPTER 29

~

The next morning, the meeting duly took place. Chuck was standing at the window of his office, looking at the water flushing out of the sky with the intensity of a monsoon. It turned out that the day before, with its moderate rain, had been what passed for a break between storms. Chuck felt a little spooked. He remembered his mantra—Is it the Vietnam highlands? Is it the monsoon season? Is anybody shooting at me? Then I'm having a pretty good day.

So, okay, he was having a pretty good day, although Kelley's appearance did nothing to improve it. Jack sat in the chair across from Chuck's desk, talking about his plans to enclose the grandstand by hanging scaffolding from cranes for the ironworkers. Chuck, surveying the downpour, thought the man daft.

He turned away from the window.

"And what about the flood, Jack?"

"What about it?"

Kelley still looked like shit, wasted, but even in this reduced condition, he remained 100 percent the company man. He would drag himself out of bed to complete the track project, the track project *über alles*.

"Maybe you haven't noticed," Chuck told him. "The situation keeps on getting worse. If we're gonna build anything, it oughta be an ark."

"Prediction's only for twenty-seven feet. Six feet below the track surface."

"At thirty feet, you'll start to have wave wash."

"We've still got several feet of leeway."

"You thought about the infiltration?" The real problem wasn't going to be water coming over the top of the job site.

"Of course."

"You mix water and sand, wha'd'ya get?"

"A quick condition." Which was a fancy term for quicksand. "That doesn't bother me."

"It doesn't?"

"No, it doesn't. I'll deal with it, the time comes. Now I'm worried about maintaining access to the job site. The road. You gonna help? Yesterday you said you would." Jack had been taking a matter-of-fact approach to the conversation thus far, an improvement on his usual self-righteous sincerity.

"You can have six trucks," Chuck told him. "The salt boxes and plows are being removed. They'll be ready this afternoon. We'll supply drivers, too. Charge you the city's going rate."

Jack nodded. He sat at a slight angle in his chair, his lips open but teeth clamped shut, his chest rising and falling as he breathed.

Chuck had not moved away from the window. A damp chill bathed the back of his neck.

"You know," Kelley finally said, "I remember something you told me a couple weeks ago."

"Oh?"

"About the dog track. You said what pissed you off was the idea of having your tax dollars used to pay for it. Remember that?"

"Sure."

"Well, guess what? If we don't keep going, if we don't enclose the grandstand, if we don't beat the flood, then there's no way we'll have a racing season this year."

And thus, no money from track operations to begin paying off the bonds. The money would have to come out of the city's coffers. Chuck understood all this, but it wasn't going to get Kelley where he wanted to go.

"My motivations are my own, Jack. They're not weapons for you to use against me."

"But you do represent the owner. How do you think the city council's going to feel about paying for the track using general revenue money?"

Chuck crossed his arms and stared at Kelley. If it had been another man, perhaps Chuck would have been more agreeable. If it had been himself, for instance, he might have decided, *Let's go for it, what the fuck, shits and giggles.* Enclose the grandstand, fight the flood, do whatever crazy thing was necessary to get the job done. But then again, Chuck's own streak of foolhardiness seemed to him an altogether nobler excess.

"Let me tell you, Jack. The city was stupid enough to build the project in the middle of winter, okay? And as if that wasn't dumb enough, they had to put it on an island in the middle of the Mississippi. Just because they happened to own some land there. A wonderful site, too, a dump, for Christ's sake, off-gassing methane. What kind of fucking reasoning is that? And on top of everything, it's a dog track you're building, a place where little old ladies can go and blow their life savings. No, Jack, no. This project deserves nobody's undying devotion."

"You think I'm crazy about it, is that what you think?"

Chuck stared at him and then laughed. "Okay, you hate it. You just happen to be a goddamn obsessive."

Kelley adjusted himself in his chair and looked down at his hands. "You still haven't answered my question. What about the city council?"

"This is not a question you'd ask me, Jack, if you knew what I think about politicians." The conversation was clearly taking its toll on Kelley. Chuck, on the other hand, was beginning to enjoy himself.

"You work for them," Kelley said.

"Do I? Or do I work for the city? Or Paul Cutler? Or the engineering profession? Or my family? Or *myself*? Perhaps I'm the only one who really counts here, Jack."

Kelley, seeing that this angle of attack was getting him nowhere, tried another. "I just want to get the damn job done. If we all help, it'll get done. But either way, it's my job to do. And I intend to do it."

"What happens when the flood gets worse? What happens, Jack? What happens when defending the track gets as idiotic as building the thing in the first place?"

"If I have to, I'll give up the effort. But I don't believe it'll come to that."

Jack had gotten to his feet. He'd decided, apparently, that the conversation was over.

"Anyway, it's too early to give up now," he said.

Chuck supposed that that much was right. Later would undoubtedly be another matter, but for the time being... So he said, "Okay, it is too early. I agree. Might as well stick it out for a while longer, on the off chance."

Kelley untangled the lapels of his coat, showing no emotion at this concession.

"I'd like to have you on my side, Chuck. I need you helping me. I don't need you down on the job site second-guessing everything I do."

"When have I ever done that?"

"But if you're against this thing, if you think there's no way it's gonna work, if you come out there and start challenging me, even in some piddly-assed way, and the contractors see that, then it's all over, I'll completely lose control. They'll stop paying attention to me. And if that happens, Chuck, then we really can forget about the rest."

"Won't happen."

"And one last thing—I need to move some money around. I'll need more in general conditions."

Chuck understood. The flood was one helluva general condition. "Fair enough. You do that. But I have one last thing, too, Jack. I won't interfere, okay, not on the job site. But if I think the situation's gotten just too damn dangerous, I'll close the project down. I've got other concerns, even if you don't. The liability, for instance. The city's damn paranoid when it comes to liability. Hell, they won't even let the firefighters ride off the backs of their trucks anymore. What do you suppose they'll think about leaving people out on the island in the teeth of a five-hundred-year flood? When the water gets up, Jack, you're gonna be standing on quicksand and the river coming at you head-on. Think about it."

"I intend to keep on working, as long as I can." With this last bit of defiance, Kelley was out the door.

Chuck still hadn't moved from the window. He was looking at the space Kelley had vacated. Still too early to shut the job down—the man had, indeed, been right about that much. Trouble was, when the time *did* come, then it might be too late.

～

Jack felt better, still so tired that staying awake took a conscious effort, but better. He took the day in stages, like an exhausted driver on a long journey.

After getting what he wanted from Fellows—more or less—he'd gone to talk with the glazier for the track work, an old friend whom Jack had once saved from going out of business and who at once agreed to begin installing the glass without waiting for the roof to be completed. He asked for no extras. They talked tactics.

Back at Steadman, Jack called around to the local crane services. When they quoted him high rates, thinking they had him over a barrel, he told them they had equipment sitting around their yards doing nothing but rusting. He'd give them enough to cover the monthly payments on their leases and their overhead. When they balked at putting their cranes out in the middle of a flood, he pointed out that the project was crucial to the economic recovery of the city. When they still hesitated, he told them he'd be sure the community knew who had helped and who had not. Jack got what he wanted.

He went down to the track and talked to Jim Bergman again. The ironworkers were already at work cobbling together the scaffolds to be hung from the cranes.

Late in the day, Jack managed to corner Tony Vasconcellos in Tony's office. First thing tomorrow, Vasconcellos told him, first thing tomorrow he was putting every available man on stubbing out the conduit from the grandstand.

No doubt, Jack thought as he left, Tony would do just that. Jack wouldn't have the pleasure of burying him. That was Vasconcellos. He made life miserable for others, then saved his own butt just in the nick of time.

Same with Fellows. Probably he'd be just helpful enough. In the end, Jack wouldn't be able to justify letting it be known in the community how lukewarm his efforts to save the project had been. People were like that. You had your good ones, and then you had the escape artists.

Outside the rain continued to fall.

After eating dinner in the kitchen, instead of going up to bed at once, Jack got a cup of coffee, the purpose of which was to keep him awake another half hour, and brought it into the dining room, where Janelle was busy on a new project and the TV tuned to the local access channel. On the screen, city council members were milling around in anticipation of their meeting. Jack explained to Janelle what he'd been doing and about his meeting with Hank Steadman the day before. Janelle said nothing, for she hadn't been talking to Jack the last two days, his penalty for checking himself out of sickbay against the advice of the attending physician.

Finally, on the tube, El Plowman gaveled the session to order. The convocation, rotating among the local clergy, had come around tonight to none other than Mike Daugherty. Father Mike, like the proverbial bad penny, just kept turning up.

Next, to a scattering of applause, the city clerk swore Plowman in as mayor and then the councilman elected to take her old seat. Finally, there being no proclamations, Harry Steadman came stepping jauntily up to the podium to give his track update. Everything is fine and dandy, his posture proclaimed.

He proceeded to give his upbeat account of job site progress. Often it sounded like he was talking about some other project entirely. Then he went on to the matter of the flood and announced his intention to mount an effort to keep the site dry and to continue working.

"You'd think he thought it up himself," Janelle observed.

"He can take the credit for all I care."

"That's my Jack."

After Harry had completed his update, Jack went upstairs and immediately to bed, pleased that Janelle was talking to him once more. And pleased with his day. Except, of course, for the damn rain, which just kept coming.

CHAPTER 30

~

Vintage El Plowman, Johnny Pond decided. Now she was about helping the other communities along the river. Not on the agenda, but no matter, she'd discuss it anyway. El wasn't a woman to be deterred. Johnny listened, faintly amused, faintly disconnected, faintly irritated as she got the other council members to agree to a clearinghouse, one-stop shopping, to put volunteers in touch with people who could use a hand. Everyone agreed, a good idea, the matter handled so quickly and smoothly that it must have been arranged in private beforehand. City personnel would be used, no extra funding required, and no resolution necessary.

The council returned to the agenda, not a long one tonight. No budget to fight over. They ought to be through well before midnight. Johnny settled in.

For a time, nothing much happened, not until nearly eight fifteen, when he heard a slight disturbance behind him. The mayor looked up from the document she had just been handed. Other council members looked up as well, toward the entrance, which was behind Johnny. He turned.

Just inside the door stood Fritz Goetzinger.

Johnny hadn't seen the ex-mayor since his resignation. Goetzinger hesitated, expressionless and unmoving, as a man might at the moment of finding himself in a strange place, before surprise has time to register. He looked left and right, barely moving his head. The cloth jacket he wore flapped open. He'd lost weight, but otherwise appeared unchanged, a little gaunter, his hair still with its odd patches of white, his dark eyes and broad, hard face as uncompromising as ever.

El Plowman stopped the proceedings for a moment. "Fritz…Mr. Mayor, how nice to see you."

He acknowledged the greeting with an abrupt nod, something inward turning about it, and then without a word took a seat at the back, saying nothing to anyone, just sitting, dour and alone, as the moment of stunned awareness in the chamber passed and council deliberations hesitantly resumed.

For the next hour, until the break, Fritz's presence seemed to become the subconscious of the room. From time to time, Johnny tilted his head and eyed the former mayor, the man of misfortune, his wife dead and he partly responsible, the company he once worked for now closed and he partly responsible for that, too. On top of this, according to rumor, his farm was about to be repossessed by the banks that held his markers. But nothing of these calamitous events could be read in his countenance, only waiting.

During the break, Johnny and several others, including El, went over to speak with him, but Fritz had little to say. Close at hand, it was more obvious that the death of his wife and the rest had taken their toll.

Johnny felt a tug on his sleeve and turned.

"I'd like a word with you outside," El said quietly.

As they exited, El leading the way along the second floor corridor, she asked, "You don't happen to know why Fritz is here, do you?"

"No. You?"

She shook her head.

"Expect he can't make matters any worse," Johnny suggested.

Determinedly, El was leading the two of them far down the corridor. "Fritz," she said, "can always make matters worse."

Johnny smiled to himself at the thought that she was right.

At the end of the hall, it turned out that she wanted to talk about Sam Turner's situation, and so, briefly, unwillingly, Johnny talked about that, El trying to spread the blame around, but Johnny having none of it. Sam was on his own. They had done what they could to help—just as they'd be bound to help other young black men who came along—but now Sam needed to make his own way.

Johnny had spotted Sam the day before looking down on the Jesse Jackson rally from the third floor of city hall, the first time he'd seen him since visiting the hospital, where he'd told him, despite his intention to keep his mouth shut, that he was a damn fool getting involved in the shenanigans of Reiny Kopp. Sam, Johnny understood now, was a man with no discernible purpose in life beyond continuing to live. In Sam, some elemental disconnect existed that neither Johnny nor El could do a damn thing about. Not that El, given half a chance, wouldn't keep on trying.

❧

El detached herself from Johnny's aura, his big man's heat, and returned to the meeting, conscious of his anger, which she guessed must mask at least a little bit of guilt over his part in the Sam Turner mess.

The meeting resumed. El sat in the mayor's chair and listened to the matters being discussed and thought about her misconceptions.

Fritz Goetzinger remained in the back of the chamber, severe in the pocket of isolation he had made for himself.

The meeting wore on. The palms of El's hands were cool and she pressed one, then the other against her forehead.

Finally, they got to the matter—Deuce Goetzinger's committee-with-no-instructions—that El had removed from the list of consent items, and a couple of the other council members agreed to get together with her to study the proposal. That disposed of, the rest of the consent items were passed en masse.

The time had arrived for public input. She glanced at her watch—10:35. Except for city officials and the press, almost everyone had gone home. But not Fritz. He sat where he'd been sitting since he entered.

Council members to the right and left of El began to gather their papers together. She could sense their relief, glad to be finishing early for once.

Fritz rose. He had taken off his jacket, beneath which he wore a work shirt. He had lost weight, the shirt collapsing in upon his chest. Deliberately he approached the public lectern. The room fell quiet. He took his time. Looking at him, El had the urge to ask questions a wife might ask. How was he taking care of himself? Why was he so thin? Was he eating properly?

He gripped the lectern with his farmer's hands, which given his thinness seemed all the more angular and powerful, and leaned forward. Unnecessarily but according to form, he told them his name and address.

"We're glad to see you again, Fritz," El responded.

He paused and regarded her, but said nothing.

"What can we do for you?" she asked.

He continued to look at her for a time, as if contemplating some sarcastic remark. Then he composed his face and leaned close to the microphone and said quietly, "What are you people going to do about the wall?"

"Excuse me?"

"The wall. The floodwall."

What was he talking about? "Do about it?"

He leaned even farther forward, his tone still conversational, his voice so familiar from over the years, the slightly rasping tone, the phrasing like probes, like a man trying to insert a pry bar under some bulky object. "Got to add to the wall," he said, leaning far forward and letting his eye roam from council member to council member. "The wall and the levees. Raise them on up. If you wait, it'll be too late. If you wait, the river'll come up, and it'll be just too damn late."

El stared at him, understanding now, her understanding, once started, coming in a rush, several ideas simultaneously clamoring for attention. None of them welcome. And worst of all, she realized that he was going to mention Walter.

Paul Cutler had turned around in his chair so he could look directly at the ex-mayor. "With the council's permission," he said, "are you trying to tell us, Mr. Goetzinger, that water's going over the wall?"

"Nobody, Fritz," El added quickly, "is saying that."

"Nobody?" he said to her.

"Who?" Paul demanded.

Fritz ignored the manager, instead waiting for El to speak. If she didn't, he would.

Damn that Walter, El thought. To Fritz she said flatly, "If you're trying to say that Walter Plowman has made such a prediction, you're wrong."

"Ask him," Fritz said.

The consequences weren't clear in El's mind. Fritz was jumping the gun, of course. A favorite ploy of his, take a position before anybody else even knew there was a position to be taken. Whatever else happened, El had to extricate Walter from the mess Fritz seemed intent upon making for him. So she said, "I don't know what you *think* he told you, Fritz, but he didn't tell you water's going over the wall. Nobody believes that's going to happen."

"Is that right?" Fritz said. "I got a suggestion for you. Why don't you go down and tell that to the people living around Five Points, why don't you tell it to the people in Little Wales, why don't you tell it to…," and he continued ticking off low-lying neighborhoods on the Flats. He still hadn't begun to shout, but his tone had become more insistent, beginning an oh-so-familiar escalation.

El didn't even know if it was possible to raise the wall. She glanced toward Chuck Fellows, sitting among the other city staffers, and decided that it made no difference, not at the moment. It was simply too soon to act.

None of the other council members, caught absolutely flatfooted by all this, had said a word yet. El wiped her hand, hot and moist, across her forehead. Damn that Walter. She felt nauseous. She thought, without a trace of satisfaction, that indeed she had been right.

Fritz could always make things worse.

CHAPTER 31

~

"Do you *ever* pay attention to just who it is you're talking to, dear?"

"He asked me a question," Walter said defiantly. "I answered it."

This fight with El wasn't nearly as much fun as the last one.

"You're naïve, Walter. You don't know how Fritz operates."

El had always thought him naïve, just as he thought her arrogant.

Somebody was rapping on the back door.

"At this hour?" she said and stopped berating him long enough to go answer it.

On the windward side of the house, the storm made a stippling and singing sound. To the leeward, in the building's small rain shadow, he could hear nothing, the silence rather more ominous than the storm's lashings on the other side.

"Do you know what time it is?" El was asking in the mudroom.

Walter couldn't make out the response. He consulted his watch—11:47. Whoever it was had been admitted, for he heard the rustling of an approaching coat.

"You see, Walter?" El said, reappearing. "This is what you've got yourself into." Behind her came the *Trib* reporter, Rachel Brandeis.

"I'm sorry," Brandeis said. "The light was on, I thought I might get a statement."

This apology was halfhearted, Brandeis already busy disentangling her notebook from the side pocket of her coat.

"The story's not just going to be about Fritz," El was telling Walter. "It's going to be about you, too. Tell him, Rachel."

"Well, he's the putative expert, if that's what you mean," Rachel said to El. The notebook was out. She opened it and looked up, composed, ready, intent.

"Hear that, Walter? *Putative.* Tell him what's going to happen, Rachel," El insisted.

Brandeis looked from El to Walter to El, then asked, "What do you mean?"

"The story. What's going to happen to the story?"

"Okay, well, I expect the wires will pick it up. There'll be a lot of interest." The reporter paused, contemplative, then spoke directly to Walter. "If you're right about how high the water's going," she said, "doesn't that mean all the flood fights up and down the river will be lost? Billions in damages. On top of what's predicted already."

"Will Walter be believed?" El asked her.

"I don't know. I suppose for other papers it's a sidebar kind of piece."

El nodded, satisfied. "So there you are, Walter. Local weatherman predicts doomsday."

"I'm not the only one thinks that might happen," Walter said defensively.

"But nobody else is saying it. Not even your friend Mick Kilmer," El snapped.

"That's right," Walter admitted. At the moment, he was wrapped up in the distinctly eerie sensation of hearing his speculations boomeranging back to him from a totally unexpected quarter.

"Fritz Goetzinger has put you on the record, Walter," El snapped. "If I was in your shoes, I'd be mad as hell."

"What did you tell him?" the reporter zeroed in.

"Did you tell him water was going over the wall?" El interrupted. She wasn't fooling around.

"No," Walter said weakly.

"You didn't?" El said.

He wouldn't have said that, although he didn't remember exactly what he had told Fritz. What he'd implied. What Fritz could have taken him to imply. The eerie quality of the situation was giving way quickly to nervousness. He knew what he believed, but no man, if he knows what's good for him, is flat-out honest. People took things the wrong way.

"What did you tell him?" Brandeis asked again. But El wasn't through.

"This is off the record, Rachel—everything I say here is off the record—but let me tell you, Walter doesn't have any official standing. He doesn't work for any responsible agency. And Fritz Goetzinger's call to raise the floodwall is way premature. You know how he operates. This should be a non-story."

"Too late to stop it," Brandeis told her and then added, "but you're right, I know how Fritz operates. Doesn't make any difference, I'm afraid."

"It doesn't make any difference that Walter didn't tell him water's going over the wall? The man's a liar."

Brandeis looked at Walter. "Is he?"

"I didn't tell him that."

"There!" El said, triumphant.

"But what exactly did you tell him?" Brandeis persisted.

Walter tried to remember. Only the gist of the conversation came back. He wasn't absolutely sure of anything. The trouble was, his discussions with Fritz in the past had always been of a speculative nature, long-term forecasts that Fritz needed in order to decide whether he should plow in the fall or could afford to wait until the spring. Walter tried to help Fritz, and that required a certain willingness to go out on a limb, but he'd always assumed Fritz understood the uncertain nature of the forecasts.

For the reporter's benefit, he repeated the conversation as best he could recall. He tried to decide if he should be mad at Fritz, but his apprehension made it impossible to think clearly. No way he could get off the hook here, not without lying himself. He should have known better. Damn!

He continued talking, telling her why he believed what he believed.

Several weeks earlier, while scouring his data, he'd found a pattern from twenty-seven years ago, almost as far back as he could go in his own stuff. He'd confirmed it with his contacts at NWS and COE. During that long-ago spring, a precip max engulfed the southern tier of states. A series of intense storms had come off the Pacific, re-formed over the Four Corners area, and hightailed east, picking up all kinds of moisture from the Caribbean and causing widespread flooding. Conditions were the same today, with two exceptions.

"Which are?" Brandeis asked.

"For one thing, the northern jet stream blocked all those earlier systems, keeping them from tracking into the Upper Midwest. But that's not the case now. Right now the jet stream's aimed right at us."

"Like a gun."

"You could say that."

"You said there are two differences from back then. What's the other?"

"Connected to the first, really. They were southern storms. There was no snowpack to worry about then."

"But we've had record snowfalls," Brandeis said.

He nodded.

"So you're telling me this is going to happen?" Brandeis asked.

"Oh, dear," El said.

"No, no, not necessarily," Walter quickly amended. As he had been talking to Brandeis, he seemed almost to remember the conversation with Fritz. "Storms track along jet streams, okay, but jet streams move around."

"So everything might be different tomorrow?" El asked.

"Yes," Walter agreed, with a mixture of relief and reluctance.

"Good," she said.

"But weather's got a memory." Walter knew he should probably keep his mouth shut, but he was primed to tell the reporter everything. If she didn't know everything, she wouldn't know what he really thought.

"Oh, no, not that again," El tried to cut him off, but he wouldn't be cut off.

"It's not a stochastic process." He stopped, frustrated. How could he ever tell these people what he'd learned, what he felt, what thirty years of thinking about weather and climate had lodged in his very bones. "We know maybe 10 percent of what there is to know."

El pounced. "So you're guessing." She was after one thing and one thing only. This made him all at once mad. In her own way, she was no better than Fritz.

He didn't answer, and then he said merely, "I don't know." Every scrap of intuition he possessed told him the rain wouldn't stop. "But you've got to understand—"

"You don't need to say any more," El told him.

"Yes, I do!" Walter yelled at her. Brandeis flinched at this sudden outburst. El merely folded her arms and waited.

Walter struggled to speak precisely. The grandfather clock in the hall chimed, the ringing seeming to recede into the distance rather than grow softer. Outside, rainwater made a tinny drumming sound in a downspout.

"It might hold. I mean, weather is a science, okay…but only up to a point, and then you have to… If you just, like, slavishly follow what the models say, that's way too mechanical. I mean, we've got this regime now, and maybe it won't last. But the weather remembers… And I've got this feeling…" He halted. Hopeless. There was no way he could communicate what he knew. It wasn't words at all.

"Won—der—ful," El said, three syllables, each carefully articulated. "Let me tell you, Walter, you might think you're only half saying what you're saying, but people don't pay attention to footnotes. You say 'maybe' but what people hear is 'probably.' And what they remember the next day is 'definitely.'"

Walter stared around himself, with the vague intention of finding something he could do besides talking.

Maybe El was right, maybe Fritz had used him. People around Walter were forever simplifying the world so they could do what they wanted.

The two women looked at him expectantly. The reporter had her right arm curled around her notepad, her wrist crooked in the manner of left-handed people. Sinister. He stared at the nub of her pen.

For months he'd been thinking about the possibility of a huge flood. A huge one. One day, he knew, the Mississippi would take back the floodplain. Maybe not this year, but sometime.

"You don't understand how serious this is, Walter. And I daresay neither do you," El added, turning to Brandeis. "This could rip the city apart."

"Maybe you should do what Fritz says," Walter suggested quietly, thinking that after all, an ounce of prevention…

"Fritz is irresponsible. It's too early to talk about adding to the system, even if it's possible. And Fritz knows that."

"Expected value," Walter said.

"What?" El narrowed her eyes at him.

"Expected value. It comes from statistics. Even when the odds are long, if the payoff is great enough, it's worth doing."

"Oh, good grief. Look, just because we've got a lot to lose here, dear, that doesn't mean we can simply go ahead and spend all this extra money. Did you mention this 'expected value' idea to Fritz Goetzinger?"

"I don't think so. I might have. I don't remember."

"Three possibilities," El said to the reporter. "Take your pick." She turned away and rubbed her temples, tight circles with the tips of her fingers. "Beastly headache." Then she turned back toward him, the expression on her face a mixture of physical pain and frustration.

"But Fritz can't know that water's going over the wall, isn't that right? Tell her that much, at least, Walter."

"Of course."

"And the odds, these precious probabilities of yours, they're long, really long, isn't that right?"

Walter sighed and gave in. "Long enough," he said.

CHAPTER 32

~

The next morning, as El was leaving the Friends of the Community weekly breakfast, Ed Ohnesorge, the director of Catholic Charities in the Archdiocese, fell in step with her.

"We do need to help the people of East Jackson," he agreed, continuing a discussion from the breakfast. El heard an asterisk in his tone.

They were making their way through the parking lot at speed.

"Yes. We do," she told him, adding her own asterisk.

The two of them were pals, if that was the correct description of the relationship, which had evolved out of work on countless community projects and was sustained by brief conversations, lasting a minute or two, just long enough.

"I haven't had a chance to congratulate you on your election," Ohney said.

"Thank you. A mixed blessing, no doubt."

He chuckled. "I know about them."

Along with briefness, these interactions were marked by understatement. The asterisks. El didn't remember how that had started, long ago, time out of mind. It had something to do with gender, with Ohney's gallant image of himself, with the fact that he was tall and thin and still, even at his age, had all his hair.

"The council meeting last night," he said.

"What about it?" She tried to think which part would have interested him and decided it must have been Fritz Goetzinger's surprise appearance. "Fritz misinterpreted what Walter told him."

Ohney said, "That can happen," then returned to the earlier matter. "We do need to help others, El, I agree. At Catholic Charities, our services are open to everyone. It's true that the people we often end up helping...trying to help, at least...aren't exactly a cross section of the population. We patch them up as best we can. We want to make them self-sufficient, too, but that's not so easy, not when you're dealing with folks who have pretty much been marginalized and oppressed all their lives."

She didn't know where this was all going. *Marginalized* and *oppressed* were favorite Catholic Charities' words.

Ohney returned to the city council meeting and Fritz Goetzinger.

"Perhaps," he suggested, "you should just go ahead and add to the floodwall."

Oh, no, here we go again, El thought, *first Walter and now Ohney*. In Ohney's case, the connection was obvious. If water went over the wall, the people flooded out would be the people who lived on the Flats, Ohney's clientele.

"It's too soon. It's throwing money away."

"Still…"

"Fritz jumped the gun. That's his way."

"Still…"

"It polarizes the situation. There's no excuse for it. I've been thinking about this, Ohney. Naturally I didn't get a wink of sleep last night, so I've had a lot of time to think, and I'll tell you what. Even if we did follow your advice—it'd be irresponsible, but suppose we did—just go ahead and willy-nilly beef up the system. It would accomplish nothing. It certainly wouldn't help the people down on the Flats. It only benefits them if water is actually going to go over the top. In that case, we *will* add to the system, rest assured. It's simply too early now. However, I'll tell you what I think the real problem is here. We've lost our sense of intimacy with the river, our sense of a shared fate. In the old days, people knew what to do. But now it almost seems to me that—for the sake of community spirit, at least—it would be better if we didn't even have a floodwall."

He considered her words. She knew that he wasn't so concerned with community spirit as with social justice, but perhaps he could at least appreciate the irony of the situation.

"Might be you're right. Of course, given the way this flood's shaping up…"

From the parking lot of the Lumberman's Inn, as they completed their walk back to their cars, the Ice Harbor scrolled into view through the half-abandoned brick industrial buildings. At the far side of the harbor, the gates remained open yet, and through them a snippet of the rising river would have been visible except for the rain.

"That's right," El agreed, "it's too soon to add to the floodwall, but thank God we've got it."

"Or too late."

"If it is too late, in the sense you mean, then we owe it all to Fritz. A fight will polarize the community even further. You can't want that."

"I suppose not. And probably you're right, probably it would have been better if Fritz had stayed retired." Ohney hesitated and then surprised El. "But then again, I've got enough shanty Irish in me to think a little fighting's not necessarily a bad thing."

"Ohnesorge?"

"It's on my mother's side. The Ryans. I come from a mixed marriage." German Catholic and Irish Catholic, Jackson's version of miscegenation.

They stood by Ohney's car. This two minutes together was almost over.

"A *little* fighting?" she said. "Is that what you think?"

He smiled. "That's what we like to call it."

"In that case, let me say I'm a *little* concerned."

"There you go." He ducked his head as he folded himself up and slid into the driver's seat.

"And I'm looking for a *little* help, too," she shouted after him, for he was already backing out. "The city's broke. We can't afford to go throwing away money. People need to understand that! Even the oppressed and marginalized need to understand that!"

He stuck his arm out the window and waved as he drove away.

CHAPTER 33

⁓

When the river stage reached fourteen feet, Chuck Fellows began to seal the city against the rising water.

He stood next to the 16th Street retention basin and watched the street department wrecker lower into place the first of the two massive trash gates, vertical bars in a steel frame designed to prevent debris from the basin being sucked into the pump used to discharge water over the levee once the gates on the river side had been shut.

Seth Brunel, the assistant city engineer, stood next to him, talking about ways of adding to the levees and floodwall, now that Fritz Goetzinger had put the idea in play.

"Maybe we can do it ourselves," Seth suggested. Chuck had set him to thinking about the matter, so naturally Seth was all hot to go ahead and do it. The kid was a ditz. Chuck set him straight.

"Plan A is to try and con the Corps of Engineers into doing it. They built the damn thing in the first place. Plan B is to wait and see if the yahoos on the city council are so chickenshit that they knuckle under to Goetzinger. As for Plan C, forget about it. We'll deal with it when and if we have to. First we make sure the system we've already got is up and running." Chuck regretted his advance planning. Served no purpose.

The storm sewer outlets to the river would be closed and storm water diverted to the retention basins and Ice Harbor, where it could be pumped over the levee-and-floodwall system. The Ice Harbor gates would have to be closed. Chuck had been putting off cleaning the sills. He couldn't put it off much longer. He needed to get his scuba gear out and check it. Still had time, still had a couple of days. You did something when you had to.

The Northland Power generating plant would have to close its discharge into the river and start pumping its cooling water over the wall. The brewery on the Ice Harbor peninsula would have to remove its motors from the basement, then fill with city water. Clean water did less damage than floodwater. Other businesses along the river would have to activate their emergency plans. And a crane would be needed to close the concrete gates in the floodwall and complete the sealing of the system.

"I'll take care of the Ice Harbor. You take care of everything else," he told Brunel. "If you have any trouble, let me know." Chuck was concerned about the floodwall gates. They hadn't been closed in the years he'd been in the city, maybe never.

Slowly, the second trash gate slid down the I-beam slot, which held it in place. They had begun.

∿

Jack Kelley waited impatiently to use the access road. Vehicles were queued up, a crane among them. The cranes were starting to arrive. Jack intended to keep going no matter what. But everything, even the simplest task, was taking twice as long to accomplish. Just getting on the job site had become a hassle. The union gate was no longer usable, so everyone had to enter through the nonunion. Jack had talked to the union reps. They weren't happy, but under the circumstances…

Down the way, one of Mitch Mitchell's scrapers hauled the last of the sand pumped by the dredge up onto to the slope of the road, where a dozer massaged it. The trucks Jack had gotten from Chuck Fellows were off-loading gravel for the surface. Jack stared at the embankment and thought about the flood. He didn't want to think about it. He wanted to reduce it to a minor nuisance and concentrate on enclosing the grandstand. But the pale sand looked so defenseless, the road at the moment resembling nothing so much as a shabby dam. When the river rose high enough to flood the island, it would flow straight into the embankment and then sluice along its base, carrying the sand away. Storm sewer pipes had been pierced through beneath the road to relieve some of the pressure. Maybe Jack would have time to armor part of it with riprap. Mostly, they'd just have to use poly and sandbags and prayer. If the road went, the job site would be completely cut off. Another burden. Every new burden just made life more difficult. Production slowed even more. He'd never finish the damn project!

He closed his eyes and tried to take a catnap. His fever was gone, he was healthy, by his own lights, at least. But the illness had weakened him. He dragged himself through the days and dreamed of sleep.

The access road haunted his thoughts. The damn road. What to do about the damn road. He didn't know. It was a simple problem, but his mind barely turned over. If he managed to add a little more stone, bring it to thirty feet at least, and the predictions didn't keep on going up and up and up...

This reminded him of Fritz Goetzinger, Goetzinger's grandstanding before the city council. There went the city trucks. Jack would be on his own.

A horn startled him. His eyes popped open.

The line had begun to move.

Chapter 34

~

Seeing in the distance a scrimmaging of birds, Deuce Goetzinger guessed that he already had his answer. He'd come down merely out of curiosity—that's what he told himself—but as he got closer, his agitation grew. He felt a fluttering in the gut. He forgot about his father.

To his right, a narrow farm field lay along the floodplain of the Little Mesquatie River. To his left, the familiar wooded spur of the bluff.

He drove gingerly over the pitted gravel, less for the sake of the undercarriage of the sports car than his own reluctance. Now he could see what he had expected, the grain wagon around which the birds were engaged in a free-for-all. The herring gulls had returned, come north with the spring.

The ridge spur ended, a narrow skirting of hardwoods and pines around its base, and the field appeared, the field his father had leased for so many years from the Fish and Wildlife Service. Deuce parked.

He looked out across the expanse. The corn picker stood exactly where he had last seen it, when he and his father had come down the morning after the blizzard, from the cave where they'd taken shelter, and encountered the search and rescue people sent out to look for them. Now the snow was gone, except in the lee of the nearby north-facing embankment, where remnants still sagged, holding pools of blue shadows. Beyond these, the field bristled with corn stubble reaching out to the combine. Behind the machine stood still-unpicked corn.

To the right, toward the confluence of the Little Mesquatie and Mississippi, he could make out a sheen of water. The river rising.

He took a pair of work boots from his trunk, put them on, and walked in the rain toward the picker. The mud sucked at his heels and beneath the slippery surface the decaying frost crackled with each step.

That the machine remained there after all this time—for the old man would never simply abandon an expensive piece of equipment like the picker—filled Deuce with a complex mixture of irritation and satisfaction.

Driftwood had become wedged between two of the snouts on the cornhead. His father had mounted a green Deere head on the red IH picker, another hybrid, like his hog-breeding experiments.

In the snowstorm, he hadn't gotten on the last set very well, and the cornstalks about to be consumed by the machine remained twisted awkwardly to one side, exactly as they'd been the moment when the wood jammed itself in the head but now matted down by the weight of the winter storms. Deuce kicked at the tree limb. In December it would have been frozen in the ground.

Half-heartedly, he pried at the wood, then stood back and looked at the head. Too damn low. No reason to run it that low. Something else that wasn't like the old man. If he'd been running it high, like he should have been, he probably would have gone right over the wood.

Deuce went back over to the harvester and, using the energy that comes with sudden anger, worked the driftwood back and forth until finally it came free. He flung it aside.

Next he pulled himself up into the cab and settled in the familiar seat. The key was still in the ignition.

Under his clothing, he felt sweat trickling down his sides. He thought about his father, about the fact that he hadn't come down to retrieve his equipment. All or nothing, that was the old man. All or nothing. Deuce remembered his sister at the funeral, her insistence on removing the gun from the farmhouse. Deuce would've left it there. Let the old man use it if he had a mind to.

From the cab of the combine, the land ringing the field lay exposed. Water had already backed up beneath the railroad bridge and flooded the drainage ditch next to the tracks. Pods of ice drifted in it.

Thinking to move the picker to higher ground, Deuce turned the key. Nothing. The engine didn't make a sound. Battery, probably. Or maybe it had seized up. Sometimes, in real cold weather, the old man used number one diesel.

Water glinted from the headlands. If he was going to do something, he didn't have much time. Contrary urges tugged at him. The old man didn't care enough to rescue the machine, so fuck him. This thought came to him at once, his knee-jerk anger. Yet after a time more worthy impulses arose, too, the simple desire to do something that ought to be done. He'd worked with machinery all his life—on the farm, at the water plant—and held it a duty to care for it. Ill-used equipment offended his sensibility. And his mother's voice, so quiet for weeks, now returned, as well. *Do this, too, for me*, the voice said.

Well, worthy motives were all well and good, but at the moment if he was going to do anything, he needed a more satisfying goad. He wrapped his arms around the steering wheel and slowly panned the scene. The more he looked, the more water he saw. It occurred to him that rescuing the machine could be perceived as an act of revenge, too. The combine, after all, like the place itself, was a symbol of his father's guilt. Rescuing the machine would be a reminder.

Yes.

In the distance, a breeze moved across the water. Shadow and light.

He continued to sit there, undecided, and watched the rising water.

CHAPTER 35

~

Chuck found the workboat pulled up out of the water and no one around, so he used it to get out to the dredge, deserted as well. On the harbor tug, he had more luck. Amid the pall of smoke and old man's odors, Bud Pregler and Albert Furlong were playing euchre with Orv Massey and his great-grandson.

"I hope you guys don't expect to get paid for doing this," Chuck told them.

"We're off duty. Ain't no more sand to dredge, boss," Pregler said. "Where's Sid? Not with you?"

"I found the workboat ashore."

"We sent him for eats."

Orv told Billy to go out and keep an eye peeled, and the others went back to their game, Chuck kibitzing, not that he knew diddly about euchre.

"As soon as we arrange for a mooring in the Ice Harbor," he told them, "we'll take the discharge line apart and move everything down there. This weekend if you guys are available. You still determined to go back to Abbey Station, Orv?"

"Expect so."

They talked about the city council meeting the night before. They talked about the flood fight starting at the dog track.

"Know what I'd be worried about," Orv said. "Once water gets over the upper end of the island, you're gonna have debris coming down the river. Trees, houses, dead cows—all manner of stuff. Could just tear the hell out of your protection works."

Chuck hadn't gotten that far. He was still half-thinking it'd be better just to shut the project down for the duration.

"I know what I'd do," Orv said. "Borrow some barges and sink 'em at the head of the island. Form a barrier. Probably wanna wait until water got up high enough so you could float 'em right up onto the island."

173

"Yeah." Chuck looked at the man, old, beyond old, his stringy arms, his remnant of hair tied in a dirty white ponytail, drinker's eyes, the cigarillo dancing in his mouth as he talked. "If Kelley's gonna do it, he'll need a tug to move the barges."

"That thought had occurred to me," Orv said, the cigarillo doing its little jig.

When Billy spotted Sidney with the food, Chuck hitched a ride back ashore.

❧

Since he was on the grandstand deck, Jack stopped briefly down in the crawl space, which was actually nine feet high, plenty of room to work in, the designation commonly used for utility spaces, whatever their dimensions, below the occupation levels in buildings without basements. The Vasconcelloses, father and son, were hopping to it for once. As Tony had promised the day before, he'd brought in a big crew to finish stubbing conduit out through the grade beam, the tubing he needed to run the electrical—for the tote board, the track lighting, the starting boxes, the railing for the bone which the dogs would chase.

"Have you taken a gas reading lately?" Jack asked him.

"Yes," Tony said at once, without a moment's hesitation, almost as if he was telling the truth.

Jack worried about the methane rising from the old dump beneath the site. You couldn't smell it, you couldn't see it. When water came through the soil, it'd press the gas up against the mud slab they'd laid down as a barrier. If there were any gaps…

"Take the readings, Tony," he told Vasconcellos.

As he continued staring at the mud slab, however, another idea occurred to him. *Might work,* he thought. *Worth a try. Good.*

Back up on the deck, it was another day too crummy for the ironworkers to go aloft. Instead they continued to fabricate scaffold-ing to hang from the cranes. As for the other contractors, nothing the HVAC guy or Dexter Walcott could do until more of the building was under cover. The plumbing crew still had work down below, but Jack wasn't worried about that. He was worried about all the stuff that remained up there on the top; that was the real problem.

As he queued up again, leaving the job site, he spotted a city car pulled over to the side and a man out of it and down on his haunches, peering back along the northern edge of the road. Jack couldn't see his face beneath the cowl of his slicker. He pulled over and got out himself.

Near at hand, the dozer surged up the north slope of the road, the side that would take the brunt of the current when water got up on the island. "I've decided how I'm gonna protect it," he said to the figure. This was the idea that had come to him down in the crawl space.

A part of Chuck Fellows's face, a crescent moon consisting of a cheek and a single eye, became visible as he turned briefly to inspect Jack.

"First," Jack told him, "I'm gonna raise the road to thirty feet. Then I'll lay mats down on the slopes and cover them with a concrete slurry."

Fellows had turned back to his view, sighting along the embankment. He spoke with his usual bluntness.

"If we add to the city's system, I'll have to pull the trucks I gave you."

"Assuming you take Goetzinger seriously."

"It's not me, it's the twinkies on the council. I'm just telling you."

"Fritz Goetzinger," Jack said, disgusted. Edna Goetzinger had been in Jack's parish. The best thing about the ex-mayor had been his wife.

Chuck glanced up again, and Jack could see his full face this time, the man's aggressiveness somehow suggested by the very regularity of his features. "I hope it doesn't happen, Jack, but I *will* pull the trucks. If I have to."

"The access road is the city's responsibility," Jack pointed out. Chuck had been pumping sand for it, but he'd clearly decided that his priorities lay elsewhere. Just how much so became immediately apparent.

"It's our road, that's right," he agreed, "but it's also a threat."

"What do you mean?"

Fellows pointed along the edge of the road, then raised and lowered his arm, his hand a blade. "Flow line. Once the water gets up on the structure, it's gonna start going thataway."

"Right. The road will be undermined if we don't do anything." But then, in an instant, Jack saw what Fellows was talking about. He would have understood sooner except he'd been thinking only about the road itself. Now, looking back toward the city, the other problem became apparent. They'd pierced the road with big storm sewer pipes, which would dispose of part of the flow, but only part. The rest would be diverted toward the city, flowing back along the road and then across the channel and straight into the levee at the point where the highway crossed onto the island. Maintaining access to the track could threaten the city's own protection system. "Shit," Jack said.

"Yeah."

"We can add pipes and divert more of the water."

"No matter how many you put in, there's still gonna be significant flow toward the levee." The inexorable destination of these observations couldn't have been clearer.

"So you're thinking about just blowing up the road, is that it?"

"I'm not gonna *just* do anything."

"You leave me no alternative. I'll have to plan on being isolated." Confronted by this new problem, another damn problem, Jack's mind swung 180 degrees. He'd do it! He'd move everything he needed out onto the job site and then maybe, by God, he'd blow the friggin' road himself. To hell with Fellows.

But now the conversation took another unexpected turn.

"Probably, that's right," Fellows said. "Probably you should expect to be on your own. At some point. As for the levee, I'll armor it, then keep an eye on things." It wasn't so much the words themselves that surprised Jack, but rather their tone, a matter-of-factness which was as good as sympathy where Fellows was concerned. "I'll let you keep your road as long as I can," Fellows said.

Jack calmed down a bit, and as the two of them stared along the embankment, he became conscious of the rain. Always the rain. But not so hard at the moment, at the moment a farmer's rain, perfect for watering the soil after planting.

"By the way," Fellows asked after a time, "you thought about debris in the river? When water gets up on the island?"

Reluctantly Jack's mind veered around in this new direction. There'd be debris in the river, all kinds of it. And no, he hadn't thought about it. He didn't want to think about it. He wanted to build the damn track. Fellows, on the other hand, was obviously getting into this flood business. Every time he opened his mouth, another situation came out.

"My position is, the crest's gonna be twenty-seven, twenty-eight feet max," Jack said. "That's the prediction, that's what I'm going with. Water on the island, but not that deep in most places. A seepage problem, okay, but nothing that can't be handled with a few well points. And as for the debris you're talking about, mostly I expect it'll either stay out in the main current or get hung up in the trees at the head of the island. All I've gotta worry about is the access road…until you blow it up, that is."

Fellows got up and rubbed the wet sand off his hands. "Okay," he said, "it's your funeral."

CHAPTER 36

~

Late that afternoon, Chuck drove down to Rock Island for a meeting, set up by his buddy Jake Podolak, at the Corps of Engineers' district headquarters. The Corps people took less than half an hour to tell Chuck what he already knew but needed to hear officially anyway. Because of the antecedent conditions, they'd been gearing up for months and now had a huge flood fight on their hands. They didn't have time for the kinds of speculations Fritz Goetzinger and Walter Plowman were trying to peddle.

Afterward, Chuck and Jake walked from the annex building back into the persistent light rain. Less rain down here. They stopped in the parking lot to shoot the shit, and as they talked, Chuck became aware that a third man had followed them out and slowly been approaching. Now he stopped, still a few paces away, and waited. He'd been in the meeting. Chuck didn't quite remember his name, only what he did—a hydrologist, in charge of the Corps' computer model of the river.

Jake paused and eyed him but didn't speak, and the guy sidled up the last few steps, keeping some space between Podolak and himself. He was short, stocky, balding. His expression suggested reluctance mixed with a certain hangdog determination.

"Mick Kilmer," he reintroduced himself to Chuck and then needlessly added, "I was in the meeting."

Kilmer looked at Podolak doubtfully, then back to Chuck.

"You were talking about Walter Plowman," Jake said to Chuck. "Mick here is an asshole buddy of his, ain't that right, Mick?"

"You know Plowman?" Chuck asked.

Kilmer nodded. "A long time." From beneath his heavy eyebrows, his eyes darted another look at Podolak, then back at Chuck.

"A bunch of us are interested in climate," he continued. He mentioned himself, he mentioned the Iowa state climatologist, he mentioned a couple of academic types. And he mentioned Walt. "We've been discussing this event on the side."

"Nutcases," Jake said pleasantly.

"And I love you, too, Podolak," Kilmer fired back but without heat. Jake winked at Chuck.

The light rain fell from the bright, clay-yellow sky. Chuck had taken his jacket off. Since Vietnam, he didn't like to have his forearms covered.

"As I said," Kilmer pressed on, "we've been talking. This has nothing to do with the Corps, you understand." He was looking directly at Chuck now. "But if you want, I'll tell you what I think."

"I want," Chuck said.

"It could happen. Water could get high enough to go over the wall in Jackson. This doesn't come from the numbers. No way the Corps could respond to it. Not yet, at least. Right or wrong, no way we could do anything different but what we're already doing."

"Nevertheless, it could happen," Chuck said, interested that someone with the Corps would be willing, even apparently anxious, to put himself beyond the pale. "So what are we talking about here? How high?"

Kilmer waggled his head and sucked air through clamped teeth. "Can't put a number on it. Once the river starts to take the floodplain back, we'll begin to go blind, lose gauging stations. Calculating discharge will get a deal trickier. Even if we knew how much rain was gonna fall... All I'm saying is maybe. This might happen. And maybe not, too. I could be dead wrong. Maybe twenty-seven feet's right on the money."

"But maybe you're right, too."

"Yeah."

Chuck crossed his arms. "Just what do you expect me to do with this information?"

"Up to you. I'm just the messenger. I just wanted to let you know that Walter Plowman isn't, as Podolak here would have it, a nutcase. No, sir. He might be wrong, but he's not crazy."

Chuck looked at Jake. "Is that what you think, Podolak? These people are up a tree?"

He expected another whimsical dismissal from Jake, but Jake surprised him, growing serious for the moment, or what passed for serious in Podolak's case.

"Not my field of expertise, ol' buddy. Mick and your TV weatherman friend there might be certifiable, but let's face it, none of us are wrapped too tight. And Mother Nature's having us on, that's for sure."

Chuck turned back to Kilmer. "But maybe you're wrong, too. Maybe the Corps' current prediction is right. Maybe even the National Weather Service. Maybe it won't go above twenty-three feet." The current NWS forecast for the crest at Jackson.

"Bite your tongue," Jake said. Corps guys didn't have much use for the Weather Service.

"Look," Kilmer told Chuck, "you gotta understand, the Corps and the Weather Service are coming from completely different places. Those people make their predictions based on rain already on the ground, or maybe, in extreme situations, they'll factor in a few days' worth of forecasted precip. So what happens is, their predictions go up as more rain comes. Toward the end, they can tell you exactly how high the crest will be and when it's coming. Trouble is, they don't give you a whole helluva lot of lead time. And frankly they don't have the experience on the river that we do."

"A bunch of numbers crunchers," Jake said.

Chuck knew all this. The Corps had been dealing with the river for nearly two hundred years. And they built protection works, so they needed lead time. They had to forecast farther out. Trouble was, neither the NWS nor the Corps was giving him diddly at the moment. It might be this and it might be that and who the hell knows.

He smeared across his skin the cold rainwater, which had beaded on the ends of the hair of his forearms. The sting of the water, at least, was something definite.

"So, tell me then, Mick, what's your best guess?" he asked again. "How high?"

"I'm sorry. I'm just not going to make a prediction."

"Shit."

"The whole point here, my friend, is to make your life more interesting," Podolak explained.

Chuck peered at Kilmer. "Okay, then, just give me what you know. Whatever might help."

Kilmer talked, and as he did, he sounded very much as Walt Plowman had on the day Chuck and Walt and Todd had tramped along the floodwall and levees.

The rain was slackening, the yellow sky brightening.

"Of course, the rating curves change at the extremes," Kilmer told him, nearing the end of his cautionary tale. "They'll flatten out some as the river takes the floodplain back." He raised an eyebrow and nodded and smiled ironically, his first smile. "And as the flood fights go bust upstream, that'll be good news for you." The water would spread out above Jackson and take some of the pressure off the city.

Chuck fought against the rising excitement. How easy it would have been to get really interested in this stuff. "How much warning will I have?"

"When the time comes, a week maybe, a little more," Kilmer said. "The rain simply won't let up."

Seven miles of waterfront to protect and a week to do it. A clusterfuck if there ever was one.

"But anything's possible?" Chuck asked one last time.

Kilmer nodded vigorously. This was the idea he obviously felt most comfortable with.

"Maybe thirty-five feet?" Chuck asked.

"Most likely, if it goes over the wall, it'll be just a skosh. But yeah, even thirty-five, even that could happen."

Jake whistled. "Thirty-five feet. Shitload of water."

"But maybe it'll only be twenty-seven," Chuck said.

Kilmer nodded.

"Or twenty-three."

Jake laughed. Kilmer just smiled and shook his head. Nothing was unthinkable, nothing, that is, except the possibility that the National Weather Service might be right, after all.

~

Chuck didn't take the highway back to Jackson. Instead he drove up the river road, where he could watch the Mississippi. He drove through the little shoreline towns, which reminded him of Vietnamese villages. Of course, they weren't like 'Nam at all. The similarity rose not from what he saw, but what he felt, the anticipation of the worst, and with that, a deep, abiding sadness.

As he drove, the rain became heavier again. He read the early signs of preparation—mobilized equipment, piles of sand, pallets of baled sandbags. The serious flood fights at the moment were occurring far to the north, in places like Benson, Minnesota, where the old ladies drowned in the elevator, but if Walter and Mick Kilmer were even half right, these people down here were in for one damn rough time.

As the towns to the north lost their fights and the river spread out over the floodplain, that would take some of the pressure off Jackson, Kilmer had said. This idea saddened Chuck, too. In a way, it was the saddest of all.

But nothing to be done. Just the way it was. Somebody else got screwed, you were saved.

The river rolled by, still contained within its banks down here, scuffed by the wind, reflecting the odd clay color of the clouds. Chuck quit paying attention and tried to make time.

CHAPTER 37

～

"Off the record," Paul Cutler said with disgust. "Do you suppose we could add to the wall off the record?"

Paul had put on a tie, but the rest were dressed casually. Chuck Fellows slouched spread-legged in his chair, arms crossed, having made his report. Harvey Butts, the city attorney, stood at the window, looking down at the Saturday morning traffic, and appeared hardly to attend to the proceedings. El Plowman sat quietly, her chair pushed slightly back from the table, hands folded in her lap, alert.

Paul was conscious of the presence of the others' unrevealed thoughts, not precisely what those thoughts were, only that they existed. He was also conscious of the isolation of each person—the different constituencies, the animosities. Baggage.

What needed to happen here was obvious enough, but that hardly seemed to matter just then. Outside Paul's office, the emptiness, city hall on a weekend, added to the weight of the moment. Yet nothing Paul had learned so far changed the situation one iota. Adding to the wall was technically feasible. Chuck had already figured out how. It'd cost four hundred grand, more or less, if they did it immediately, and who knows how much if they waited. But four hundred was more than enough.

El asked, "There's no way the Corps will act now, Chuck, you're absolutely sure, no way at all?"

Fellows shook his head. "They said no advance measures. On the other hand, it's their project. Once the prediction's over thirty feet, they'll do something. And, as I said, they seem to think they could get the job done in time."

"That's it, then," Paul interrupted, with the dim hope of speeding things along a little. "If the Corps can handle it, let 'em."

"But if the flood gets that bad," El wondered, "will they be too busy? Can we really count on them?"

"Could be a flood of record all the way down to the mouth of the Ohio," Harvey Butts observed from his post at the window.

Paul, disliking this turn in the conversation, said, "Don't you think the Corps knows that? I'll tell you one thing, folks, if they say they can do the job, we better have a damn good reason for second-guessing them."

"We can call Hus," Harvey suggested, "see if he can put some pressure on from his end. That's what congressmen are for."

Fellows snickered.

"I've already got a call into his office," Paul said. "I'll try." He had his doubts. After all, the dike had been built with exactly this kind of event in mind, leaving Jackson snug behind its wall while the Corps and FEMA and so forth were freed up to help the less-fortunates along the river. And anyway, Paul added with a sigh, Ed Hus was a two-term congressman in the minority party without any committee assignments that might give him leverage on the Corps. Iowa's two senators weren't likely to be of much help, either. There'd be a lot of empathy, of course. Disasters were marvelous opportunities for politicians to show how much they cared.

"What if we do the job ourselves?" El wondered out loud. The inevitable question.

Paul looked at Fellows. "Did the Corps say anything about picking up the tab if we do the work?"

"Sure, if the water actually goes that high. But coitus interruptus doesn't count. The feds don't pony up any money unless you actually get fucked."

Paul was satisfied with the contents of this comment if not its packaging. Fellows certainly had a way with words.

El had looked down and seemed to be examining the stitching on her clothing. "Perhaps," she said, "this isn't the time for a cost-benefit analysis."

"Well…," Paul began, and then left the word hanging.

"If we do nothing, and the Corps isn't able to act in time…"

"A few days ago," Paul said to her, "you were horrified when Fritz Goetzinger made his demand. What's changed?"

"I've been thinking about the people on the Flats."

"I see. Yes, of course."

Paul was pleased on occasion to toss something into the council's lap and let them take the heat. He was even tempted now. And if his own fate hadn't hung in the balance, maybe he would have. Instead he turned the thing around slightly, so they could inspect another facet.

"Let me remind everyone that we wouldn't be having this little conversation if it wasn't for Goetzinger. Do you really want to let him call the tune here?"

"Call the tune?" El said at once.

She inspected him coolly, and he looked back and said, "Okay, let me rephrase it. Does anybody here actually believe Goetzinger? The man's made a career of going off half-cocked. Is this really any different?"

"The stakes," Harvey Butts drawled from the window, "are a tad bit higher, I'd say. It appears our friend Fritz, whom we'd left for dead, is very much alive and kicking."

"Yes," Paul said, seizing on this, "and it burns me up, it really does. Absolutely irresponsible. After all the man's been through," he continued sourly, "you'd think he would've learned a little, I don't know, humility."

Nobody touched this comment.

"Guy's got brass balls, say that much for him," Fellows observed by way of an aside.

Paul took a deep breath. "Look here, folks," he said, deciding it had been pointless to bring Goetzinger up and he might as well speak directly to the issue, "suppose we raise the wall and suppose the crest is, indeed, twenty-eight feet. That's the highest *reputable* estimate we've got at the moment, let me remind you." He leaned hard on the word *reputable* and stared at El, unsure how much credence she gave to her husband's predictions. "So suppose we *do* add to the system and then nothing happens. We're left high and dry. We've dropped four hundred grand or whatever. And, of course, provided a major photo op for the press." Every paper in the country could be counted on to run a picture of the emergency work that wasn't needed.

"I'm worrying about the people who might have their homes destroyed," El said. "Don't talk to me about photo ops."

"You think I'm not?" he shot back. "But there are a lot of considerations here. And the city's image is not irrelevant. We've already had enough bad press over all this racial stuff. Do we want to end up looking like idiots, too?"

El snorted. "I've spent a good deal of time the last few months looking like an idiot, Paul. Believe me, you get used to it."

Paul clamped his jaw shut to keep from saying something he'd regret. Then he thought, *Fuck it*, and turned to look at her again. "Maybe that should tell you something."

"Oh," she said, unfazed, "it does...but not what you think."

"I don't even want to know what that means," Paul said.

"Under the circumstances," El added, going back to the subject of the floodwall and making her case not to Paul but rather to the back of Harvey Butts, "perhaps the best thing we could do would be to spend some money *needlessly...*"

"You're kidding," Paul said.

"Well," the lawyer observed, "as we all know, a patient's sense of therapeutic effect is directly proportional to the cost of the medicine."

This was silly. It was stupid. Paul interrupted again. "I wasn't hired to spend money needlessly."

Harvey turned around at the window. "Not part of your program, is it?" This brought Paul up short. He tried to remember when he'd used that expression with Butts. Oh, yes, of course. The lunch at the country club. When Harvey surprised him by coming out in favor of young Goetzinger's proposal for a committee with no instructions. So Harvey had made a point of remembering that, had he? Well, all right.

"Tell me, Harv, suppose we just go ahead here and add to the damn wall, add to the levee, whatever, and suppose the water tops out at twenty-eight feet after all. Would that open us up to a suit, do you think? Could Joe Citizen, less impressed than we seem to be with the rantings of Fritz Goetzinger, suggest we'd been derelict in our fiduciary duty to the city? Could he?"

"Expect he could," the city attorney conceded.

"So, yes, you're right, that's not part of my program."

Butts nodded slowly, impassively, at this retaliation. Paul turned toward Chuck Fellows, who hadn't been saying much. "What about you?"

Fellows got off on being contrary, but Paul wasn't unmindful of the fact that he was supposed to be the technical expert here. His position carried some weight even if the man himself was a barbarian.

The muscles of Fellows's forearms bulged where he had crossed them. "Been thinking. Either way, add to the system or not, people won't leave their homes. Some will, maybe, but not most. A lot of dim bulbs down on the Flats. If water goes over the wall, people will still have some time to get out, not a lot, but a little. But as you raise the system, the situation changes. You lose the safety factor built into it. You increase the chance it'll fail catastrophically. And then..." Fellows spoke matter-of-factly.

Paul, for his part, thought, *Yes, good, that would be the worst case of all.*

"So you're suggesting maybe we don't want to do anything, no matter what happens."

"That's not an option," El said curtly.

Chuck shrugged and continued blithely onward. "Anyway, you act when you've got enough info, which we ain't. And you're always prepared to accept the consequences, to take a flood if it comes down to that. Sometimes you end up in the middle of a shit storm. Just the way it is."

Paul scratched along the line of his jaw. Wonderful. Fellows did indeed have a way with words. "Let's hope to hell it doesn't come down to that."

El said, "It's not going to, Paul, believe me."

"Nobody wants it to, El." Paul turned toward the others. "The question is, what do we take outside this room?" The management team would get together Monday morning, then emergency response people. Goetzinger had tossed a rock into the water, and this meeting was the first of the ripples that would spread outward from that.

"Chuck," Paul asked, "your advice is to wait?"

Fellows nodded.

"Harvey?"

Butts had turned his attention back to the street. "I suppose, for now."

"El?"

She stared at Paul, not answering at first and then slowly nodding, her eyes cool and withdrawn. "For the moment," she said.

CHAPTER 38

~

They tilted the green corn head, snouts up, against the side of the truck carrier and then went back for the combine. Deuce had his doubts. The carrier had been big enough to haul the little city bulldozer, but the combine?

J.J. had eyeballed the flatbed of the truck, then, in the distance, the picker. "No sweat."

He drove the dozer and Deuce splashed along next to it. A veneer of water now lay across the field, peppered by raindrops, like seeds being sown. In a few days, the combine would have been lost to the floodwaters. Deuce had half expected to return and discover his father rescuing the machine himself. He'd been preparing himself for the encounter. But still no sign of the old man. Probably run into him at the farm.

They hooked the towing chain to the undercarriage of the combine, and Deuce stood back, idly picking an ear of corn as J.J. climbed back onto the dozer and cinched up the chain. The shuck crackled as Deuce peeled it back, exposing the rows of hard, yellow kernels beneath.

He looked up at the snap of the chain coming taut, water leaping off it. The combine shuddered, then seemed to settle back, like a puller in a tug-of-war, straining against the chain and only grudgingly beginning to give ground. Deuce climbed aboard, into the cab, to steer.

They swung in a wide, slow arc toward the gravel access ramp.

When the machine was finally aligned on the roadway behind the truck carrier, J.J. drove the dozer around and out of the way, then went back to the carrier and tilted the hydraulic flatbed up and played out the wire come-along. To Deuce, the picker still looked too big.

"Corn gone bad?" J.J. asked as the cable slowly reeled in, pulling the combine inchwise toward the lowered lip of the truck bed.

"Field dried. Be okay until the water gets to it."

The combine hesitated, then began to climb up onto the bed.

"Could rescue the corn, too," J.J. suggested.

"Probably a lot of loss, deer wintering in the bottomlands. Raccoons, turkeys, jays, you name it."

"Not enough left to make it worthwhile?"

That wasn't quite true, but the point here wasn't to be high-minded and do the old man a good turn. The point was to make him feel like shit.

"By the time somebody got back here," Deuce hedged, "water'd be too high to put a picker into the field."

"Do it by hand, then. Got a buddy out near Holy Cross does some farming. We can start a phone tree, get plenty of folks down here pronto, I bet."

Deuce reminded himself that J.J. was occasionally subject to enthusiasms.

"Be my guest."

"Oh, no. I'm not going to do this by myself. Fritz's your old man."

"You think that makes any difference?"

"You're rescuing the picker."

"That's another matter entirely."

"Oh?"

"Hate to see good equipment ruined."

J.J. wasn't buying. "That's not the only reason, my friend. You can't kid me. You're as moralistic as my dentist."

"Yeah, right."

The picker climbed the last few feet up onto the bed, the hydraulic winch winding to a stop.

"We could have ourselves a husking bee," J.J. said, half to himself, obviously quite taken with his proposal.

"The trouble with you, Dusterhoft, is you like people too much."

"I find them fascinating," J.J. corrected him. "It's a mystery to me what God thought He was trying to accomplish when He made us." He had reached into the cab of the truck carrier to lower the bed. The picker sat on it like a fat man on a barstool.

"We'd better tie her down," J.J. said, "just in case."

Finally under way, a red flag flying off the hind end of the rig, they pulled cautiously out onto the highway, J.J. driving.

"We're illegal as hell, of course," he noted for the record. "Load this wide requires a special permit. Probably should have had you bring your vehicle along to use as a pace car, just to make it look like we're on the up-and-up."

"Misuse of city equipment," Deuce added. The truck and the dozer J.J. had borrowed from the city garage.

"Goes without saying."

"Must be a law against driving this slow, too."

"Undoubtedly."

The idea of all this illegality seemed to lift J.J.'s spirits. He hummed a little tuneless tune and kept his eye on the rearview mirror. Deuce, for his part, took up where he had left off, anticipating the encounter with his father.

He hadn't seen him since the funeral. The empty feeling in the pit of his stomach surprised him. He'd imagined that, finally, he had a grip on himself where the old man was concerned. He was an adult, for Christ's sake. But here he was, queasy as hell. Not a good sign.

On Brick Kiln Road, winding up the bluff toward the farm, the diesel engine surged and he felt the weight of the combine behind them.

"So," J.J. said as they rounded the bend at the north side pumping station, "the city's taking a serious look at your committee-with-no-instructions scheme, after all."

"Yeah. Plowman, at least."

Despite the uproar over his father's demand that the city beef up the flood protection system, the old man at it again, Deuce had not forgotten the other thing of interest that had happened at the city council meeting: the mayor's apparent adoption of his proposal to inject a little democracy into the workplace. How strange was that?

"Aggie working behind the scenes," J.J. suggested.

That had to be it. "Cutler must be royally honked off."

"A safe assumption. Our friend, no doubt, has been on the receiving end."

Deuce had already figured this out for himself. If Aggie had been championing the scheme, they were both on Cutler's shit list. Aggie's attributes mounted. What all this might mean for the relationship between the two of them he couldn't imagine. Of course, strictly speaking, they didn't have a relationship, not since he'd abandoned the union negotiations. So most likely it all meant nothing. Although, curiously, he found himself reluctant to actually talk about Aggie, even with J.J., who continued after a pause, "At no small cost to herself, she's done this thing. We must think of a way to show our gratitude."

Deuce finally said, "She's welcome to the idea."

"Ah," J.J. remarked, and they traveled in silence for a while.

It was taking forever to get to the farm, and Deuce wanted to get this over with.

"So okay, then, what's next, Mr. Deuce?" J.J. asked as he downshifted and waved a car by that had come up on their tail. "Tell me that."

Deuce was happy to stop thinking about the past.

"Next?"

"Now you've had this uplifting union experience, leading the membership in their struggle against the forces of evil. Surely, you're not going to leave it at that."

"Watch me."

J.J. wasn't buying this, either.

"Like it or not, my friend, you're born again, although, admittedly, who the hell knows as what."

Deuce laughed. "Sometimes you're so full of shit, Dusterhoft. What am I gonna do? Go back to playing poker, maybe. Or maybe I'll just sit on my ass. Who says I gotta do anything?"

J.J. contemplated this rebuttal and nodded his head wisely. "A good deal to be said for that. People who do things are betraying their sense of inadequacy. I've always said that."

Deuce laughed again. Dusterhoft was a piece of work.

Finally arriving up at the farm, they rolled the combine off the flatbed and into the equipment shed. The old man's pickup was gone. Deuce felt deflated. He'd psyched himself up for the confrontation, and now the old man wasn't even there.

They climbed back into the truck and headed down to fetch the dozer.

As they drove, Deuce realized that he'd counted on his father being there, to see the expression on his face. Or maybe he wanted to tear into the son of a bitch. Whichever, the business between the two of them wasn't finished. It'd never be finished as long as Deuce stayed in Jackson. Maybe that was what he should do, get the hell out of the city, go somewhere else, anywhere else, get away from the old man.

He thought about the corn.

"You say you know a guy out around Holy Cross?"

"Should I call him?"

"Yeah, what the fuck." Deuce knew some farmers who had bought breeding stock off his father. "Expect I've got a few names to throw into the hat."

"Now you're talking."

They drove on. "I hate to see good corn go to waste," Deuce added, feeling some justification of this about-face was required.

J.J. looked at him with raised eyebrow and the beginnings of a smile. "Sure you do," he said.

CHAPTER 39

~

Saturday night. No beer in the fridge. The dredging finished, Chuck could go off the wagon, but he simply hadn't gotten around to it. He'd stopped smoking years ago. He could give up booze, too, he supposed. The regimen appealed to him. Getting rid of stuff appealed to him. Discard the booze, then while he was at it the rest, too—job, property, friends, wife, children. Walk into the woods and keep on walking. He had thought he'd be dead by thirty-five, and here he was, nine years later. Maybe he'd end up like Orv Massey and live forever.

Diane offered him some of her wine, and he accepted. He had his scuba gear spread across the kitchen floor and was scrubbing the oil off the lens of a new mask. The kids were in bed, Francine gone back to Waterloo for the weekend. Diane brought the glasses over and sat at the table across from him.

"I talked to Kitty Kelley today."

"You two are getting pretty thick."

"You might say we share a problem."

Chuck looked up and smiled. "And what might that be?"

Diane smiled back, one of her nice-try-Romeo smiles. "According to Kitty, her father intends to mount a flood fight out on the island. I thought you said you were going to close the project down until the flood was over."

Chuck had told no one of his thinking on the matter except Jack...and Diane in passing.

Diane crossed her arms, a way she had of satirizing his favorite pose, and gave him a canny look. "So which is it?"

Chuck went back to working on the mask with pad and scouring powder.

"There'll be a flood fight. But if things get too dangerous, I'll shut the site down."

He had a vision of the river in full flow, current rushing along like a class-three rapids on the Colorado, access road long gone, Orv Massey ferrying the construction workers over to the city levee before the track was overwhelmed. Assuming, of course, that Orv would still be available—the Coast Guard would close the river at some point—and assuming that Kelley pretty damn quickly started to take the problem of flotsam seriously enough to talk to the old man about positioning barges at the head of the island, assuming these things and a thousand others, as well.

"Kitty seemed to think you'd close down the job just to spite her father."

"She can think whatever she wants."

"Of course, I don't think that." Chuck concentrated on the mask, working carefully around the edge of the lens, but he felt Diane watching him. "What I think is that your dislike of Jack Kelley will lead you to do something stupid, something you wouldn't normally do. You won't intend for it to happen, but it will."

Chuck carried the mask over to the sink and rinsed it off and held it up to the light, looking for the telltale refractions that would betray leftover oil. He came back to the table and put the mask down and took a mouthful of wine as he decided which piece of equipment he would check out next. Then, instead of deciding, he sagged back in the chair and stared half-seeing across the room.

≈

Three-quarters of an hour later, nearly ten thirty, he drove along the access road to the track. He'd tried to reach Kelley at home and been told by his wife he was down at the job site. The lurid white glow of light plants set up at either end of the grandstand illuminated the iron skeleton of the building.

He parked. The construction trailer was empty and so he hunted through the hard hats until he found one that fit without the hassle of adjusting the headband and then headed out onto the site. From a pair of cranes nodding past each other hung scaffolding that suggested the gondolas of hot air balloons, gondolas with their sides replaced by railings and roofs added. A third crane was hauling material aloft, insulation at the moment, which ironworkers wearing harnesses and working from the makeshift scaffolds unrolled in baskets in preparation for installing the roofing.

"Slow going," said a voice behind Chuck as he watched the elaborate choreography. Jim Bergman, the foreman for the steel erector, stepped up beside him. "It'll speed up a bit as the coordination between my guys and the operators improves."

"Never going to get very fast."

"Nope. Rather work in the dry."

"What are you doing about mold?" The insulation would get wet before they could get the roof on.

"I've got a chemical I use. Kills it on contact. We're also bringing in some temporary heat from the below and working a small area at a time. Brute force approach, like everything else. Should work."

"Sounds about right." Redundancy. "You seen Jack?"

"Around here somewheres."

Chuck watched the work for a time, then continued his search and found Kelley coming back from the kennels.

As Jack approached, Chuck thought about what Diane had said. He didn't believe that his attitude toward Kelley would influence his behavior, but he wasn't absolutely sure on that point. Who could be absolutely sure about anything? Anyway, his dismissive attitude toward the man, which to tell the truth he rather enjoyed, was a luxury he couldn't afford at the moment. Liking Kelley might be out of the question, but he had to work with him. He had to bend over backward to work with him. There'd be plenty of time to return to a more convivial relationship later.

CHAPTER 40

~

Jack finally went back to Sunday Mass at St. Columbkille's, having missed one week because he was so pissed off at Mike Daugherty and another because he came down with the flu. He still felt tired, and he felt frustrated because he felt tired, tired and inefficient and even incompetent, forgetting stuff he had no right forgetting, sick or not. Illness reminded him of childhood. It seemed atavistic, like a childhood sickness come back to plague him rather than anything adult. He hated it. And so, exhausted though he was, he got up and went to Mass with Janelle and Kitty, and the obligation to go was only part of it.

In church he made a special effort to concentrate on the words, the service divided into brief involuntary naps and episodes of a fierce commitment to the meaning of the sacrament.

On the way out, Father Mike accosted him.

"Have you got a second?" Mike asked under his breath as the Family Kelley arrived at his post in the narthex, it being too rainy to greet the exiting communicants outside as he normally liked to. It seemed Jack could never leave Mass except that Mike had to have a private word with him.

Before Jack could reply, Mike said, "It'll just take a sec." He raised his hand, traffic-cop fashion, to hold up the proceedings while he drew Jack aside and said what he had to say in a single breath.

"Can you come to the rectory sometime this afternoon? Any time, whenever it's convenient. Just you. Won't take long. It's got nothing to do with Tony Vasconcellos or anybody named Vasconcellos. Come. Do. I'll be there. Almost no chance I'll get called out, not on Sunday afternoon. Call ahead if you want. Or not. Whatever."

"I don't know, Mike."

"If you can."

And the priest had turned back to the others before Jack could think of anything else to say.

In the car driving back home, Janelle made no comment upon the priest's importuning of Jack. Sometimes he felt he ought to put in a good word on Mike's behalf, a kind of preemptive strike, even when Janelle hadn't opened her mouth. But not now.

Instead he drove without a word, trying to decide whether he would go see Mike, wondering what could be so important—aside from the Vasconcelloses—that the priest must see him. They were still on the outs, hadn't dealt with the issues piled up between them, and it could be, Jack supposed, that Mike had decided the time had come to do that. Yet the priest's anxiety had seemed of a different kind somehow, more something new than old.

And what about himself, Jack wondered. Did he want a heart-to-heart with Mike? With the flood coming and the future uncertain, he supposed it was a good time to clear the air. Probably it was. His exhaustion undermined his resistance to this idea. And a couple of blocks farther along, it even occurred to him that his illness might have changed the situation slightly between the two of them. He might even be able to talk to Mike about the state of his faith now. Of course, what else would you talk to your priest about? Not Jack. Not with Mike. It was the last thing he would have discussed with him. He'd rather have hashed it over with Janelle, Janelle of all people.

He glanced at his beloved. She rode peering ahead, moving her head just enough to miss nothing, impressive in profile, all her force of authority gathered in her prominent, resolutely straight nose. Face on, she was so thin that you might contemplate putting one over on her, but when you saw that profile, you knew.

Jack sighed and turned away. Janelle? No, no way. He had no one to talk to, and wasn't even sure, as a matter of fact, that he wanted to talk to anyone. To do it properly would take a lifetime, he imagined. For a long time, he'd struggled against the erosion of…not his faith, for that remained, would always remain, even though he had lost any ability to articulate it. Faith didn't depend upon your ability to talk about it. Atheists, he thought, were people who had lost this ability but felt compelled to go on talking anyway. For Jack, faith remained, even if much of its substrate had vanished, the hardpan of his literal childhood beliefs eroded away, the mineral grains scattered.

During his illness, when he had seemed most childlike and help-less to himself, his first faith had momentarily returned, the lived experience. Just in flashes. It couldn't survive the thinking about it. By a kind of trick of the mind, he clung to it, but only for ever-briefer moments and only tainted by the effort. An insight came. Even as a child, he seemed to recall something tentative in his acceptance of the teachings. God had not spoken to him, only human beings had. Even then, even as a five-year-old, his toy faith must have changed, grown, waivered on the basis of the string of priests and nuns and laity that he had encountered, each person different, each haunted in some way, their human frailties like being possessed. A child must wonder on some level. Life was such a curious business, how could he not? And hadn't Jack wondered, even at that early age? He seemed to remember so.

Perhaps that was it. Faith didn't descend from the ether, but must be built and rebuilt and rebuilt again, an act of the will. He could talk to Mike about this. Or rather, he could *maybe* talk to Mike about this.

He could certainly go and see him. Yes, that much at least.

CHAPTER 41

~

"What a week!"

El spoke to the walls. After two months in which Sundays had consisted of church and campaigning, never a moment to herself, she was gloriously alone. Walter had gone up to the lock and dam. Tows were still being locked through despite the rising river. Then he was going to the Ice Harbor, where the gates were being closed. Then to the railroad bridge where he and the fellows sent by Mick Kilmer were to take their readings, then somewhere else, maybe down to the Herrigs to look at his instrument shelter, maybe to the station despite the fact that he had a girl who did the forecasts on weekends. Walter was beside himself, gathering his beloved data by the bushel basket.

El, on the other hand, wanted nothing so much as a little time to herself. She felt like the mayor of the *Titanic*. God willing, nothing would go wrong for a minute or two. After finishing the Sunday paper in the kitchen, she'd made another mug of tea and taken it up to her room on the second floor of the tower of their Queen Anne. She settled herself in the comfortable rattan reading chair and picked up the murder mystery she'd started many weeks earlier and opened to her bookmark. She read a few lines and realized she'd forgotten who was whom, and she'd have to go back, which at the moment seemed like too much of an effort. So instead she sat with the book closed on her lap, doing nothing, which was what she really wanted to do. "What a week!"

On Tuesday she'd been elected mayor and already that seemed like another era. The flood was rushing down upon them. And here was Fritz, turning up again, trouble as always.

She found her mind slipping irresistibly back toward her public burden. And caught herself. She wasn't going to think about that. She was going to take a few minutes for herself.

Stuffing the book into the side of the seat cushion, the tough, smooth fibers of the wickerwork rubbing her knuckles, she picked up her tea mug and held the rim against her lower lip without drinking. She'd always loved that room. Round rooms were so much more… healing. What a blessing to live in a house with three of them, the sitting room directly below and Walter's study overhead and this, hers.

She closed her eyes, feeling the mug against her lip, and wondered if she should at last take Walter up on his offer to switch with her. To give her the top-floor view. From the second floor, the nearby houses interfered, and looking down on the city was like reading a story with pages missing. She opened her eyes, sipped the lukewarm tea, and set the mug back down.

The doorbell rang.

She started at the unexpected sound and then thought, *Oh, no*, and then, as she waited, *It was too much to hope for.*

For several long moments, nothing happened. Maybe the person would go away.

The trouble was, she realized, that she'd left her car out. She hadn't put it in the garage and closed the door as she should have. If she wasn't there, why was her car there?

The doorbell rang again. It was the back door. Strangers usually came to the front.

Still, she might wait the person out. She got up and went over to the window on the driveway side. A mistake. As she looked down, she saw a woman standing next to the car and staring up, right at her. The jig was up. So much for her pleasant few hours alone.

Downstairs she opened the back door and said, "You."

Rachel Brandeis stood outside. Talk about trouble.

"Walter's not here," El told her.

"I came to see you."

There was, of course, no reason to find that surprising. El was mayor, after all.

"Well, you're just getting wet standing out there. Come in."

In the kitchen El turned on the overhead light as the reporter fished her notebook out from beneath her raincoat. The two of them remained standing, chatting briefly until, in the normal rhythm of such encounters, the moment came to put pleasantries aside.

"I understand there was a meeting at city hall yesterday morning," Brandeis began.

"Is that a question?" El asked, partly to cover her surprise.

"I've been told you were there, along with the city manager and Chuck Fellows and Harvey Butts."

"Who told you?"

"I don't reveal my sources."

Of course she didn't. El was thinking furiously. For the moment she didn't worry about who the source had been. She could deal with that later. More important now was what Brandeis knew, or thought she knew.

"What can I do for you?" El asked her.

"There was a meeting?"

El nodded.

"Can you tell me what happened?"

"It was not a public meeting."

"I understand you considered a number of options with regard to the city's flood protection system. Is that correct?"

El regarded the reporter intently. When Brandeis had come to Jackson in the fall, young and bright and untested, there had been something appealingly open and uncertain about her, along with her obvious intelligence. Then, for months, she had covered the death throes of the meatpacking company. That experience seemed to have done something to her. She was a bit more seasoned now, but a good deal less appealing. Perhaps her youth had something to do with it, an unwillingness to expose herself to the manipulations of people older than herself. Perhaps, later in life, with even more experience, she'd become a little less...El wasn't sure, a little less single-minded, perhaps.

The story she'd written about Walter had, as El feared, painted him as this eccentric local weatherman predicting a flood of biblical proportions. Rachel had told them it would probably be picked up by the wires, and it had been. People were starting to call from all over the country. Walter was as much to blame as Fritz and Rachel, but still... Anyway, it was over; it made no difference now. This new story the reporter had her teeth in was likely to be even worse.

"Ask me," El said, "the question you came here to ask."

CHAPTER 42

~

Chuck Fellows listened to his breathing, the higher pitched rasp of the intake, the dying away as he exhaled. A wreath of cold encircled his face at the edge of the neoprene hood. He balanced in the water, kicking just hard enough to overcome the downward tug of his weight belt and continue his slow glide along the sill. Even with the underwater lamp, he could barely make out his surroundings, only a few feet to the front and sides.

The business of closing the Ice Harbor gates was taking too long. After three dives, the effort had begun to tell on him, his muscles cinching up, his stomach beginning to churn.

He found the problem this time, a wedge-like slab of rock he'd somehow missed before, probably not even on the sill earlier but kicked up somehow during the earlier attempts to close the gate.

He swam out toward the river and dropped the stone, a small cloud of black muck rising up and enveloping it.

Then he waited for his nausea to settle before kicking slowly back over the rubber boot at the base of the gate and into the harbor, policing up trash and depositing it in the wire basket he carried for the purpose. No sign of fish. He tried to breathe slowly, conserving oxygen. He had always prided himself on the length of time he could stay down.

Feeling a calf beginning to cramp, he stopped and reached back to tug at the toe of his fin, stretching the muscle until the tension unlocked. Then he started swimming again, but realized at once that he'd become disoriented. He paused, staring at the featureless silty bottom and taking long, slow breaths. His stomach seemed okay for the moment, and so, arching upward, he began to make his way back toward the surface. If he'd been in the Caribbean, he would have been swimming with a buddy and toward the light, but here, in the murk, he swam alone and against the weight of his belt, until he broke the surface.

His chin at water level, the harbor spread away from him like a vast plain, at the far side of which lay the dredge at anchor, surrounded by its skirt of floating discharge pipes. The rain fell haphazardly, fusillades here and there, kicking up bomb craters, the noise almost musical, but muted by the hood of his wet suit.

He hadn't wandered far. He added some air to his buoyancy control device so that he could rest. He'd drunk some river water and was out of shape, but he shouldn't feel this lousy.

Glenn Owens, who normally supervised the drafting room, now manned the dredge's workboat, in which they'd rigged a pump with suction and discharge lines for Chuck to use for the initial cleaning of the sills. Kenny Nauman, a draftsman normally, stood above on the machine shed platform, next to Walt Plowman. On the other side of Plowman stood the cameraman he'd brought, who had draped a plastic sheet over his equipment to protect it. Their story about the closing of the gates was improving at Chuck's expense.

He circled his hand over his head, the signal to take another crack at it, and Nauman disappeared into the shed.

Chuck tried to turn off the air valve at the top of his tank, but couldn't reach it. With the effort, his nausea returned.

He took a deep breath and then lumbered past the workboat and over to the concrete landing, where he unbuckled his weight belt and slung it onto the haulout, then pulled himself up and wriggled out of the scuba tank and shut off the valve. Glenn moored and disembarked and the two of them climbed the stairs back up to the platform above, Glenn hauling the trash basket and Chuck his scuba gear, panting as he'd slowly climbed, feeling worse and worse.

The cameraman was busy shooting the gates as they closed. Walt had out his microphone and was coming forward to resume the dialogue they'd begun before Chuck entered the water, discussing the sealing of the city against the rising Mississippi.

In the heart of the concrete beneath him, the gears and cables strained as the gates swung shut inchwise. The vibrations rose up through the soles of his feet and into his queasy stomach. He felt rotten.

"Looks like you ain't much of a fisherman," Walter said, observing the basket with its rusted cans and bottles and other debris.

At the moment, Chuck wasn't interested in lighthearted exchanges, his stomach roiling. His balance was none too certain, either. He'd never felt this bad after a dive. When Walt started to ask a question, Chuck held up his hand and shook his head.

He was breathing through his mouth. His stomach was pushing up against his diaphragm, and he was sweating.

"Always thought I might like to try this," Glenn Owens was saying as he inspected Chuck's scuba equipment.

"Way I feel right now," Chuck told him, "you could buy a set of gear real cheap."

The gates continued their transit, their leading edges creeping toward each other. From the machine shed issued the high pitch of the electric engine and all around him, it seemed, the groaning of cables and gears.

Chuck's insides surged violently upward, and he rushed to the edge of the platform, barely making it before his stomach turned inside out, the vomit spewing down the wall and onto the steps below.

He heaved again and again. Finally, spent, he leaned hard against the railing, sucking in air.

He could feel the presence of the others behind him.

"You okay, boss?" Glenn said softly.

Chuck stood up and wiped his mouth with the sleeve of his wet suit.

"Probably drank some river water," Walt suggested. "Full of all kind of stuff not fit for human consumption."

Chuck shook his head and took another deep breath, sweat pouring off him.

The two gates swung slowly, patiently toward each other, almost closed.

To push aside the sense of awkwardness he felt, Chuck closed his eyes briefly and leaned on the railing and tried to remember what he had to do next. The brewery. He had a meeting set up. They were right next to the levee and needed to think about pulling the machinery out of their basement and filling it with city water.

When he looked up again, the harbor gates had silently seated themselves.

Kenny Nauman came back out of the shelter, where he had been keeping his eye on the motor.

"Look okay this time?" he asked Chuck.

"Yupper," Glenn said.

"Looks fine," Chuck agreed, still breathing through his mouth.

He felt the cool of drying sweat on his forehead and swallowed again, tasting the acid. But he felt okay now, except for a residue of embarrassment. The others, however, after their initial sympathy, had said nothing more about it, as if it had never happened.

With them, he gazed at the barrier zigzagging along the waterfront, continuous now, separating the city from the river. As his eye traced the path of the wall, Chuck became conscious of something new. He turned his head away, then looked back. Yes, he could sense it, something that had been absent before. The flood fight, up to that moment, had been hardly more than an abstract engineering exercise. At this river stage, do this, at that, do that. Stick to the drill. Let the local yokels go bugfuck. But the river had spread over its embankment and was creeping steadily upward toward the battlement raised against it. The floodwall itself seemed unsubstantial, even a joke. He knew the strength of concrete and knew the safety factor built into the system, but nevertheless the wall, barely a foot wide, appeared such a flimsy barrier against the great hydraulic power of the Mississippi. Now, with the closing of the gate, with the wall sealed, the flood had finally become something beyond a technical matter, become a living, gut-level reality, a mindless force against which to pit his meager human intentions.

The others perhaps felt something similar, for they all stood saying nothing, just staring at the scene before them.

"Pump her down to eight feet," Chuck finally told Kenny Nauman. Storm sewers north and south would now be closed, to keep the river from backing up onto the city, and runoff from storms be diverted to the harbor where Kenny could pump it over the wall.

❧

After answering Walt's questions on camera, Chuck changed back into his civvies, stowed his gear in the 4x4, and started toward the brewery. As he drove along the nearly deserted road, a car passed going in the other direction, something vaguely familiar about it.

The focus created by the task of closing the gates began to dissipate, and beneath his stronger emotions a familiar, weaker one revealed itself: his dissatisfaction. He thought about losing his lunch. Maybe it had been the water, but he was thirty pounds overweight and way out of shape; it could have been that. Or it could have been something else. Who knows why things happened?

He drove, nursing his dissatisfaction, and only when he glanced in the rearview mirror and saw the car behind him, the same one that had passed a couple of minutes earlier going in the other direction, did he realize that he was being followed.

He pulled over and climbed out and, still under the sway of his annoyance with himself, slammed the door shut.

CHAPTER 43

~

A nd so Jack went to see Father Mike after all.

Sister Ursula answered, but even as the door swung open, Jack heard quick steps on the stairway inside and Father Mike's voice, "I've got it, sister." He came into view, a little breathless, and laid a hand on her shoulder, removing it at once. "It's for me."

Sister nodded, accepting, observant but unquestioning, and took herself off. The relationship between Mike and Ursula had always been a little mysterious to Jack. She taught math at the parish school, one of the last nuns on the faculty, and cooked and cleaned for Mike, a kind of working wife without the sex.

Almost gleefully, Mike led the way into the east parlor and when Jack started to head for his usual chair said, "No, no, back here," and continued on, into his cramped study, a triangular room fashioned from one of the leftover spaces in the rectory-cum-octagon house.

"Can I get you something, Jack?"

Mike always asked. Recently, while they'd been clashing over the Vasconcellos business, Jack had made a point of refusing, but now he said, "How about a cup of coffee?"

"Leaded? I'll get us each one. Back in a sec."

Left alone, Jack shifted one of the chairs to give himself more leg room, then sat and looked about. Whatever Mike had on his mind, he apparently didn't want Sister Ursula to overhear.

A minute later, Mike hustled back in. "It's on the way."

Jack said, "You remember the last time I was in this room, Mike?"

"Not sure. Last September?"

"Last September." When Jack had come bringing the half-formed idea of unburdening himself to the priest, and before he could, Mike had dragged Tony and Angela Vasconcellos into the conversation.

Now Mike said, "Not to worry. Nothing like that will happen this time."

"What *will* happen?"

"Let's wait until the coffee comes." Mike enjoyed his mysteries. "Tell me about the track. Is it true? You're really going to mount a flood fight down there? How fascinating."

"*Fascinating* isn't the word I would have chosen." Jack described his preparations. Mike asked questions. He'd always been interested in such matters, in almost all matters. He had the gift of being interested; that was one thing you could say about Mike Daugherty. Because of him, St. Columbkille's was a hive of the parishioners' enthusiasms brought to life—the midweek revival lunch, the historical wall in the school cafeteria, the peace tree, the returnees' monthly potluck, and so on and so forth. There wasn't an idea so crackpot that Mike couldn't figure a way to make it materialize.

Thus he asked eagerly about the track, and Jack elaborated, and in the process found his own commitment to the flood fight acquiring a bit more of an edge. He recalled for Mike's benefit the discussion he'd had with Chuck Fellows the night before, Fellows playing the role of Cassandra, but at least trying to be helpful for once. First reluctantly and then more readily and finally losing all sense of time, Jack elaborated on the measures already under way and the various dangers posed by the rising waters.

Sister Ursula had long come and gone, the coffee already growing cold before they arrived at the reason Mike wanted to see him.

Mike tapped a fingertip on the saucer, a musical ting-ting-ting-ting, and looked past Jack, his eyes going suddenly dull. The tinging stopped.

"I'm leaving St. C.'s."

"What?" Jack was shocked.

"I'm being transferred. The personnel committee, in its infinite wisdom."

"Where? Why?"

"St. Dominic's in Maquoketa."

This news so startled Jack that he didn't know quite what to say. "But why?"

"The official reason or the real one?"

"Both."

"Officially. Well, as you know, a lot of Mexicans have come north to work in the new meatpacking plant down there. The parish has been overrun with them. So they need some help. I'm going down as the associate." He shook his head. "Can you believe that? The associate. Like some kid straight out of seminary."

"Frankly, no, I can't believe it. How's your Spanish?"

Mike just smiled. "This has nothing to do with my linguistic abilities, believe me. I'll tell you what's really going on. The Chancery has had me on their watch list for a long time now. I've been too successful. Priests in other parishes don't much like losing their seed stock, and they've been complaining. Of course, no one will admit it, but that's what's happening. They've been looking for an excuse. Now they've found one." Jack had heard that there were complaints, too many people from other parishes opting into St. C's, but it was common nowadays. People crossed parish lines—looking for a better school, a jazzier homily, a priest who sympathized with the ways modern Catholics cut corners. That couldn't be the only reason. There must be more to it.

"I just don't know what to say, Mike."

"Say nothing, then."

"Does Sister know?"

"Oh, yes. Probably before I did."

Jack didn't quite understand, then, why Mike insisted on talking to him in private, if Ursula already knew. Complaining to a member of the laity wouldn't be good form, perhaps that was it.

Jack said, "There'll be a protest."

"I'm going to discourage that sort of thing. It'll accomplish nothing, just get a story in the paper, more dirty linen. The Church has enough troubles… Anyway, I wanted to see you, to make everything okay between you and me."

"Of course."

"As far as the Vasconcelloses are concerned, I don't know. I'm sorry it's been so hard on you. Spillover effects. Although, in all honesty, it couldn't be helped. I'd do it all over again. The Vasconcelloses are still together. Dysfunctional as hell, but still together. Sometimes that's the best you can do. But I am sorry, Jack."

"Forget it," Jack found himself saying.

Mike nodded. "Thank you."

In the silence that followed, Jack felt the oddness of such an end to their relationship. It had been unhappy of late, certainly, and perhaps it would have gotten even worse, Jack didn't know. But he'd always assumed it would continue. It should have continued.

"I'm sorry, Mike. If what you say is correct, the personnel board should be brought to account."

"Oh, it's correct all right. And I'll tell you, Jack, just between the two of us—I wouldn't say this to another soul in St. C's—if the

Church was just the Chancery, if it was just the damn hierarchy, I'd leave the priesthood. You're shocked? Well, it's true, I would."

Jack was shocked, although less that Mike harbored such feelings than that he'd reveal them to someone like himself. The two of them had never been *that* intimate. On the other hand, Jack had no idea whom the priest might actually take into his confidence. He'd never talked about priest friends. He seemed to know everybody and nobody.

Mike regarded Jack closely, stripping away the space separating them. "Part of the trouble between us, Jack, between you and me, is you have in your mind the idea of what a Priest, capital P, should be. No, let me finish. Of course, I can't know what you really think, not for sure. But I bet I'm right on this one. You measure me against this ideal you carry around in your head. Even when you imagine I might have sinned, the sins you assign me are the ones of other priests. There are lots of sins, Jack. Human beings are subject to them all, and I'm a human being. I'm no more a priest than you're a construction guy. This is a job, not the vocation it used to be. I'm middle management. Like a lot of priests, I came out of a blue-collar family, and my parents thought of the priesthood as a step up. It is, in a way. And don't get me wrong, I'm not without my gifts. I bring something to the Church. They need guys like me. I know how to grow a parish. I understand that the Church is a community of believers. But the truth of the matter is that the priesthood is no longer set apart. I know that…"—he jerked his thumb in the general direction of the Chancery—"…but those guys, forget about it. They think priests are still married to the church, pawns to be manipulated in their little power games."

Jack didn't care about the hierarchy. Or Mike's obvious bitterness. Jack cared about Mike himself, sitting there, looking like Mike always did, thinner but still a little chunky. He carried the weight well. Some men were not meant to be thin but filled out, looking prosperous and pleasant and only so complicated, looking, in fact, like the middle manager out of a blue-collar family that Mike claimed to be.

"You never felt called?" Jack asked, and in asking the question he realized that he did measure Mike against his idea of what a priest should be.

"As a matter of fact," Mike said, "I did." He hesitated, continuing only after a thoughtful pause. "Let me tell you a little story. About a year ago, I was down in the Quad Cities and ran into one of the fellows I went to seminary with. He'd left the priesthood. Sometime in the seventies, when it wasn't so hard to get laicized. He wanted to talk, so we went and got something to eat. A very strange conversation. But revealing in its way. He was anxious to tell me that he hadn't lost his faith, that he still saw the many ways in which God operated in his life. But it turned out he didn't belong to any parish or go to Mass anymore. He was thinking of starting up again, he said, and running into me was fortuitous, whatever that meant. We had a long talk. He told me all about his life since the priesthood. He'd gotten married and gone into social work. You know, the typical ex-priest's shtick. But what he most wanted to assure me of was all the ways that God was still present in his life, an astonishing variety of ways, it turned out. I'm sorry, I shouldn't be so sarcastic. Maybe it wasn't all baloney. But what struck me, listening to this litany, was just how…naive, primitive, I don't know quite the word for it. Like the faith of a seventeen-year-old just entering the seminary, that's what it was. Like it had been preserved under glass or something. Like the kind of thing an archaeologist might dig up."

"Maybe he really believed," Jack suggested, remembering his own recent visit, courtesy of the flu, back to his childhood faith.

"Might be," Mike conceded. "But he wasn't going to Mass, Jack."

"Not fulfilling the obligation."

"Not *practicing*."

"But given the drawbacks of the institution… Consider your own situation."

Mike smiled. "Well, yeah, the institution's totally fucked up, we all know it. But that's not the point."

"Which is?"

"The guy came to me for confession. That's what it amounted to. Three Hail Marys and four Our Fathers, go and sin no more. As if I had the power. For what ailed him, Jack, there was no absolution. But you and I, we're still here. We haven't gone anywhere. Life keeps on getting more complicated, but we're hanging in there. See what I'm saying?"

Jack had been feeling increasingly uncomfortable as he listened, for he knew what this was all about. Not just Mike. Not just the call, which he had once had but which had apparently become misplaced somewhere along the way. Jack recognized Mike's generosity in broaching the matter in this delicate way. But it made no difference. Want to or not, Jack realized that he still wasn't ready to talk about the chaotic state of his own faith, a labyrinth with no entrance.

And he didn't want to hear what Mike had just been at pains to tell him, either. He didn't need a confidant. He didn't need someone trapped in the same complexities Jack found himself in. He needed a Priest.

Chapter 44

～

On Monday morning, when El came downstairs, Walter had already left. The morning paper lay unfolded on the kitchen table so that her attention would be drawn to the lead story. Hardly necessary. She already knew about it. The only question was how bad.

She stared at the paper, pondering whether she should get something to eat first. *How bad, how bad, how bad?*

The three-column headline, visible from across the room (*To Fight or Not to Fight—City Ponders Flood Options*) wasn't a hopeful sign, although El supposed she had seen worse heads. Given her druthers, she'd have all headline writers lined up against a wall and shot.

But, of course, the problem here wasn't the head, it was the fact that the story existed at all. The meeting in Paul Cutler's office on Saturday morning had been behind closed doors. It should have stayed that way. Paul would think she was the leak. It had to have been either Chuck Fellows or Harvey Butts. *It couldn't conceivably have been Paul himself*, she thought, although on the other hand she didn't believe Chuck or Harvey would have done it, either. Perhaps one of them had inadvertently talked to someone else, who had in turn gone to Brandeis. Either way, a very, very bad business.

For half a minute, she stood across from the offending article. If she'd gone to get something to eat at once, maybe she could have delayed the reading, but each intervening thought had added to the burden of her impatience. She went over and seized the paper and read.

"City officials, meeting in private over the weekend, refused to rule out any option in the coming flood fight, including allowing water to go over the protection system."

El groaned. Just as she'd imagined. The worst. Everything lost in the very first sentence.

She read on, although it seemed hardly necessary now, the rest merely a string of footnotes—her claim that they'd never let water go over the wall, that the Corps of Engineers had committed to adding to the system should predictions for the crest rise above thirty feet. Most of the quotes were from Chuck Fellows, who for some reason had laid out the particulars of the meeting for the reporter's benefit. After Fellows got through, the reader might as well have been there. Brandeis, of course, had gone to Fritz Goetzinger for the expected zinger. Harvey Butts, at the opposite extreme, wasn't quoted at all, whatever that might mean. Lawyerly discretion. Nor was Paul, but El knew that he had taken his daughter to Des Moines to participate in the state high school orchestra. He might not even know the story existed.

El tossed the paper down and stood thinking, not as distraught as she would have expected. The story had been perfectly dreadful, and damn that Rachel Brandeis for wringing every ounce of sensationalism out of it, but still, as El mulled over the situation, she realized that she didn't feel that bad. Not good. She didn't feel good.

She remembered her conversation with Ed Ohnesorge after the Friends of the Community breakfast the other day. Ohney was hardly a neutral observer and nothing he said had been new, but perhaps that exchange had nudged her toward the possibility of adding to the flood-wall without assurances the city would be repaid. Or perhaps it had nothing to do with Ohney's argument. Perhaps she'd simply acquired a taste for experiment and risk-taking over the past several months. El had no idea, really, what set the mind off on a different track.

She picked up the paper again and leafed through it until she found the weather map and laid the page out and stared at the big low pressure system moving northeast from the plains states, almost on top of them, and the trailing one in the desert southwest. It helped, seeing the map. From Walter she got weather reports all the time, of course, but that was Walter.

She went out to the back door and looked at the rain and the charcoal pall of clouds overhead. Where would Walter be at the moment? At the station? Down at the Herrigs, checking his instrument platform? When he went to the Herrigs, it was usually at this time of the day.

But, she decided, she'd try the station first.

CHAPTER 45

◆

At the Okey-Dokey next to city hall, Paul Cutler stopped and bought a cup of coffee and a sweet roll and the morning newspaper, folding the paper without a glance. He carried his purchases across the plaza. Another gray day, another storm bearing down on them. Wonderful.

He let himself into city hall and relocked the door behind him. It was just after 7:00 a.m., and the building wouldn't be open for business for another hour. Upstairs, in his office, he left the door open and hung up his raincoat and took a couple of aspirin and a bottle of eye drops out of the top drawer of his desk. He fanned the items he had brought with him across the end of the conference table, the paper still folded, then swallowed the aspirin without water and tilted his head back and squeezed a couple of drops from the bottle into each eye. He stood blinking until his vision cleared, then sat down at the conference table and took a bite of sweet roll and sipped the coffee and sat perfectly still for a minute, conscious of his resistance to the day.

Finally, he opened the paper and read the headline and, quickly, with ballooning uneasiness, the first paragraph of the lead story— "City officials, meeting in private over the weekend, refused to rule out any option in the coming flood fight, including allowing water to go over the protection system."

He took the paper, folded it twice over, slammed it three times against the edge of the table—*Shit! Shit! Shit!*—then flung it across the room. "SHIT!" The pages, unfolding in midflight, began to come apart and dived, like a shot quail, toward the floor.

Paul stared, his mouth working, in the grip of his anger, even as his mind told him again what he had been telling himself for months. He should have left Jackson while he had the chance!

❧

"Conditions are getting worse," Fellows told Paul matter-of-factly as soon as he was through the door. Paul had left a message that he wanted to see Fellows the minute he arrived.

Paul smiled. "Is that right?" He held up the newspaper, retrieved and reassembled. "You didn't happen to see this little item, did you?"

"The story about the meeting? Yeah." Unceremoniously, Fellows planted himself in one of the chairs. "Whoever leaked it should be shot."

"It wasn't you?"

"No way. If I want to fuck somebody over, I don't do it behind his back."

"I'm sure that's commendable. Please explain to me then why you felt called upon to describe the whole damn meeting to Brandeis."

"She already had the story. Had some of her facts screwed up, too. I set her straight."

"I'm not going to ask why you did that. I don't want to know." Paul didn't understand Fellows. The man was a Neanderthal. "Tell me, Chuck, are we going to let water go over the wall?"

"No."

"That's right, no. That's the story here, Chuck, the whole…fucking…story. All this other stuff is irrelevant. What in God's name were you thinking, man?" Again, he brandished the newspaper.

Fellows sat with his arms crossed, bellicose and cocksure as usual. Paul always suspected such people of being drawn, like moths, to oversimplification, and he listened with rising irritation as Fellows described his rationale. Which didn't take long. Fellows never bothered to nuance anything he said, just laid it all out, so many slabs of meat on a butcher block. He finished by repeating that he didn't know where Brandeis found out about the meeting in the first place. Probably Plowman.

"Frankly," Paul told him, "I don't give a damn where she got it." He picked up the receiver of his phone and pressed down the plunger as he continued to talk. "Where she got it is irrelevant." His anger renewed itself sentence by sentence. "There should've been nothing for her to get. For Christ's sake, man, use your head!"

Disgusted, he dialed the newspaper and asked for the city editor.

"We've got a problem, Neal."

Paul proceeded to tell him that Brandeis had misinterpreted what Chuck had told her, that the city had never, even for a moment, contemplated letting water go over the wall. The meeting had been nothing but a brainstorming session, everything on the table to begin with—that was the nature of such get-togethers—but the idea of simply letting water go over the wall had been dismissed immediately after it was raised.

As he made his points, he listened to the silences and brief noncommittal questions at the other end of the line.

"I would've told all this to Rachel Brandeis if she'd bothered to wait for me to get back to her. There was no story here, Neal. I can't tell you how much damage you've done."

"Perhaps it was a matter that shouldn't have come up at all," the editor suggested mildly.

"C'mon, Neal, give me a break. You know how these meetings go. All kinds of crackpot ideas get discussed. That's the whole point. People can say whatever comes into their heads precisely because it's *not going to go public*. You know that." It really torqued Paul off. Fellows was right about one thing. Whoever leaked the information should be shot. If it was El…

He continued to argue, managing to extract a commitment to run a follow-up story with Paul's interpretation of the meeting. Not that anyone would believe his interpretation.

He hung up. "Maybe that will help. Probably not."

Fellows slouched in his chair, arms folded, barely contrite.

"What the *hell* were you thinking?" Again Paul's voice climbed word by word. "Now we've got no credibility in the city at all, not a shred!"

Fellows stroked his jaw and finally said, "Shit, yeah," which was as close, it turned out, as Paul got to an admission that Chuck had screwed up. Just totally fucking screwed up! Nothing to be done, Paul decided, calming down a little. Chuck Fellows was a lost cause. The sooner he was gone, the better.

Unless Paul was shown the door first.

CHAPTER 46

❧

Picking the corn was in no way an orderly exercise, J.J. Dusterhoft noted. The pickers consisted of local farm families, a band of 4-H kids, and a Boy Scout troop, but mostly a ragtag assortment of the young and old from who knows where, truants from school, escapees from rest homes, drawn here perhaps out of a sense of solidarity with Fritz Goetzinger or perhaps merely for a bit of fun, the opportunity to pick corn the old-fashioned way.

The two wagons crept through the water at a distance from one another, pickers clustered around each, lobbing corn into the boxes. Other people worked alone or in small, chummy groups wandering here and there, husking the corn with the antique hooks and pegs the old-timers had scrounged from attics and cellars and barns and storage sheds. Former husking champion Fred Stanek—who had regaled them with stories about the days of open-pollinated corn before all the high-yield varieties and mechanical harvesting—possessed many of the devices, which he drew one after another from the deep pockets of his foul-weather gear.

Most everybody seemed to be having a good time, and J.J. was tickled that he'd goaded Deuce into organizing it, although at the moment his friend could hardly be said to be entering into the spirit of the occasion.

One of the wagons was drawn by a team of handsome black Percherons, prancing even in a foot of water, show horses on a lark. A bangboard, on the same principle as the backboard for a basketball hoop, had been erected along one side of the wagon to catch errant tosses from the pickers. The second wagon was an altogether sadder affair, resurrected from the far precincts of some barn where it had lay moldering for who knows how long. To it were harnessed a mismatched pair of horses, the equine version of disgruntled old retirees pressed back into service.

J.J. and Deuce and Stanek and a drove of others were lobbing ears into the wagon drawn by the Percherons.

J.J. had stationed himself where he might see both Deuce and, in the distance, Deuce's father. Fritz moved through the splintered and canted stalks, not picking corn, but rather passing from person to person, young and old, shaking hands and saying a few words to each. His trajectory and that of the group around the Percherons intersected.

Only the highest ears of corn on the stalks were being picked, those well above the water, which hadn't yet had the nutrients leached out of them. The river sloshed about the calves of J.J.'s waders, and he felt it creeping up to his knees, although he knew that that must be an illusion since it was rising too slowly to be perceived. The mud beneath sucked at the soles of the boots.

Deuce hadn't shown much interest in the different husking devices, but J.J. noted that he had picked up the technique from Stanek right away, and he moved along stripping the husks aside, snapping the ears clean from their shanks and tossing them into the wagon with a single fluid motion. A natural athlete. Unlike J.J., who was always much too interested in the why and the how of a thing to ever become one with it.

Deuce seemed to be ignoring the progress of his father from picker to picker. The ex-mayor spoke to everyone, even the youngest, coming to a full stop each time and bringing his total attention upon the person.

He was getting quite close now. Deuce fired an ear hard off the bangboard, showing his displeasure.

The rain had begun again, not hard, but steady.

J.J. stopped for a moment and rubbed and rotated the shoulder of his throwing arm, bitching pleasantly. Deuce said nothing.

Husking again, J.J. went a little slower, a little stiffer.

Fritz was right on top of them now, expressing his gratitude to Stanek, taking an extra minute to chat with the old man, seeming more outgoing than J.J. remembered him from before all his troubles. Stanek dug into his pocket and produced yet another husking hook, which he gave to Fritz, demonstrating the proper technique.

The two men walked side by side as Fritz practiced. Deuce in the meantime had picked up his pace, grabbing corn left and right, husking it almost savagely. He started to swing out and past his father, and it appeared for a moment as if he might avoid Fritz altogether, but as he moved to go by, Fritz, without even looking at him, reached out a hand and grasped the sleeve of his jacket.

The moment had come.

Fritz, still looking at Stanek, took a step farther along before his gaze swung around on his son.

Because Deuce didn't offer to shake hands, his father reached out and took up his hand himself, holding it as he spoke briefly. Deuce had his back turned, so J.J. couldn't see the expression on his face or hear what he had to say, if anything. The father had moved close to the son to speak his few words. Just a few.

And then he moved on, turning and coming back toward J.J. himself now, having spent barely more time with Deuce than with any of the other pickers, far less then with Fred Stanek.

Near at hand, Fritz appeared different, lacking the presence he had seemed to possess at a distance, as if, perhaps, his consciousness still lay back with his son.

"Thank you...thank you," he said as he clasped J.J.'s hand, awkwardly because of the husking devices they wore. Fritz had only a feed hat on his head, despite the rain, and his slicker flapped open. His eyes rested momentarily on J.J.'s, coming into focus the way a penny set ringing on a table twirls around and then thumps into place. He nodded and hesitated a moment longer, taking a second look, before moving on.

J.J. listened to him splashing away behind, and then the sound of the splashing ceasing as he paused to thank the next person.

Now, his father having passed by, Deuce waited for J.J. to catch up and then passed judgment on the passage.

"Tell me the son of a bitch isn't running for office."

They continued picking, and J.J., with leisure to meditate upon the matter, wondered at this unremitting animosity from son to father. Deuce had rescued Fritz's combine and now he was picking his father's corn, and still must needs slam the man at every opportunity.

Yet, upon further reflection, it wasn't just the son who had betrayed a contrary streak. Fritz had been more subtle, perhaps, but he'd had a hand to play, too, when he doled out to Deuce exactly the same amount of gratitude he'd given everyone else, as if blood was no thicker than water.

On visualizing again the brief scene between father and son, J.J. seemed to remember something more, a certain extra intensity in Fritz's grasping of his son's hand, something in his look meant to call forth a further interaction if only Deuce should want it. Or to under-line Deuce's failure to want it.

And yet... and yet Deuce had helped Fritz, that much was to be said. And Fritz had been grateful, if perhaps not properly so.

When all was said and done, though, the interchange must have been unsatisfactory, whatever those unheard words passing between them had been. J.J. would never have imagined that charity could be warfare by other means, but in this, obviously, his imagination was deficient.

Ah, he thought, *families!*

CHAPTER 47

~

A s city council members made their way to the emergency meeting that night, rain hammered on roofs and asphalt and car tops,
choking downspouts and running in sheets over the tops of gutters,
the torrents swirling down streets into whirlpools at storm drains.
The streets were drowned. The wind-like sound across the windless
landscape died away only to swell with renewed fury, a fearful noise
that reached into people and touched some secret, forgotten reservoir
of fear.

On the main stem of the Mississippi and the major tributaries
to the north—the Minnesota, St. Croix, Chippewa, Wisconsin—and
the numberless smaller streams, the water continued to rise. A Presi-
dential Disaster had been declared in Minnesota and Wisconsin, and
still the water continued to rise.

~

Walter Plowman stood at the lectern, answering questions.

"Thirty-six hours ago, this storm was centered over western Kansas," he told the council members. El had asked him to speak, the
emergency meeting called so quickly that few members of the public
were present. Walter was talking to the council and the city officials
and the press, and that was about it, except for whoever had happened
to turn their TV on to the local-access channel.

"It's been complicated by a mass of cold air working its way down
from Canada," Walter continued. "It could have nudged the new
storm south of us. What happened instead—the storm kept coming
and rode up over the cold air mass. As warm, saturated air rises, it
cools. Water vapor condenses. This intensifies the rain." He was using
no visual aids. The storm outside was all he needed.

"Talk about the other storms coming, Walter," El said.

He had become her expert witness. The whole business had for him an eerie, unreal quality. Here El was, after all the times she had wormed admissions of uncertainty out of him, suddenly insisting upon the worst.

For the council's benefit, he tracked backward along the still stationary jet stream, from the present storm to the next one coming in from the Four Corners to yet another one just now approaching the California coast.

"What causes a major flood," he explained, "is when heavy rainfall comes after the smaller tribs fill the channel and valley storage. That's happened. This rain is on top of that. There's no storage anywhere in the system anymore. It's got no place to go but into the Mississippi and the major tributaries.

"What about all these reservoirs on the river?" the newest council member, elected to fill El's old seat, asked. "Aren't they for flood control?"

"The headwaters reservoirs? Flood control and recreation," Walter told him.

"Won't they mitigate the flood?"

"Yes. But you've got to understand, they only control about 10 percent of the drainage area. At the beginning of the winter, the Corps of Engineers draws them down to accept melt the following spring. And they usually break up one to two weeks later than the Mississippi, so the runoff is delayed. That's another thing—the timing. For instance, on the Chippewa, you usually have about a week after melt before the crest gets to the Mississippi, but it's been delayed this year. It looks like it might coincide with the crest coming down the main stem. When crests are added to each other like that, the flood gets worse."

He continued, answering questions at length, and El let him talk, never once telling him to get to the point or go on to something else. This freedom to keep on talking felt as eerie as everything else, and Walter at first thought that she must believe him now. Yet as he elaborated, keeping one eye on her, he seemed to detect an increasing impatience and decided it must be a tactic, allowing him to go on and on. She must feel that all these details bolstered his credibility in the eyes of the council. She didn't necessarily accept them. She was putting up with them was all.

"So tell me," Roger Filer said, "this new figure—twenty-eight feet—still a couple of feet below the top of the wall. Just how accurate is it?" Filer didn't seem to have quite gotten over his defeat at El's hands yet, and had been silent up to that point. But Walter was glad for the question and said so.

"As you move downstream, your predictions get better because you have more data points. To miss by two-tenths of a foot, a couple of inches, at St. Louis might mean that the forecaster had done a sloppy job, whereas in a small headwater stream, your prediction might be off by as much as two feet."

"And here?"

Mick thought he could hit it within a half foot in Jackson, but Walter had his doubts. They were already starting to lose gauging stations and go blind. And Mick had his share of the Corps of Engineers' can-do bravado. "I'd say a foot," he told Filer.

"So, twenty-nine feet then. And the Corps still won't act?"

From his seat back among the other staffers, Chuck Fellows said, "No advance measures below thirty feet."

"So we're almost there."

"But the Corps wouldn't accept the twenty-nine-foot figure, would they?" asked Bill Pfohl, another of the men on the council. El and Sister Jean had been letting the men do all the questioning.

"No, that's right," Walter agreed. "The prediction's twenty-eight feet. That's what they'll go with."

"But when it gets to thirty," Filer said, "then they'll act?"

"That's right," Chuck answered.

A brief lull descended upon the meeting, until El said, "If there are no more questions for Walter…" She looked right and left, then back to Walter. "Thank you very much for your time."

Out in the hall, on his way back to KJTV to prepare his ten o'clock cast, Walter paused to listen to the muffled voices on the other side of the chamber door. Moments earlier, has he had left, he and Chuck had acknowledged each other with slight grimaces and nods as Chuck approached the podium, taking Walter's place. Now, listening to his friend's indistinct voice, knowing what he was saying, Walter remembered the moment last fall when Chuck had arrived for the first time at the TV station, come to ask Walter about the possibility of a spring flood. No, that wasn't right; it hadn't been about a flood. Chuck had wanted to know about freeze-up on the river, when that would occur. He'd been concerned about the dredging for the dog track. It had only been afterward that they'd talked about the sequence leading to a big spring rise. And since then, one after another, these events had come to pass. Walter and Chuck had watched, just the two of them at first. For months, the spring flood had been theirs alone. Now, it belonged to everyone.

Walter listened to the voice on the other side of the door, telling the council what the two of them had known all along.

$\sim$

After further discussion, the Jackson city council voted unanimously to add emergency flood protection to the top of the city's existing system.

PART IV

Chapter 48

~

Seven days later, Chuck Fellows and the others leaned into the storm as they left the construction trailer on the Ice Harbor peninsula and made their way toward the dike.

The normal landmarks dividing the day into periods for work and play and sleep had been obliterated. Now Chuck worked, catching a bite to eat or a few hours of shut-eye when he could. As public works director, with an emergency declared, allowing the city to implement its emergency plan, he led the flood fight. The city council and the city manager remained officially in charge, but when there were decisions to be made, Chuck made them.

The weather had also blurred the days into a sameness. Overhead, clouds packed the sky, creating a permanent dusk. This storm was salted with snowflakes, large and ragged, slashed at by the rain, and on impact turning in a moment from white to gray to light to nothing.

The small group walked along Fourth Street, which cut diagonally across the peninsula. Once it had been the main entrance to the city, before the elevated Mesquatie Bridge had been built across the river to East Jackson. Now the old artery carried almost no traffic. It had been stubbed off at the levee, the Fourth Street Bridge long since torn down.

Walt Plowman led the way. Chuck had asked him to talk about the history of the Ice Harbor area, which was not irrelevant to the matter at hand. They neared the convergence of the road and the railroad bridge and levee. To their right stood the brewery where trucks were unloading malt in bags so the company could stay in production. On the other side of the railroad tracks, beyond the shot tower and the grain terminal, the coal pile at Northern States Power smoked. Rainwater carried oxygen deep into the pile, feeding the combustion already present.

They had to huddle around Walt to hear what he was saying above the pounding of the storm against their rain gear. He had stopped and momentarily lifted the hood of his slicker free of his face so that he could take his bearings. "When Excelsior and the other big lumbering operations started up, there were still sloughs out here. Gradually they got filled in and built over. The fill tended to be whatever they had to get rid of."

Sandy Norquist, the contractor out of Madison hired to do the emergency floodwall and levee work, drew the obvious conclusion. "Sawdust."

"That's right," Chuck said, "this whole area is a boil waiting to happen."

"We're standing right on top of one of the old sloughs," Walt said. He indicated a line beginning where the railroad track and Fourth Street converged, passing beneath their feet, and heading at an angle across the peninsula toward the harbor. "This is a natural line for the seepage to follow."

"What about under the floodwall?" Norquist asked.

"No." This from Lin Jiang, the Corps of Engineers' flood area rep, operating out of Clinton, but up here for the day. "Borings were taken before construction. Any bad fill would have been replaced with hydraulic material. But that doesn't mean all kinds of bad things can't happen. If you get a lot of seepage under the levee, for instance, you could get raveling at the toe, you could get slumpage at the top, the inside slope could shear off. All very bad."

In the distance, through a gap between grain terminal buildings, Chuck watched Norquist's men work, adding panels to a section of the floodwall. Behind him sounded the warning bell of a truck backing along the crest of the levee, where, under Norquist's direction, city crews and volunteers were building mud boxes to raise the levee's height.

Chuck's beeper went off, and he tipped it away from his belt so he could read the number in the dim light. The city's emergency operations center.

"Here, use this," Norquist said, handing Chuck a cell phone. Chuck stepped away from the others to make the call.

The storm had eased for the moment and water dripped from the hood of his slicker as he talked to the EOC. A short distance away, the others continued the discussion of the threat of sand boils, the wind blowing away all but fragments of their conversation. From the freight yards, a railroad work vehicle hove into view, a pickup truck mounted on iron wheels.

As he finished the call, Chuck looked at his watch. Moisture had condensed under the crystal. He went back to the group.

"One way to do it," Lin was saying, "is to supercharge the soil. You force the seepage to travel farther before it comes to the surface."

Chuck returned the phone to Norquist, who asked, "Anything I need to know?" The question was brusque. A good man, Chuck thought. Very low bullshit quotient.

Chuck shook his head. "The EOC got a call from some clown claiming we're getting flooded from behind, down through Mercy Valley."

"Mercy Valley?"

"North side of town. An old abandoned valley of the Little Mesquatie."

At Chuck's words, the side chatter died down. He told Norquist and the others, "We shot elevations out there. No way the flood's gonna backdoor us." He'd go out and take a look, but it'd be a wasted trip.

Walter had abandoned the group and was climbing the railroad embankment toward the hybrid RR work vehicle. In the back was piled the equipment the Geological Survey people used to measure discharge in the river.

"Let's finish up here," Chuck said.

A brief time later, he walked away. He would go out to Mercy Valley, but not to see if it was flooding. He wanted to find whoever had started the rumor. That's what he wanted. Chuck lived now on the edge of anger. People had always thought he was difficult. They didn't know difficult. Anyway, he'd go out to Mercy Valley. He'd deal with the situation.

CHAPTER 49

❧

A half dozen trucks were waiting to unload in front of him, so J.J. Dusterhoft put on his hat, got out, and moseyed up to the next guy in the queue. Wisconsin tags—a cheddarhead—with Norquist & Sons lettered on the side door.

"What's the good word?" he said to the elbow sticking out the window.

A face appeared above the elbow, not a particularly friendly face, but J.J. didn't require an amicable countenance before he'd engage in conversation.

"Are you Norquist or one of the sons?" he asked.

The guy laughed, a sort of humorless laugh. "You'll never see anybody named Norquist driving one of these rigs."

"Just a grunt, huh?"

"You got that right."

The cold front was well by, the temperature easing back into the fifties, the rain tapering off, mist drifting in the thick air. The weather had been alternating between storms and the expectation of storms. J.J. was still trying to make up his mind what he thought about it all.

"You a local?" the guy asked.

"Born and bred."

"Got a question for ya. The clay we're hauling, what's this business about the mayor wanting to give it to the city for nothing?"

"Ah, yes, that." A rumor. J.J. was something of a connoisseur of rumors. "You mean the ex-mayor, though, not the current one." Fritz Goetzinger apparently had a source of good fatty clay up on his farm and had offered it to the city gratis, but the city council, ticked off at him for making them look like shit in the public eye, had told him to drop dead. That was the rumor. J.J. considered it and said, "If there was an offer and the city took him up on it, we'd be hauling clay from

232

way the hell and gone at the other end of town. Cost more than we'd save by getting it for nothing."

"That right?"

"Yup. And, of course, it doesn't help matters that the city's buying the stuff from a local developer that isn't well liked. Makes no difference. Ten cents a yard from the Devil himself would be cheaper than nothing from Saint Jude." Jude being the patron saint of desperate situations.

The fellow nodded, more or less accepting J.J.'s explanation.

Rumors had been floating in with the rising water—various scurrilous reasons that the city fathers secretly wanted to take a flood, a claim that the wall was going to fail no matter what they did, another that some disgruntled soul from downstream or East Jackson across the river—depending on which version of the rumor was being passed along—was going to dynamite the floodwall, in the spirit, J.J. supposed, of leveling the playing field.

The sources of rumors were great mysteries, with as many suspects as you could possibly want. People had reasons that reason never heard of. But despite all this, rumors themselves charmed J.J. They sustained interest in the way the truth never could. Rumors of God and the Devil, that sort of thing, for rumors were not lacking in moral scope. But they could be modest, as well, a matter of the most delicate innuendo. They might even be true, nothing was impossible, although J.J. generally suspected that they revealed more about the teller than the told, their truth or falsehood pretty much beside the point.

The truck had been creeping ahead as they talked, so J.J. said finally, "Well, better go fetch my vehicle and take up the slack."

Five minutes later, with the warning bell singing and reverse gear whining, he was wheeling the truck briskly backward along the levee toward the work site, where a guy with an illuminated baton waved him to a stop, then with small jerks of the baton brought him back the last few feet into position. "Okay, drop it, drop it!" he yelled.

The box tilted slowly upward. The load of clay hesitated, as if making up its mind, then slid out in a rush, rasping against the metal bed. In the rearview mirror, J.J. watched the carpenters building the lumber walls on either side of the levee, between which a backhoe was placing the clay and volunteers spreading it in lifts a few inches thick, which a small dozer packed down.

From below, the river slowly rose toward the permanent levee, almost on it now. But they had plenty of time. Maybe all the time in the world, in fact, since the question still remained whether the water would ever reach the emergency work. Near at hand, silt and soil stained the river brown, but farther out the reflections of the sky laid a screen of light across the water. The only reason people thought water was blue, J.J. supposed, was because of the reflections of the sky.

"Move it out, move it out!" the guy with the baton yelled at him as soon as the rasping noise ceased, and J.J. lowered the box on the fly, enjoying the chance to shift up through the gears like an Indy 500 driver as he raced along, the truck chattering over the furrows cut into the top of the levee, the first stage in the work.

As he turned off, the next truck, reversed and poised for the backward dash, had already begun to move. He glanced at his watch and saw he'd been on top for less than three minutes.

Swinging past the line of waiting trucks, he headed toward the borrow site for the next load.

Chapter 50

～

"H ow old are you?" Aggie Klauer asked the young man.
"Eighteen."

"Okay, then, let me ask the question a little differently—what school do you go to?"

The young man, stocky and with a slightly insolent manner, might have gotten away with it, but he'd brought some of his chums along to volunteer with him, and taken together it was obvious these were high schoolers. Their leader hesitated, deciding what he was going to tell Aggie.

"Fill out the forms," she told him, "you and your friends. We've got all the volunteers we need at the moment, but we're taking names just in case." They were going to use college kids before high school, just about anybody before high school. But you never knew. If it got bad enough...

El Plowman, who had been standing nearby and going through completed forms, came forward, up beside the slightly insolent young man, and pointed at the form Aggie had just handed him and said, "I'm particularly interested in this and this." Aggie knew what she was pointing at, the question about whether the volunteer had a truck that could be used to help evacuate people and the one about whether he—or obviously his family in this case—might be able to house evacuees.

Aggie was handing out the forms to the others. "You can use the tables over there. When you're done, return the forms to me." The leader of the band was inspecting his sheet with a trace of disgust, as if she'd just handed him a test to take. But finally he started off toward the tables, his gang trailing after.

As personnel director for the city, Aggie had been put in charge of the volunteers and then, almost as an afterthought, of the entire mobilization effort. The emergency operations center, from which Chuck

235

Fellows directed the overall flood fight, was located uptown in space donated by the phone company and connected by several dedicated phone lines to the various functions housed down at the civic center, Aggie's domain, at the moment a bedlam, people all over the place.

Not like six days earlier, when she had stood in the empty and silent ice rink with the center director and talked about whether the ice needed to be melted before they laid down the flooring used normally for basketball games but soon to become the mobilization center. She had been petrified at this sudden responsibility. In no time at all, she had to organize literally thousands of volunteers to help people evacuate, to patrol the levees and floodwalls, to fill sandbags, to do who knows what else. She was really just this little personnel director trying to deal with picayune class/comp issues, help people with drinking problems, negotiate contracts, do a bit of organizational development on the side. Biblical floods weren't part of her job description.

The echoey silence in the rink, like the ghosts of past hockey games, gave her the shivers. Or maybe it was just the cold curling up around her ankles. Or maybe it was just that she was a little chicken. *Okay*, she ordered herself, *make a decision*. Making a decision was always good. So she did. They'd start out by melting the ice. If people were going to be spending hour upon hour there, no need for them to end up with chilblains, too, or whatever it was you got from having cold on your feet all day long. One decision made, she felt a teeny bit better. Then she called her buddies in the local chapter of Women in Management and pretty soon had her first volunteers, a group of executives to help her set up and run the center. She felt a little better yet.

And now, six days later, the ice rink had been transformed, with stations set up around the perimeter for the Red Cross canteen, first aid station, the public health nurse, a distribution center for rain gear run by the St. Vincent de Paul Society, a Salvation Army table, and a table for the city finance people. The finance director had established procedures to keep track of expenses in hopes the city would later be reimbursed. Forms had been created, and in the center of the room there were rows of tables for people to fill out those forms. A classroom had been established for volunteer orientation, including a display explaining the proper way to fill sandbags. Around Aggie were the radio dispatch operators, the motor pool table, and her own reception tables. A bank of phones had been installed with the idea that the citizens would have a single number to call for all flood-related matters. She had phone lines to fire, police, the sheriff, the county, the state EOC. She was connected.

At the far end of the huge room, behind everything else, rows of cots had been unfolded, with blankets, so people on the rapid response teams could sack out while they were waiting for sand boils or other emergencies. Buses were parked outside to shuttle them to and from the work sites.

Aggie chaired her all-woman committee, which ran the operation. And finally, the whole business reduced to a set of routines, she had begun to think that, yes, she could do this. She felt exhilarated and amazed at her own competence.

The exhilaration and amazement lasted approximately ten seconds. The rest was work. Less than a week into it, and already she was exhausted. Already she felt half sick. She kept telling herself it was just the miserable heating, the gusts of cold air from doors left open with people continuously coming and going. Spend a half hour in the place and you felt like you were getting pneumonia.

She hunted around in her shoulder bag, stored under the table, for some throat lozenges and, as she sucked on one, she watched the schoolboys looking at each other's forms like kids cribbing on a test. Behind her, El, who had developed the habit of stopping by several times a day, was sorting through the forms already completed. Another potential volunteer stepped up, no kid this time, and Aggie asked him the preliminary questions and handed him a form to fill out.

As he left, Chuck Fellows came striding into her line of sight.

"Word," he said to her.

Aggie got one of the other women to spell her and stepped aside with him, El coming along, too, the three of them moving into the vacant space between the desks the high school kids were using and the rows of chairs that had been set up for volunteer training.

"How many inspectors so far?" Chuck asked.

"Six hundred. We could have had more, but I cut it off at that number, as you asked."

"Good. That should be plenty. And the theater?"

"I'll make sure it's open at eight tomorrow morning. That's when I told everyone to come." He needed a bigger space to conduct his orientation for the people who would be patrolling the levees and walls looking for leaks. Six hundred little Dutch boys and girls to plug their dike.

"I'll need the theater opened before eight," Chuck said. "For setup. Sam Turner will be doing it."

"Okay."

This matter disposed of, El brought up the subject of evacuations.

"Have you talked to the National Guard yet?" she asked him. If they could get people to evacuate, they'd need National Guardsmen to patrol the area. "Or should I talk to them myself?"

"No, no, shit, I'll do it. Sorry."

"Thanks."

"Anybody left yet?" he wondered.

"No. But it's still early."

"Good luck," he told her, meaning she had her work cut out for her.

"I know," El agreed, "it's difficult. I plan to talk to Fritz, see if I can't get him involved. That would help. If we can just convince a few people to leave, that might have an effect, start the ball rolling."

"Yeah." Chuck nodded. He and El weren't exactly on friendly terms, but they'd put their differences aside for the moment.

"Tell me, Aggie," El asked, "could we get Lucille to leave?"

"Who's Lucille?" Chuck asked.

"My mother," Aggie told him.

"Where does she live?"

"Little Wales."

He nodded. Little Wales. Everyone knew about Little Wales, just about the lowest point on the floodplain, Death Valley without the sand dunes.

"She might leave?" he asked.

"Never," Aggie said, and then, feeling some defense of her mother was called for, added, "She's lived her whole life in that house. People who haven't always lived in the same place wouldn't understand. She was born there. It's as much a part of her as her skin."

Chuck rubbed vigorously behind one ear, listening with intense impatience. "Her choice," he said, and turned to El. "Get as many out as you can. We'll use Guardsmen to secure the area." Then back to Aggie, "Make sure the theater's open by seven. It'll take Sam some time to set up."

And he was gone, moving quickly away.

The high schoolers had returned with their completed forms, which El collected, looking for the information she was interested in. Aggie told the leader, the one with an attitude, "See the chairs over there? There'll be a short orientation." She was going to tell them to go back to school after that, but on second thought she had a better idea. "What school do you attend?" she demanded, and seeing that she meant business, he told her. "Okay, when we're through, we've got buses outside. We'll give you a lift back."

After they were gone, El said, "With all the snow days they've lost, they'll be in school until August." She waved the completed forms. "There are a couple of possibilities. I'll make copies, if you don't mind." Aggie had set up copy machines along the folded-up bleacher seats. El started toward them, and then turned briefly back. "You're absolutely, positively sure Lucille won't leave?"

"You'd have to carry her out."

El nodded. "Her and just about everybody else." Evacuating was going to be a tough sell.

Aggie relieved the woman who had taken over for her at the registration desk, and El went to make her copies.

CHAPTER 51

∽

At the dog track it was raining, but there was no wind, what Jack Kelley now called good weather. The ironworkers were aloft, wearing harnesses, their scaffolds hung from the cranes flocking along both sides of the grandstand. In the dim midafternoon, the arrays of lamps mounted on trailers sent columns of white light streaming up through the rain and ironwork.

Jack had climbed to the framed-in judge's stand and was finishing a conversation with the steel foreman Jim Bergman. The stand rose above the roof on the north side of the building. Bergman's people having finished with the west end, the glaziers had taken over. They worked on top of scissors lifts, installing glass.

Many of the tradesmen had been on the site through the winter cold and snows, and now rain and soon a flood. It had been a plagues-of-Egypt kind of job.

"How you coming with Eddie Blue?" Bergman had asked.

"Nothing so far. Gonna try again."

Blue, the architect, didn't like to change his designs. He claimed to see Jack's point—if they installed glass between the grandstand and clubhouse areas, half the building could be sealed and it would be possible to accomplish the inside work quicker— but besides making sympathetic noises, the architect had done nothing.

"Guys like Eddie Blue are a mystery to me," Bergman said.

Jack told him, "Don't get me started on architects."

From the judge's stand, they had a panoramic view. The place finally looked like a racetrack, the kennels finished, paddock building, too. The track oval had been roughed in, and beyond it, at the northern edge of the site, the tote building stood with cutouts for the electronic displays to be mounted later.

Farther to the north, beyond the job site, the flood had begun to invade the island. Through the trees, the patches of visible water appeared to Jack like pure energy.

He climbed back down to the deck and returned to the construction trailer and turned on the AM/FM radio with the weather band and listened to the current forecast.

He'd become a weather addict. The radio was equipped with an emergency warning alarm in case the National Weather Service issued a severe storm watch or warning. Jim Bergman had the same setup in his trailer. The two of them conducted a more or less ongoing discussion of the weather conditions. Jack also talked regularly with the NWS meteorologist out at the airport. When he was home, which wasn't often, he turned on the weather channel, much to Janelle's annoyance. He found himself studying the sky and feeling the breezes and listening to the sounds that storms made.

The weather forecast hadn't changed. He told Sean, "Keep an eye on things. I'm going uptown to get on Eddie Blue's case." He'd do it in person this time.

Before he got into his car, though, he checked on the progress with the well points. A ring of pipes—excess lengths cut off the pilings that had been driven for the buildings the previous fall—now girdled the job site, driven ten feet into the sand at one-hundred-foot intervals. Jack intended to drop submersible pumps into them to handle the seepage. He chatted briefly with the guy doing the work. It had taken less than a day. A nothing job. No charge. Jack thanked him, then went over to spend a couple of minutes talking to the volunteers that were laying polyethylene sheeting, held in place by sandbags, as an extra layer of protection over the riprap.

Satisfied, he headed for his car. Eddie Blue notwithstanding, a lot of people had gotten behind Jack's attempt to protect the site and continue working. Granted, with less to do at the moment, contractors like Tony Vasconcellos and Dexter Walcott had trimmed their crews. That had reduced the chances for friction, but Jack expected cooperation to hold after he had half the building sealed and the pace of work picked up again. The flood at least ought to take people's minds off other grievances. If Blue didn't come through, he was determined to rig up some sort of temporary barrier himself to enclose the west end. Anything to keep going.

As usual, he had to wait to drive along the access road. The last of the concrete slurry was being placed on the nylon mats Jack had found to lay along the road's embankments. A concrete truck blocked the roadway as it crept along, hosing the slurry down the mats. It wouldn't be completely cured before the water reached it, but good enough, Jack judged.

He closed his eyes, contemplating the pleasure of a catnap, and his mind, slipping its constraints, began to float pleasantly toward the void. It would be so nice to sleep, just for a little while…

Into this doze, the image of Father Mike Daugherty popped unbidden. It occurred to Jack that he hadn't been thinking about Father Mike lately. Not at all. Or his faith, either, although that was a somewhat different matter. The dog track, everything was the dog track. He'd stopped going to the morning Masses at the Cathedral. No time. No time for anything but the track.

He wasn't angry with Mike anymore over the Vasconcellos business. They'd patched up their differences. He remembered how he'd once liked the priest. He liked him again. But he was afraid of him, too, afraid of where any more conversations with Father Mike Daugherty were likely to lead. Beware the modern priest. Better to wait for the next one the archdiocese assigned to St. C's. Jack felt a little guilty about this impulse to avoid Mike, but he decided, yes, better to wait for the next one.

Finally, he was able to edge around the concrete truck, and, once again on the move, his thoughts quickly returned to the press of immediate concerns.

Chapter 52

~

"Nineteen point six. Two hundred and three thousand."
Every day now, Walter was going out with the Geological Survey technicians as they did the first of their two daily measurements off the railroad bridge. And every evening, he announced to El the current stage of the river and the volume of water passing under the bridge. Over two hundred thousand cubic feet every second now. Two hundred thousand. Who could comprehend such a figure?

El didn't like the way Walter looked. He'd been doing too much. And she wished he wouldn't go out on the bridge, which seemed dangerous to her. "You're not so young anymore, dear," she reminded him.

It was 1:00 a.m. and they were getting ready for bed. Except on weekends, they only saw each other early in the morning and late at night, their marriage held hostage to the public lives they led.

"I'm okay," Walter said, sitting slump-shouldered on the edge of the bed in his underwear. "It's good for me. Exercise."

His long, graying sideburns, in a style out of fashion for many years, announced his indifference to conventional opinion. His face remained smooth despite his fifty-seven years. He resembled a young man aging around the edges, the young Walter still clearly visible, not like El, who was getting old all over. Of course, Walter didn't pay any attention to this. Aging was neither here nor there as far as Walter was concerned.

"I'm still afraid something might happen," she told him. "You're not used to handling heavy equipment." Both of the Geological Survey men that Mick Kilmer had arranged to come to Jackson had bad backs. Bad backs, it seemed, were an occupational disease of such people.

"The stuff's not that heavy," Walter reassured El, "not with four of us." The railroad man was apparently helping, too. But El didn't care how many were helping; she still didn't like it.

They'd had this conversation before. When El got very tired, she became more concerned about Walter, or rather it became harder to keep her mouth shut.

Beneath her nightgown, she wriggled out of her underwear, aware of her body, while Walter across the room stared past his paunch and between his soft, pallid legs. "Don't worry, Ellie. The Survey guys are doing most of the work. And I'm careful." He looked up and smiled, his guileless smile one of true pleasure, something else that had not changed in all the years they'd been together. "If I was gone, who'd collect my data?" She had been talking only about him getting hurt, but he understood her greater fear.

"Just watch out, okay?"

The problem was that Walter sometimes forgot to be conscious of the world around him, absorbed utterly in whatever had captured his attention at the moment. What interested him interested him absolutely. But El thought the river had become like the seventh wave on the ocean, the sleeper that could drag an unwary man out to sea.

Nothing to be done, she knew, nothing to be done. Except hope for the best.

CHAPTER 53

～

"I want to thank you for volunteering," Chuck said, staring out at the hundreds of men and women filling the orchestra seats, some even in the balcony of the ornate old theater.

"On the top left corner of the written handout you received, you'll find a number. That's your team. Below the number is the name of your team leader. And below that, your assigned watches. Some of you have one, some two, based on your stated availability. If you cannot fulfill your assignment, for whatever reason, see Sam Turner at the end of the orientation and he'll make the necessary changes. Sam, raise your hand so people know what you look like. Back there, in the middle aisle, that's Sam. He'll be out in the lobby when we're through." Chuck stopped pacing back and forth long enough to say, "If you can't do it, now's the time to get out. Let me remind you, this isn't just a week or two we're talking about here. Mississippi River floods take their sweet time. It'll be weeks, it could be months. So you're signing on for a hitch. Get out now, or plan to stay for the duration.

"If you do stay, I'll expect you to perform. Understood?

"Each team will be assigned to a quarter-mile section of the system, either floodwall or levee. That's your section, you're responsible for it. Your job is to make sure the water stays in the damn river where it belongs. I expect you to go on your watches with an attitude. I expect you to take it personally. We lose the flood fight in one place, we've lost it everywhere.

"The first slide…"

A large map flashed onto the movie screen, showing the alternating sections of floodwall and levee along the riverfront.

"As you can see, the system's a patchwork, each section different. When we're through here, we'll go outside and there'll be buses ready to shuttle the teams to their mobilization points. You'll mobilize at these before each watch. You'll go on watch as a team. If someone's missing, your team leader will find a replacement. There's a number to call if you absolutely cannot make it for some reason.

"This morning, everybody's going to walk their section of the system and become familiar with it. In the handouts, you'll find a blowup of yours. Study it and make notes as you go along—drainage penetrations, seep ditches at the landside toes, places where the levees have been patched, where levees and floodwalls abut. Any place the integrity of the structure has been compromised, even a little bit, might be a point where failure will begin. Believe me, people, water is sinister damn stuff when it comes to a situation like this.

"I expect you to maintain visual contact with at least one other member of your team at all times. To contact your team leader, use your handheld, which will be assigned to you before you go on watch. Notify him if you see anything suspicious. There'll be flying squads with sandbags and other fighting materials positioned up and down the system and ready to respond. Speed is essential. Absolutely essential.

"Keep unauthorized people off the levees and out of the area. When you're up on a levee or walking at the base of one of the floodwalls, that's where you live, that's your home. Anybody else shows up, he damn well better be the plumber come to fix a leak.

"You understand what I'm saying? We're not fooling around. We've got a city to protect. You people are on the front line. The first line of defense. It's your responsibility." He paused and surveyed the room, taking a long moment, picking out one set of eyes, then another, first the orchestra, then the balcony.

"Next slide.

"I'm going to talk about the levees first, then the floodwalls… Okay, here's a typical cross section. To begin with, you have to understand that levees can fail in a variety of ways…"

CHAPTER 54

❧

El called ahead. Fritz was home, and so she drove up to see him. The last time she'd been at his farm, he'd ended the exchange by killing a hog in front of her. The memory of that still disturbed, although less the brutality of the act than its calculated nature, Fritz trying to shock her, as if she didn't recognize the world for what it is.

She could have ignored him. Being part of the problem seemed a point of honor with Fritz. And he was merely a citizen now. He had no standing. He represented nobody but himself. She could have ignored him.

The farm lay dour and colorless in the rain. Her car rocked up the steep, muddy drive, tires spinning, and she parked and picked out a crooked path between pools of standing water up to the back door. Fritz came and, with what she took for tired resignation, led the way inside. El shucked off her rainwear on the porch and followed.

In the kitchen she looked for signs of change—of the husband who had become a widower. The place seemed more spartan, although she had seldom visited the Goetzingers when Edna was still alive. The changes in Fritz himself, however, couldn't be mistaken.

"There's some coffee left over from earlier," he said. "I'll heat it up if you want."

"No. Thank you. Nothing. I'm fine."

He shifted two of the kitchen chairs away from the table so that they could sit facing each other.

"Thank you for offering the clay to the city," she said. "You understand why we didn't take it?"

"Of course."

"It wasn't personal."

"Of course."

"Good." He sat erect, hands on his thighs, his terseness seeming to indicate that he was just there to listen. His gauntness struck El. He had lost weight, like someone who had fallen ill. His blue work shirt, faded almost to white, sagged on his reduced frame. His asymmetrical features remained, the patchy whiteness of his hair, the black now shot with gray, his eyes that did not quite match, the prominences of his leathery cheeks, his mouth canted at a slight angle. Except for his hair, the differences were slight, but strong enough to suggest contrariness, or complexity, or a life subject to the continuous pressure of distorting forces.

"How are you doing, Fritz? I know we've had our moments, but I do worry about you up here all by yourself."

"Got my youngest with me. In school now."

"Yes, of course. Well, that's good then." She leaned toward him. "But how are you? Really."

"Gonna lose the farm."

The rumor had been around for months, but still the reality possessed the power to shock, and the casual bluntness of Fritz's announcement, too. She reached out and would have touched him if they'd been sitting closer. "I am sorry. Isn't there something that can be done?"

"Expect not. Banks have been carrying me long as they're gonna."

"What will you do?" The man had lost his job, his wife, and now this. No wonder he looked like he did. "It's dreadful, it truly is, on top of everything else."

He shook his head. "When Edna died, that was bad. This…" He made a gesture of indifference, then changed the subject, asking what she wanted, why she had come up there.

El leaned back and exhaled and looked at this man who was not prepared to be comforted. Given the history of their relationship, she supposed she couldn't blame him. And from her point of view, he was hardly a more sympathetic character now, in pain, than he had been before all these Job-like misfortunes. He remained the same old Fritz.

"I have a favor to ask," she told him, "but first, I want to catch you up on what we've been doing. After all, you started it," she couldn't resist adding. "It's still not clear, by the way, that the extra protection will be necessary."

As she began to describe ongoing activities, Fritz sat up even straighter and interrupted. "If this is gonna take time, I've got something to do."

"I can cut it short," El said. "I thought you'd want to know."

"Let's go out to the barn. You can talk as we go."

Remembering the last visit, El said, "Not another pig."

He smiled, the first smile since she'd entered. "Not today."

As they left the kitchen, El took one last look around and the emptiness now appeared to her more like that of somebody preparing to move.

Out in the barn, corn had been piled into a tall stack, still on the cob, and around it were scattered stools and a variety of old-fashioned corn-shelling implements. It seemed that the people who had picked and husked the corn for Fritz in the field down by the river had neglected to finish to job, and El found herself briefly pressed into service using one of the old shellers as she detailed the city's flood fight.

Fritz left the barn door half open so they could watch the rain.

"That was wonderful, what they did, harvesting the corn for you," El told him.

"My son organized it." Some energy had come back into Fritz's voice.

"Your youngest?"

"No. Fritz, Jr."

"He did?" Since Senior and Junior didn't get along, this was news. "Well, good for him."

She mentioned the negotiating his son had done for the union and his scheme for the committee with no instructions. Democracy in the workplace. "Some people thought that it might have been your idea."

"Woulda never thought of something like that."

"Aggie believed all along that Deuce…your son had come up with it. It didn't belong in the contract, but I do think it's worth a try. So we're going to."

Sitting there and shelling corn was certainly more pleasant than following Fritz around as he prepared to shoot a pig. The shelling machine she was using looked a little bit like a kitchen meat grinder mounted on the side of a box. She inserted each cob nose first into a hopper on the top and turned a crank at the side. She didn't hold the first cob tight enough, and it twisted around in her hand as she cranked. She gripped it tighter and could hear the raspy noise of the mechanism as kernels of corn spilled out a spout into the box. She selected another cob and removed the leftover husk and silk.

"The reason I came, Fritz, was because I want to encourage people to evacuate from the Flats until the danger is past."

He was picking through the implements, selecting one for himself. "Premature."

"Perhaps. But Chuck Fellows says that once water gets up on the emergency additions, the safety factor will be lost. It might fail all at once, like a dam."

"No one will leave."

El took a deep breath. Of course, it was unrealistic to expect Fritz to be cooperative.

"Not at the moment. I understand. But that doesn't mean people can't start thinking about it. Perhaps moving some of their belongings out of harm's way. Make arrangements for where to go if the time comes. There's lots that can be done."

"Is the city prepared to pay for these?"

"We're arranging with schools and churches and other institutions for storage and shelter space. We're going to use the motherhouses. Sister Jean suggested it. They'll be perfect." There were almost no women religious anymore, the huge old buildings practically empty. "But we need all the space we can get. We expect refugees from across the river and from Abbey Station and maybe from other places, but certainly some of the Flats people could make use of these facilities, too. Most will find relatives or friends to stay with, that's what we expect. I'm also putting out a call for people who would be willing to open up their homes. We can do a lot now, Fritz. And you could help. If you encourage people to start preparing, they'll listen to you."

When he responded, it wasn't to this last statement but the one immediately before it. "You expect people to let strangers into their homes?"

"I don't know. I hope. Some have indicated a willingness. Of course, it'll have to be done with care. That's the value of starting now."

He had abandoning his shelling and sat gravely, hunched over on his stool, forearms resting on his knees, slowly shaking his head.

"I don't doubt you mean well," he said.

"We calculate that if the flood crest is as high as thirty-three feet and the system fails, as many as 4,500 people will be displaced. We simply couldn't handle that number all at once."

Fritz said, "It's too soon. And anyway, these people don't have any money. They live from paycheck to paycheck. They can't afford motel rooms and such. Why do you think I made the city add to the protection system in the first place? It sure as hell wasn't so people would have to move."

She saw it was hopeless. She'd never learn. Fritz always, always looked for the reason something wouldn't work, and, by God, he found it. This visit to the farm might have been more pleasant than the last one, or rather less unpleasant, but El would accomplish precisely what she'd accomplished last time.

Her hand, the one gripping the ears of corn as she turned the crank, had begun to cramp up and she stopped and opened and closed it several times. "If the folks down there don't start thinking about what they're going to do, Fritz, too soon might become too late."

To this, all he had to say, as he chose another shelling implement and another ear of corn, was, "I got no doubt, Eleanor, that you mean well."

CHAPTER 55

~

Once a week, Deuce had the first shift. His life had been geared to the nighttime for so long that he found the daytime tour of duty the most difficult, although, as with everything else, he made a point of not minding. A few minutes before 3:00 p.m., he performed his end-of-shift ritual, going down to the pump room and wiping the machines and the floor around them, cleaning up the small spatters of oil from the last eight hours. Afterward he went back upstairs and finished his paperwork. Then he waited for his relief.

The union negotiations had failed. His halfhearted attempt to revenge himself upon his father had failed. His valued possessions at the moment were two, or three if he counted the RX-7. He had his job, and he had his bitterness. About the job, well, he took his samples and made his tests and watched his gauges. He walked the plant, checking machine bearings and adjusting chemical feeds and measuring the thickness of the beds in the basins and backwashing filters and performing the dozens of other routine tasks. He had a certain genius for the routine. He almost liked the work.

As for his other possession, the bitterness, he finally understood the simple fact that it was his alone, just as whatever guilt his father felt because of the death of his mother was the old man's alone, Deuce powerless to add or subtract. His father would never change, and Deuce would hate him for what he was and what he had done. And it didn't make a fucking bit of difference.

Finally his relief arrived. As he was leaving the building, he heard voices in Wayne Gourley's office and stopped to see what was going on. Wayne was there and the other water plant brass and a couple of the maintenance guys...and Chuck Fellows. They were talking about the flood.

Nobody told Deuce to shut the door on his way out, so he leaned against the jamb and listened.

The conversation bounced around. Not much had happened at the plant so far, but people had obviously been thinking about the thing, and everybody had a pet concern. They'd need to install a portable chlorination unit at the head of the plant in order to maintain the chlorine residue throughout the treatment sequence. Could they run the plant flooded? The chemical feeders and switch-gear were high enough, but they'd have to figure a way to protect the pumps. Then there was the matter of how much water they'd have to truck in if they could no longer treat. They crunched the numbers—at five gallons per day per person, they'd need 300,000 gallons every day or 93,000 cubic feet of water. Assuming they used milk trucks to haul it, that would be thirty-seven trucks every day. Plus distribution points. If the plant stayed on line, a more pressing need would be chlorinating just prior to putting water into the distribution system. They'd have to figure out how to inject it into the reservoir, a pressurized system. That would take some thought.

Fellows was obviously growing irritated at this pinball chatter. "Talk about the wells," he interrupted when he'd had enough. "That's what I'm worried about at the moment."

"Right," Wayne agreed, "we need to look at them first." Wayne always agreed with everybody, but in this case he was actually right, he and Fellows. The wells were the concern. They were located nearby, but outside the flood protection system, on the man-made peninsula built to provide for a marina and boat ramp. Nine shallow wells out there. If the water went high enough, the wellheads would be flooded even if the city wasn't.

So they talked about that. The wells had submersible pumps, which would not be affected, but high water would threaten the transformers on top of the wells. They would have to be elevated.

"I'll tell you what I'd worry about," Deuce put in, his interest piqued.

Fellows's head swiveled around. "Yeah?"

"The electrical lines out there. They're thirty or forty years old. They were just laid in trenches. If they end up sitting in the water table, they could short out."

"That's right," Wayne agreed. "We'd never do it that way today."

"What about bringing in power overhead?" Fellows asked. "We can get Northern States to set some poles for us."

"We could," Wayne agreed.

The conversation continued, and Deuce listened with growing interest. The flood was something a little different to do, he decided. Why not?

He could get to the rest of his life later.

CHAPTER 56

~

When Chuck Fellows stopped back at city hall, he picked up his messages and then went over to fill Paul Cutler in on the day's activities so the manager could go hold the hands of the city council.

"So it's twenty now?" Cutler asked.

"Higher—20.7, as of this morning. Going up a foot a day, a little more. Got the figure from Walter Plowman. He's been helping the Geological Survey guys who are doing stage-discharge readings off the railroad bridge."

"Eleven days?"

"That's right."

"And the crests of the Minnesota and Mississippi are going to be synchronized?"

"Yup."

Cutler looked glum, probably as much because the manager had become a bit player as because of the magnitude of the disaster. There was nothing here he could hope to manipulate to his satisfaction.

"They've just given up the flood fight in Red Wing," Chuck told him. As the water rose, one community after another had conceded defeat, these defeats descending the river like the flood itself. Many thousands of people already displaced. Hundreds of millions of dollars in damage and just a start. After it was all over, though, and the river back in its banks, the thousands would return, back to the floodplain, back to rebuild. It was never just a matter of what made sense.

"River's rising a foot or more a day, you say?"

"Went up 1.1 yesterday."

"And it could start going up faster?"

"Could."

"If the crest isn't for eleven days, won't that take it over thirty?"

"Near the crest the river flattens out. Could be going up a half foot a day or less."

Cutler nodded unhappily. "And when are you going to be done?" he asked, meaning the emergency work.

"Eight days, give or take."

"Not that it'll make any difference." Water might never touch the additions to the walls and levees that Chuck was throwing up. The prediction was sitting right at thirty feet, right on the design flood, the highest crest the protection system had been designed to handle. All this extra work might be money down the rathole. Chuck could almost sympathize with the manager.

"And the new storm won't change anything?" Cutler asked.

"It's already been factored in. Of course, it could be worse than expected. And there's another one behind it, and that could be worse than expected, too. Possible."

The city manager eyed him and then held one hand up, making a two-inch gap between thumb and first finger. "That's all I ask. And pray to God nobody else loses a flood fight because of it."

CHAPTER 57

～

As Aggie drove by the water plant and turned onto Cardiff Lane where her mother lived, she was reminded of Deuce Goetzinger. She hadn't seen him since the time in the cafe. He'd no doubt gone back to his old life. Of course, he'd been nothing but an irritant. And they had nothing in common. He spent his free time playing cards and chasing women. Probably he was a drinker, too. Aggie was done with drinkers. She'd learned her lesson. And, as if that wasn't enough, Deuce never believed in the committee thing, even when he was busy championing it. He'd admitted as much, said it was better not to believe in the thing, then you couldn't be disappointed. Well, maybe, and Aggie certainly knew a thing or two about disappointment. But what did it say about a man if he refused to expose himself to the possibility of regret?

Cardiff dipped down sharply for a few feet, then leveled off, the dip back in time as much as space, into the heart of Little Wales and the house where she'd grown up and where Lucille had grown up before her. The neighborhood looked nothing like it had when she was a kid. The houses had been spiffed up, the street landlocked when they filled in the slough and built the industrial park. Almost all the old river families were gone, only John Turcotte and Lucille left.

Aggie parked and turned off the motor, the windshield glazed with water the moment the wipers disappeared. She sagged back in the seat and stared at the bleary scene. And, anyway, she thought, he was lower than her on the organization chart.

She got out, fetched the first grocery bag out of the backseat and braced herself against the wind. The storm rose to a momentary crisis and swirled around her. The old fishnet decoration rattled against the siding of the house.

"Phew," she said as she came into the steamy kitchen, and deposited the groceries, "it's ugly out there, Ma."

Lucille sat in the rocker, knitting and smoking, the remains of an old-fashioned on the tray table beside her and Phil Donahue on the television across the room. The dogs were snoozing on the floor, making almost a perfect circle around their mistress.

"You're early," Lucille said.

"Can't stay long. Gotta go back to Five Flags."

Aggie went outside again and brought in the second bag and put it down next to the first.

"I'll put them away," Lucille told her, holding the cigarette as she knitted, ignoring Phil Donahue. "Don't drip on the floor. I put the coat rack out in the sunroom."

Aggie left her rain gear where instructed and returned.

"I like the rain," Lucille announced, ever the contrarian.

"You should go outside, Ma. Then you could really enjoy it."

"Hmm," Lucille said and with two smart taps knocked the ash off her cigarette.

Aggie considered unpacking the groceries, but then decided she'd take her mother at her word. Always best to take Lucille at her word.

Aggie chatted about all the volunteers pouring into the mobilization center and about plans to station inspectors up and down the levees and floodwalls, this a lead-in to what she really wanted to talk about. "They're discussing evacuating people, too, just to be on the safe side."

"I hope you don't expect me to go anywhere," Lucille snapped, knitting a little faster.

"No, Ma. I told them you'd lived here all your life, and you'd never leave. They'd have to carry you out."

"Fucking right."

In fact, Aggie couldn't conceive of her mother living anywhere else. The old aura of the river folk who had once lived there might be gone from the neighborhood, but it still lingered inside that tatty old house—the faded furniture, the sentimental illustrations on the walls, the rooms as small as cabins on a ship, the odors so complex they seemed to form their own ecosystem. It was easier to imagine a turtle without its shell than Lucille without her house, even for a little while.

"But I've been thinking, Ma."

"Have you?" Lucille was on her guard now.

"Maybe you ought to get flood insurance. That way, if something happened, you'd have money to repair the place."

Lucille did not react at once. She sat ticking like a clock and fiercely tapping her cigarette against the edge of the ashtray, having dropped her knitting in her lap. Finally she merely said, speaking the words with deep suspicion, "Flood insurance?"

"Why not? Just as a precaution. It won't cost much."

"Who do you get it from?"

"It's a government program."

Lucille went on ticking, but she appeared to be coming to grips with the idea. "Let me get this straight. You can sit around on your keister until a flood's almost on top of you, then run out and buy flood insurance? The government will actually let you to do that?"

"You have to take precautions. I mean, the city has to. Like build a floodwall. But once you do that, yes, you can buy insurance." Aggie had imagined that this idea might be reasonable enough to appeal to Lucille, but she saw that she had been mistaken. Of course, her mother didn't have much money, there was that.

Anyway, whatever, Aggie couldn't just back down now. Backing down simply made the next encounter more hopeless. Lucille already thought Aggie was a wuss. Like father, like daughter. No need to make matters worse. So she said, "If you've done what you can to protect yourself and conditions get even worse, then it's not your fault and you should be allowed to get reimbursed for your losses. That's the theory, Ma. It's not unreasonable."

"Hmm." Lucille gave Aggie a canny look and her eyebrows jumped a couple of times. "Suppose I give up these." She waved the cigarette. "Suppose I get cancer. You think someone's gonna give me health insurance then?"

"No, of course not, but this is different. Nobody's saying the house is going to get flooded. It's just a precaution."

"I thought that's why they're adding to the levee there—just for a precaution. And you're telling me they're gonna try to evacuate everybody. That's another precaution. Now you want me to buy insurance. How many fucking precautions do we need?"

Lucille smiled a gotcha smile at her daughter, and Aggie thought, *Rats*.

"Why don't I just move to Los Angeles there," Lucille suggested.

"Good grief."

"I'll tell you what the problem is, Agnes. People don't have the stomach to take chances anymore. They want everything 100 percent guaranteed. Country's gone gutless." Lucille picked up her old-fashioned glass and looked at the fruit in the bottom as if she was contemplating another drink. But Aggie knew that she wouldn't. Lucille had her rules. Just like she always got dressed to watch her TV shows, as if she was going to be in the studio audience. She was a woman of regular habits, even if many of them were bad.

"The trouble is, Ma, the flood keeps getting worse. Nobody knows how high the river's going to go."

"Is that right?" Lucille had picked up her knitting again, but she put it down at once. "Well, you just hold on to your britches there. I got something to show you."

She got up and shuffled straight into one of the dogs, Little Caesar, who rolled lazily onto his back. A moment later, understanding that a tummy rub was out of the question, he lumbered to his feet and out of the way.

When Lucille was feeling put-upon, she had a huffy way of walking, a haughtiness that would have made an English Victorian gentleman proud. In the catchall drawer next to the fridge, she began rooting around. *Good grief,* Aggie thought.

This was so typical of Lucille, who knew what she knew with a godlike certainty. Aggie, when confronted with all this confidence, had had a long history of losing her tongue. Aggie and her father before her.

Lucille continued rummaging through the drawer.

"They're talking about a two-hundred-year flood, Ma. Maybe worse."

"Shit, where is it?" said her mother. "Ha!" Triumphantly, she extracted a 3x5 card out of the midst of the debris. Arm ramrod straight, she dangled it a few inches from Aggie's nose. Aggie took it. In her mother's hand was printed, "wasps, twenty-seven feet."

"What's this?" But she knew at once. Walter Plowman's mud daubers.

Lucille grabbed the card back and clutched it to her bosom, smiling over it with dreamy satisfaction.

Oh, criminy, Aggie thought, count on her mother to remember the folk beliefs Walter used to spice up his weather forecasts. "So that's what you think, Ma, the river's only going up to twenty-seven feet?"

Lucille waggled the card at her daughter. "There's more wisdom in the world than what you know, dearie."

"But Walter doesn't believe that anymore." He probably never did, although with Walter you couldn't tell for sure. "He's saying water could go over the wall."

Lucille dismissed this with, "Bah, he's just all caught up in the thing himself." Using a fish magnet, Lucille pinned the card to the refrigerator door. "You just wait." She tapped the card. "We'll see who's right."

In some things her mother's willfulness seemed positively loony. But, on the other hand, what difference did it make? Either way, Lucille wasn't going to evacuate, Aggie didn't even want her to, and if Lucille didn't want insurance, that wasn't going to happen, either. And what was more, people were entitled to their opinions, even her mother.

Aggie took a deep breath.

"Okay, Ma, we'll see who's right. As for the insurance, that was just an idea. You can do what you want."

Without thinking, Aggie began to unpack the groceries. After a minute, Lucille joined in, and they did it together.

Chapter 58

⁓

S am Turner had been assigned a section of the southern levee, where
the emergency work hadn't begun yet. Beneath his wet-weather
gear, he wore a jacket with a city logo on the breast and a baseball cap
with the logo above the bill, and he had been given a flashlight and a
handheld radio transmitter, which he could use to communicate with
the captain of his watch.

At one end of the section, the floodwall began, and Sam would
shine his light along the seam joining levee to wall, mindful of
Chuck Fellows's warning about weak points. At the other end, where
the levee continued on, he sometimes encountered the inspector
coming from the other direction and they might chat briefly before
returning to their vigils. Other people patrolled at the base of the
levee, called the toe, where an inspection trench had been dug in
case of seepage.

The light faded—the long Northern dusk. Across the water,
sounds carried from the flood fight in East Jackson. In the distance,
he could make out the splashing of the power plant's spent cooling
water being pumped over the wall. And below his feet, the darkening
river crept up the embankment, the surface of the water filled with
chop and disappearing into the rising night. From it, billows of cold
swept across the top of the levee.

Sam felt better. He seemed to be clothed in glass and, during
moments of the chill upwelling from the river, in ice, perfectly trans-
parent.

Earlier, waiting to go on his first watch, he'd fallen into conversation with one of the other inspectors about the big flood they'd had
back in '65. The fellow had asked Sam if he'd been in Jackson then.
No, Sam said, Chicago. He didn't remember much of anything from
1965. What he remembered from his youth was the 1968 Democratic
Convention, the riot. He'd gone uptown and watched it happen.

And so the two of them jabbered on about these things, Sam the riot and the other fellow the flood, sharing their different stories of the 1960s, two guys talking.

Later, on top of the levee, a lady had come up the embankment with a cage, inside which was a furry animal about the size of a wiener dog. Groundhog, she told Sam. Sam had never seen a groundhog close-up before. A live trap, she said. She told him she'd release the animal in the Mines of Spain, where he wouldn't dig holes in the city's levee anymore. She was a middle-aged woman, stocky, with strong forearms. Sam watched as she lugged her burden away, the cage swinging as the groundhog paced, back and forth, back and forth, looking for a way out.

The night became darker. The beams of lights from the flood fighters in East Jackson broke up in the chop and were carried away by the victorious river. On his side, the flashlights of the inspectors played back and forth along the foot and crown of the levee.

Sam had imagined that some momentous event might change him, some great thing would happen and without him doing hardly anything, he'd become a new man. What a motherfucking joke, who was he trying to kid? He'd been in the papers, the *New York Times*, he'd been on national television, he'd been beaten up, nearly killed, and he was still just Sam. Soon he'd be laid off. Soon people would forget about him, and he had no idea what he'd do. It was like he'd been living under a spell all these years, and now…he didn't know. When you broke a spell, it was broken, that's all.

He'd eaten hardly anything over the last few days. After a time he wasn't hungry anymore. He stopped thinking about eating. He didn't think about anything in the future.

That was all right, he decided. Next he had to forget about the past. The past, the future. He thought of himself as becoming a specialist in giving things up.

His legs were tired from walking. He would have liked to sit down and rest, but he had a job to do. He liked this job. And if he stopped walking, the good feeling would go away. His leg was still not entirely healed, but like the hunger, the aching had passed away, leaving only a stiffness and the desire to rest, which he would not do.

Below him, in the pauses among other noises, he could hear the river lapping up against the bank, the water perfectly dark now, except where the reflections of lights from the other side were broken up and dragged along and sank into the black current.

CHAPTER 59

~

River stage: 24.6 feet

Deuce finished his shift on the pumping side at 7:00 a.m., then went down to help out at the river. He drove through the gates of the water plant and stopped to wait for a passing car, his mind untethered so that the car had already gone by before he realized that Aggie Klauer had been behind the wheel. She was already turning into Cardiff Lane and in a few moments had disappeared in among the cottages.

Deuce stopped at the head of Cardiff, peering along the low, narrow street, Aggie's car nowhere to be seen. He hesitated, then backed up and turned down into Little Wales himself and drove slowly along until he found where she had parked, in the driveway of the only two-story on the street. A number on the mailbox, no name.

He drove farther and turned around and drifted back and would have stopped if he could have thought of a plausible story to explain his sudden appearance. The house had obviously been a single-story bungalow at one time, identical with the others in the neighborhood. On top of the clapboard first story, a board-and-batten second had been added, of indifferent workmanship, in need of a paint job. The plantings around the place looked old and leggy, and in the driveway, Aggie's red Honda blocked in an ancient Dodge Dart. What business, he wondered, could she have in such a place at this hour of the morning?

Fearing she might spot him, he tapped the gas and, once back on the main drag, resumed his journey out to the river, thinking about his former duelist from the negotiating table.

At the National Guard checkpoint, he showed his pass. Then he drove through the gap left in the emergency levee so that water plant employees could finish sandbagging the wellheads on the peninsula outside the flood protection system. Chuck Fellows was there, talking to somebody Deuce didn't know. Every time he opened the newspaper, turned on the tube, went somewhere, there was Fellows.

The protection works now behind him, he drove down onto the peninsula, man-made and the size of several football fields. The wellheads were scattered about, eight of them ringed already, the ninth and last being worked on by volunteers and plant employees. They'd also sandbagged the emergency electrical poles the power company had set.

Normally the peninsula, with the Mississippi on one side, a small boat marina on the other, and a boat ramp at the far end, rose fifteen feet or more above the river. But floodwater had climbed its embankment, foot by foot, and in a few hours, a day at most, would cover the field. At the marina in the distance, men were sandbagging buildings. The boat ramp was drowned. And to the east, toward the river, nothing but water, disappearing into the fringe of trees far on the other side.

Deuce was not a man to be frightened easily, but the river frightened him. Every day he'd been down there helping, and every day the water had been higher. It rained and the river rose. It stopped raining and still the river rose. Other men would take a break and go out to look at it and talk about it with awe. That was not Deuce's way. He didn't try to put his feelings into words, not even to himself. There were no words.

He parked and got out and went over to the flatbed truck stationed next to the last well, the same truck he and J.J. had used to haul the old man's picker back to the farm, but now piled with sandbags that had been filled down at the city garage. A Northern States Power truck was there, too, and a crew busy lifting the well's transformer to the top of a pole that they had raised. A couple of porta-potties had been brought in, as well, and would have to be removed as soon as they were done. Nearby stood an empty table, which would have coffee and donuts on it as soon as the water plant secretary brought them on her way to work.

Deuce made a place for himself in the sandbag brigade, and set to work.

～

Chuck Fellows stopped at city hall long enough to get his messages from the day before. Paul Cutler wanted to see him. People's

Natural Gas had confirmed the meeting set up for that morning. And so on and so forth, down to a request from Aggie Klauer for the elevation at her mother's home.

"Where does her mother live?" he asked Joyce, the public works girl Friday.

"Little Wales."

"Right. I knew that. Okay, tell Howie to put it on his list." Chuck had what he needed from the survey crew. Now they were shooting elevations for civilians.

He went over to Cutler's office and gave him a rundown. Another storm coming in.

"So it's twenty-four now?" Cutler asked.

"Closer to twenty-five. Water will be up on the peninsula next to the small boat marina today. They're finishing ringing the wellheads up there. We're also chlorinating at the head of the plant."

"Good."

"Tomorrow or Sunday we'll top 26.8," Chuck added, but Cutler wasn't interested in this particular fact, the highest stage recorded since the white man had come west and started keeping track of such things.

"Don't talk to me about setting records," he said. "I've never understood why people are so fascinated by them. What about the crest, still thirty?"

Every day he asked about the crest.

Chuck nodded. "Eight days."

"I don't see how it can't go over thirty."

"Probably will. But nobody's willing to say it. My guess is that the Corps doesn't want to predict anything higher because then most likely they'd have to pay for what we're doing, even if it doesn't happen. They'd rather we wasted our money."

"I'm sure."

"The storms might peter out or miss us entirely. Or the Corps' prediction might simply be wrong on the high side. They're trying to extrapolate their models way the hell beyond the historical record. Nobody knows what the fuck they're talking about."

Cutler was just shaking his head. "And the Weather Service?"

"Twenty-eight. Anyway, predictions for us are irrelevant. We've got our protection. The river can do what it wants."

But Cutler wanted the comfort of a prediction. He wasn't the kind of man to build on spec.

"They've given up the flood fight in Prairie du Chien," Chuck told him. "Mostly towns everywhere have abandoned their first lines of defense and are putting their efforts into backup levees. Saving anything they can."

Cutler was nodding. "And you're how close to being done?"

"Three days. Four, max. Then I'll start our own backup work."

"The water plant first."

"That's right."

"Whatever else happens…," the manager said.

After the issue of who was going to pay for the emergency work, what Cutler worried about was the city water. Chuck was too tired to worry about the water or anything else.

"We'll do what we can," he told the city manager. The rest would just have to take care of itself.

∼

From the northern edge of the job site, Jack Kelley watched with Chuck Fellows as, in the distance, two men scrambled out of the last of the barges that Orville Massey, the skipper of the harbor tug, had positioned across the head of the island. The barge began to sink slowly into the floodwaters. Because of the current, the job of forming the barrier to protect the track site against debris in the river had proved trickier than anticipated. They'd been at it most of the morning, one barge at a time. Now the last one descended into the river chop, coming to rest at an awkward angle.

Massey had jockeyed the phalanx to divert flotsam back toward the main channel. Now, obviously dissatisfied, the old man swung the harbor tug around and spent several minutes attempting to nudge the final barge into a more upright position. Finally Chuck called him on the two-way and said forget it, it was good enough.

Shielding his eyes, Jack could make out the water forcing its way past the barges. Nearer, the river pushed through the thickets, making wakes behind the trees. As he stared, the trees themselves seemed to start moving. The sensation grew stronger, everything beginning to strain against the massive inundation, the construction site, the island itself, as if struggling to make headway against the onrushing current.

Chuck was still on the radio, thanking Massey.

Massey's ancient voice crackled back, "Got anything else you want done, speak now or forever hold your peace."

"That's it, Orv," Chuck told him. "You better get off the river." It'd been over a week since the Coast Guard had closed the Mississippi.

"You got any particular place you want me to drop your people off?"

"Small boat harbor."

"Wilco. Then I guess I'll be heading on home."

"Don't hit your head on any of the bridges," Chuck joked. "I owe you. You need anything, you know my number."

"Yup. Come on down to Abbey Station after this is all over, and we'll hoist one."

"Will do."

"Ten-four."

The radio went dead, and Jack watched as the small tug turned toward the harbor, which was awash in floodwater but where it was still possible to put people ashore.

Below Jack's feet, the flood lapped against the sides of the construction platform. Except for the access road, only the job site now rose above the river, water everywhere. And the crest still two hundred miles upstream.

People talked glibly about acts of God, but as Jack looked at the massively swollen river descending upon him, the flood did indeed seem like the Lord's work. And the dog track project even more unworthy. He could almost envision a latter-day Noah building his ark and Jack not invited, Jack busy constructing his pleasure palace, which the deluge was coming to wash from the face of the earth. Of course, such thoughts were vacuous. Jack wasn't like one of those little old ladies who went around sprinkling her house with holy water before an electrical storm. He didn't believe God acted in the world except through the hearts of men.

"I can send you a flatbed with filled sandbags," Chuck said, breaking the spell. They turned away and started walking back toward the construction trailer.

"What about volunteers? Can you spare some more?" Jack asked. "I hate to use tradesmen. It means splitting up crews."

"No problem," Fellows said. "Got more than I know what to do with."

They were moving quickly because they both had things to do, Jack the weekly contractors' meeting already under way without him, and Chuck off to somewhere. One of Mitch Mitchell's graders swung by, skimming sand from the top of the site to use for the levee Jack was building for extra protection. In the distance, the roofers and glaziers and other laborers continued to work on the grandstand in the light rain. At the kennels, converted into bunkhouses for the people now living on the job site, a panel truck was unloading provisions. And beyond, at the far side, stood the semi-mounted generator Jack had rented along with 8,000-gallon tankers of fuel in case power to the site was lost.

Near the trailer, he and Chuck went their separate ways.

~

"Yes, but suppose you don't turn the gas off?" Chuck asked. He'd driven out to Tri-State Natural Gas on the west end of town to talk to the people in charge of the company's gas distribution system.

"That's right," agreed Dave Solis, the company's technical chief, who had taken the lead in the meeting. "Still," he reiterated, "if water doesn't go over the wall after gas is cut off and commercial firms start to lose product and the food in homeowners' freezers goes bad.... But you're right, liability is even greater when you don't shut it off, and say a big fire results."

Chuck noted the tension in the room. Like everybody else, the gas people faced stark alternatives. Anybody that liked to hedge his bets was shit out of luck.

One guy had said nothing. Frank Dunn, the CEO, sat angrily at the head of the table. Chuck liked the look of the fellow. Under these crisis conditions, efficiency implied anger, anger kept in check, just barely.

The company's floodplain map had been mounted on the wall. Dave, the technical guy, pointed here and there and talked about shutdown areas.

"In an emergency we can bring people in from the outlying districts. It'd take about an hour to shut off all the valves in the affected area."

"You won't have an hour," Chuck told him.

The bluntness of this assessment had a dampening effect on the conversation for some moments.

"The city's trying to get people to evacuate, isn't that right?" the company's PR guy finally piped up. Chuck had been introduced to him, but couldn't remember his name. He'd met scores of people over the last couple of weeks and mostly remembered faces but not names.

"If people are leaving their homes, they can at least shut off the gas first. We can work with the media to get the word out, have them publish diagrams of typical gas shutoffs."

This idea sounded sensible to Chuck. But diagrams in newspapers? "If you want to make sure gas gets turned off, you've gotta do it yourself."

They talked about this halfway measure, which, as Chuck thought about it, seemed as much a PR gimmick as anything else. Probably it had liability ramifications, too. Just about everything did. But it made one big assumption: that people would actually evacuate.

Chuck looked at his watch. This seemed to be the signal for Frank Dunn, the CEO, who abruptly cut off the cross talk that had arisen around the table, told the PR guy to contact the media, told Dave to assign a tech to do shutoffs, then turned to Chuck. "No way we can turn off the gas down in the Flats. If you told me the dike was gonna fail tomorrow, were absolutely certain about it, then maybe, just maybe, but we got customers to service, and by God, we're gonna do it. And hope to hell you can keep the damn river out of the city."

During this exchange, Chuck's beeper had gone off, and he borrowed an empty office and a phone to call down to the EOC. He had an urgent call from somebody named Chuck Fedders, who didn't or wouldn't say what it was about, just that it was very urgent.

Unless Chuck saw actual blood, he wasn't of a mind to think much about matters that were merely "very urgent," with no specifics attached, but the guy's name was Chuck and, in a mindless sort of way, that counted for something. So he called the number the clerk at the EOC had given him.

"Beneficial Credit," a cheerful feminine voice said on the other end of the line.

"Fedders," Chuck said.

"Which Mr. Fedders, please?"

"Chuck."

"Can I say who's calling?"

Chuck identified himself. Already he didn't like this.

"Hello, Mr. Fellows, thanks for calling back," said a male voice, equally cheerful.

"I understand this is urgent," Chuck said.

"Yes, indeed, sir. Yes, indeed. It's my understanding you have a Mr. Jason Earl working for you."

"Never heard of him."

"He's a trucker, Mr. Fellows. I'm told the city has hired him to haul clay, you know, during the emergency."

The city had hired some independents, to augment the city's own crews and the people provided by Norquist.

"Maybe we've hired him," Chuck told Fedders. "Anybody with a truck can find plenty of work now."

"Well, yes, sir. And that's the whole point, isn't it?"

"What are you talking about?"

"Anybody can get work now. I don't want to cast aspersions on Mr. Earl. Just let me say that he has taken out a sizable loan from Beneficial Credit and is substantially in arrears with respect to the repayment."

"Nothing to do with me," Chuck said. He saw the drift here.

"Not directly, no, sir. But we would be much appreciative if the city would inform us when Mr. Earl is paid for his current work with you."

"You want us to be your collection agency?"

"Well, no, not at all. We'd just like to know when Mr. Earl's paid. I mean, there's an emergency and all that, we fully understand that. But, you know, business—"

Chuck cut the son of a bitch off. "Look, if Earl works for us, he'll get paid. But you're right, there's a goddamn emergency on. I don't have time for this bullshit."

And he hung up.

As he returned to the meeting, muttering under his breath about dirtbags like Chuck Fedders, his beeper went off again.

~

After the contractors' meeting, Jack Kelley walked over to the grandstand and watched the last of the plastic curtains being installed, sealing the west end of the building so that the inside work could begin in earnest. Not that the space was absolutely watertight. Far from it. But, as with the skewed placing of the last barge earlier, it was good enough. Good enough was all Jack asked for.

Eddie Blue, the track's architect, had finally come through with the design change that Jack been badgering him for, and the glazier had expedited the work. Now glass separated the grandstand area on the west end of the building from the clubhouse seating still open to the sky on the east end. The curtains had been hung off the ironwork to shield the concourse, offices, restaurants, and betting counter areas. A jackleg arrangement all around.

Dexter Walcott and Tony Vasconcellos and the other contractors with interior work to accomplish had their crews back. At the meeting, they'd all groused about the conditions and lined up their excuses, but Jack could sense the excitement, too. This was a project they'd talk about for a long time.

Which was interesting, because Jack didn't think he would. He just wanted the whole business to be done, through, over with, so he could go on to something else. His attitude now wasn't all that different from Chuck Fellows's, he supposed, although their reasons couldn't conceivably be the same. Not that Jack knew exactly why he felt the way he did. It wasn't merely the ultimate triviality of the project, although that must be part of it. Or even the pain his lackadaisical Catholicism caused him, belief without intensity. He just didn't know why.

He could still, it was true, take some satisfaction from watching the crowd of laborers now set loose on the guts of the building. But the feeling lacked the old intensity. As hectic as his life had become, as determined as he remained to finish the project, he felt some part of himself withdrawing, almost like the beginning of withdrawal from life itself.

Dexter Walcott was on the way over. Jack, glad at the prospect of getting out of his own morbid thoughts for the moment and dealing with something practical, went to meet him.

∾

With all their gear loaded on top of the hi-rail—the one-ton pickup equipped with rail wheels that the railroad maintenance people used nowadays instead of handcars—Walter Plowman and the other three men drove on the Illinois Central tracks out onto the railroad bridge, stopping at the first of the thirty stations where they'd take velocities and soundings. For the next three hours, they'd unload and set up the equipment, the GS technicians would take their readings, and everyone would pitch in to haul the apparatus from station to station.

Fortunately, railroad traffic was light. The Illinois Central sectionman that accompanied them had no trouble getting what he called track-and-time authority from his dispatcher. That part had been easy. Taking discharge readings off the railroad bridge, however, had turned into a major hassle, the two Geological Survey techs, with their bad backs, glad to have Walter and the IC guy along to help with all of the bullwork.

"Cold front coming in tomorrow, gentlemen," Walter announced as they were unloading. "Thunderstorms. Severe, looks like, although it depends on how fast the front's moving."

They discussed the effect this might have. Working in the rain had become routine. A day like today, misty and warm, seemed almost eerie, like the eye of a hurricane.

They mounted the framing between the tracks and railing, then carried the counterweights over to hold it in place. Next came the crane, which extended beyond the railing, and finally the velocity meter and two-hundred-pound weight and reel.

Walter was already sweating. He stood back as the GS techs unreeled the meter and the weight until they just touched the surface of the floodwater below and then read off the figure on the dial and did the quick calculation to determine stage.

"Twenty-five point three." Getting close. Barely a foot and a half below the flood of record.

Next, to estimate depth and discharge in that section, the counter was zeroed and the bomb-shaped weight with the meter lowered farther, disappearing into the choppy brown water. Having a little time to himself, Walter stepped several feet away and leaned on the railing and watched the flood sweeping past.

He would join in the chatter about jobs and families and so forth, but as they moved from station to station across the Mississippi each day, he liked these moments by himself, a chance to meditate upon this, the greatest event in his life. He never got tired of watching the river. The water had a lot of debris in it, which wouldn't slack off until the crest or later. Even today, with the mist prickling his nostrils, he smelled the peculiar odor, partly not an odor at all, but only the cold shed by the water. At times the great plain before him seemed to be boiling rather than moving. Even directly beneath his feet, where the current's velocity was most apparent, it hardly resembled a rapids, the water moving at barely three miles per hour, perhaps twice that at midstream. The power wasn't in its speed but its momentum, the great mass of the water flowing by—290,000 cubic feet per second according to their calculation the day before, more now. For all its evident presence, the real power of the river remained hidden. In the distance, the water itself disappeared, the sense that you could see it an illusion, for all you were looking at were the gray reflections of the clouds sliding by overhead.

Walter had been out there so much over the last week, watching the Mississippi rise by degrees, that the floodscape had become almost commonplace, like a beautiful picture seen too many times. But it made no difference; he didn't want to miss any of it. And each day, when he first stepped away from the others to gauge the change over the last twenty-four hours, the impact of the scene returned with renewed vividness. Although he had predicted the flood and his prediction was coming to pass, he realized now how little he had truly understood.

When the others had finished, Walter returned to lend a hand and they wrestled the gear to the next section across the rough surface of the roadbed.

~

Norquist, the contractor for the emergency work, was inspecting the truck when Chuck arrived and walked up to him on the crown of the levee.

"What happened?"

"Driver claims his brakes seized up as he was backing."

The dump truck canted off the landward edge of the levee. Chuck and Norquist squatted down to look at the broken rear axel.

"We could just bulldoze it over the edge."

The truck didn't belong to the city or to Norquist.

"Whose is it?" Chuck asked. He was remembering the conversation he'd just had with Fedders.

"Don't know. Hey!" he yelled over to a cluster of laborers who had come for a look-see, "what's your name?" One of them detached himself from the others and came forward.

"Duane Coulter," he said.

Norquist told him to repeat his story to Chuck. After he finished, Chuck, having the vague idea that incompetents ran in packs, asked him, "You know an independent named Jason Earl?"

"Never heard of him. Why?" the trucker said.

"Not important." Chuck turned to Norquist. "Is there a wrecker on the way?"

"Yeah."

"If he can manage to move this thing, okay. If not, go ahead and bulldoze it. You better get the clay out of it, first, though, whatever you do."

"My idea exactly."

"Hey, wait a second," the trucker complained.

Chuck told him, "We'll try to get it out of there, okay? But we can't waste a lotta time." He looked at Norquist. "Okay?"

"Okay," Norquist said.

❧

As Dexter Walcott ran toward the site, he could see Jack Kelley coming at a run, too, stumbling as he ducked through the sheeting hung up on the deck to isolate the work area. They arrived almost at the same instant. Several fights had broken out—or scuffles, didn't hardly deserve the name of fights—but the main event was between Acey Blake, Dex's man, and one of the electricians. Acey had the white boy's shirt pulled up half over his head. Each man was attempting to pin the other's arms while freeing his own in order to flail away. It reminded Dex of one of them hockey fights. Acey would get his arm free and lay a couple of uppercuts on before the white boy managed to corral him again, then they'd switch roles. Mustafa had closed in on Tony Vasconcellos's son and was having a discouraging word with him. There was plenty of shoving and yelling, too, but nobody would've confused it with the Friday night fights. These boys didn't much like each other, but that didn't turn them into what you'd call fighting machines.

Dex looked at the scene, shook his head, and then waded in, and he, Jack, and the elder Vasconcellos managed to restore order after a while. What had happened turned out to be simple enough. Outside, the sandbags were being offloaded from the flatbed truck that Chuck Fellows had sent over. The white boy had been watching and called it "nigger work" within the hearing of Acey, Acey being of a prickly temperament. Words were exchanged. Acey made a negative comment about the white boy's mother, and that led directly to fisticuffs. Upon inspection, Acey had got the better of it, having landed at least one blow flush on the peckerwood's bugle, which was bleeding copiously.

Jack, who had been so determined to keep the lid on, stormed around, livid. Dex, however, took a somewhat mellower view of the matter.

The CM dragged him and Vasconcellos aside.

"If this was a war," Kelley steamed, "those two guys would be shot. And as far as I'm concerned, it is a war, and I want them both off the job site."

"My man didn't start it," Vasconcellos claimed.

Nobody was better than Acey when it came to hanging drywall, so Dex wasn't of a mind to lose him. "The white boy used the word *nigger* within my man's hearing, Jack. These boys have been raggin' on us since day one. Not when you're around, of course. And not to our faces. Subtle-like. I haven't bothered to complain. We expect this sort of thing. But these people do it enough, my boys are gonna start reacting. It's just human nature. You understand what I'm saying? And as for who threw the first punch, it wasn't my man."

Jack said, "I don't care who started it. Does this look like a courtroom?"

Dex had to laugh at that. "Not any courtroom I'd wanna be tried in," he said.

"Those two guys are gone," Kelley told them.

Dex didn't want to lose Acey, but since Jack wasn't prepared to be reasonable, a choice had to be made. As Vasconcellos tried to make his case more forcefully and got nowhere fast, Dex considered the situation. Finally he said to Jack, "Maybe we can get somethin' done here, but first I gotta talk to my men."

"Okay, but you understand—"

"I understand," Dex acknowledged. "This ain't no courtroom, you ain't no judge, you the executioner."

As Dex took his people aside, they were grinning and talking the talk. Acey was the hero of the moment. Dex, however, was not so happy with Acey, and as soon as they were far enough away to have a little privacy, he laid into him.

A half hour later, he found Jack in the construction trailer with his man Sean and Vasconcellos.

Dex said, "I've talked to my boys and it's all right with us if Tony's man stays on, just so long as I can keep my man, too."

Kelley shook his head. "No way. They're both gone. We could be isolated from the mainland anytime, and I'll be damned if I'm gonna have troublemakers on the job site in the middle of a damn flood."

Vasconcellos was saying nothing, but something in his expression suggested to Dex that he was prepared to go along with Kelley. Dex was not surprised. He saw the writing on the wall. But he wasn't prepared to lose Acey unless these boys understood a thing or two.

He turned a chair around and sat down and made himself comfortable.

"You boys ever heard of the dozens?" he asked.

~

Muscles sore from slinging sandbags, Deuce had returned to his apartment to take a shower and try to catch a few hours sleep before he had to go back to work. But the image of Aggie Klauer turning into Little Wales continued to prick at him, and so finally he got up and called the library and asked the woman at the reference desk to check the city directory and tell him who lived at 37 Cardiff.

Lucille Klauer.

Deuce thanked the woman and hung up and stood drumming his first two fingers on the countertop, as he might drum while waiting for some clown at the poker table to call or raise or fold, except that at the moment he was the clown and it was his choice. Raise or fold?

He had a name. Lucille Klauer. Lucy. Aggie's mother? Sister? Sister-in-law? Cousin? Impossible to tell. He needed more information. The obvious person to ply with questions was J.J. Dusterhoft. That would be easy. J.J. was probably out on his truck hauling clay for the emergency work. Deuce could call Peg down in the comm center and get patched through. Sometimes it proved useful having ex-girlfriends in low places.

But wait a second. Did he really want to call J.J.? To call J.J. was to announce his interest in Aggie.

Just thinking this thought brought him up short. *Was* he interested in her? He liked her intelligence, certainly. He liked someone who could play the game. And he also liked the way she looked at him. And she improved upon acquaintance, that too. But if with most of his former girlfriends, part of the trouble arose from the fact that it was all too easy to see what a future with them would be like, in Aggie's case the problem was precisely the opposite. He could barely conceive what their next encounter might be like, much less anything beyond that.

At any rate, he didn't want to raise or fold, not just yet, and J.J., for all his virtues, could not be counted on to keep his mouth shut. Some other way had to be found.

Assuming Lucille Klauer turned out to be Aggie's mother, that would be easy enough to establish. Aggie was a native, so he could go down to the recorder's office in the county courthouse and look at her birth certificate.

First, he needed some sleep. He set the alarm.

∼

Five hours later, in the dark, he drove down Cardiff for the second time that day. Aggie's car was not there, but he didn't expect it to be. No point in waiting for her reappearance, which could be whenever. He parked behind the Dodge Dart and got out and in the darkness picked his way over the soggy ground to the back door.

Lights burned downstairs, so someone was still up. He rang the bell and a dog inside barked—a single, rather listless bark—and then nothing. He opened the storm door and rapped on the window, which induced a couple more barks, as pro forma as the first. Eventually he heard movement inside and a raspy woman's voice telling him to keep his britches on. The outside light came on, and the door swung open.

The house exhaled, a billow of food and cigarette odors engulfing him. Inside the door, a cigarette in one hand and a drink in the other, stood the ghost of Aggie Klauer.

Chapter 60

~

Walter woke up at 4:00 a.m. and couldn't go back to sleep. He lay on his back and listened to the silence immediately outside and the night traffic sounds farther away and, from the distant waterfront, the faint ruminations of construction equipment. At 4:15 he climbed quietly out of bed. El turned and groaned, but said nothing. He couldn't tell if she was awake.

He dressed in the darkness, putting on the clothes he'd worn the day before, then went downstairs and closed the doors to the kitchen so the breakfast smells wouldn't spread. He was very hungry, but as soon as he had filled the coffee maker with water and got the beans out of the freezer and the grinder from the back of the counter, he realized he was too impatient to eat.

He left the stuff where it was and drove rather than walked to the Jackson Building. The security man let him in and activated the elevator so that he didn't need to walk up the nine flights to KJTV. He let himself into the station and waved to Abe, the engineer who filled the hours between the late-night talk shows and morning news with reruns of local programming and old movies. Terry, the young woman who produced, wrote, and anchored the local inserts into the network morning news feed, was dashing around in her usual controlled frenzy. Walter showed up at the station at all hours, so they weren't surprised to see him.

He chatted briefly with Terry, then went into his cubicle and turned on his radio, tuned to an all-news station out of Chicago, and his TV, the weather channel. Next he ripped off the latest product from the National Weather Service wire. He turned on Hazel and called up the current radar image from Waterloo, then dialed a private number he had for the NWS office in Des Moines and talked to the guy on duty out there.

When he was satisfied, he looked at the time—5:23. Still pretty early, but he didn't give it a second thought.

The night clerk at the motel where the Geological Survey people were staying patched him through, and after a couple of rings Duane's groggy voice came on the line. Walter didn't bother to identify himself. He merely said, "The storm has picked up speed. It's already over the western part of the state. Lightning, hail the size of walnuts."

On the other end of the line, Duane yawned enormously. "Give us forty-five minutes," he said.

Walter hung up. Who else? Arnie, the Illinois Central sectionman. They needed to make sure they could get track-and-time clearance. He made the call. Then he sat staring at Hazel and wondering who else he should contact.

~

Chuck Fellows dropped the receiver back into its cradle. Diane, waking up and flopping onto her back, asked who it was.

"Walt Plowman. Storm's speeded up. Gonna be ugly—hail, lightning, maybe even twisters, all manner of shit." Incoming.

"The people on the waterfront."

"That's right." He looked at the clock on the bedside stand and decided how much time he had to tell the foremen doing the emergency work to shut down their operations and get their men under cover. Same thing for the inspectors. Once things settled down, they could go back out again.

He rose at once, against the mounting exhaustion of the long days. Diane was up, too, and they could hear Francine in the guest room, dressing to go out to the job site. It being Saturday, Diane would be on kid duty.

Downstairs they found Francine dressed not to go out to the dog track, but to return to Waterloo. Dexter had told her to go home; he didn't want a woman on the job site when it was cut off from the mainland.

Francine was prowling glumly around the kitchen, appeal in her voice as she said, looking first at Chuck, "I can take care of myself," and then at Diane, "Any man tries something with me, he live to regret it." Chuck didn't doubt it for a moment. In a feminine outfit, her designer jeans and cowgirl blouse, Francine looked every inch a woman ready for steer wrestling or whatever else came up. Some asshole would make a serious mistake if he misinterpreted her normal deference.

"So it's back to Waterloo?" Diane asked.

Francine hung her head. "Hate leaving like this, you know, in the middle of things."

"Stay, then. Chuck's probably got something for you to do."

"Help with the mud boxes, I suppose. Another chance to piss off white construction workers."

"And you could help with the kids, too," Diane suggested. "That would free me up to spend more time down at the mobilization center. You could help out there, too."

And so, in a few moments, it was settled. Francine whooped.

Diane had already set about scrambling some eggs. Chuck wolfed down the food standing up, listening as Francine recounted an incident at the track site from the day before. Then he filled his thermos with coffee and headed on out.

∾

Aggie detoured by her mother's on the way to Five Flags and told her that a big thunderstorm was on the way, lightning and hail and lots of wind. Sure enough, Lucille had windows open all over the place, less to get rid of the stale cigarette smoke than simply because she liked to keep the windows open.

She wasn't in the house when Aggie arrived, however. She had dragged a kitchen chair out to the driveway and was sitting there in her mauve sweater, the one that had gotten so baggy and stretched out of shape that it reached to her knees. She was smoking and drinking her coffee and observing the world in detail. The dogs were out and about.

"You want I should go in and close some of the windows, Ma?" Aggie suggested. "That way you wouldn't have to get up."

"I have no intention of getting up, and you can leave the windows be."

"Okeydoke," Aggie said. The point of the visit, besides making sure that nothing had happened to her mother overnight, was to let Lucille know the storm was coming, for she did not pay attention to the news in the morning.

In the old days, when the slough was still there and people hadn't started to move away yet, others would have been outside, too, even at that hour of the morning. Now Lucille sat there mostly alone, although every once in a while someone from one of the other houses might happen to appear briefly, taking out the trash or whatever, and exchange a few words with her, a matter of courtesy. And sometimes John Turcotte would stop, and they'd chat about the old days.

Lucille, of course, was not a Klauer, Klauer being an uptown name. Bernie Klauer had married Lucille Duccini, of the river-rat Duccinis, and therein lay a tale. Except for the drinking, Aggie was her father's child. Another tale. That was Little Wales, filled with tales.

"Those people you sent were here yesterday," Lucille said.

"People?"

"From the city."

"The survey crew? That was quick. I just asked on Wednesday. What did they tell you?"

"That I live in a hole. As if I didn't know."

"How high will the water go? I was thinking that we might move some stuff upstairs, just to be on the safe side."

Lucille did not respond to this. Instead she said, "Your friend was here, too. The mayor's son."

"El? She doesn't have a son."

"The other mayor, the one that resigned."

Aggie's heart seized up for a moment. "Deuce was here?"

"That's what I said."

"What did he want?"

"Who knows? Looking for you, I suppose."

Could it be true? Aggie wondered.

"Said you and him negotiated with each other over one of the union contracts."

"Don't you remember, Ma? I talked about that."

"Kinda cute," Lucille said. She still had an eye for the men.

"What did you talk about?"

"This and that. He wanted to know if I needed any help evacuating. I set him straight. Then we started talking about the cellar. Don't know how we got on that. Anyway, he asked what I was gonna do about seepage, on account of I'm not that far from the river. That made some sense. I told him about the sump pump. That's about it. Then he went off to work. Said he worked down there at the water plant."

"That's right. How strange." Aggie didn't know what to make of it. "What about the survey crew, Ma? What did they tell you?"

Lucille threw the lighted cigarette down, and it sizzled momentarily in a small puddle, sending up a last-gasp thread of smoke.

"Water up to the eaves. Suppose I could crawl out onto the roof there, like you see in pictures. Me and the dogs."

So much for Aggie's idea of moving stuff up to the second floor. Her mother was looking at her, waiting for her to say something. Aggie, however, didn't have any more time to serve as Lucille's punching bag. She reminded her mother about the coming storm and then got back in her car to continue on to the mobe center.

As she drove, she tried to figure out just why Deuce might have shown up on Lucille's doorstep. Aggie was still officially mad at him for walking out on the negotiations. The coward. But still... Her temptation was to come up with an explanation flattering to herself, but she supposed the real reason must be much more prosaic. Probably he had merely stumbled onto the fact that her mother lived down in Little Wales, right near the water plant, and as a gesture decided to offer to help her move if she wanted. That *must* be it. If he had actually been interested in Aggie, he would have called her up. Wouldn't he? Of course. He'd dated all these other women. It was simply inconceivable that his standard strategy involved approaching their mothers first. The idea was laughable. *Yes*, she decided, *good*. This reasoning relieved her anxiety for the moment. A relationship with someone like Deuce? Out of the question.

But it had certainly been nice of him to offer to help Lucille. It was an aspect of himself that Aggie had never expected.

~

Once more, Chuck and Jack Kelley were side by side on the prow of the job site, watching the river come at them full bore.

"I handled it the way I saw fit," Kelley said. "If you don't like it, that's just tough."

"Dex's man didn't start the fight." This argument was pointless. Chuck didn't have the time. So he added, "But it's your call, Jack. You know and I know you're just trying to get through the project."

"We've been lucky so far. Yesterday was the first time, and I don't intend to have a repeat. But you're right, I'm just trying to finish the project. That's all. That's what I care about."

He said this almost matter-of-factly, as if speaking solely for himself, not trying to wrap it up in some greater good, some grand rah-rah sentiment, the community or whatever the hell. Chuck had found recent exchanges with Jack more satisfying, Jack having finally abandoned the idea that Chuck, against all evidence to the contrary, might be brought around, might even be a nice guy after all, if Jack could only figure out the formula.

"You ever hear of a game called the dozens?" Jack asked.

"Yeah. It's an insult game. Played in inner cities."

"Right. And whoever throws the first punch is declared the loser."

"What about it?"

"Apparently some of the white workers have been baiting the blacks, not directly, waiting until they're near enough to overhear and then saying certain things. The blacks, according to Walcott, have been letting it slide. Up to now."

"But no more?"

"That's right, no more."

"So it's the dozens, is it?"

"Just what I need."

The whites would be no match for the blacks.

"You can ask a man to turn a deaf ear only so long," Chuck said.

Jack said nothing and then, "I suppose."

Chuck nodded toward the western sky, where towering black clouds were massing.

"Better be ready to get your guys down off the steel," he said.

"Yeah," Kelley agreed, "I know."

Leaving the job site, Chuck stopped on the access road and got out to watch the floodwater flowing along the embankment. He stopped again near the bridge back to the mainland and inspected the warring currents funneling into the narrow underpass, where all the shit flowing down Kiakiak Channel ended up. More brush and lumber and other debris had piled up. He needed to get a crew down there again. The stone he'd used to reinforce the levee seemed to be holding up, that much at least.

As he got back into his vehicle, however, he reminded himself that problems cropped up where you least expected them. You worked your ass off dealing with some situation you knew about, then got blindsided.

Not that it much bothered Chuck.

In fact, he rather liked the idea.

~

They weren't going to beat the storm. The GS guys were rushing to finish the readings at the twenty-sixth section. Walter ignored the river. He was watching the lightning strikes on the bluffs behind downtown Jackson. One seemed very near his home, and he wondered where El was. She worried about him being out there on the railroad bridge in the middle of the flood, the storm bearing down on them, guns blazing, but Walter paid attention. El was the one with the flippant attitude toward the weather, as if it was nothing to her. She was capable of rushing out into the middle of a lightning storm for no reason better than she'd left something in her car or suddenly took it into her head she had to fetch in the mail. In all their years together, she treated the weather about the same way another woman would have treated the sports her husband watched. He felt his familiar irritation rising at these thoughts. But mostly he was worried, not knowing where she was.

He could see the rain now. No, not rain, it wasn't rain.

"How much time, gentlemen?" he asked.

"Just the two-tenths."

"Better hurry. Hail on the way."

The winds were gusting around them. The lightning seemed to be skirting north and south, but not the hail, which fell not like rain, but a vast meteor shower. He could no longer see the houses on the bluff.

"Better cut the time down on the meter," Walter warned.

"Okay. We can do a half count." Which was twenty seconds, measuring the number of rotations of the meter's cups for half the normal time.

Walter could hear the first reports of the hail from the far end of the bridge, a pinging sound.

"Better make it a quarter count," he warned.

The hailstones closed in, banging against the steel trusses and ricocheting at crazy angles. One clipped his ear, stinging. They were all around him now, and the pings had turned into sharp metallic reports.

"Ow! Shit!" one of the GS guys said. The racket of the storm continued to rise.

"Leave it!"

"No! We might lose it!"

Cursing as the hail slammed into them from every direction, they all four dragged the meter and weight and boom back onto the bridge and then sprinted for the hi-rail. Walter scrambled in, but not before something slammed into his lower back, a sharp pain. Crowded in the cab, he held his back, his eyes tearing. The hail continued to come, cracking against the glass and metal, so loud they had to shout to hear each other.

And then the rain began.

~

The clouds marshaled overhead and a nighttime blackness fell across the city. Chuck drove the waterfront, yelling at laggards to get the hell under cover. As the hail began to fall, he picked up several men still out in the open and drove toward the mobilization center. The storm intensified, the individual concussions becoming a continuous din. The landscape disappeared in a whiteout, forcing him to slow way down as the hailstones rebounded from the windshield and hood and street.

At Five Flags, as they waited in the vehicle for the hail to end, a stone the size of a baseball hit the windshield flush and a crack streaked across the glass. Chuck cursed, then thought, fuck it, why should he be spared.

Finally the storm paused and they made a dash for Five Flags. Aggie Klauer and the other people inside the building were crowded around the entrance, looking out at the ground littered with hailstones which crunched underfoot as Chuck ran. Torrents of rain had begun to fall. Aggie and the others made way, and then Aggie followed Chuck inside.

"Wild," Aggie said, her voice bright with amazement.

"Cracked my windshield."

"Sorry."

He waved the sympathy away, looking toward the phone bank, where as quickly as a phone was put down it started to ring again. One of the operators put her hand over the mouthpiece and gestured toward them, and Chuck and Aggie went over. They were starting to get calls that nobody knew what to do with—people whose homes had been damaged by the hail and were demanding that someone come at once and make repairs to keep the rain out.

Chuck counted to three and thought, *People are morons*, then took the phone and talked to the caller himself, informing the woman who she was speaking to, asking her to describe the problem, and then telling her that until the storm was over, she would have to deal with the situation herself. She should put cardboard or any other available material in the broken windows, then go up in her attic to look for leaks in the roof and put buckets under any she found. Under no circumstances was she to go up on the roof herself or attempt to get anybody else to go up on the roof. Did she understand? When the storm was over, she should listen to the radio for information about the extent of the damages citywide and just whom she should contact to get help. "There are a lot of people with problems. We can't get to any of them until the storm is over. I need for you to understand this." The woman agreed reluctantly. "Thank you," Chuck said and hung up. "Handle all calls the same way," he told Aggie. "I'm going up to the EOC."

Back in his vehicle, he drove through wind and rain to the center, located in donated space in the phone company building, where Seth Brunel—now pressed into service as the EOC coordinator—gave him a sitrep. Most of the activity so far had been to the northwest of the city. The NWS had broadcast a flash flood warning for the Little Mesquatie valley. An intense cell was sitting on top of the basin out there. One of the ham operators, brought into the EOC with his two-meter rig, had talked to someone who'd seen a funnel cloud. All hell was breaking loose.

Chuck tried unsuccessfully to reach Walt Plowman, then called the NWS meteorologist on duty out at the airport, who told him that the squall line reached from Maquoketa in the south to the Turkey River in the north and would clear out in about a half hour. But intense rain lay behind it.

A short time later, as Chuck was jawing with the director of disaster services for the county and the reps from fire and police, a flash of lightning filled the room with a vivid neon glow, and a moment later an explosive thunderclap detonated practically on top of them. Chuck flinched. The lights in the room went out, leaving them almost in total darkness despite the fact that it was the middle of the day. Then the lights flickered back on. Chuck went to the window. He could see lights nowhere else. He pressed his cheek against the glass, peering toward the end of the block. The traffic signals were out.

"Call the power company," he told Seth, then changed his mind. "I'll do it." They had a dedicated line, so he got through immediately. The company's maintenance chief told him it appeared that the

Eighth Street substation had been hit. They had a crew on the way. As soon as they knew anything, they'd call him back.

For the next couple of minutes, an unnatural calm descended. The phones fell silent, and Chuck had a vision of people across the city hunting around for the candles they failed to have out and ready. There'd probably be traffic accidents, too, drivers who didn't know the protocol when the signals were out.

One of the phones rang. The operator passed the call on to Seth, who said, "It's Kenny," and handed the receiver to Chuck. Kenny Nauman, down at the Ice Harbor.

"What's up?" Chuck asked.

"The electricity's off down here."

"Off all over, looks like. The Eighth Street substation probably got fried."

"That right? I got a problem. The generator didn't come on. I ran through the checklist. Don't see what's wrong."

Chuck thought for a second. Did he want to call the repair guy they had lined up? No, he'd take a look himself first. "Hang on. I'm on my way."

He told Seth to hold the fort, he knew where to find Chuck if he needed him. A minute later, he was back in his 4x4 and heading for the Ice Harbor, glad to put the EOC behind him. He spent as little time there as he could.

The rain continued to pour down, and he was drenched in the short walk to the machine shed next to the harbor gates. Inside, Nauman was poking around with his flashlight.

Hardly had Chuck gotten through the door before his beeper went off. He tilted it out and Kenny flashed his light on it. The EOC.

He called at once. The man who answered immediately transferred him to Seth.

"What?" Chuck asked.

"We just got a report of flooding through the Mercy Valley."

"Shit, not that again. Forget it, it's nothing."

"I dunno, Chuck. The guy seemed pretty definite. He said water's streaming down Couler Ave., heading for town."

That would be the Little Mesquatie, backing up into its old, abandoned channel, but no way could it backdoor the city, a rumor that simply refused to die. Chuck tried to envision what was actually happening.

"Okay, Seth, this is what you do. Call Hank Kraft down at the city garage and tell him to send two of the flatbeds with sandbags and all the people he can spare out to Couler and Diamond. That'll be where they need to sandbag. Keep one of the flatbeds there and send the other on to Greenwood Estates. If there's water, that's the other area that'll be having a problem. We'll need maybe thirty people at Diamond, the rest, as many as you can get, at Greenwood. Call Aggie Klauer at Five Flags and have her put all her standbys on buses and send them on up."

"Gotcha," Seth said and rang off.

Chuck now turned his attention to the balky generator.

"The engine seems okay," Kenny said.

Chuck began by checking the circuit breakers. He always assumed if there was a problem, it was the most obvious one. They'd run out of fuel oil. The battery was dead. Someone had pulled the plug.

When he'd satisfied himself it wasn't anything trivial, he ran quickly over Kenny's checklist and then immediately got on the horn to the generator repairman they had on retainer. He needed to get his ass down there pronto. Half the storm water in the city was flowing into the Ice Harbor. If they couldn't start pumping it over the wall again pretty damn quick, they were gonna have a flood on their hands that didn't have anything to do with the river. The guy said he was out the door.

Then Chuck called Bud Pregler and told him to contact the Furlong brothers. The city was taking water fast. If they couldn't get the pump up and running, they might have to use the dredge and figure out a way to pump water over the wall. He'd know in a couple of hours. If so, he'd arrange for more manpower for them.

"There's something else, boss," Kenny said as soon as Chuck hung up. "I don't know if you want to deal with it now."

"What?"

"The gates."

"What about them?"

"Best you take a look for yourself."

"Okay, but make it quick."

And so they went back into the drenching rain, Kenny leading the way out onto the harbor gates. As soon as Chuck set foot on the catwalk across them, he understood what Kenny was talking about.

"When did you notice?"

"Just before you came. After the generator failed, I came out here to look at the water level in the harbor."

Beneath Chuck's feet, the gate was vibrating. About halfway out to the point where the two gates met, Kenny stopped and pointed down with his flashlight and Chuck could see where water was bubbling up on the harbor side. Some sort of gap still existed, most likely down at the sill. "It'll have to be caulked, or maybe shimmed," Chuck said.

He'd have to get his scuba gear out again. And he'd have to work from outside the gates, so getting down to the water would be a problem. Probably he should hire the work out. Although, on second thought, if he sent somebody down and something went wrong... Did he want to put on his gear again after all the trouble he'd had the first time? Shit. One way or another, he couldn't wait. As water rose on the outside of the gate, the pressure would build and the task get more difficult. The gates wouldn't fail, he was sure of it. On the other hand, if they did, he could go find another line of work.

But he didn't have time for that now. He told Kenny not to worry, he'd deal with it, and then headed for his vehicle.

When he got to Couler and Diamond, he had the satisfaction of seeing that he'd guessed right. Water was flowing down the shallow swale next to the road and threatening a neighborhood of working-class tract homes. The sandbagging crews were already on duty, a brigade formed and rapidly placing bags to choke off the flow. Nearby, where the homes were already being flooded, volunteers had split off from the main group and were lugging sandbags through the water to seal doors and basement windows.

Chuck told the fellow left in charge that as soon as they'd staunched the flow, they could back the flatbed around and use more people to protect the houses. Somebody would need to remain there until the water started to recede. "Do you have enough sandbags?"

"I think so."

"If you need more, call down to the garage for the last flatbed."

He hoped the hell they didn't have to deal with any sand boils down on the peninsula. The worst possible time.

He climbed back into his vehicle and headed for Greenwood Estates. There he found Glenn Owens, normally the supervisor in the drafting room, but now in charge of Chuck's rapid response team of sandbaggers.

"I talked to your guy at Couler and Diamond."

"One of the volunteers. A good man. Very low bullshit quotient." Glenn's smile acknowledged the borrowing, one of Chuck's pet expressions. Since Glenn was lending a hand, lugging sandbags with the others, Chuck pitched in, too, for a short time.

As at Couler and Diamond, he'd been right about the problem here. The nameless creek that normally ran behind these more upscale homes and into the Little Mesquatie had become a lake and was attacking the buildings through their backyards. Floods, unlike more equal opportunity disasters, tended to wreak havoc on the working class, those people who ended up living on the lowest tracts of ground, but given the chance, they'd inundate the more affluent, as well. Two buses were parked nearby. The floodfighters had dispersed, working in small teams and helping individual homeowners. Chuck grabbed a couple of bags and walked with Glenn over the muddy ground and into the floodwater. They talked as they went. The rain continued to pelt down.

~

Deuce had the day shift at the water plant, which let out at three o'clock. The rain had slackened as he exited the building. The power was still out, and he'd spent the shift keeping a close eye on the emergency generators, but for all that, it had still been a pretty routine eight hours. He decided to check whether water was up on the peninsula yet where they'd ringed the wellheads. But first he'd go pay a call on his new friend Lucille Klauer. He had some news for her.

As he drove down Cardiff, he spotted Aggie's car in her mother's driveway. He stopped and considered turning around and going away. Instead, as he had the day before when he'd first seen Aggie turn down the street and had followed her, he eased by the house and then turned around and drifted back. He felt like a negotiator unprepared for a session. The whole point in buddying up to the mother had been his interest in the daughter. How juvenile was that? What did he think he was trying to accomplish? He had no idea. But just driving away would have been chickenshit. And so he stopped. He'd have to brazen it out.

He knocked and Aggie came, pulling the curtain aside in the window of the back door before opening it. She was holding a candle.

"Well."

Deuce could smell the candle wax. Candle wax and cigarette smoke. "I've got something to tell Lucille," he said matter-of-factly, unable to come up with anything witty as a starter.

"Come in, then." She matched her tone to his. "Someone here for you, Ma! She's upstairs. She'll be right down."

"Thanks." Deuce was feeling very uncomfortable. He forgot about brazening anything out. This was a bad idea. The whole business had been a bad idea. He had nothing to say to this woman.

Aggie had put down the candle. In the gloom, he couldn't make out the expression on her face, just the curve of one cheek and tip of her nose, illuminated by the weak daylight shining through the back door. She seemed to be looking at him intently. He heard steps on the stairway, Lucille coming down one step at a time. Dogs coming down, too, down and up and down again.

"You quit," Aggie said.

The possibility that she might jump on him for abandoning the negotiations had occurred to Deuce, but for some reason he'd forgotten about it. Now he felt the sting of the accusation. He had to defend himself.

"J.J. could handle the rest better than me."

"You should have finished."

"It was over. I thought Cutler had won. I had no idea El Plowman would take up the idea."

"It was a good idea."

Lucille had reached the bottom of the stairs. The dogs spotted Deuce and came bounding over, looking for attention.

"You ran away," Aggie said and then louder, "Deuce has something to tell you, Ma."

Lucille was approaching, peering into the dimness. "Young Goetzinger, is it?"

"Hello, Lucille."

One of the dogs had nudged its nose under Deuce's hand, and he took the hint and patted its head. He was okay with the dogs at least. Lucille had seized the candle and was tilting it toward a side table, the wax dripping off. She found what she was looking for, a package of cigarettes. "I suppose this is about the cellar," she said.

"It's about the cellar."

"He wants me to fill it with water," Lucille, lighting up from the candle, said to Aggie.

"Won't cost you a cent," Deuce told her. Since the two women were ignoring them, all three dogs had crowded around Deuce, who squatted down among them with the vague idea of showing his generosity toward animals. "The city's going to pick up the tab for anyone who wants to do it. Some of the businesses along the river already have."

"Agnes here was telling me just the other day you can buy flood insurance in the middle of a flood. Now you got the city giving away water. Expect it's easier to be generous when it's someone else's money."

Squatting, Deuce was none too steady on his haunches, and one of the dogs, jostled by another, knocked against him and he went down on his ass. As he scrambled to his feet, he said, "I don't know anything about insurance, but seepage is dirty and will do a lot more damage than city water. We want to encourage people to use it."

"Makes sense to me, Ma," Aggie said.

"Hmm," said Lucille.

"Why don't we go down for a look-see?" Deuce suggested.

They descended into the musty cellar odor, Deuce first with the flashlight, then Aggie, then Lucille, finally the dogs, Lucille telling Deuce she'd had the sump pump checked and the man had assured her it could handle any seepage she was likely to get. "It's old, but it still works. Like me." There was no pump sound at the moment, of course, with the power out.

"What was the prediction for the flood crest when he told you that?"

"I don't remember."

Near the foot of the stairs, Deuce stopped and swept the beam back and forth.

"What is it?" Lucille asked from behind Aggie.

"Water." A slick of gray lay across the concrete floor like glazing on pottery.

Lucille edged by her daughter and down next to Deuce. "Doesn't look too bad."

"Depends on how long the power's off."

He stepped down. It was maybe an inch deep. "Where's the pump?"

"Over in the corner there." As he went for a look, Lucille asked, "Tell me, you got any other name besides Deuce? What were you called at home?"

Great, Deuce thought, just what he needed. This whole visit seemed designed to cut him down to size. He didn't know what to say to Aggie. He fell on his ass trying to pat the dogs. Now Lucille wanted to know his other names.

The sump pump was, indeed, old, its cover missing, the gleam of oil showing that it had been recently serviced. As he returned, he said, "If you decide to use city water, you'll want to seal the pump outflow. My full name is Fritz Goetzinger, Jr. No middle name. My parents called me Junior. My friends call me Deuce."

Aggie said, "Junior," as if testing the sound of the word on her tongue.

"Agnes," he whispered as he passed her on his way upstairs.

She accompanied him out to his car. He half expected her to drag his absconding from the union negotiations into the conversation again, but she didn't. Instead she thanked him for helping Lucille out.

"If she takes my advice."

"She might. Ma has to get used to an idea. And you're a man, that helps. She always defers to men." This was obviously a sore point with Aggie. "Tell me, Deuce, how did you happen to find out that Lucille lived in Little Wales?"

Another unexpected question. And this one even more loaded than the last, and delivered with frankness that would seem to call for frankness in return. But, of course, telling her the truth was out of the question.

So he said, "Everybody knows about Lucille, don't they? She's a well-known local character."

"You never mentioned her before," Aggie noted suspiciously.

"Introduce her into the negotiations? Now there's an idea."

"In the cafe when I talked about her, you never said a word."

"I don't believe you mentioned her name. If you had, of course…"

"Of course." Aggie remained suspicious.

"And there are lots of Klauers." Which, conveniently, was true in Jackson.

Aggie conceded the point. "I suppose." Her voice lost the liveliness of moments earlier, and he regretted he hadn't been quick enough to sustain the exchange a little longer. Negotiations were like poker in that regard. The point was not simply winning or losing. Winning and losing were merely the occasion. And whatever was going on here, their entire relationship up to that point had consisted of negotiations. Could this be any different?

Inside, the lights popped on.

"Power's back on," he said.

"Good."

"Right. But you might want to check to make sure the sump pump's come back on, too."

"I will." They stood silently until she asked, "Where are you off to now?"

"Out to take a look at the wellheads."

"I understand you've been putting sandbags around them. You're done?"

"Yup."

"It'd be dreadful if we lost the water."

He was considering whether he should ask her if she wanted to come out to look at the wellheads with him, an offer that seemed approximately as lame as everything else out of his mouth over the last half hour. He might have done it anyway, except that she beat him to the punch. "I've got to go back to Five Flags. Just wanted to see how Ma was doing."

Disappointed, Deuce wondered if there was something, just one thing, he might say of interest, but the cupboard was bare. He looked at Aggie. She was dressed way down for her emergency work, wearing almost no makeup, just a touch of lipstick. She looked good. "I'll be going then," he said.

"Okay."

"If your mother decides to take me up on the offer, I'd be glad to help you move stuff out of the cellar."

She smiled. "I'll work on her. But she's pretty stubborn."

"Aren't we all," he said.

CHAPTER 61

~

The next morning, Jack Kelley took a chance and left the job site long enough to go to Mass. He stopped at the midpoint of the road and got out in the rain to admire the concrete facing he'd used to secure the embankments. The road would be overtopped in a couple of days, but it had given him extra time. He stood on the rock surface, feeling for uncertainty through the soles of his shoes and watching floodwater creeping up toward the top. When he got back from Mass, that was it, he decided. All ashore that's going ashore. They had what they needed, it was time to stop pushing their luck.

At the bridge across Kiakiak Channel, the road was partially coned off and a crew preparing to remove trees and other material that had become lodged against the overpass. Jack had to wait to get by. The rain was steady and cold now, miserable working conditions for everyone. Around the parapet at the north side of the bridge, several men in hard hats were talking, Chuck Fellows among them. Floodwater had begun to pile up behind the debris. Dangerous work. Jack found himself becoming interested, but before he got a chance to see how they were going to proceed, the flagman had waved him on.

He met Janelle and Kitty at St. C.'s, glad to be at Mass, although his concentration, of course, wasn't there. Too much going on. And he couldn't push aside his fear that the road would wash out in his absence. Other problems, real and conceivable and far-fetched, crowded out thoughts of Our Lord's sacrifice for humanity. During the reading of the Gospel, it occurred to him that maybe Chuck Fellows was right after all, maybe he should have allowed Vasconcellos's and Dexter's men to remain on the job site.

Outside, shaking hands with Father Mike, Jack apologized for his attire.

"No apologies required," Mike said. "Glad you could make it. I thought you were trapped out on the island."

"Not quite yet."

"Tell me, Jack, what are you doing for religious services out there?"

"On the island?" The question startled Jack. He'd never considered the matter, the job site being about as secular as places came. Yet some of the men would undoubtedly be practicing Christians.

"If you want," Father Mike suggested quietly, "I could come out."

"I'm shutting down the road. Too dangerous."

Mike said, "Just a sec" to the people standing behind Jack, and pulled him aside for a quick word.

"What about this afternoon? You want, I can be there almost immediately. It'd give the men a chance to pray together before the worst."

Jack thought about this, about his own failure to think of such a possibility—no doubt the tradesmen out on the island weren't all heathens, and some might truly be in need of spiritual comfort—and decided this was another symptom of his own skewed priorities. He said, "We've probably got some Protestants, too."

Mike lowered his voice even further. "Doesn't make any difference. I can do ecumenical."

"Not a Mass, then?" The Mass being open only to Catholics.

Mike thought about that, but not for long. "Well, we won't call it that. We'll call it Holy Communion." Mike smiled slyly. "What can they do, Jack, ship me out to Maquoketa?" Then he became serious, and perhaps not wanting to cast himself entirely in the role of a renegade, he added, "Extraordinary times, Jack. It's the right thing to do. I'll call Rangel at First Presbyterian. He'll be game. We can conduct a joint service. That ought to be kosher enough."

Jack remembered how much he had liked Mike before the Vasconcellos business came up. He looked at his watch.

"One o'clock?" he asked.

"We'll be there."

Jack went home for the extra clothes and so forth that he'd need since he was moving onto the island with the others now. He felt good about Mike's suggestion, felt the rightness of it.

Janelle drove him back. No reason to have the car stranded out on the job site. They passed over the Kiakiak Channel bridge, where debris removal continued, and turned toward the job site. Jack was looking left and right, inspecting the edge of the access road, when Janelle hit the brakes and he lurched against his seat belt.

In front of them, the road was gone.

❧

Even hard against the Ice Harbor gate, Chuck Fellows felt the power of the river. The water flowed around the rim of his scuba mask as he kicked slowly downward past the steel x-framing and edged along the foot of the gate, searching for the void where water was surging back into the harbor. The current snooped around him, like a wrestler probing for a better hold.

Above, as he had been preparing to dive, descending the outside of the gates on the rope ladder they'd rigged up, the rain had eased a little, the day brightening, not that it made a helluva lot of difference. Every dive in the Mississippi was for all intents and purposes a night dive, although it was true the water seemed to have cleared a little since the last one. Or maybe it was just his imagination. The beam of his light made a clay-brown bowl around him. He kept the gate just off his shoulder.

From the upwelling on the harbor side, he knew approximately where he'd find the trouble, near the leading edge of the right-hand gate, and he moved gingerly toward it. Inside, the water surface lay twenty feet below the river stage, a differential pressure of 1,200 pounds per square foot, give or take, not exactly the power of a fire hose, but enough to take it easy.

The vision of the water's brown solidity began to break up, becoming fluid and flowing away from him. He moved up slightly and glided above the lower edge of the gate, beneath which the water was quickly vanishing, the gap made visible by the silt load, like dye injected into a hydraulic system to detect a leak.

He placed his hand against an I-beam and felt the sharp vibration. For some reason, the gate hadn't seated properly along a length of several feet.

He moved closer and reached down to gauge the height of the opening. The force of the jet sucked his fingers inward, pulling his forearm hard against the steel framing. He yanked free and, holding his wrist stiff and the blade of his hand at right angles to the rushing water, estimated the distance to the sill. Two or three inches, no more. Amazing the power water could generate.

He moved a few more feet along the gate and measured the depth of the opening again. Less, but still too wide for the caulking. They'd have to use shims.

He paused, ready to ascend, and suddenly became aware that he had frozen, his body suddenly rigid. Something…

His mind reeled with nowhere to focus. For an instant, a fraction of a second, he remained suspended, his body locked, and then something hit him, driving him against the steel framing.

He found himself on his back, a sharp pain in his left side. The gates!

He struggled to right himself. The pain encircled his chest. He had trouble breathing. He wanted to panic, but some small part of his mind held on, resisting the urge to spit out his respirator and crawl desperately upward.

He realized at once that he'd been wrong, that the gate hadn't ruptured. He would have been flung into the harbor in the surge of floodwater. Hadn't happened. He still clung to the gate, to the steel flange he'd been thrown against.

He breathed slowly, the pain squeezing his chest, like the air being knocked out of him.

Everything was as before, as if nothing at all had happened. The water had gone back to its ceaseless snooping. He continued to grasp the flange tightly, not sure other blows wouldn't follow.

Then, slowly, painfully, he began to ascend, not swimming, but climbing hand over hand up the gate face.

~

In Little Wales, Aggie Klauer heard something. What, she couldn't tell. Like a medicine ball being dropped on a wooden floor. She cocked her head, waiting. Nothing followed, only an odd, particularly intense silence.

She went back to the dishes. Other people were taking care of the mobilization center for a few hours so Aggie could begin to move things up from her mother's cellar. Keeping busy was the trick of spending time with Lucille.

Lucille, of course, believed none of it. If Aggie wanted to clean out the basement—that's what she called it—and fill it with the city's water, that was just fine so long as Lucille didn't have to pay for the water. But she'd not lift a finger herself, nosiree. What she was doing at the moment was smoking her ciggies and drinking her coffee and watching pro wrestling on the tube, still wearing her Sunday-go-to-Mass clothes.

Aggie waved away the smoke as she went to gather more of the dirty dishes. On her way back to the sink, she heard a car horn in the distance, not a single honk but repeated, as if someone had just gotten married or won a big game. She stopped, holding the dishes, and listened as the sound receded in the distance.

She continued her task, but now her nerve endings were tingling. She turned on the radio, tuned always to KJAX. Perhaps fifteen seconds later, a door slammed nearby, and Aggie started.

Then the sirens began.

"The levee!" she yelled.

Nearby, another car door slammed and she heard it accelerating away, horn blasting. Aggie rushed to the front window, but couldn't see any water. Hard to make out anything in the rain.

The phone was ringing and Aggie rushed to it. One of the people at the mobilization center. There had been an explosion near the grain terminal. The floodwall had collapsed.

Aggie slammed the receiver down. Back in the kitchen, Lucille hadn't moved.

"Let's go, Ma, we've got to get out of here!"

Lucille took a puff of her cigarette. "What's going on?"

In short bursts, Aggie told her what had happened. Lucille listened without much apparent interest.

Aggie wanted to grab her mother, but that wouldn't do, and so she merely crouched before her, hands turned upward, fingers crooked like prongs, pleading, "Please, please, please!"

Lucille didn't say anything but irritably stubbed out her cigarette, then leaned forward so she could use both hands to get up.

Aggie danced excitedly about as her mother made her way to the sunroom and stared out the window in the direction of the river.

"Don't see nothing," she said skeptically.

"If you see it, Ma, it's too late."

Aggie was calming down herself, now. Okay, okay, this was absurd, but what else was new? Her whole life as a daughter had been ridiculous.

"Can we go now, Ma? Huh? Just in case, okay?"

"Let's go outside. We can see better from there."

"Why don't we go up onto Garfield?" Garfield would be dry if Little Wales flooded.

"Why don't we go outside," Lucille said and opened the front door and walked out under the wedge of roof which, like a visor, shielded the steps. Aggie followed and scanned the back lots of the industrial buildings toward the river, the scene still walled in by the rain. A car, its headlights boring into the downpour, raced along the road through the industrial park.

No sign of the approaching floodwaters, but the section of the wall that had collapsed was at least a mile away.

Aggie rushed inside for the portable radio and brought it back.

"We could save some stuff, Ma, while there's still time."

"Where's the water?"

"It'll get here. Then it'll be too late."

"Hmm," said Lucille.

Aggie still felt a little jumpy, but in the face of her mother's intransigence, she had calmed way down. Nothing to be done. Lucille was her fate.

The two of them stood listening to the radio…and waiting for the water that never came. The sirens stopped. Gradually, the truth was revealed to them.

~

A bruised rib, Chuck guessed. Maybe cracked. He didn't care. He'd go and have a picture taken later. Now, distraught, he walked with the others out onto the railroad bridge and searched the floodwaters, as if there was any chance that Walt Plowman and the photographer who had fallen into the river might still be near.

One of the shaken Geological Survey men was describing what had happened. At the exact moment that the fuel tank, floating in the river, probably mostly empty except for fumes, hit the north side of the bridge and exploded, the TV photographer had been leaning over the railing to get a good shot of the weight and meter being cranked down into the water. It was just incredibly bad timing. A minute later and the photographer would have had his shot. Walt Plowman had reached out to grab him and they'd both gone over. Must have been the weight of the camera. The cameraman probably hit his head because he didn't seem to be conscious in the water. Walt had stayed with him, trying to help. When they disappeared downstream, Walt was still with him, still trying to help, still in the middle of the current.

The others went over to the opposite side where the tank had plowed into the cutwater of the bridge pier.

Chuck stayed where he was. His life had been filled with deaths. He would gladly have taken Walt's place. Perhaps Walt would be found alive, he thought and then put such a hope out of his mind.

He gripped the railing and stared at the empty river.

Part V

CHAPTER 62

~

River stage: 31.9 feet

The jet stream hadn't budged, storms tracking over the northern basin, seventeen straight days of rain, the crest pushed higher and higher as the Mississippi, gathering the offerings of its tributaries and taking back the floodplain as it came, continued its massive watery procession toward the city.

Paul Cutler had gotten his wish. The city would be reimbursed. The river had reached the emergency protection works. He took the thinnest satisfaction from the fact. There comes a point… The city should have wasted the money and other communities been spared.

When Chuck Fellows stopped in with the morning report, Paul asked where the crest was.

"Minnesota-Iowa border." Fellows had been working on little sleep for weeks, and the exhaustion damped down his normal aggressive edge. "Three days."

"How high?"

"The Weather Service is saying thirty-four feet."

Paul smiled wanly and shook his head.

"Water plant?" he asked.

"We'll finish ringing it sometime tomorrow."

"And then it's just wait?"

"More or less. Still plenty to do."

Fellows had also become quieter; Paul would have said more introspective if that hadn't been a concept that seemed so alien to the man. Paul assumed it had something to do with the loss of Walter Plowman.

Chuck described what, besides backup at the water plant, he intended to accomplish during the next twenty-four hours and then asked, "Anything else you want?"

"Yes." Paul made him wait before saying, "I suppose I ought to go down and take a look at the river. At least once." He'd been attending to the routine tasks of his office and keeping tabs on the money they were spending on the emergency work, making sure the necessary paper trail was in place. He hadn't gone down to the waterfront. It had been a conscious decision. He wouldn't go down to the corner to see a traffic accident, either.

"Up to you," Fellows said.

"What about tomorrow morning?"

"Up to you."

Nothing had changed really, Paul needn't go. But at some point— in his own mind, at least—the virtue of attending to the day-to-day business of running a city had, Janus-like, turned into a craven shrinking away from the beast at the door. Which didn't magically transform witnessing the flood into a positive act, only something that couldn't be avoided.

"Tomorrow morning," he told Fellows. "First thing."

CHAPTER 63

~

Aggie drove up the steep driveway and parked. El had told her that she didn't need to come, had even become annoyed with her for showing up "every two minutes" to see how she was doing and whether there was any news. Well, Aggie thought, that was just tough; El could get as annoyed as she wanted.

On the first day, there had still been hope that Walter might be found alive. Characteristically, El threw herself into the mechanics of the search effort. She had maps of the river spread out on her dining room table, and men who knew the currents explained to her where Walter and the cameraman might have managed to get ashore, although the normal flows would have changed because of the flood.

On the second day, semi-fantastic scenarios, the stuff out of adventure stories, had been concocted to explain why the two men might still be alive but unfound. One of the search parties discovered the corpse of an unidentified woman, but no sign of Walter and the cameraman. El had gone out searching, too, saying she had to do something. When she got back, she started talking once more about the need to get people to evacuate from the Flats.

On the third day, the well-meaning said things like, "Miracles do happen," but mostly a somber mood marked the period between the end of hope and the beginning of acceptance. Beyond what had to be said, El stopped talking about Walter. When she showed up at the mobilization center, taking up the evacuation effort with an energy that seemed to Aggie just short of hysteria, the loss of Walter and the not knowing enveloped her in the manner of a dark aura.

And so on the fourth day, as Aggie got out of her car at the Plowmans', she trembled to think what she might find.

She knocked and entered the silent house without waiting and called out, announcing her presence. El sat in the kitchen, a teacup before her, across the table from Walter's empty chair. Seeing Aggie, she merely frowned and shook her head. No sign of him, not yet, not ever, don't ask.

"There's no coffee," she said.

"That's okay."

Aggie sat down and, as a substitute for what she really wanted to talk about, described the situation down at the mobe center.

There was no evidence that El had eaten anything, no food smells, no dirty dishes, although Aggie knew that the fridge was stuffed with dishes brought over by the neighbors. El's intelligent gaze had gone dull, washed out and lined with sleeplessness and lack of food and anxiety, but she had changed her clothes from the day before and fixed her face, so that was something.

The tea appeared untouched. She might or might not have been attending to what Aggie said, impossible to tell, but it made no difference, Aggie soon ran down, and they ended up sitting silently together.

Aggie tried out various encouraging words she might offer, but they all sounded phony. El was looking at her hands, rubbing them, and turning them over. She stopped and stared briefly off to the side, then toward Aggie. She began to speak.

"Walter's gone."

Aggie leaned forward, but El raised a hand a few inches, a warning gesture.

"He's gone," she repeated.

"Yes."

El dropped her hand disconsolately into her lap and stared wide-eyed with grief at Aggie.

"You can't imagine, Aggie, how bad it is. One moment he's here and the next… No good-byes. Nothing. I always assumed we'd be able to say our good-byes. You always assume that."

"I know."

"But that's not the worst. You're with someone all these years and you think you know him, you really do. But you're wrong, you don't, not at all. You underestimate him. You're so used to making allowances for his shortcomings. You've decided he's a certain way, so that's what you see." El took a deep breath and began shaking her head, briefly mustering a more conversational tone when she resumed.

"Walter and I had several conversations about him going out on the bridge. I didn't want him out there. I don't know, it just made me nervous. Walter could be so…absentminded. I imagined him getting all wrapped up in whatever he was doing and not paying any attention to the river. I imagined it would be his carelessness. It never occurred to me he might die trying to help somebody else. It never entered my mind. I just thought, 'Walter can't be trusted to take care of himself.'

"I was wrong. I didn't give him enough credit, Aggie. That's what hurts so much. I didn't give him enough credit. How can I make that up, Aggie?" Tears had finally started coming. "I always discounted him. I always thought, 'Well, that's Walter, what can you do?' And now he's gone, and it's too late. It's too late, it's too late, and it hurts so much."

Aggie made another gesture to go to El, but El held a hand up to stop her.

"Why didn't I see? He was capable of enormous self-sacrifice. Self-sacrifice, Aggie. Tell me why I didn't see that in him."

There was a knock on the back door.

At once, El got up and headed toward the mudroom, drying her eyes with the backs of her wrists. Over her shoulder, she said, "We don't honor one another the way we should."

From the other room, Aggie heard the door opening and then a sentence fragment, a man's voice, and then El saying, "Come in." She returned, followed by Fritz Goetzinger. Aggie hadn't seen the ex-mayor in months. Deuce's father.

Fritz nodded to her. To El, he said, "Would have come before. Didn't want to intrude." Beneath his raincoat he wore a suit. Aggie didn't remember ever seeing him in a suit. Certainly he'd never worn one at the council table.

El was still drying her eyes, making no attempt to hide the fact that she'd been crying. "It's okay," she said.

"Walter was a friend," Fritz told her.

"Thank you." Fritz had been hanging back at the door, and El told him, "Please. Come in. Sit," and motioned to the chair she had just vacated. "I've been thinking about you. About what happened to Edna. The dreadful coincidence."

A number of people had commented upon the eerie similarities between the two deaths, first of Edna and now, apparently, of Walter, the spouses of the last two mayors.

"Since it happened…," Fritz started and then stopped.

El went over to the fridge and took the dishtowel hanging on the door and finished the job of drying her eyes. "Yes? Please. Sit."

He did as told, taking up only the barest edge of the chair, his hands balled up between his thighs. He was staring at nothing in particular, at some inward vision, perhaps, and Aggie noticed for the first time his state of agitation.

"The last three days...," he started again and stopped again. One of his hands, a pattern of white and red, seemed to be trying to crush the other. "The waiting..."

El must have grasped his meaning at the same instant that Aggie did, for she said, "I'm sorry, Fritz." This wasn't about Walter. Not just about Walter.

"It always happens to the good ones," he said.

"I didn't really know Edna—" El started. Fritz didn't let her finish.

"She was a wonderful woman."

"I'm sure she was."

"Nobody knew her like I did. They didn't know her qualities."

In the pause before he continued, Aggie exchanged an astonished glance with El, Aggie struck almost with horror at the thought that only now, months later and with Walter's death, had Fritz Goetzinger finally arrived at a place where he could truly begin his own grieving.

Chapter 64

~

After the access road went out, it had taken Jack Kelley the rest of Sunday to get back out onto the job site, eventually finding a local sport fisherman willing to put his boat in the water long enough to give him a lift. The small craft skittered nervously across the top of the flood and its owner, anxious as soon as he launched, could hardly wait to get back to shore and haul out again. Jack wanted to explore around the point where the road had gone out, but the man said, "Do I look like a cruise director?" Jack settled for the ride.

Other people had been off the job site when the road went out and found one way or another to get back, or mostly didn't return at all. It was Monday night before Lonny Vasconcellos made it, using a rowboat he scrounged from somewhere. His father stayed in town. Fine by Jack, who announced that the rowboat would henceforth be used to put ashore anyone who got into a fight. Whether the whites and blacks were playing the dozens, Jack didn't know, but if they were and if somebody threw the first punch, he was gone. Working in the middle of a damn five-hundred-year flood ought to be enough excitement for any man.

In the meantime, the four-foot levee girding the site had been completed and polyethylene sheeting thrown over it and held in place by sandbag counterweights. That was pretty much it. They had their protection. It would be good enough or it wouldn't.

Rain kept falling. The ironworkers and glaziers set product when they could. Jack concentrated on the work in the half of the grandstand that had been enclosed. The weekly contractors' meeting had become a sort of progressive meeting, ongoing as Jack adjusted schedules on the fly.

"If you get to an area and that's your next phase, then you proceed," he told everyone. "Until the whole building's buttoned up, we're gonna be tripping all over each other. Can't be helped. Fifteen or sixteen weeks is a long time to put the guts in a place like this. I want to do it in half that time. That means dogs on site and training races beginning five weeks from today."

"Hell," the sprinkling contractor said, "the flood won't be over in five weeks. We'll still be camping out in the kennels." He was the newest denizen on the job and hadn't earned the right to bitch yet.

"I understand," Jack told him, "that greyhounds make good pets." That got a laugh. "Eight weeks, gentlemen, assuming we don't get washed down the river first."

Jack appointed himself judge and jury of all coordination problems. The rest of the time he was on the radio, talking to his boss, talking to Chuck Fellows, talking to the consultants, and doing the logistics, which meant beating the bushes looking for a helicopter he could hire to ferry material out to the island.

But once or twice a day, like everyone else, he would knock off long enough to go out and stand with the volunteers that Chuck had sent him and look at the Mississippi. The water had reached the top of the riprap and begun to mount the emergency levee. Apple Island, except for the job site, now lay at the bottom of the river, the crest of the flood still seventy-five miles upstream, the river still rising.

But, as Jack reminded himself again and again, he'd done what he could. An end loader sat ready to dump a bucket of filled sandbags into any rupture in the levee. The volunteers continued to prepare more bags. In the worst possible situation, they could drive the end loader itself into a big breech and sandbag around the machine. If it came to that. Mostly Jack worried that the levee would be overtopped. At some point, human effort would simply be inadequate.

He second-guessed himself. He should have sunk more well points to drain the seepage. He should have made the levee higher. He should have simply closed the site down and waited for the flood to pass like Fellows wanted.

In every direction, to the farthest reaches of his vision, lay the swelling breast of the river, the barges they had sunk at the head of the island now invisible, buried beneath the waters, the drowned trees bending in the current as if in a great wind. It gave Jack the willies to look at that plain of water, rising almost to eye level, and to smell the cold smell of it and to feel in his bones its awful determination. For it did feel like determination, as if the river acted with a purpose, as if only in a situation this extreme could someone like Jack sense the underlying consciousness in events.

The rain stopped falling for a moment, and behind him he heard a metallic pounding from among the ironworkers up in the framing of the grandstand and a bell-like clangor that would be the cables banging against the boom of one of the cranes as it swung to pick up another load.

He turned away from the river and went back to work.

CHAPTER 65

~

The rasping of the hacksaw made conversation impossible for the moment.

With her cup of coffee in her lap, Aggie was sitting on a dilapidated kitchen chair in her mother's basement as Deuce finished disconnecting and capping off the oil and water lines of the ancient steam boiler. Having come straight from a shift at the water plant, he was wearing his work clothes, dark blue trousers and a lighter blue shirt with a water symbol above the pocket. The clothes fit him as neatly as if he'd had them custom made. Perhaps he had. Perhaps he was vain, too, along with all his other defects.

She'd brought up his father's surprise visit that morning to El Plowman, not knowing how he'd react. He hadn't reacted at all.

His cup was on top of the water heater. In the far corner, the sump pump continued to bang away, but it was losing its own personal flood fight, seep water covering the floor and creeping higher.

Volunteers would soon arrive to help Deuce haul the boiler and the water heater out of the cellar, before filling it with city water. Lucille would have to heat water on the stove and use space heaters. Aggie remained amazed that her mother had agreed to do even this much, but Deuce was cute and a man, both of which counted with Lucille.

"So, what next?" she asked.

"What next?"

"The next chapter in Deuce Goetzinger's life."

"Don't know. Not much left for me around here."

"Off to see the world, then?"

"Maybe."

Aggie felt a pang at this possibility. If he went away, perhaps that would be all for the best, but the pang had nothing to do with her better judgment. Here poor Walter was drowned. So many awful things had

happened. And now Deuce leaving. Not that she and he had a relationship or anything like that, Aggie quickly reminded herself. Deuce
leaving wasn't anything important, not compared to all the rest.

"Could stay, too," he said. The frankness of his gaze lasted only
a few moments, then he looked away, his expression going vague
although a slight remnant of a smile remained, for his eyes and mouth
seldom agreed. "But I don't know. Probably not."

"What would you do, then?"

"Go on the road."

"Become a hobo?"

"Not quite."

She raised her eyebrows and tilted her head, a silent question.

"Poker," he said.

"Ah." Poker. Of course. She felt a keen disappointment. "I think
being a hobo would be more interesting."

"You're probably right," he agreed.

They heard steps, Lucille and her canine retinue. Every few minutes, she came down and stood on the bottom step, to see how the
work was going or to complain about something, but mostly, Aggie
knew, because Deuce was there. Aggie almost felt that she and Lucille
had become rivals for Deuce's affection. It was all pretty pathetic.

Now her mother watched the work silently for a brief time, smoking, one arm folded under her bosom and serving as a prop for the
elbow of the other, the cigarette pinched between her first and second
fingers in front of her mouth, its ashes getting longer and longer, tilting down before they fell off into the water, one after another. The
cellar was filled with the hacksaw sound as Deuce finished cutting off
a section of pipe where the threads of a coupling had become hopelessly frozen.

As sound died away, Lucille said to him, "Got a question for
you."

"Shoot."

"Musta heard it four or five times."

Deuce waited.

"People are saying there's a weakness in the floodwall somewheres."

Deuce bent the pipe section back and forth a couple of times and
it came free. "We've all heard that one, Lucille."

She took a puff. There was something both furtive and aggressive in
the way she smoked. Aggie was always reminded of World War II spies.

"Explain a lot," Lucille said. "For instance, why the city didn't want to add to it in the first place. If it was just gonna fail anyway…"

One of the dogs, Domino, was sniffing at the end of the pipe Deuce held.

He said, "It would also explain why I wanted to move your boiler and water heater."

Lucille nodded sagely. "And all this business about the mayor trying to get people to evacuate."

Deuce offered the pipe to Domino, who decided it held no further interest.

Aggie said, "The city wouldn't do that, Ma. If they knew there was a weakness somewhere in the system, they'd fix it."

Lucille, of course, ignored Aggie, assuming that nobody would ever tell her anything. And anyway she worked for the city and so was hopelessly compromised. Deuce worked for the city, too, of course, but he was a man and cute.

"It would explain a lot," Lucille repeated, studying Deuce closely.

With the nail of his thumb, he scratched above one eye. "Dunno, Lucille. The rumors are all pretty vague."

She considered this. "Still…"

"Tell you one thing," he told her, nodding toward the boiler, "reason we're moving this sucker got nothing to do with the levee failing." He toed up a small splash of the seep water, in which the discarded pipe section lay half buried.

Lucille took a puff. "Nothing would surprise me."

"You're not a woman easily surprised," Deuce said.

"Damn right."

A short distance away, Little Caesar lay down in the water, and Lucille ordered him to get up. Reluctantly he obeyed, and with the other dogs followed her back up the steps.

When she was gone, Aggie said to Deuce, "There's no secret weakness in the system. You know that as well as I do."

"Not one that anybody knows about, at least. But you can't tell Lucille."

"You can't tell Ma anything."

Deuce was putting some sort of goop around the end of the pipe that he planned to seal. He glanced at Aggie with a little gotcha grin. "Lucille's okay."

"Ma's a pill. You never had to live with her."

"Always an advantage," he conceded.

But Aggie didn't want to talk about Lucille. She wanted to talk about Deuce leaving Jackson. So she said, "What about the union? If you go away, who's going to organize your, you know, the democracy thing, the shadow government, whatever you want to call it?" Even if El could get the city council to go along with the idea, making it work would be as tricky as bringing democracy to some third world country.

"You and J.J.," Deuce told her. "The two of you are more interested in it than me."

She wanted to contradict him, except for the inconvenient fact that he was undoubtedly right. Probably, if Deuce abandoned the crusade, she would arrange to have a little chat with J.J. on the side. Still…it would've been nice to have Deuce as part of their cabal.

"Too bad," she said.

He stood at ease, his arms hanging at his sides, a pipe cap in one hand, the brush he had been using to paint the end of the pipe with the goop in the other, his narrow poker player's gaze the only spark of alertness at the moment.

"And so you're going to be a card sharp. I'd think the fun would go out of it awfully fast if you were doing it all the time."

"That's right," he agreed. "And, if you want to know the truth, I did the union thing pretty much because I got bored with cards."

"Then why go back to playing?"

He shrugged. "I dunno. One less illusion to get rid of later, I suppose."

She shook her head, confused. A slight flicker of irritation, or perhaps it was merely impatience, had passed over Deuce's face. "No matter," he told her.

But Aggie wasn't ready to go on to something else.

"So this poker playing of yours, then, it's a kind of—I don't know—a job, just another job, is that it? A way to make money."

"Not quite. But hard work, anyway."

"Okay, but if you don't do it for the joy of the thing, then why bother?"

"Sometimes there's joy. Although I'd probably call it something different."

"What?"

He shook his head.

Aggie tried to put herself in his place. All those dreadful motels and card games with strangers. She looked for an analogy with her own life. What occurred to her might or might not have been relevant, but she said it anyway.

"Once, I don't know, I must have been twelve or thirteen and, by definition, confused and miserable and idealistic and all those other things a twelve- or thirteen-year-old girl is, and I decided to become a nun. I had no vocation, just my misery and idealism and so forth, and I would've made a perfectly dreadful religious. But I can't say that the life you appear intent upon taking up seems any less extreme."

"I don't think the Church would consider poker playing a proper vocation."

She laughed. "No, I'm sure they wouldn't. Which means, I suppose, that it would be worse for you. You'll have the deprivation, but get none of the approval."

He smiled. "There you go."

As they talked, she was conscious of how carefully each of them chose their words, tightrope walkers with language their balancing poles.

"So we'll never see you again," she said finally.

"Don't know."

Having regretted his departure, she now wondered what might bring him back. To play poker with people he'd played with, and presumably beaten, for years? To visit friends? For his father's funeral? Deuce was not the kind of person to return to a place once he had left, she decided.

She told him anyway, "If you do come back, stop in and see me. I'd like that."

He smiled and nodded but did not speak, his way of acknowledging the offer.

In the silence between them lay the boundary they had never crossed.

CHAPTER 66

~

At the eastern horizon, the clouds lifted, exposing a strip of white, a fringe of slip beneath the gray dress covering the rest. J.J. Dusterhoft thought this, but he was so tired the image came to him as a dream vision might. In the other direction, across the prairie fields, things didn't look so good. More weather coming in. Unbelievable. He closed his eyes for a moment and began to dream, the dream an afterimage of what he'd just seen. He was not asleep, not awake…in some jagged seam between.

The cab of his truck vibrated, tossing him back onto the shore of wakefulness. At once he began to slip back off. A minute later, or perhaps only an instant, the truck vibrated again, rolling him once more up onto the fringe of the waking world. Somebody was yelling at him.

Jed, the guy operating the front-end loader at the clay face, had pulled his machine around to the cab of the truck and was circling his hand in a roll-down-your window motion, his image distorted in the rain-streaked glass.

For once in his life, J.J. didn't feel like talking. He lowered the cab's window anyway.

"You're all set, J.J."

J.J. let his tongue loll over his lower lip.

"Know just how you feel," the other sympathized.

"Beat." J.J. yawned hugely. From the yawn, he extracted a particle of alertness, like a traveler lost in the desert tipping up his canteen and letting the few remaining drops of water fall on his tongue.

"They say the crest's near Prairie." Prairie du Chien, Prairie of the Dog.

J.J. was too tired to much care where the crest was. As he swung the truck around to head back, his eye passed over the graveyard and he envied its inhabitants their sleep.

He drove down Presentation Boulevard following the clay that had fallen from the treads of a thousand other truck runs that had gone before, a river of clay diverging into a half dozen tributaries at the foot of the boulevard, leading toward the various construction points along the city's dike. At Rhomberg, he turned and headed toward the water plant.

The backup levee now encircled most of the plant. Along the outside of the completed sections, volunteers had unrolled polyethylene sheeting, overlapped at the bottom and pinned in place with sandbags.

J.J. parked at the back of the short line of trucks waiting to unload. Things were winding down.

Two dozers and a small roller shaped and compacted the six-foot structure snaking around the plant buildings. In the bright dullness of the rain, the clay had turned a viscous, almost organic brown. The mist lay close to the ground in some places. In others, it rose and drifted and glowed a hoary white.

J.J. closed his eyes, another two-minute nap. And another dream. His life was filled with dreams, a myriad of bizarre concoctions to accompany the fighting of the flood. This one a courtroom drama. He was the defendant, guilty of fishing with a permit. A reasonable mistake, he tried to explain to the judge, since he'd been fishing with a permit all his life. The judge gaveled him into silence. J.J.'s lawyer was talking about changing his plea to one of innocent by reason of government employment. Somebody mentioned lethal injections with a certain fondness. The judge continued to pound his gavel.

J.J. struggled back awake, the gaveling changing to a rapping on the window of his truck. He opened his eyes and rolled his head toward the sound.

Deuce Goetzinger was peering into the cab. Raindrops bounced off the hood of his rain gear. He seemed happy.

J.J. rolled down the window.

"Sorry if I interrupted your little snooze," Deuce told him.

"I'm sure you are." Goetzinger was just the sort to disturb a fellow's sleep.

"Got something we need to discuss," Deuce said.

"Um."

J.J.'s mind was working so slowly that everything had the quality of being something remembered. And so he remembered what he'd noticed a few moments earlier, that Deuce didn't look all that bad. In fact, he seemed pretty damn chipper, considering.

"Why don't you look like shit like the rest of us, Goetzinger? You been getting sleep on the sly or something?"

"Been working, like everybody else."

"If you say so." J.J. didn't quite believe it, but analysis was beyond him at the moment. "This ain't a game for us old codgers, I guess."

"Been working rotating shifts for years, Dusterhoft, plus the all-night poker. My schedule's just naturally fucked up. This here flood's nothing but business as usual."

J.J. nodded. He hadn't thought of that.

"I got a little proposition for you," Deuce told him.

"I'm beyond propositions. Go find somebody else."

"Nobody else will do. You're my man."

J.J. laid his head against the back of the seat and closed his eyes. "I'm going back to sleep," he announced.

Deuce made a stab at reassuring him. "It ain't much. You can handle it."

"Ain't much is too much."

"You'll like it."

"No, I won't."

"I'm going to ask, anyway."

"I'm asleep now," J.J. informed him. "I can't hear you anymore."

But it made no difference. J.J. was Deuce's man.

Chapter 67

~

Dusk and the new storm came on together, darkness accelerating, the rain stalking across the land. Chuck Fellows paused and looked toward the west and reminded himself that it was just another weather system, nothing to take personally.

Behind him, the volunteers had finished the last plank runway up the levee, another escape route should the levee fail. The 2x12s were laid across hickeys, small wooden devices that acted as shims, leveling the planking as it angled up the steep slope.

Chuck got in his vehicle and headed south toward the Ice Harbor peninsula to verify that the brewery building remained open and the security guy had shown up. Inspectors working behind the floodwalls had no high ground to scramble up, but some of the nearby industrial buildings had upper stories that could be used. He'd cut deals with several businesses—they provided access, he took care of security.

On the floodplain behind the walls and levees, the controllers had been removed from the traffic signals and replaced with four-way stop signs. Firefighters had attached poles with flags to the hydrants so they might be located underwater. Techs from the gas company were shutting off gas lines wherever they could and power company crews raising transformers and sandbagging the repaired Eighth Street substation.

The new storm crept over them, the rain falling harder. The next seven days were critical, the flood crest itself not the event of a moment or an hour, but stretching twenty-five or thirty miles along the river. It would last the better part of a day and only then the river begin to inch back down, only then would the enormous hydraulic pressure slowly begin easing.

Chuck had been flashing on 'Nam, the wasted feeling, the same kind of marrow-deep exhaustion he'd experience after a couple weeks on recon duty playing tag with the NVA. After a certain point, all that mattered was getting it over with. That was all he cared about now, getting it over with. And not losing anybody else.

His beeper went off and he pulled over and looked at the number—city garage.

He called at once. "What is it?"

"Sand boil on the peninsula," the dispatcher told him.

"Where?"

"Fourth Street, near the grain terminal. A flatbed's on the way."

"So am I."

A minute later, he pulled up near the truck, which was piled with sandbags and angled across the road to facilitate rapid unloading, although at the moment nobody was doing anything.

Glenn Owens left the others and came to meet him.

"Glad you're here, boss."

"What's it look like?"

"See for yourself."

The others made way for them. Beyond, a faintly uneasy glistening lay along the sandy shoulder of the road, not circular as Chuck would have expected but a long oval. In the lousy light, it was hard to make out much of anything. He glanced in the direction of the river, about a hundred yards away but invisible, of course, behind the protection works. That was how far the seepage had traveled underground.

"Who found it?" he asked.

A fellow who had been standing among the sandbaggers stepped forward, one of the team captains. "My man did." He and Chuck shook hands. "He was patrolling along the course of the old slough and sure enough."

Right where Walt Plowman had predicted they'd get boils, the old sloughs filled with sawdust by the nineteenth-century lumber mills.

"What's your guy doing now?"

"Back inspecting."

Chuck nodded. "Tell him 'good going' for me."

"I will."

Glenn was kneeling down on the asphalt next to the boil. "Look at this," he said, and reached down to scoop up handfuls of water.

Chuck knelt beside him and they peered at the water as it ran through Glenn's fingers. Then Chuck dipped some up for himself and tilted it this way and that in the dimness. Finally he dumped it out and rubbed the palms of his hands, feeling for grittiness.

"Clear."

"Yupper," Glenn agreed.

Which was the reason they hadn't immediately set to work ring-ing the thing.

Chuck and Glenn stood up, and Chuck spoke to him but loud enough so the others could hear.

"As long as it stays clear, we're not going to do anything." Water by itself was no problem, but when it started eroding the substrate away, that was another matter. "We'll leave one of the sandbaggers here for the time being." He addressed himself to the team captain. "When I get back to the mobe center, I'll tell the watch commander to make sure there's somebody here at all times." He turned back to Glenn. "As long as it stays clear, okay, but the minute there's sand, soil, whatever, ring the sucker."

"Yupper. You want I should leave the flatbed here?"

If the truck stayed, the sandbaggers might as well, too. Out in the rain.

"No, go back to the garage. Need be, you can get back here fast enough. If you do ring it, make sure you don't stop the flow of water." Otherwise, the hydraulic pressure could simply force more failures nearby. Might anyway, since the whole area lacked integrity.

"Yupper," said Glenn, who knew all this.

Chuck spoke to the group again, telling them what he'd been tell-ing all his people. "The crest is late tomorrow night. The water's gonna be way the hell up on the emergency work, over if this goddamn rain doesn't give us a break. Either way, a shitload of pressure on the sys-tem. The safety factor the Corps built into it is gone. It could fail at any time, no warning.

"Every one of you, I don't care where you are or what you're doing, I want you to know at all times where the high ground is—on top of a levee, in a building, wherever. You're not sure where you should go, ask your team captain. If you see a problem, you report it. Depending on how serious it is, you wait for help or you get the hell out of there. If you hear the civil defense siren, you haul ass, period. That's an order. Got it? No fucking heroes here, folks."

Chuck got back into his car and went to check on the brewery.

CHAPTER 68

~

E l went downstairs and lay on one of the sofas in the front parlor, a room she and Walter never used. The humpy settee was like trying to sleep draped over a termite mound, but she didn't care. Sleep was an impossibility. She only wanted to breathe a little easier.

As soon as dawn light began to color the shades, she got up and climbed back upstairs to dress. Because it was too early to go anywhere else, she drove down to the mobilization center and spent an hour talking to people and listening to the latest rumors. Then she went over paperwork.

More people were evacuating from the Flats now that Fritz had come out in favor of it. Many still refused to budge. El didn't understand it. If they thought the protection system was going to fail...? Perhaps the ones staying weren't the same ones spreading the rumors.

After she'd satisfied herself that all the documentation was in order, she drove up to the storage facility for her daily meeting with Sister Beth DeVries, her procurement and distribution director, who used to do the same work for the Mount Carmel Motherhouse back in the order's heyday.

"Any word, my dear?" Sister asked.

El shook her head.

"I shall continue to pray," the nun said.

They walked up and down the aisles of food and other provisions, Beth with her inventory and usage sheets, bringing El up to the moment. The food distributor had been giving them some problems. Beth said that the account rep she'd been working with was "a dear, although awfully young." Sister herself was in her late seventies, and it wasn't clear precisely what she meant by "awfully young."

El picked a can off a shelf and looked for the expiration date.

"I suppose there's no point to looking for another vendor. Just so long as they understand that we might have to expand our operation in a hurry."

After she finished at the storage facility, El visited the mother-houses where she was putting up many of the evacuees. Odd to see so much activity around these massive old building complexes after their years in decline.

Driving between them she would wonder where Walter was and have to resist the urge to imagine he might still be alive. He wasn't alive. All that remained was to find his body. It had taken them about this long to find Edna Goetzinger, but that had been different. People who drowned in the Mississippi sometimes were never recovered. The idea of Walter ensnared in some cold, foul recess in the depths of the river filled her with loneliness and sorrow.

Later in the morning, when she finally arrived back down at Five Flags, she had to make herself get out of the car.

~

"I'm glad you're here," Aggie told her as soon as El was through the door.

"What?"

"I just got off the phone with a woman up in Guttenberg. Red Cross. They've got several very sick people living in tents. And a pregnant woman due anytime. I told her, you know,"—Aggie was shaking her head, her mood somewhere between unhappiness and irritation—"that our resources are limited, and so many people are homeless now. We simply can't help everybody. I told her, but she was pretty insistent." What Aggie wouldn't have revealed to the woman was that they were trying to save some beds for the people of Jackson should the protection system fail after all.

"If the people are in extreme need," El told her, "there has to be someplace for them up there, convalescent homes, even private homes. What about their clinic?"

"They've lost it to the flood. She said they'd moved as many people as they could into shelters, wherever they could. It's just gotten so bad."

They were getting calls from up and down the river, as far away as McGregor and Prairie, Jackson in everybody's mind suddenly the shelter of last resort, ready to gather the drenched and homeless masses to her bosom. El had wanted to help, but she couldn't help everybody. She'd end up offering to many nothing but disappointment. You try, and where does it get you?

"Call the woman back," she told Aggie. "Work with her. Try to find someplace else the people can be taken, someplace inland maybe. If you can't…"

"Okay." Aggie nodded, obviously relieved. El's mind, however, continued to dwell on the negative.

"I suppose we should just keep on putting people up until we run out of space. Then, if the floodwall fails…"

What difference did it make? You did what you could; that was all you could do.

❧

Later, in the rain, El walked along Green Street, which would become a shoreline should the worst occur. With her were Chuck Fellows and the director of public transit and the chief of the city's survey crew, who was tracing out for their benefit exactly where water would reach on the basis of the latest predictions from the National Weather Service. The crest was below North Buenie, less than twenty miles upriver. It would get to Jackson sometime after 2:00 a.m. the next morning, in less than thirteen hours.

They talked about picking up people who would be fleeing from their homes in the event.

"Almost nobody's going to be on foot," Chuck was saying. They had stopped at the corner of Twelfth Street and were looking toward the river. In the distance, furniture was being loaded onto a pickup truck. Nearer, a low sandbag dike had been constructed around a ground-level doorway.

"Rubberneckers," Lou, the transit guy, said.

"Right," Chuck agreed. "Place is gonna be a zoo."

"I need to be able to get my vehicles down here, and park them so I can pick up people. Maybe I should do it now. I've got a couple of buses I could spare."

El smiled. Lou was a nice guy, but a little tone deaf, politically speaking. "People already think we know the system's going to fail. Do we want to advertise?"

Chuck said, "You can park in the middle of the street, it comes to that."

The rain started to fall harder; they stepped into the entrance of a store to get out of it and continued talking.

～

In midafternoon, El drove up to Mount Mercy Center, the last of the motherhouses they were opening, and toured the facility with the sister-in-charge and Ed Ohnesorge, head of Catholic Charities for the Archdiocese. Ohney had been smoothing El's way. No doubt he would have done it anyway, but he'd inadvertently placed himself under an extra obligation when he'd taken El aside after the Friends of the Community breakfast and told her she should add to the protection system no matter what, as a kind of symbolic gesture of solidarity with the people in the Flats. As it turned out, of course, they would have had to do it anyway. But that was neither here or there.

"There are no locks on the doors," Sister said as they walked down a corridor so long that El wondered that there had ever been a time when there were so many Catholic religious in the world. Sister opened a door. "And the rooms are small."

Ohney stuck his head in and inspected the monastic cell. "I suppose it's not going to kill someone to get a little taste of the ascetic life." He grinned back at Sister. "Think of the recruitment possibilities."

As El drove back downtown later, thinking of Walter and still under the influence of her visit to the motherhouse, she got a call on her car phone from the airport administrator. At the instant the ringing began, she had been fretting over her loss of income with Walter gone, which was grossly practical, but something that must be considered. There was much, she decided as she listened to the ringing, to recommend the simple life. Surely she could simplify her life. She didn't need to take vows to do that. On the third ring, she answered.

"We just gave clearance to a military transport to land," the airport administrator told her. "It's carrying cots and bedding. What am I supposed to do with the stuff?"

"I'll take care of it." She called the commander of the National Guard unit in town and then Chuck Fellows and before she'd turned into Airport Boulevard, she had help on the way.

Driving up the entrance road, she tried to remember the last time that she and Walter had been at the airport together.

CHAPTER 69

~

The night before, when she'd come down to see how Lucille was doing, Aggie had made the mistake of looking into the cellar, filled with city water. The surface lay startlingly close and dead still, gleaming dully up at her, like reflections from an ancient cistern. She'd immediately closed the door. The vision gave her the creeps.

This time, as she drove up to her mother's, the people next door, a young family, were just finishing packing their station wagon before they evacuated.

"We don't know what to think," the wife, who was pregnant, said. Aggie thought about the pregnant woman up in Guttenberg. In disasters there always seemed to be pregnant women all over the place.

"Probably it's going to be all right," the husband said.

"Probably," the wife agreed, tilting her head and smiling defensively.

The husband finished stuffing some blankets into a vacant cranny in the car. He dusted off his hands. "Better safe than sorry."

In the wife's apologetic tilt and the husband's hint of irritation, Aggie detected a detente. "Where are you going?" she asked.

"They're opening a new shelter in an unused wing at Mount Mercy. We understand that's a lot nicer than the Sisters of Presentation," the wife said. "Although Mount Carmel is supposed to be nice, too."

A little enviously, Aggie watched them driving off with their two children and dog and belongings.

Her mother sniffed when Aggie told her about the young family. They weren't the third or fourth generation in Little Wales is what the sniff meant. Not river rats.

"They seemed nice," Aggie commented.

Walking around inside the house, she was conscious that just a few feet below lay the dead-still pool of water, like an omen. A boil order had been issued for the Flats, and Lucille had a couple of large pots

heating on the stove. Boxes and other stuff were piled all around, giving off their cellar odor. The dogs sensed that something was seriously
the matter, for they had started to wander around in the distracted
way dogs sometimes had.

Every fiber in Aggie's body told her that Lucille should get the hell
out of there. But it would never happen. The fact that the people next
door had left became another argument for Lucille staying put. Or
not even that, since Lucille didn't feel the need of arguments.

Aside from scaring the stuffing out of herself and fulfilling the
role of dutiful daughter, Aggie didn't know what she expected to
accomplish coming down there. She'd been telling anybody who'd
listen that her mother would never leave. Lucille was grafted onto
that house. She'd never leave. It was true. And besides, Aggie had
spent years learning to give Lucille the right to be herself. Lucille
would rather be sitting on top of the house with floodwater all
around it than warm and comfy in somebody else's place, including
Aggie's. Especially Aggie's.

Aggie knew all this.

But finally, it made no difference. "You need to get out of here,
Ma."

Lucille said nothing, just kept her eye intently on the tube. She
was watching the flood on TV, interested in the fate of other people.

Aggie took a deep breath. "It doesn't make any sense to stay. Look
at the dogs. They know something's wrong. They know this is not the
place to be just now. The water's way up on the emergency works. The
safety factor is gone. Everybody says so. It could fail, just like that, no
warning. You don't have to leave for long, a few days. You can stay
with me."

Still no reaction. And, it had to be said, even as she continued to
badger her mother, Aggie felt like a traitor. Lucille's life was her own.
What right did Aggie have to try to get her to do something she didn't
want to do? And wouldn't do, no matter what Aggie said.

"If you won't go, it's just pigheadedness. A week ago, two weeks
ago, whenever, you told me it wasn't going above twenty-seven feet.
Remember, Ma? Now it's over thirty-three. I don't care what you think
you know about the river, nobody's ever seen anything like this. It's
just crazy, staying here."

The situation had oh-my-God written all over it. Still, Lucille said
nothing. Aggie could tell, though, that her mother was working herself up into a response.

Well, Aggie decided, she had one more tactic she could try.

"If you don't want to leave, then I'm moving in," she announced.

That did it. "The fuck you will."

"I won't have you down here by yourself if something happens."

"You won't, huh? Well, I've lived here alone since your father died. I guess I can take care of myself."

"No, mother, that's the whole point. If something happens, you won't be able to take care of yourself."

"I don't care if something happens," her mother snapped.

"Well, I care! All I've asked you to do is move out for a few days, until the danger passes."

"I'm not the one who's going to leave," Lucille said and smiled. "You are."

"Ma!"

Lucille stopped smiling. "Frankly, I've had it up to here with you coming around and hounding me."

"I haven't been hounding you." Aggie had been making constructive suggestions; that was the way she viewed it.

Lucille pointed at the door. "Out."

"Good grief. You're acting like a child, you really are."

"Don't you talk to me that way, missy."

A surge of anger had suddenly taken possession of Aggie. She was right, and she was really pissed, and it felt good.

"Grow up, Ma! This isn't a joke. You could get killed."

"Get out!"

"Baby, baby, baby!"

"Get out! Get out!"

Her mother had heaved herself up out of the chair and begun an advance across the kitchen, as if she contemplated the use of force. Caesar began to whine.

"You get out of my house!" Lucille yelled.

Aggie stood her ground, expecting her mother to stop at any moment, but she continued to bear down. Now she started pushing Aggie, saying over and over, "Get out, get out!" Her eyes were shiny with rage.

Aggie, seeing the hopelessness of the situation but still angry at herself for bringing the subject up at all, even madder at the headstrong old woman for refusing to listen to her, fetched her raincoat from the sun porch. She stopped briefly at the kitchen door and looked back. Her mother stood, her feet spread, in a kind of half crouch in the

middle of the floor, jabbing a finger at her and repeating, "Go, go."
All the dogs were making whimpering noises now.

"Okay, Ma," Aggie snapped. "Suit yourself. Stay here. See if I
care." She slammed the door behind her.

Chapter 70

~

As day settled into night, Chuck Fellows kept on the move. Seven hours to the crest.

He stopped at the city garage and discussed shifting the sandbagging operation to another location, somewhere out of the floodplain. Most of the city vehicles had already been moved. Response time would be increased if they did. There was no obvious place to set up a new operation. Even if the system failed, they were far enough away to save whatever needed to be saved. They'd stay put.

On the Ice Harbor peninsula, where a series of boils had now been ringed, he walked along the course of the slough, filled so many years ago with the waste of the old lumber mills. Water migrating through the unconsolidated material had sought out the many weaknesses and forced its way to the surface. As sand and soil, the decayed fill, forced its way up, the crews had ringed one boil after another, the series of sandbag enclosures like the volcanoes of a chain of oceanic islands.

At the Ice Harbor, he checked in with Kenny Nauman, making sure that the pump was managing to keep up with all the city storm water pouring into the harbor, forcing it over the wall and into the flood moving down the Mississippi. While he was at it, Chuck went out on the catwalk on top of the harbor gates, holding on to the plywood sheeting used to add four feet to the height of the gates. The gap he'd found at the bottom of the gate hadn't been fixed. He pressed his hand against his sore ribs, not cracked, just bruised by the explosion. After what had happened to Walt, he regretted that he didn't have cracked ribs at least. He had no time to fix the gates, to go down and do the job himself. He wasn't going to ask anybody else to go into the water. Standing out near the middle of the span, he judged the vibrations no worse than before. Probably the gates would hold. No safety factor anymore. Meant nothing. The safety factor was gone everywhere.

Next he stopped up at the EOC, then went down to Five Flags to talk to the watch commander. Diane was there, helping out, one of Aggie's crew of women execs. With the preparations complete, nothing much was happening at the moment, but Diane had stayed on with the others, waiting for the crest. Aggie and El Plowman, too, and scores of volunteers, scattered across the converted hockey rink, drinking coffee and chatting or reading books brought to pass the time or sacked out on cots, more rows added in case they were overrun with evacuees. They were like people waiting for midnight on New Year's Eve.

Chuck stopped for a word with Diane.

"Where are the kids?" They weren't with Francine. She was down at the garage filling sandbags.

"Neighbor's," Diane said. "How are you doing?"

The question, he understood, was personal, asked with evident concern, but he had little interest in matters of self-consideration.

"I'm fine." He turned his attention to El. "Walt was right about the Ice Harbor peninsula. One sand boil after another."

"Walter was often right," she answered. Chuck had changed his mind about El Plowman.

"How many left in the Flats?" he asked.

She rattled off the figures. There were still over 1,900 people either refusing to leave or unaccounted for.

"Can you deal with that many?"

"I hope we don't have to find out."

"Yeah."

Chuck and Diane went aside to talk privately for a minute, and then he climbed back into his 4x4 and continuing his restless patrolling along the seven-mile front he had raised against the flood.

❧

On Apple Island, Jack Kelley was on the move, too, but hemmed in, trapped on the scrap of land still struggling to hold itself above the floodwaters. It took him only a few minutes to complete another circuit of the breastwork. Pitch dark now. The wind had started to come up, pushing down from the north like the flood itself. Jack didn't like wind at night. Even without it, the rain was too heavy for the ironworkers to be overhead installing the roof. The other trades had knocked off, too, gone back to the kennels where Jack had installed cots and TVs and coolers for beer and chow, and where he didn't intrude. He was no housemother. Whether the blacks and whites had been baiting each other, whether there had been more fistfights, he didn't know. Or care. He'd ceased to care. Maybe he'd care later. At the moment, as long as the work continued, as long as nobody wrecked the kennels, they could do whatever the hell they wanted when he wasn't looking.

The volunteers were still at it, filling sandbags in the shelter built for the purpose on the backstretch of the track oval and hauling the bags over to reinforce the north levee, which was taking the brunt of the flow. Many of the tradesmen had joined them. One of the light plants had been turned around so they all could see what they were doing. They moved with the step-by-step doggedness of exhausted men.

Jack talked to the fellow in charge, who told him that he didn't like this wind, pushing the water higher.

"Only a few more hours," Jack told him. Crest was due sometime after two a.m. "You're doing a good job. Hang in there. A little longer."

The man repeated, "I don't like this wind."

Jack went out and climbed the planking laid diagonally up the levee and looked down at the water. Still a sliver of freeboard left. The levee looked okay to him, too. It looked like it ought to hold.

He felt the freshening wind. The lights behind him reflected from the whipping rain, a kind of blindness. He thought, for the hundredth time, *There's nothing more to be done*. He'd done everything he could do. It was in God's hands. It was time to let go.

He closed his eyes and considered praying but did not. Or perhaps he did.

After a while, he climbed down, followed the track railing around to the homestretch side, and passed the darkened grandstand without so much as a glance. Probably, he thought, he should have everything moved from the kennels up onto the deck, the cots and bedding and so forth, in case the site was overtopped. The deck was already jammed with construction material, though, and moving everything else up there seemed like a kind of giving up, like tempting fate or the utter loss of faith. He could, of course, abandon the construction trailer, move his own cot up out of harm's way, although why should he be safe if the rest weren't?

In the trailer, he called Janelle on the radio and briefly caught her up—the crest would arrive in a few hours, the levee was holding. Then he told Sean to wake him at midnight and turned in to get a few hours' sleep.

CHAPTER 71

~

Jack woke up. He lay staring at the near blackness, wondering where he was until his mind, like an upset boat, righted itself. Yes, the job site. He could hear voices. He listened to the wind and the strafing of rain against the side of the trailer, felt the canvas of the cot beneath him, smelled the air, damp and stale with cigarette smoke.

The voices closed in, the trailer rocked slightly, and the door swung open.

"Wake up, Jack!" Sean's voice.

"Am awake. What is it? Is it midnight?"

"No, 'bout nine fifteen."

Not midnight. He threw off the blanket and swung upright with a groan. "What?"

"You'd better come."

The hard frame of the cot cut across his thighs as he pulled on his boots. The luminous dial on the alarm clock read 9:09. He struggled into his slicker, and he and Sean and the other man set off at a dogtrot toward the northern edge of the site. The rain peppered Jack's face, and he seized his hat by the brim to keep it from flying off.

"Started blowing like this a few minutes ago," Sean said, raising his voice to be heard above the storm.

Both light plants were turned around and directed at the levee, where water oozed over in a dozen places, the volunteers and tradesmen trying to add one more layer of sandbags to the top, slamming the bags down on top of the water.

"It's the wind!" Sean yelled.

Slipping on the planking that he'd climbed hardly more than an hour ago, Jack scrambled to the top of the levee. The remaining strip of freeboard appeared and disappeared as the waves mounted against it, the wind scooping water from the wave tops and dashing it against him.

Jack took one look and climbed back down and ordered any tradesmen left in the kennels rousted out and the kennels emptied. Everything up onto the deck of the grandstand—food, sleeping bags, clothes.

Five minutes later, a line of men could be seen hauling their gear across the sand and up onto the deck. Then Jack and everyone else, ignoring rank, ignoring racial differences, set to work filling sandbags and flinging them across the top of the levee.

The crest was still several hours away. The wind kept blowing.

❧

Chuck Fellows couldn't reach Jack Kelley on the radio. He couldn't raise anyone out at the job site, so he drove north, through the National Guard checkpoints, and stood at the sandbag barrier closing off the bridge out onto Apple Island and trained his binoculars on the site. The floodwater, chest high, partially blocked his view, and he imagined at first that the track had already been swamped. But the work lights continued to shed their intense beams, and he could make out some sort of activity, hard to tell what. The wind screamed out of the north, driving the flood before it.

He tried to reach Jack again. No luck. For a moment he cursed the man for his damn heroics. For a moment he thought, *If the flood gets Kelley, the son of a bitch deserves it*. He thought this and then, irritated, pushed the desire aside. So Kelley was an asshole. So he'd done this stupid thing just because he wanted to finish the job on schedule. So what? Kelley might be an asshole, but he wasn't alone. They were all assholes. Chuck, too. He didn't exempt himself. And what difference did it make? Not a goddamn bit. They were here. They were in the middle of this huge friggin' shit storm, and Chuck cared only about one thing. He didn't want anybody else to die, not Jack, not anybody.

He tried to reach him again and failed again. Nothing he could do. Jack was on his own. *Hope to hell he'll be okay*. But nothing Chuck could do, not a damn thing.

❧

At the mobilization center, people had gone dull with waiting. The lights had been turned down for those who wanted to sleep, creating a twilight atmosphere. Everything that needed to be said had been said, and said again, and said again, the only flurries of activity when another group of the standby sandbaggers were called out to fight another sand boil or more evacuees arrived and had to be assigned to housing.

The operators were on the phones, calling in more volunteers, and as they arrived singly and in small groups, Aggie and her assistants would make sure they had filled out the forms and had their shots and learned how to properly fill and stack the sandbags.

For Aggie this was hardly more than busywork by now, and in the periods when she wasn't thus occupied, she and the others would sink at once back into their private thoughts or take their catnaps, waiting for the crest. It seemed like they had been waiting forever.

A short distance away, El sat on the edge of a cot, slumped over as if asleep sitting up. Farther away, Diane Fellows had gathered the latest batch of volunteers around her and was instructing them in a low voice. She'd been doing a wonderful job. All the women Aggie had recruited to help run the center had been doing a wonderful job. Thank God for the women.

Aggie sat behind the check-in desk. She had an unopened book on her lap. She was trying not to worry about her mother.

～

The band was cut off the last bundle of sandbags, the bags grabbed off in handfuls and hauled to the filling sites behind the levee. Jack had stopped filling himself and now paced back and forth, his eyes sweeping the crest of the emergency work. The flow was stanched in one place only to spring up in two or three others. The wind-blown floodwater had begun to spill around the ends of the north-facing section and water was coming across the flanking sections in several places.

Sandbags were filled and placed almost in a single motion. The water, blocked for an instant, would spatter, then begin to seep around the edges until more bags were jammed into place, and two feet or five feet or ten feet along the levee, another spill would appear.

As his alarm grew, Jack walked faster, then began jogging. Then stopped dead. In the center of the levee, water had ceased spilling in seams and now swept over in a broad sheet.

He started yelling, "It's too late! It's over! Everybody up on the deck!" He started running, yelling, his call picked up and relayed by others. In a ragged line, the flood fighters began to retreat.

Some kept on working. Jack ran at them. "Too late! Too late!"

Others abandoned the effort. "Save the unused sandbags," Jack told them.

One last person continued to work in the distance and Jack headed for him only to discover it was Lonny Vasconcellos, with a sour intensity continuing to fill bags and fling them onto the levee. Lonny, ever contrary.

"That's it, Lonny," Jack told him. "Nothing you or anybody else can do now."

Young Vasconcellos continued to work doggedly for a brief time and then, without looking at Jack, threw his shovel down and walked away.

Jack grabbed the shovel and began retreating, walking backward, watching as water breached the wall at one place after another. It was over. They'd done all they could. It was over.

~

Nearly ten o'clock, Sam Turner's tour of duty almost finished. He stopped long enough to huddle beneath his rain gear and install new batteries in his flashlight. Then he began walking again.

The stiff wind sprayed floodwater over him, the river on the other side of the mud box so high that he had to hold his arm up to skim the beam across its surface, filled with waves like he used to see on Lake Michigan, the water almost near enough to touch. He couldn't see much. In the morning, he watched the sweep of the river, and it was a fearful thing. At night, like now, it was different, only a small area visible, his relationship with the flood more intimate, as it spit at him and the waves rolled by, curling as if about to crash into a beach.

He kept on walking along the landward side, on the lip between the mud box and backslope, the path he'd made over the last four hours a confusion of imprints in the mud.

He remained alert, as fresh as if he'd just begun. Sam didn't pretend he could understand it. He should have been tired and bored. But he wasn't. He felt fine, with a kind of slow attentiveness, which was a little bit like indifference. He moved deliberately, the ground slippery, and let his free hand play long the top of the mud box planking, shining the light here and there.

At the northern end of his section, where industrial buildings nosed down close to the river and the levee had been tied into a section of the floodwall, he stopped for a few moments, as he always did, to check around the elaborate polyethylene diaper wrapped over the juncture between the flashboards added to the wall and the levee's mud box. Then he ran the beam down the tops of the flashboards until the light could reach no farther, had become nothing more than a vague glow reflected back by the storm. Water squirted beneath the panels and pushed up to within a few inches of the top, half a foot maybe. Waves surged over in pulses.

Another of the inspectors would be walking at the base of the wall, but Sam couldn't spot him in the intensity of the storm. He turned and began to walk back along the levee, and had taken a couple of measured steps before something caused him to turn back.

Later, he would wonder what it had been.

～

Chuck finally reached Jack Kelley by radio.

"It's over," Kelley told him.

"Where are you?"

"Up on the deck. We're all up here."

"Good," Chuck said.

"No," Jack told him, his voice scratchy over the radio, "it's not good. But water's pouring over the levee, and it couldn't be helped."

"All right, Jack. But you did the right thing."

"It couldn't be helped. What about you?"

"Okay for the moment. I'm down on the Ice Harbor peninsula. Boils all over the place, but as long as the damn river doesn't go much higher…"

"I hope to hell it doesn't."

"Gotta go."

"Yeah."

"I'm sorry, Jack. You tried."

"Yeah. For all the good it did."

Chuck rang off. The team captain for that stretch of the floodwall was coming toward him. The man was running, a strange awkward kind of running, like that of someone who hadn't run in years.

～

When the sirens began, Lucille had just returned to the kitchen, after making another trip out to inspect the water welling up in the back yard. She'd marked out the puddle as worthy of her attention that morning. Of course, there were puddles all over the fucking place. But this one kept on growing and she'd noticed a small spot at its hub, which seemed to be boiling. The puddle was more or less at the edge of where the Kiakiak Slough had been before they filled it in to make the industrial park. That was another reason Lucille noticed it. She knew about boils, of course, which were nothing more than the river returning to its ancestral pathways. In the mind of the river, the slough still existed. Any idiot that imagined he could get rid of it simply by filling it in was as ignorant as a stump.

Lucille had gone back to the kitchen where she now stood listening to the siren, her hand on top of her head, and thinking, *Shit, not again.* The dogs were swishing back and forth, looking to her for guidance.

"I suppose we'd better check it on out," she said to them, and they all traipsed back to the sun porch, where Lucille peered through the rain this way and that. Hard to make out anything.

So she put on her slicker and grabbed her flashlight and pushed out onto the front steps after telling the dogs to stay put. They crowded behind her, and she flapped her palm against Gino's nose, Gino always the one who wanted to go bounding out for a bit of a smell-around.

She still couldn't see anything. There was something, though. Beneath the racket that the rain was making, not to mention the siren, she heard something. A low, steady noise. Not something she was familiar with. She swung the beam of the light toward it. Nothing. She turned her attention back to the puddle, which had grown during the day, now pretty much covering the whole back yard. She probably should call somebody about it. She swung the flashlight here and there. Sure was a fucking lot of water around.

Lucille shivered, suddenly colder. The noise had intensified, a kind of rubbing sound, steadily swelling up. Again she shined the light in the direction it seemed to be coming from, to the northeast, toward what would have been the entrance to the slough in the old days. Now she could almost see something. That's what it seemed like, the moment before seeing.

For an instant she was aware only of her own alarm, and then she spotted the thread sliding toward her like a snake, sliding and coiling and disappearing into the standing water. Behind it came more, now the back of a broad serpent, a low wave sweeping along and tumbling and mounting higher.

Lucille supposed she could stop worrying about the puddle now. Now the puddle was the least of her problems.

"Time to leave, dogs," she told Gino and the others.

She went inside and stood considering. Her boots, she didn't have her fucking boots on. She wasn't going anywhere without her boots.

While the dogs charged around, Gino barking, Lucille wondered what she should take with her, but then decided she probably didn't have time to take anything. She sat and laboriously pulled on one boot and then the other. She wasn't as young as she used to be, and putting on boots had got to be a pain in the ass. She told the dogs to hold their horses, she was coming.

∼

After he finished his brief conversation with Chuck Fellows, Jack had gone over to the northern edge of the grandstand deck, walking down through what would be the seating area, intent on marking the progress of the floodwater as it enveloped the site. He'd made several such trips, compulsively, heartsick, but with growing acceptance, too. And perhaps they'd get lucky, perhaps the flood wouldn't wash away all the sand that had been dredged to form a platform for the construction work, although he had a vision of the sand gone, the track buildings in midair on their pilings like some Polynesian village raised on poles above a lagoon. It couldn't be helped. It must be accepted.

Now he stood at the window, peering out and shifting back and forth as he tried to get a decent view through the glass.

Strange. The water slick on the windows could almost be mistaken for the floodwater covering the site, but beyond that... Something was wrong...

He loped back up the steps to the top of the deck and grabbed his coat.

"What is it?" Jim Bergman asked.

"Don't know."

Bergman followed, and several of the others. As Jack left the building at the southeast corner and went around toward the north side, a siren began in the distance. He slowed his pace. He could see well enough now. Floodwater was no longer pouring in a single sheet over the levee. Streams overflowed here and there at low points, and water flew across the barrier like salt spray at sea. Puddles were scattered everywhere, but that was all.

"Hey, all right," said one of the others who had come out.

The crest of the flood was still hours away. The rain was still streaming out of the sky, the wind howling from the north. Jack looked at Bergman, who looked back. Their eyes met, a moment of powerful intimacy that they would both remember for the rest of their lives.

A couple of the men started to cheer, but Jack told them to shut up, there was nothing to cheer about. Water should have been pouring over the barrier.

Everybody quickly understood. The track had been saved, but at a dreadful cost.

❧

Water was all around the house now. Lucille heard the phone ringing back inside. A car sped along Cardiff, and she listened to the water splashing up around its tires.

"Get in, get in," she ordered the dogs as soon as she had the door to the Dart open.

She got in herself and settled behind the wheel and with a certain irritation, a certain sense of being unfairly put upon, jammed the key into the ignition. The car was old, like Lucille, and cranky and not always in a mood to perform.

She turned the key, and in an instant the motor had turned over and begun a steady murmur. Lucille said, "Good."

She put it in gear and backed up, stopping at the end of the driveway to make sure no other idiot was charging down the road trying to get away. The engine hesitated, but then surged strongly as she swung backward into the road.

She shifted into forward. The motor wheezed and died.

"Shit," Lucille said.

She tried to start it again. The engine turned over and turned over, but wouldn't catch. She sat hunched behind the wheel. The light from the headlamps rippled over the top of the floodwaters rolling toward her. Well, this was a fine how-do-you-do.

"Okay, everybody out. We're going to have to walk."

She opened the door and stepped into the water, surprised by how deep it had already gotten. Gino went bounding away.

"Not that way, you dumb dog!" she yelled after him. Gino ignored her and in a few moments had disappeared into the murk. Caesar and Domino were wading back and forth. "Let's go," she told them and started trudging toward the end of Cardiff. They were going toward the rising water, but there was nothing for it. That was the only way out.

The water filled her boots. It crept up her calves, cold as ice water, and began to lift the hem of her dress. The current wasn't that high or that strong, but it was hard to walk anyway, and she wavered and almost fell and after a few steps halted, irresolute. The water had found the hollows behind her knees, sensitive spots where it stung mightily.

"Fuck!" Lucille snapped. This was no good. She'd never make it. "You do what you want," she told the dogs. "I'm going back in the house."

She turned and made her way toward the driveway, the rising water carrying her along and making it even more difficult to keep her footing. The dogs were sticking close, swimming now.

In the driveway, or maybe along its edge, she stepped into a hole and pitched forward and staggered back to her feet, the front of her clothing sopping. She walked the rest of the way with her legs spread apart and crouched over.

At the back door, the water had already reached the top step. The dogs' wet flanks brushed against her as they all tried to go inside at once.

Lucille turned on the lights and stripped off her raincoat and pulled the bodice of her dress free and shook it. A deep chill began at her shoulders and cascaded down her to her feet. She must change. Soon as she'd called.

She dialed 911. Busy. *Of course*, she told herself. *Don't be an idiot.* But she tried it again anyway, just in case. As she listened to the busy signal a second time, she heard a sizzling sound and the house went black.

⟨∼⟩

When the sirens had begun, a low moan rising quickly into an anguished wail, Aggie flinched, head turned toward the sound, palms pressed against the edge of the table, finger lifted.

Lucille!

Her immediate impulse was to fly off to her mother. It was happening. Oh my God!

She leaped up. All around her, the room was coming to life. El, up off her cot at once, came rushing forward. The steady wail of the siren was like panic itself.

Wait a second, wait a second, Aggie told herself, *wait a second, get ahold of yourself.*

She turned abruptly and went to the phone, the dedicated line she had up to the EOC. As she was reaching for it, it rang, and she seized the receiver. The person on the other end started talking at once. She recognized Seth Brunel's voice.

"There's been a break in the system."

"Where?"

"One of the wall panels behind Tri-State Power."

Aggie was horrified and relieved at once. The worst had happened, but it wasn't near Little Wales, Lucille would have time to get out.

El was standing right behind her, others crowding around, too, more coming quickly from across the vast room.

"Well?" El demanded.

"The floodwall behind the power company."

"Damn," El said, then, "Okay." She turned around and, yelling to be heard above the sirens, told the others what had happened. She started moving through the throng. "Everybody knows what to do! Bus drivers first! Listen up!" She was making the quick adjustments in their standing instructions to take into account where the break had occurred. The phone rang again. Seth again.

"What?" Aggie asked.

"Second break."

Aggie caught her breath. "What? Are you sure?"

"Yes."

"Where?"

"The road to the lock and dam."

That was near Little Wales! "Where on the road?" Aggie asked.

"That's all I know. Get back to you."

As Aggie hung up, the operator who had been assigned to call Lucille the moment something happened came rushing over and told her that there was no answer.

El, who had finished barking out her instructions, approached. "What was that?"

"Another break!"

El immediately called after the retreating bus drivers and their helpers, her cries repeated across the room until everyone had heard and returned. She told them what had happened and diverted some of them at once to the pickup points established toward the North End.

Aggie was wondering what it meant that her mother hadn't answered her phone. Probably she had already left. Probably. Although with Lucille you could never tell. She might have thought it was Aggie calling and didn't answer because she didn't want to have to admit Aggie had been right all along. Aggie had a vision of her mother sitting in a chair in the middle of her house, in a foul mood, as the floodwater rose around her.

Nearby, El was repeating to the bus drivers, "If people keep coming, don't leave until you've got a full load. But if there's a lull, bring whoever you've got."

After they were gone, she returned to Aggie and peered carefully at her.

"How's Lucille? Has she left?"

"Couldn't reach her. Probably she's gone. I don't think she'd stay."

"Why don't you go find out?"

"All the people are gonna be coming." Aggie couldn't desert El. Lucille was probably all right. If she'd still been home, she surely would have answered the phone. Aggie was sure of it. Aggie was almost sure of it.

El was staring at Aggie, her Dutch-uncle look. "I've been preparing weeks for this. You think I can't handle it? Get out of here. Come back when you know she's safe."

"Thank you, thank you," Aggie told her, enormously relieved, and grabbed her coat and ran.

She started driving toward Little Wales, but she wasn't thinking clearly. She'd never been good when it came to spur-of-the-moment stuff. Now she thoughtlessly took the shortest route toward Cardiff Street and quickly realized her mistake. The traffic got heavier and heavier, and in a few blocks she'd become hopelessly stymied among cars streaming away from the Flats area, people fleeing on foot, people wandering around in the middle of streets trying to spot the approaching floodwater, cops and National Guardsmen blocking off one way after another. She was forced to turn around and drive not toward, but farther away from her mother as she tried to think of what back-streets might take her around to Little Wales.

Ma!

❧

Chuck could hear water moving, although none was visible yet. The break had occurred on the other side of the railway embankment leading up onto the bridge across the river, the one from which Walt Plowman had fallen. Chuck could hear the water, but he couldn't see it.

"No!" he screamed at several of the volunteers who had started running away from the river. "Into the brewery!"

He continued yelling and waving and pointing at the brewery, until all but two of the men had heard and obeyed.

He swore. The 4x4 was a couple of hundred yards away, no time to go and get it.

Nearby Glenn Owens was herding his sandbagging crew toward the building. Chuck yelled at him to get the radio out of the 4x4 and haul it into brewery; he was going after the last two guys.

Then he took off, running parallel with the embankment and listening to the water hurtling along on the other side. He ran at an angle to the others and on the roadway, so he had better footing, but the extra pounds he'd put on over the years and the weeks with almost no sleep had taken their toll, and he was quickly sucking wind and finally almost blind from the effort. He cursed that he'd let himself get so badly out of shape. He cursed because he hadn't gone back to get his vehicle. No way he'd catch them. No way, no fucking way.

Summoning his remaining scrap of energy, he pushed himself into a brief sprint and then stumbled to a halt and screamed at the fleeing figures.

"Stop!!!"

One heard him and obeyed, looking back, and then the second stopped and looked back, too.

"This way!" Chuck panted.

They didn't move, looking at him, uncomprehending.

Chuck pointed beyond them. "Look!"

At the end of the railroad embankment, where it sloped down toward the old railroad station and freight yard, the water had appeared, moving fast, cutting off their escape. Finally they understood.

His hands on his knees, panting, Chuck waited for them to get back to him.

"Sorry," one of them said.

"Save it," Chuck told him and waved back toward the brewery, and the three of them started running again, the water in pursuit.

By the time they got to the building, the flood had caught up and they were splashing through it, the water coming so fast that Chuck decided several of the panels of the floodwall must have failed.

Inside, he climbed to the third floor, where he found the team captain for the inspectors in the area and Owens, and together they took attendance, making sure that everybody was accounted for. Some of the inspectors were still out on the levee, but they should be okay. They could stay put or walk out along the tops of the mud boxes until they found a way back to solid ground.

Chuck got on the radio and started to call around to make sure all his other people were safe.

~

Lucille figured that Aggie would never let her live this down. Very irritating. She and the dogs had retreated to the second floor because the first was now filled with water. It had already begun to cover the upstairs floor. Very irritating.

They'd have to get on the roof somehow. The dogs were whining, and Lucille told them to shut up, don't be pansies. There was no way she was going to be able to climb out the window and up on the roof. There was nothing for it but to wait for the water to get high enough and then float on out, and let the water carry her higher and swim if she had to. She used to swim, forty years ago, and supposed she could still manage a few strokes, enough to get around to where she could climb up on the roof.

As the water inched up, tickling her legs first and then turning them to ice, she tried to decide whether she should have more clothes on or less. She'd changed after her futile attempt at flight and put on jeans, more appropriate wear for the occasion. Maybe a light jacket, she decided now, and waded over to the closet and felt around for something that would work and settled on the jacket of one of her old formal dresses. She'd look stupid, but what difference did it make?

It took her several tries before the window budged. Water, higher outside, came rushing in and knocked her with a splash on her keister.

"Fuck," she said.

As soon as she'd struggled to her feet, however, she realized that the water was too high and if she was going to get outside before she got trapped, she'd have to step on it. The dogs were swimming around, not sure what to do. She herded Caesar over to the window and pushed him through. When she went for Domino, however, Caesar swam back in.

"Dumb dog," Lucille said.

She dealt with Domino, aiming him in the right direction and giving him a shove on the rump, she following along, holding Caesar by the collar, yelling at Domino to encourage him. Finally the dogs were outside, but the water had climbed too high for Lucille to escape without ducking under, so she held her breath and let herself sink and gripped the window frame to pull herself through.

The dogs were swimming in circles. Outside there was nothing to hold onto, so Lucille paddled around the end of the gable to where the roof was sloping up. Nothing to hold onto there, either. She tried to climb up, but kept on slipping and finally just managed to jam her fingers under one of the shingles.

The effort had exhausted her. She could barely maintain her grip and felt weak and infernally cold. The dogs had clambered up onto the shingles and were exploring and stopping every once in a while to look at her just hanging on there, all her strength gone. They seemed to be wondering why she didn't climb up there with them. It wasn't hard. "It's no use," she told them. "Old women weren't designed for this sort of thing."

The water continued to pluck at her. She could only tell she was still hanging on by looking at her hands, pincered on the edge of the shingle, the feeling gone. She was going stiff.

She could hear traffic in the distance, not far away. A hundred yards? Two hundred? She didn't know. Not far. Was a time she would have swum for it, no trouble. The roofs of the other houses on the street would be underwater, or she might try to swim from roof to roof. That probably wouldn't have worked, either. She was an old woman. She was past derring-do.

The water rose. She reached for a higher shingle, jamming her thumbs under it and holding on as best she could.

The time for practical considerations had passed, she decided. Too late, it was all too late. This was it for old Lucille Duccini. She'd never been a Klauer. She'd just married one. Always a Duccini. River people. And now the river would take her.

She was afraid, a little afraid. She didn't mind dying, was even looking forward to what was coming next, but she didn't like the idea of drowning. Something undignified about it. She wondered if there was some other way she could put an end to things, but her options at the moment seemed pretty limited. No matter, it was a sin to take your own life, even if you were about to die anyway. She'd lived by her faith this long, stupid to change now.

She was shivering violently, couldn't control herself. She just wanted it to be over. She watched her hands let go. She sank, getting a mouthful of water and struggling back to the surface, but finding that the water had carried her out of reach of the shingles. She tried to swim, but the roof refused to come closer, and again she went under and swallowed more water and only just managed to get her chin back up into the air this time. She struggled, gagging, not wanting to go down for the third time. The third time was the last.

But she did go down again, desperately thrashing her way back to the surface, suffocating and petrified.

And then something happened. She heard a strange noise, like a great windstorm, and imagined it must be an angel, come to take her to heaven. She relaxed, and let the water close over her, although in some far corner of her mind she thought it strange, not at all what she would have expected. But then, who could know about such things?

❦

Walking along the top of the mud boxes, sinking into the earth fill up to his ankles, Sam Turner joined the other men who had been patrolling along his section of the levee. One, a guy named Ralph, was talking on his handheld to their team captain, who was holed up over in the brewery, and informing him everybody was present and accounted for. The captain told them to stay put, which everyone thought was pretty funny. Ralph asked him just where the hell did he think they were going to go. Both ends of the levee were butted into floodwalls, the wall at one end having now failed, the wall at the other still intact but its flashboards so skinny it'd give a tightrope walker second thoughts.

Sam and Ralph and the others set about waiting the thing out. The rain continued to fall and the wind to blow, but the flood had gone down some, a little bit, the damage done. And their job done, too. They had nothing to do but wait, and so after a few minutes, the time began to stretch out and the cold and wet to seem colder and wetter. No place to sit down, the earth fill being saturated. They stood or crouched, sinking into the muck. It was like being in a swamped, earth-filled boat. But this boat, at least, was solid beneath them. All they needed to do was hang on, and eventually someone would come get them.

The storm peppered them with grapeshot. It was pitch black. They were several men huddled together, and nobody could see the color of another man's skin. Under the circumstances, it didn't mean a helluva lot, but Sam was conscious of it. The others were bitching and trying to figure if there might be some way off the levee after all and wondering what was happening in the rest of the city. Sam was content with the way things were.

After a while, he described how the floodwall had failed, for he was the one who had witnessed it and called in the alarm. As he had started to walk away from the joint where the levee and wall met, something—he didn't remember what—had caused him to turn back around. The wall remained intact. As he looked, however, the flashboards separated nearby, pulled apart as abruptly as paper is torn, and the wall began to slide, not shatter or overturn, but slide backward and around like a giant door opening, the tower of floodwater shoving it aside and rushing past. Sam, as he grabbed for his handheld, had stared at the gap where the wall stood and at the waterfall tumbling through it, astonished by the apparent effortlessness with which the barrier had been thrust out of the way, as if it had hardly existed at all.

~

Aggie got to within a few blocks of her mother's house and could go no farther. She ran the rest of the way to the water's edge, where she hurried back and forth, asking people if they'd seen Lucille, calling her name, and finally wading into the water to a point where she could make out the entrance to Cardiff in the lights shed from the water plant, itself now surrounded by the flood. Uncertain, helpless, she waded forward and suddenly stepped off a dip in the road and fell into the water and came up sputtering. Wet now, determined, she started to wade toward Cardiff when she felt a strong hand grab her arm.

She staggered, and the hand pulled her upright, saving her from another fall. It was J.J. Dusterhoft.

"J.J.! My mother!"

"I know," he said. "C'mon, come out of the water." His arm was around her waist, pulling her back.

"My mother!" she said, and attempted to free herself.

"It's okay," he said, "wait, it's okay."

"What do you mean? Is she safe?"

She was half still trying to escape, half letting herself be dragged backward.

"Wait," he told her, "it'll be okay."

J.J. continued to pull until they were out of the water. He kept his arm around her and they huddled, sopping.

"I didn't see you," Aggie said.

"Just got here."

"Ma's okay? How do you know?" She was shivering violently.

He pulled her closer. "Don't worry, hon. Everything will be fine. It's in the cards."

A minute later, above the racket of the storm, above the sirens, a faint machine noise could be heard, and almost immediately a johnboat came surfing out of the entrance to Cardiff and, skittering sideways, made a wide turn toward Aggie and J.J. It was driven by a large fan mounted in the back.

"An airboat?" Aggie said.

"Mine."

"Yours?"

"Mine. Clearly, the fellow at the helm doesn't know what the hell he's doing."

As the boat got closer, Aggie could see two dogs in the bow, noses up, ears blowing in the wind.

"It's Caesar and Domino!" she cried.

Then she saw Deuce standing at the wheel. And then a forlorn little figure huddled amidships.

"It's Lucille! Ma! Ma!" Aggie waved excitedly toward her mother, but Lucille made no gesture of recognition. "Is she okay?" Aggie asked J.J., although, of course, how could he know? But she was alive, she was alive!

"Probably none too happy about having to leave home," J.J. opined.

Deuce cut the motor too late and the boat came barreling up onto the asphalt, half out of the water, throwing its occupants forward. The dogs jumped clear, and Lucille seemed too dispirited to do much more than bob back and forth like some abandoned rag doll.

"Nice landing," J.J. said.

"Ma, Ma." Aggie climbed into the boat. Lucille barely moved, but the small change in her expression suggested that she wasn't glad to see Aggie.

Aggie looked toward Deuce, who seemed a little shaken himself by the abrupt end to his trip. She leaped up and hugged him and whispered, "You saved my mother."

"Got to save the mothers," he said.

"Oh, Deuce." Aggie kissed his cheek, but, still overpowered by her concern for Lucille, immediately returned and started urging her to get up. J.J. helped and finally the two of them managed to get Lucille to her feet.

"Where's Gino?" Aggie asked.

"Ran away," Lucille mumbled. "Dumb dog."

J.J. wrapped his arms around her and lifted her bodily over the side and set her on her feet, but didn't let go. "How you doing, Lucille?" he asked. "You're a little unsteady on your pins, I imagine, after your nautical adventure."

"Fuck," said Lucille.

"Guess she ain't feeling too bad," he said to Aggie.

Aggie was still mystified by the whole business. "How did Deuce get your boat?"

J.J. shook his head. "Plenty of time for that. Your friend Deuce and I gotta go look for anybody else might could use a little boat ride."

"Where's your car?" Deuce asked Aggie.

"A few blocks." She waved in the general direction.

He dug down in his pocket and tossed her a set of keys. "Take mine. It's the Mazda, right over there."

"Here are mine, then." Aggie gave him her keys in exchange. She couldn't remember which street she'd left her car on. She told him the model and color and license number.

"Don't worry, I'll find it," he said, raising his voice to be heard above the scraping sound as J.J. pushed the airboat back into the water.

"Nothing personal," J.J. said as he climbed aboard, "but what say I drive?"

And in a few moments the great fan in the back of the boat was spinning and the two men racing away in a deafening backwash of wind.

❧

El Plowman stood at the entrance to the mobilization center, welcoming the new arrivals, making sure each family got a number and explaining that that would allow them to be called in order without having to stand in line. She pointed out where they could sit and where they could get dry clothes if they needed them, how to find the johns, where there was hot coffee and cocoa. Later, the Red Cross would be bringing sandwiches. She also kept her eye out for anyone who might need medical attention. They had city EMTs ready to assist people and transport them to the emergency room at St. Luke's if necessary.

For hours, people arrived by bus, by car, on foot. Despite all the planning, chaos engulfed them—questions no one had anticipated, people needing attention that El didn't notice and nobody pointed out, lost family members still not located, demands overlapping, swamping each other, jostling, pushing, a punch thrown, angry insistent voices spiraling into the dim trusses high above.

During the brief lulls, El walked among the refugees, trying to damp down the rising tensions by explaining what would happen next. People knew about the Catholic motherhouses, of course. El said that she was sorry, but they wouldn't be using them tonight. Too many people had been forced out of their homes all at once to make that possible. Some would be going out to the fairgrounds, some to auditoriums at schools. But they had enough cots and bedding for everybody. In the upcoming days, as many as possible would be moved into convents and private homes. What could be done would be done, but she asked everyone to be patient and understanding.

Even in the confusion, there were moments when people thanked her with a touching sensitivity, grateful for what she was doing for them during this time of her own grief. There were bad moments, too, when someone became accusatory or demanding or even too desperately thankful. She got away as quickly as she could from such people, feeling worse and even more exhausted.

After families had been processed, they were transported to their temporary shelters. The displaced continued to trickle in late into the night. More missing persons reports, as well, with searches immediately mounted. As the crowd thinned out and food and drink were replenished, the suffocating press of earlier eased and people began to accept their new reality. Most of the troublemakers were finally dealt with. Exhaustion at last replaced adrenalin.

Many community leaders came and went, trying to help. Some stayed. Paul Cutler assisted people with the necessary paperwork, joking with them that of course there was paperwork, there was always paperwork. Johnny Pond and Rachel Brandeis and other reporters came to interview people and take pictures. Members of the city council and the county's board of supervisors walked among the evacuees. Fritz Goetzinger, too, who had been down helping people as they fled from the rising water but finally came up to the mobilization center, where he and El walked together, talking to the people. Aggie returned and told El what had happened—Deuce's rescue and Lucille now unhappy and shy one dog, but safely ensconced in Aggie's condominium. Fritz listened to the account gravely and nodding, but without comment otherwise.

Very late the men and women who had been inspecting the sections of levee and floodwall began to arrive and tell their stories. Chuck Fellows came in last, having made sure that all his people were safe. Morning neared. People were exhausted. It was still raining.

Someone happened to mention that the crest of the flood had arrived. In fact, it had arrived several hours earlier. Nobody noticed.

PART VI

CHAPTER 72

~

From the bathroom, Aggie heard the buzzer. Somebody down in the entrance foyer. She looked at her watch. Still not six yet. Who would come so early? She thought of Deuce, then dismissed the idea. Ridiculous. He didn't even know where she lived, did he?

Her mother called out, a disconsolate complaint—poor Ma—from the other room.

"Yeah, Ma, I hear it," she said as she walked out to the landing, flicking lights on before her. Exhausted from working all night, she held the railing to keep from tumbling down.

"Who is it?" she said into the little grating of the machine.

Through the intercom came a muffled, faraway voice. "You lose a dog, lady?"

~

He stood there, saying nothing at first, his mouth slightly open, the possibility of words. The spell of silence.

Aggie knelt down to embrace Gino, who was drenched. "Where did you find him?"

"Didn't. He was sitting outside when I got here."

Aggie ruffled Gino's ears and kissed him on his wet black nose. "You're not so dumb, are you?"

The other dogs had been aroused from sleep and now were running excitedly about, uncertain whether they were more interested in Gino or Deuce.

Aggie knew which one she was more interested in. She stood up and looked at him.

"Did you find more people?" she asked.

"Handful. Mostly, we spent time ferrying the inspectors trapped on top of the levees." Aggie noticed the modesty of this. He was looking at her. "You're dressed," he said.

"I've been helping at the mobe center. Got to go back. It's a zoo. I just came to check on Ma."

He held his arms slightly open, indicating the sorry state of his own attire. His clothes were filthy and his face smeared with dried-on dirt, hair snarled, a mess, and Aggie had never seen anybody as beautiful in her life.

"How's your mother?"

"You saved her."

He smiled and shook his head. "How's she doin'?"

"She's fine. No, that's not true, she's miserable. Her house is her life, and now it's underwater."

"We'll clean it up for her, afterwards."

It occurred to Aggie that she ought to thank him, so she did. They were looking at each other.

Aggie said something else, the words half forgotten even as they were spoken. Then she said, "You came," as if this had been planned all along.

He seemed to have come closer. They were very close. He smelled of the river.

The dogs were crowding around Deuce, looking for attention.

"They like you," Aggie said. "Do you have dogs?"

"Apartment house doesn't allow them."

"Would you, if you could?" She didn't quite know what she was saying. She could barely recognize her own voice.

"Maybe," Deuce said. "Prefer cats."

"You could have some of both."

They were very close. Aggie stopped talking. From somewhere in the back of her consciousness, all the arguments against having anything to do with Deuce nattered at her, but she ignored them. An unsoiled lock of silky hair curled against his forehead. His eyes, such a vivid gray… His lower lip, so plump and pale…

"I have to go back," he said quietly. "I wanted to stop here first."

"To see about Ma?"

"To see you."

His words were spoken awkwardly. In his now uncertain eyes she saw something she had only seen once before.

"You wanted to see me," she said softly.

"Yes."

His exhaustion after all the work had allowed him to do something that his strength would perhaps never have permitted, and she held the moment, trembling slightly.

Slowly he leaned over and kissed her, their lips barely touching.

She was so happy and, for some reason, so sad, too, that she didn't know what to say, but she wanted to say something, to give him some words, a present from her to him.

"I'm thirty-four," she said.

"I know. I went down to the recorder's office. That's how I found out Lucille was your mother."

"And you're thirty-three," she said.

Aggie could feel the dogs brushing back and forth and wished, for once, that they'd go away. Deuce was smiling at her, his eyes and mouth agreeing.

She wanted to say something more, but couldn't quite. In his arms she shivered and then pressed herself closer to him, into his body heat. She reached up into the curls of his snarled hair and pulled his face down to hers.

CHAPTER 73

~

Technically the river remained at flood crest, but it had in fact fallen several feet since the moment the night before when, as the wind blew water in sheets over the top of the levee, Jack had abandoned the flood fight and ordered everyone up onto the deck of the grandstand.

Throughout the night, the construction people and volunteers had listened to the spotty accounts of the lost flood fight in the city. Jack eventually managed to raise Chuck Fellows on the radio and tell him that the track remained dry but that a number of the tradesmen on the job site had relatives living in the flooded area and wanted to get ashore to see that they were all right. Also, they wanted to keep a few of the volunteers, but most could go home. Chuck said that he'd see what he could do.

Now, midmorning, a brilliant blue sky beyond the clouds overhead and the crews beginning to return to work, Jack stood outside the construction trailer with a cup of coffee. He needed to get back to work himself. Much to do. With the flooding of the city, the project would become that much more important. He could already hear the politicians' speeches on opening day.

Curious. The future, so opaque just twenty-four hours ago, now seemed laid out clearly before him. Even his own.

Behind him rumbled the semi-mounted generator supplying power to the site. Nearby, seepage water pumped up from the well points splashed back into the river. And in the distance, through the trees on the western margin of Apple Island, sections of the city's levee were visible. From his vantage, the levee and the city behind it appeared undamaged.

As he slowly swept the scene, trying to pick out some small giveaway of the flood behind the failed protection system, a boat came into view, nosing along the levee and then turning toward the construction site, following roughly the course of the drowned access road. Jack walked toward it. A large fan mounted on the stern drove the small craft, which picked up speed as it approached and then abruptly slowed and settled back into the water and drifted the last few feet up to the levee. Several people were on board, Chuck Fellows among them. But it wasn't Fellows who drew Jack's attention.

The boat nudged directly into the embankment where sandbags had been used to seal off the entrance to the road. The passengers began to climb gingerly over the bags and onto the site.

Father Mike Daugherty grasped Jack's hand warmly. "I believe I promised to conduct a service out here." Behind him, Edgar Rangel of the First Presbyterian Church clambered over the levee and shook Jack's hand, too. "I hope this is okay," he said.

"I don't see why not," Jack told him, stunned by this bold stroke on Mike's part. Mike, of course, was enjoying his little surprise.

"These gentlemen were kind enough to give us a lift," he told Jack, indicating Fellows and the boatman, the latter looking vaguely familiar although Jack couldn't quite place him. Before coming ashore himself, Fellows handed over the satchel in which Mike carried the articles he required for the service, which made him look like a doctor come on a house call.

Jack decided he was glad to see Mike. "Good," he said. Mike grinned.

"I need to have a word with you, Jack," Chuck Fellows said. He stood off to the side and looked absolutely wasted, out on his feet.

"All right," Jack said to him. "Let me get these guys squared away."

In a minute, Sean had been summoned. Work would be halted long enough for the service. Sean was to take the priest and minister around to decide on an adequate site and spread the word. Anybody could attend who wanted. It would be an ecumenical service.

That accomplished, Jack turned to Fellows. "Okay, now for you."

Jack might have been exhausted, but compared to Fellows he was as fresh as a daisy. Chuck's skin had a bleached, sickly pallor, his eyes ringed as if he'd been in a fight, and he was breathing through his mouth, his lip sagging and exposing his bottom teeth.

"How's your protection holding up?" he asked.

"Fine. Now. We got lucky, if you can call it that."

"Let's take a walk around." To the guy piloting the airboat, Chuck said, "Be right back, J.J. Don't go away."

As they walked the perimeter, Chuck inspected the levee, which the volunteers had straightened up some since the frantic last-minute efforts of the night before. *Inspected* was perhaps not the right word. Fellows seemed barely able to pay attention to what he was doing. His eyes shifted from object to object without apparent interest, like a bored clerk taking a warehouse inventory.

Jack couldn't help twitting him. "Little tired, are we?" It was pleasant, seeing Chuck this way for once, not the cocksure master of the situation.

Chuck blew out a puff of air and shook his head. "Hit me last night. Had to chase down a couple of idiots were trying to outrace the flood."

"Catch 'em?"

"Yeah."

Jack heard a noise coming from the south and looked in that direction. A helicopter was sweeping toward them. As it neared, the letters WGN painted on the underside of its fuselage became visible—the big Chicago TV station. Must be one of its traffic choppers sent out here on assignment.

"Great," Jack said.

Chuck squinted up into the glare as the bird ranged past, and for a moment Jack thought it might continue on north, but it swung back toward them, beginning a circuit of the job site. Chuck said, "Of course, you realize, Jack, that you've mounted the only successful flood fight on the river."

"What I realize is that you lost yours and that's the only reason we're standing here right now."

"Ancient history. Like it or not, Jack, you're the man of the hour."

What Fellows was saying might be true enough, but Jack didn't want to hear it.

They continued their circuit of the site, and Jack asked about the failures of the floodwall and the levee. In clipped sentences, Fellows described what was known. "Section of the wall that failed, it slid backward, then went over. One of my people was there, watched it happen. Failed according to design. We'd lost the safety factor. Textbook."

"What about the levee?"

"Who knows. I'm gonna go up and take a look. Probably have to wait for the water to go down to tell much. Maybe not even then. Corps took borings before they built the thing. Might've missed something. A lens of weak material maybe. Can't take borings every-where. Always miss something."

The helicopter was sashaying back and forth overhead.

"I'm sorry," Jack said.

Chuck stood staring at the shelter where the sandbags had been filled. He said, "Sometimes shitty things happen. But nobody died, Jack, so far as we know. Got all my people out. As for the rest…" He held his hands up, a gesture of indifference.

"Shits and giggles?"

The shadow of the helicopter passed over them.

"Shits and giggles," Chuck agreed. He had to raise his voice to be heard over the racket the chopper made. It was putting down in a patch of open ground nearby. He eyed it distastefully. "I'm outta here. Leave the press to you." He managed a shit-eating little grin. "Gonna be a star, Jack."

Jack didn't care for his tone, so he said, "And fuck you, too."

Chuck continued grinning, leaning close so he could be heard. "But you saved the bastard, Jack. I would've pulled everybody, let the river have it."

"That's right, you would have. But I'd rather the track been lost and the city saved. Something worth saving."

Chuck made a gesture, not a matter he was going to waste words on. He pointed at his watch. "Back in an hour. Pick up your priest and the other guy. Anyone else that wants to go ashore." He cast a last distasteful glance toward the chopper before turning and beginning to retrace his steps.

A smartly dressed woman, followed by a man with a camera, came ducking under the still-rotating blades, her microphone out.

"I'm looking for the man in charge," she said.

Jack stared at her, at her eager, confident expression, ready to turn the last month into a two-minute story. Sometimes he wished he had the personality of someone like Chuck Fellows. Or Janelle? Yes, Janelle would do quite nicely. She'd know what to say. Nothing that could actually be passed along over the airwaves, perhaps, but something that would leave the reporter with no doubts as to what Janelle thought about her two-minute story. Jack had always been too much the company man. He kept his thoughts to himself. People were bound to misunderstand.

"I just work here," he told the woman. "There's the fellow you wanna talk to." And he pointed toward Chuck's retreating back. The reporter, taking the bait, scurried off in pursuit of Fellows, trailed by the cameraman.

Jack stared after them for a long moment, pleased with himself. Then he went to find Father Mike.

CHAPTER 74

~

The sun had come out. A nearby maple cast a shadow of spring buds around Paul Cutler, the day almost perfectly still. A robin looped from one tree to the next, its brief flight like a garland inscribed in the air, leaving behind a memory of grace. Paul was reminded of his daughter, Zoe, playing her clarinet. The bird perched briefly on a thick lower limb, intent upon its business, and Paul was struck by the idea of how little the flood mattered to it.

He leaned against the fence, watching the watchers. Perhaps fifty, perhaps seventy-five people were strung along the rim of the blufftop park, some leaving, others arriving, a constant coming and going, like voters at a polling place or mourners at a wake. They stood singly or in small groups, occasionally pointing something out in the floodwaters below and saying a few words, but mostly, in the face of that spectacle, silent and astonished.

After a time, Paul turned and looked down himself, at the river filling the valley, in places from bluff to bluff, half the downtown under water. The floodwall and levees, with their emergency work, remained visible, suggesting an atoll, the floodwaters forming a lagoon behind them.

Out in the middle of the river, the dike around the dog track still held. A helicopter looped slowly up and away from the construction site.

The track would, in fact and symbolically, represent the city's commitment to its future. But at the moment he wasn't thinking about that. He was thinking about all the workmen and volunteers out there who still remained at risk, debris of all sorts sweeping along in the floodtide. Risk meant liability. The volunteers had signed waivers, of course, but he didn't imagine they'd be worth much in the eventuality.

Someone walked up and stood silently next to him. He glanced to the side.

"El," was all he said before turning back to the scene spread out below them.

"People have been telling me I should come up here," she said.

They stood silently at first, then talked about the spectacle below them, then of practical matters. Volunteer cleanup crews would need to be ready as soon as the water started to go down. They would forgive the water bills for a couple of months. Looters would be a problem.

Fair weather clouds drifted by, like puffs of smoke over a now-silent battleground.

"How's Brenda holding up?" El asked. Since she seldom asked about Brenda, this question seemed curious, perhaps a surrogate for how Paul himself was getting along, considering...

"We're all doing fine," he told her, then added, responding to what had not been asked, "Sometimes there's an advantage to having an old-fashioned marriage."

She lifted her chin slightly, acknowledging the intended humor.

Brenda was not well liked among city employees. Was a time she would have hampered his rise through the city manager ranks.

"Let me say again," Paul told El, "how much I regret what happened to your husband."

El's expression changed and Paul turned his head away.

Eventually she said, "If it had to happen, Walter would have wanted it this way. Like being buried at sea, I suppose. He could have appreciated that."

Buried at sea. Yes, Paul could see why that might be preferable to someone like Walter Plowman. Brenda's parents owned plots in a cemetery back in Mount Prospect. He thought about himself, the sense that he had, in moving from job to job, of losing contact with any one specific place. The time came, his ashes should be scattered to the four winds.

He and El talked about the latest rumor going around town, that the emergency protection works had failed because they'd been constructed too hastily.

"The emergency works didn't fail."

"I know," she agreed.

"If we'd acted immediately after Fritz approached the council, the result wouldn't have been any different."

"I know."

She was looking down at the flooded neighborhoods, being patrolled by coastguardsmen in their bright orange punts.

"Yes," she said, "the result wouldn't have been any different." Although she had repeated Paul's words, her tone lacked his finality. "But history didn't begin when Fritz Goetzinger made his demand. And anyway, people remember our reluctance, not the fact that the work was done on time."

"Yes," Paul agreed. People couldn't see a thing for what it was. That had been the reason he was hired, and now it'd be the reason he was fired.

"Another of life's small murders," he said.

"What?"

"Nothing." As he talked, his bitterness became more vividly present to him. "I waited too long to leave."

"Probably you're right."

"I did nothing wrong."

She considered this and said, "You lived by your code."

"I'm not going to apologize for that."

"Of course you won't."

They leaned against the railing, looking down, the animosity between them revived, his bitterness revived. He remembered why all this had happened.

The day had suddenly turned quite warm, a foretaste of summer. Even that high, he could smell the peculiar odor of the flood, pungent, an odor he had never smelled before. Almost directly beneath them, water being pumped from the basement of the water plant splashed over the backup levee. Farther away, like punctuation marks, sandbags ringed the wellheads.

The water tied everything together. It reflected the sky, as if the buildings had been released from their earthly hold and become a kind of celestial city. It was, he thought, quite beautiful in its way.

CHAPTER 75

~

Chuck had tried to sleep, but couldn't. He lay on the bed, listening to the clock in the hall, like the steady drip of water, and when he got sick of that, he went back downstairs and spread papers on the floor and started treating his work boots with neat's-foot oil.

By the time that Diane came home, he had abandoned that effort and sat slumped in the chair, ankles turned outward so that his legs were like bowling pins being knocked over. Some internal organizing principle seemed to have let go and his body lost all its integrity.

Diane took one look at him and came around the back of the chair and kissed the top of his head and put her arms around him. "You've come home. Good."

"Sent home. Hit the wall." He'd been up for three days running. He hadn't gotten more than three or four hours of sleep a night for the last six weeks.

"You should be upstairs sleeping."

"Tried to. Too tired."

"Where are the kids?"

"Francine took them. Left a note. They went up to The Heights to see the flood."

"She did? Well, that's good, I guess. It's supposed to be quite a spectacular view."

"Yeah. Whatever." Chuck hadn't seen much of the kids lately. He'd have to make it up to them.

"I'm just here for a little while," Diane said. "I have to go back. We're still trying to get people settled in." She was looking at Chuck speculatively. "You should go upstairs and *try* to get some sleep, at least."

"Uh."

"When was the last time you ate?"

He couldn't remember and didn't answer. He supposed he was hungry, hard to tell.

Unasked she got a beer from the fridge. She poured herself a half glass of wine and brought the drinks over. Chuck made the effort to move his chair around so he could sit at the table.

"What a dreadful time," she said as she put the drinks down.

Except for Walt Plowman, Chuck didn't think it was such a dreadful time. Not a wonderful time. It wasn't the monsoon, although pretty damn close. Anyway, he wasn't out humping in the Central Highlands and nobody was shooting at him. "The protection system fails here," he said, "it takes a little pressure off the towns downstream."

Diane looked at him and her expression softened. "I love you," she said.

Chuck didn't know what that was all about. He answered, "Hmm."

They stared at their drinks. Diane took a sip. Chuck didn't feel much like a beer at the moment although he appreciated the possibility of one. And he liked being with Diane. He liked sitting with her in their old companionable way, although he wasn't much of a companion just then.

"So what now?" she asked.

"When the water starts to go down, we'll blow a hole in the levee at the south end of town." Otherwise, the water wouldn't all drain back into the river, the elevation being lower down there.

"I dread the cleanup," Diane said.

"Mud dries, it's bitch to get off. Lot to do. Something else, too."

"What?"

"I can start looking for another job."

Diane remained quiet.

"Cutler's as good as gone, too," Chuck told her.

"Every cloud has a silver lining."

One of the things he'd noticed about his wife lately was that she had more of a mouth on her. A definite improvement. Less of the silent-treatment horseshit that used to be her specialty. And she'd probably already figured out that he might be made the scapegoat here. He and Cutler. They were outsiders.

"So it's on to Yellowknife, is it?" Diane asked.

"You'd go up there?" he replied, surprised, for the tone in her voice had somehow been collective.

"If it comes to that."

"Why now and not last fall?"

She smiled. "Who says I wouldn't have gone last fall?" He stared at her and wondered if that could be true. Had she bluffed him and won? She was still smiling. "I knew what you were like when I married you, dear. I had nobody to blame but myself."

Chuck was busy trying to reconstruct the conversation from the previous October or November, when she'd threatened to take the kids and leave if he tried to force her to go to "that godforsaken place."

"You're bullshitting me."

"Am I? You'll never know."

"I've been thinking Colorado," he said, "maybe Montana." In fact, he didn't want to go to Yellowknife anymore. He'd been reading the want ads in the professional mags. The Pacific Northwest was a possibility, too, except it rained too damn much out there. He'd seen enough rain to last him a lifetime.

"What about Maine?" Diane asked.

Chuck knew what that meant. Diane had family in Connecticut. Connecticut was an easy drive from Maine. Maine was her idea of a compromise.

And maybe it was.

They continued to sit there pleasantly together until Diane said, "I'm going upstairs." She took her wine glass over to the sink and rinsed it out. "Come up in a few minutes. I've got an idea might help you get to sleep."

Epilogue

~

El and Aggie were together in the kitchen after their walk, their first since before Walter's death. There had simply been too much to do, all the business with the evacuees, frustration upon frustration as the floodwaters inched downward, and then the weeks of cleanup, still not completed, far from completed, and uncounted bureaucratic snarls with federal and state agencies, nonprofits, all the helping organizations. Today promised to be chock-full of stuff, too, but they'd treated themselves to one of their old jaunts along the blufftop.

On the south side of the room, the intense Saturday-morning sunlight poured in the kitchen window. On the other, a breeze drifted through the screen door, through the mudroom, faintly soiled by the odor of the boots and coveralls El had been wearing as she helped muck out the houses down on the Flats. The first day of deep summer weather after the long, chilly spring.

The river was finally back in its banks. The men and women who fought the flood were to be honored. In a couple of weeks they'd have the first race at the dog track, although it was going to be a pretty makeshift affair. As temporary levees were taken down, the material was being hauled out for use as fill at the track.

With the change of seasons, El thought about Walter. She missed him more than she could say. Walter, like the weather itself, would always be with her.

Almost everything reminded her of him, a quality of absence that she'd never experienced before. It seemed to get worse rather than better, the earlier grief superficial for all its intensity and gone now, mostly gone, and what lay underneath so much more painful, the fruitless attempts to replace Walter himself with her memories of him. She missed the very oddness of him, his obsession with the weather and the climate, his massive collection of facts, many of them random, his curious ways of showing his affection. El missed them all.

Aggie sat spraddle-legged, comically at ease, happy. She and Deuce were now an item. If they eventually got married, what the marriage would be like was anybody's guess. Aggie had set about working on him, trying to get him interested in the committee being formed to take a whack at introducing workplace democracy. Deuce was proving a reluctant revolutionary.

El looked forward to a wedding a lot more than she had to the memorial service for Walter. From that, what she most remembered, oddly enough, were words of Chuck Fellows, who had told her in private, "Walt lived his own life. He died living it. No man can ask for more."

That seemed about right.

His body still hadn't been found. They'd found the other man's, several miles downriver on the Illinois side. El had talked to his widow, and they'd made vague plans to get together. Where Walter's remains were no one could guess. At first it had been important to find him, and then less important, and now she hoped he was never recovered. Walter didn't belong in a casket. Let him become part of the river he so much loved.

At the moment, El had one of her houseplants on the table before her and was picking dead leaves off it. The whole situation was filled with irony, too. Despite everything, she'd been sleeping well. She felt a little guilty about that. No doubt all the physical work had something to do with it, and no doubt it was temporary. Her depression could be counted on to return, too. But for now she had a sunny Saturday morning and memories of Walter, and that was enough.

The kettle began to whistle, and she got up and had just finished fixing another cup when she heard the footsteps coming up the driveway and toward the back door.

"Who do you suppose?" Aggie asked.

El closed her eyes briefly, not ready for other people just at that moment. She waited for the knock, then set the tea down on the stove. Walking through the odor in the mudroom, she cleared her throat.

At the back door stood...El couldn't at first put a name to the face, or remember quite where she'd encountered the woman before.

"Yes?" she said as she pushed the screen door open. "Can I help you?" The woman wore inexpensive clothing, but had taken care with her appearance, a dressy white blouse and flared skirt, carefully arranged to hide the fact that she was overweight.

"You won't remember me, Mrs. Plowman."

But suddenly El did. "Jane, isn't it? Janey."

"That's right. Janey Roche." Her face lit up with the pleasure of having been recognized. "I came to visit you last winter."

The memory of that evening and conversation came sweeping back in vivid detail. "You'd fallen and hurt your poor knees. See, I do remember. You wanted the city to cut the budget across the board."

"That's right."

El smiled at her. "What a pleasant surprise. How are you?"

"I'm okay." Janey dipped her head, as if slightly embarrassed. "I want to say, right off, how sorry I am about what happened to your husband."

"Well, thank you."

"It was tragic."

"Yes. Thank you. Come in, won't you?"

"I'd better not." Janey Roche's joy at being recognized had vanished, replaced by something between distraction and determination. "I've got a lot of places to go just yet."

"Places to go?" Janey carried a clipboard.

"I'm going around getting signatures."

"I see. What about?"

"I thought, being as how...you know..." Janey hesitated, suddenly irresolute.

"May I?" El asked and reached for the clipboard. Janey readily relinquished it.

Signatures already filled most of the page below the block of type at the top, which announced the subject of the document. El glanced quickly through the printed matter to get the gist of it, then read it more carefully, interested. She'd heard that such a petition was beginning to be circulated, but hadn't actually seen it until that moment—a move to change the form of government in Jackson, to get rid of the city manager and replace him with a full-time mayor. The drive had obviously been orchestrated by the friends of Fritz Goetzinger.

El laughed, and Janey recoiled slightly from the force of it.

"I must say," El told her, "don't you think I'd be just about the last person you'd expect to sign something like this?" She thought about the assertion for an instant and then amended it. "Well, on second thought, I suppose Paul Cutler is absolutely the last person who would sign. But I've got to be pretty close."

"I'm sorry."

"Don't be."

Janey said shyly, "When I came before, you were nice. You listened."

"Of course."

"And then you even recommended it, I mean, to the city council. Cut everything the same, you said."

"Yes, I did, and where did that get us?" El smiled at her and, feeling a hint of pressure on her back, turned to discover that Aggie had appeared, coming out to see what was what. El introduced the two women, and explained to Aggie just who Janey was, and held the clipboard so that Aggie could peruse the petition as well.

Janey had found her tongue now and started listing the petitioners' grievances—the plan to bring blacks to Jackson in violation of the American ideal of individual choice, the refusal of the city to participate in a buyout of the meatpacking plant the previous fall, which led to the closing of the plant, the cutbacks in transit and other essential city services, and finally and more generally an unresponsiveness to the needs of Jacksonians. A complaint for every taste.

The document had been carefully crafted, and El wondered exactly where the language had come from. The proposal was not only for a mayoral form, but a strong one to boot, with veto power over the budget, authority to appoint key officials, and other powers typically associated with a strong-mayor government.

El returned to the list of bitches and said, "As for bringing blacks here, it's true, I handled it badly. I don't regret trying to do something—we do have a problem, Janey—but I should have approached it in some other way. As for the rest…"

Janey, confronting this resistance, rushed to plump up her argument, "A lot of people feel the city could have done more about the flood."

"How?"

"All the out-of-towners who got to stay in the best places while city people had to live in tents."

"That's only partially true. Many of the Jacksonians who got flooded out were also put up in, as you call them, 'the best places.' Anyway, I did what I could. If people are unhappy…"

"That's not what I feel, Mrs. Plowman. But a lot do. And they think the city knew the floodwall was weak and that something could have been done if you acted sooner."

"We knew no such thing. And acting sooner would have made no difference."

Janey hesitated, then shifted her ground slightly and moved briskly past the obstacle. "Well, maybe not, but people think different. And maybe, you know, the city could have done something anyway."

Janey was looking at the petition, which El still held. El wondered, should she sign the thing anyway? She wouldn't, of course, the renegade thought merely a companion to the occasional impulse she had to violate propriety—to drop a cup she was holding and let it shatter on the floor or to tell some particularly obnoxious petitioner before the city council to go fuck himself.

Aggie seized the clipboard. "I'll sign," she said.

"Aggie!"

"I don't care." She bestowed a look of mock defiance on El. "We don't need a city manager. We'll make you mayor, a real mayor. Why not?"

"Except it won't be me. It'll be your prospective father-in-law."

"Whatever." Aggie took the pen offered by Janey and signed with a flourish. "And anyway, you didn't think you'd win the last time, remember?" She leaned closer to the petition to print her name and address, the pink tip of her tongue just poking out of the corner of her mouth.

One thing was sure. If enough signatures were obtained, the referendum would pass—pretty much a sure thing, El guessed, and then immediately cautioned herself that Aggie was right, take nothing for granted. She had no data, as Walter would have been glad to point out.

If it did pass, though, Fritz Goetzinger would be elected mayor. Of that she *was* sure. El didn't even know if she'd bother to run again. She envisioned Fritz moving into Paul's office in city hall.

Aggie handed the clipboard to her, and she handed it back to Janey. "If you want me to sign," she told her, "I'm afraid you'll have to come up with better reasons."

The clipboard back in her possession, Janey visibly relaxed, and said, "Maybe she's right"—meaning Aggie—"maybe you'll be elected again."

El just smiled.

A minute later, she and Aggie stood watching Janey walk off, an overweight, middle-aged woman, no doubt with enough personal troubles to last a lifetime, and yet...

She passed by the rose bushes and disappeared around the corner of the house, on her way toward the driveway she'd fallen down the previous winter. She wouldn't fall today.

El's eye lingered on the roses. She'd removed and stored their winter protection but done nothing else for them, and they seemed to be going wild.

Back in the kitchen, she lifted the teabag from her cup. The tea was too strong and getting cold. No matter. Aggie had flopped back down in her chair. El squeezed the juice out of the teabag and folded it over the lip of the cup.

"So," she said to her friend, "where were we?"

Acknowledgments

~

Almost all of the scenes in volume three of The Loss of Certainty take place in the fictional community of Jackson, based loosely on the city of Dubuque, Iowa, but in order to mount a creditable flood fight, I interviewed many officials elsewhere, including those in the U.S. Corps of Engineers, the National Weather Service, the U.S. Geological Survey, and the Federal Emergency Management Agency. Many were helpful, but one in particular needs to be singled out for his continuing support and encouragement for my project. This was Bill Koellner, Chief of Regulations in the Rock Island District of the Corps of Engineers. Bill described the methods used to measure and predict river stage and provided the scenario for a worst-case flood in the Upper Mississippi River. His contributions were key to my understanding of the river dynamics during times of high water. A number of other COE officials were also helpful with flood and other matters, including Dick Atkinson, Wayne Currier, Lyle Davis, Vern Greenwood, and Dick Sharp. Also helpful were COE officials in Minneapolis and Kansas City.

Dean Braatz and his staff at the North Central River Forecast Center of the National Weather Service were very generous in describing NWS methodology for forecasting river stage.

From the St. Paul office of the USGS, I was able to go out into the field to help measure stage and discharge with Duane Wicklund and Greg Stratton. Also providing assistance were Joe Hess and Greg Mitton.

For weather forecasting, I'm indebted to meteorologist Tim Heller, and former Iowa climatologist Paul Waite provided much useful information about long-term weather patterns.

Dick Atkinson of COE and Ernie Roarig of the City of Dubuque engineering department were excellent sources of information about the existing floodwall/levee system in Dubuque and such systems in general.

I'm grateful to all these people I've mentioned, as well as the many others who helped out along the way. Any technical errors to be found in this and either of the other volumes of The Loss of Certainty are my responsibility entirely.

And finally let me once again thank the people who have offered critiques during the long composition of the trilogy, most notably Elisabeth Jones and Laura Baker. It's only with their help that I've managed to distill the mass of research material into a coherent work of fiction.